Something to Die For

Will Jordan's Ryan Drake novels draw on extensive research into weapons and tactics, as well as the experiences of men who've fought in some of the world's most daunting combat zones. Other books in the series include *Redemption*, *Sacrifice* and *Betrayal*. He lives in Fife, Scotland, with his wife and sons.

D1077960

Also by Will Jordan

The Ryan Drake thrillers

Redemption
Sacrifice
Betrayal
Black List
Deception Game
Ghost Target
Second Chances (novella)
Shadow Conflict
Trial by Fire (novella)
Downfall
Something to Die For

WILL JORDAN
SOMETHING TO DIE FOR

CANELO

First published in the United Kingdom in 2020 by Canelo

Canelo Digital Publishing Limited
31 Helen Road
Oxford OX2 0DF
United Kingdom

A CIP catalogue record for this book is available from the British Library.

Print ISBN 978 1 80032 201 1
Ebook ISBN 978 1 78863 716 9

Look for more great books at www.canelo.co

Printed and bound in Great Britain by Clays Ltd, Elcograf S.p.A.

For everyone who believed in me

Abbottabad, Pakistan – May 1st, 2011

It was a quiet night in the suburbs of Abbottabad in north-eastern Pakistan, with a light breeze and a clear sky studded with stars. A thin sliver of moonlight cast its pale glow on a gentle landscape of small, cultivated fields, fast-flowing rivers and trees heavy with spring blossom. The roads were deserted, windows shuttered and residents fast asleep.

Most of the properties in this district were generously sized and well-constructed, and were owned by educated professionals, prosperous merchants and wealthy entrepreneurs. It was a popular, desirable, though quite unremarkable area.

But there was one curiosity amid this bland suburban conformity. At the end of a dirt road that set it somewhat apart from its neighbours was one property in particular. Made up of several smaller plots amalgamated into one sprawling triangular compound, it had been constructed from similar materials and of broadly similar design to its neighbours.

But it was the little details that marked it out as different. The outer walls, topped with barbed wire to deter thieves, were higher than most would have considered necessary – up to 18 feet tall in places.

The main building was also larger than normal, even for the extended families common to Pakistani culture. A third floor had been added in recent years, complete with a private balcony. Indeed, privacy seemed to be of great concern to the owners. The main dwelling contained few windows; those that did exist were rarely opened.

The residents ventured out infrequently, playing no part in the local community. They didn't speak with neighbours, didn't allow their children out to play, and didn't let anyone inside.

Waziristan Haveli, as it was informally known, was the kind of place that invited speculation and gossip. Rumours of shady business, illicit drug deals and money laundering lingered around the place. Some even entertained the wild theory that the compound served as a private retreat for some famous actor or public figure.

None of this speculation came to much. Unsociable and mysterious they might have been, but the residents of *Waziristan Haveli* did nothing to anger their neighbours.

Let them live quietly behind their high walls if that's what they want, the men in local tea houses concluded philosophically. *A man is entitled to his privacy. And if he causes no trouble, then who cares?*

None of them could possibly know that, before the night was over, *Waziristan Haveli* would become one of the most infamous places on earth.

It began with a low, rhythmic thudding noise coming from the north-west, barely audible at first and easily dismissed as the sound of the distant highway. But rather than fading away into the night, the sound grew in intensity slowly but steadily.

A stray dog, asleep in a dried-up drainage culvert nearby, stirred and looked up at the night sky as a pair of massive dark shapes swept past, accompanied by the shriek of engines and a sudden gale that stirred up clouds of grit and pieces of discarded litter. Startled, the dog cowered, yipped in fear and darted off into the night.

The two Black Hawk transport helicopters, both heavily armed and outfitted with stealth adaptations to reduce their noise and radar cross-sections, descended on *Waziristan Haveli*. One took up position over the main yard while the other prepared to land in the more distant north-east corner of the compound.

Inside the first Black Hawk, a dozen heavily armed US SEAL team operatives in full body armour got ready to deploy. They had been preparing for this moment for weeks, training relentlessly, memorising every detail of the intricate assault plan.

The crew compartment door slid open and fast descent ropes were hurled out into the night, the first men taking up position in the doorway as they prepared to deploy. That was when things started to go wrong.

The downwash from the Black Hawk's massive main rotors kicked up a storm of dust in the yard below. Normally this would present little concern, but the compound's high defensive walls prevented the downwash from dispersing, creating a dangerous air vortex that began to pull the Black Hawk downwards.

As the pilot fought to maintain altitude, the aircraft's tail swung to port, striking the compound wall. A violent bang shivered through the fuselage as one of the tail rotor blades sheared clean off. Unbalanced by the sudden change in the complex dynamic forces holding it aloft, the chopper began to yaw dangerously. Alarms blared and the men in the crew compartment grasped at restraining harnesses to keep from being hurled out the open door.

With mere seconds to act, the pilot took the only option open to him and shoved his control column all the way forward, bringing the ailing helicopter down in a barely controlled crash landing. The impact shattered one of the landing struts and pitched the chopper over at a precarious angle, but it was still in one piece.

More importantly, so were the men inside.

Shaken and battered by the crash, the assault team hastily composed themselves, leapt out of the stricken aircraft and advanced across the open yard, pressing on with their mission despite its inauspicious start. Lights were coming on in nearby buildings as local residents, awoken by the noise and commotion, stumbled out of bed to gawk at the drama unfolding.

The SEALs paid them no heed as they swept in against the building, weapons up and ready. A secondary unit peeled off to breach a smaller structure on the south side of the yard, while teams from the other chopper quickly scaled the inner defensive walls, but the main force advanced on the central three-storey residence.

That was where their target would be.

Breaching charges were planted against the door, and barely a second later they detonated with a resounding boom, the shockwave shattering windows in the upper floors.

'Flash out!' the team leader cried, hurling a stun grenade in through the smoking doorway before ducking back behind cover.

The lightning flash of the grenade explosion was accompanied by a deafening bang that seemed to roll up through the very core of the house.

'Go! Go!'

The first three-man assault team went straight in, their night vision devices illuminating the darkened interior in a ghostly green. Adrenaline was coursing thick in their veins now, heightening every sense as they advanced inside.

This was it. This was the most important mission of their lives.

First door on the right. A single hard kick sent it crashing open. A woman and two children screamed in terror.

'Get down!' one SEAL yelled. 'Down on the floor!'

Civilians. Unarmed. They were no threat, though one of the SEALs shoved the woman to the floor, securing her hands behind her back anyway. Even civilians could throw a hand grenade or detonate a suicide vest.

'Room clear! Move up!'

The team pressed on. More shouts and screams were coming from other rooms. Chaos and confusion everywhere. The air was thick with acrid grey smoke.

Suddenly the booming chatter of automatic gunfire resounded from their left, and a door splintered as a burst of 7.62mm AK rounds tore through it. Instinctively the nearest SEAL dropped to his knees, avoiding the lethal but inaccurate gunfire. The powerful kick of an AK-47 caused severe muzzle climb, meaning shots often went high.

The answering burst from a pair of HK416 assault rifles suffered no such impediment. There was a scream and a heavy thud as a body hit the ground.

Forcing their way inside, the SEALs found a man sprawled on the ground, middle-aged and heavily bearded, blood from a trio of gunshot wounds staining his white nightclothes. He was feebly trying to reach for his fallen weapon.

A second burst ended his struggle.

'Tango down!'

The rest of the assault team was advancing up the central stairway to the upper floor. Their hearts were pounding, a thrill running through their bodies as they ascended. They were close. The man they'd been hunting for so long was now just yards away.

The faint padding of footsteps on the landing above caused them to freeze, waiting and listening, their weapons trained upward on the closed door at the top of the stairs.

And then, slowly, the door edged open to reveal a tall, slender figure clad in a loose-fitting nightshirt, a greying beard trailing down to his chest, his thinning hair in disarray. He peered out into the stairwell, and for a heartbeat his gaze fastened on the SEAL team below.

It happened so fast that each of those involved would struggle to recount exactly how it played out. The lead SEAL team member raised his assault rifle, took aim just as the target tried to retreat into the room, and uttered a single word.

'Contact.'

With that, he squeezed off a short, sharp burst. The weapon rattled against his shoulder, and a shower of wood fragments exploded from the door.

They heard the heavy thump of a body hitting the floorboards, accompanied by the shriek of women screaming.

'Tango down!'

'Move up! Go!'

Rushing up the stairs, the three-man team forced their way into the room beyond, having to shove the door open because the weight of the wounded man was partially blocking it. Beyond, they found two women crouched over the target, wailing and crying. Wives grieving for their dying husband.

'Get down on the floor! Down now!'

In response, one of the women leapt up and launched herself at the team. A single shot rang out and she fell heavily, screaming in pain. Blood seeped from a bullet wound on her thigh.

Moving forward, one of the SEALs grabbed the other woman and hurled her aside, allowing the team a proper look at their target for the first time. The man whose face they'd seen on countless news broadcasts and websites for the better part of a decade. The man responsible for the deaths of thousands of their countrymen.

That man was lying splayed out on the floor in front of them, blood soaking his nightshirt, his breathing coming in shallow, strangled gasps, his face contorted in pain. His eyes held the look of a cornered animal. These men were here for one reason only – him.

For a second or so, an eerie standoff ensued as the three SEALs stared at their target, struck by the power and significance of the moment. Everything they'd trained and prepared for had all come down to this.

This was the most important moment of their lives.

A volley of gunshots echoed around the room as two of the SEALs opened fire simultaneously. The fallen man jerked and writhed as the rounds tore into his body, then with a final exhausted gasp, he lay still.

The men lowered their weapons, smoke still trailing from the barrels. Neither of them spoke a word. They had just made history.

Snapping out of it, the fireteam leader hit his radio transmitter and calmly spoke the code phrase they'd rehearsed for this moment.

'For God and country – Geronimo, Geronimo, Geronimo.'

Their mission was complete. Osama bin Mohammed bin Awad bin Laden, the most wanted man on the face of the earth, was dead.

Part One

Something to Lie For

Of all the liars in the world, sometimes the worst are your own fears.

Rudyard Kipling

Chapter 1

Ryan and Jessica Drake stood rooted to the spot, neither saying a word. The world around them waited in silent anticipation; even the breeze seemed to die away as brother and sister faced off, each taking the measure of the other.

It had been nearly two years since Drake had last set foot in this doorway. Two years since he'd left his sister behind, knowing he was unlikely to see her again. He'd told himself it was for her own safety, that he'd put her through enough already. That she couldn't follow where he was going.

And yet here he was. After all the battles he'd fought, the enemies he'd overcome, the friends he'd lost and the terrible secrets he'd uncovered, he was back.

He couldn't help but gaze at the woman who had been a part of his life for as long as he could remember, comparing the face before him with the one that lived in his memory.

Physically she hadn't changed much at all. Her dark hair was cut shorter and styled differently, her complexion was pale after a winter of cold days and long nights. But she possessed the same slender yet deceptively athletic build, the same facial features that reminded him more and more of their mother with each passing year, the same eyes, identical in colour and shade to his own.

They might not have changed, but what lay behind them certainly had.

The seconds stretched out, the silence growing taut and uncomfortable. Seeking to break the standoff, Drake took a step forward.

'Jessica, I—'

He saw her hand whip around and braced himself inwardly, felt the sudden explosive impact as the slap connected hard with the side of his face. It was harder than he'd expected, and the blow left his cheek stinging.

He didn't try to dodge or shrink away from it, just as he didn't try to stop her lashing out with her fists, thumping and punching anywhere she could in a sudden frenzied attack. Instead he took the hits, letting her get it out like he knew she had to, until finally she exhausted herself and collapsed into his arms, her body convulsing with sobs.

Drake didn't speak. That would come later. For now, it was enough to let her cry.

–

Some time later, Drake was seated at the kitchen table, watching the weak February sunlight filter through the wisps of steam rising from his tea. The table at which he sat was old, heavy and solid, its design simple, its finish coarse and unrefined.

It was the kind of furniture, the kind of environment, he'd grown up with. It should have felt familiar and reassuring. Instead it felt foreign and unnatural.

On the opposite side of the table, a newspaper lay discarded, its front page emblazoned with images of the unfolding civil war in Libya. The so-called Arab Spring had spread across most of North Africa by now, threatening to topple regimes even as far as the Middle East. The images were a chilling reminder of the mission that had brought Drake here.

'I thought you were dead.'

Drake looked up at Jessica. She was leaning against the kitchen counter on the far side of the room, her fingers wrapped around her mug, her face pale, eyes still red from tears. They were the first words she'd said since she'd finally let go of him in the doorway and retreated inside. She'd needed space and distance in order to see the problem more clearly.

The problem, in this case, being himself.

'I know.'

'I mourned you. Told myself you were gone.' She caught herself, her voice threatening to break. 'I *made* myself believe it, as much as it hurt. It was better than fearing you were alive, always wondering where you were, what you were going through.'

'Jess, I—'

'The things they said about you on the news… The car bombing in Washington. That factory in Brazil…'

'That wasn't me,' Drake said firmly.

There was, of course, a great deal more to that story than he was able to share with her, but what he said wasn't a lie.

'But you *were* involved.'

He sighed. 'Yes.'

Jessica watched him in silence, her expression troubled. She understood the dark world her brother inhabited, knew why he'd been forced to go into hiding two years earlier. She'd even been caught in the crossfire herself once.

'What the hell happened to you, Ryan?'

Drake shook his head. 'It's a long story.'

'I have plenty of time,' she said, gesturing at their isolated surroundings.

'I don't.'

He could practically feel the fleeting spark of hope die inside her, could feel her withdrawing once more. 'Then why *are* you here?'

'Freya.'

He couldn't quite bring himself to use the word 'mother'.

'What about her?'

'She was part of this,' he explained. 'This thing we've all been caught up in – Cain, Anya, the Agency, all of it – she worked for the people behind it. That's why she was killed.'

Jessica straightened up, clearly disturbed by what she was hearing. Freya's murder two years ago had cast a dark shadow over her already troubled life, robbing her of the only parent she had left, and leaving her with no clue to the killer's motive or identity.

'What do you mean? Who killed her, Ryan?' she asked, her voice hardening now.

Drake looked at his sister. 'You sure you want to hear this?'

'My mother's dead. My brother's on the run from the police, the CIA and God only knows who else. And every day I wake up wondering if I'm going to be next. So yes, yes I fucking want to hear this.'

Drake knew his sister well enough to trust her judgement. In any case, he needed her cooperation, and keeping her in the dark was no way to get it.

'There's some kind of... cabal in the US intelligence service. A secret society, a shadow organisation... whatever you want to call it. We've come to know them as the Circle. They're like a cancer, infecting agencies, the military, even the government. Anyone who tries to stand against them gets eliminated.'

Jessica's eyes narrowed. 'Why? What do they want?'

Drake spread his hands. 'Money? Power? Influence? All of the above, or none of it. Nobody's gotten close enough to find out. But there's almost no limit to what they can do,' he carried on. 'They can start wars and revolutions, overthrow entire governments...'

'Ryan, you have to know how this sounds.'

Seizing the newspaper from the table, Drake held it up with the front page, and its chilling images of war, facing her.

'See for yourself,' he challenged her. 'I was there in Tunisia when it all began. I even interrogated one of their operatives. They made it happen, they've been planning it for years, setting up their pieces, waiting for the right moment. And if this is what they can do today, what's next?'

The immeasurable complexity of the planning and preparation needed for something like this almost defied belief. Engineering a coup in just a single country required an immense effort, but to trigger simultaneous revolutions across an entire continent was on a whole other level.

Jessica was pondering the same thought, albeit from a different point of view. 'If this is all true, someone would have discovered them before now. Someone would have leaked it online. They can't silence *everyone*.'

'They don't need to. Do you have any idea how many bullshit conspiracy theories are floating around out there? How many nutcases spend their days ranting and raving about this stuff?'

'Like you, you mean?'

Drake gave her a disapproving look. 'If they control the right people, they can influence the flow of information online. They can make sure only *their* version of the truth gets spread and amplified, and everything else gets shut down or silenced.'

'How do you know?'

Drake looked at his sister frankly. 'I worked for the CIA, Jess. People don't care about the truth anymore – they care about reinforcing what they already believe. Give them that, the rest takes care of itself.'

Like a herd of animals, all it took was a little manipulation at the right place and time to get them moving.

Jessica shook her head, dismissing that for now. 'And you're seriously telling me that Mum… *our mother*, Freya Shaw, was part of this group?'

Drake looked at his sister hard. He understood her anger, and her doubts. He'd harboured both in his time. But that didn't mean he was wrong.

'Yes.'

'Why?'

'That's what I'm here to find out.'

Jessica laid her mug down and folded her arms. 'Go on.'

Reaching into his coat pocket, Drake laid an object on the table with an audible thump. A key, highly unusual in design, with three blades instead of just one. A series of numbers had been carefully etched into all three sides.

'Very pretty,' Jessica observed dryly. 'What does it open?'

'That's what I've been trying to figure out. There were no instructions about where to use it. No map, no directions, nothing. Just her letter to me.'

The brief missive, written by his mother shortly before her death, had been more of a personal apology to him and an effort to provide closure than any kind of instructional document. It mentioned no places or individuals for him to seek out. Or so he'd believed.

'The answer was in front of me the whole time, only I didn't make the connection,' he said, holding up the key for inspection. Abandoning her position on the far side of the room, Jessica moved in beside him, examining the unusual device.

'What do you think the numbers mean?'

'It's a code. And to break the code, all you need is the right cipher.' Drake looked at her. 'Do you still have the letter she left me?'

Believing the document had only sentimental value, Drake had left it in his sister's care when he departed. Only recently had he seen the error of his decision, his failure to recognise that both items were required. That mistake had cost him a great deal of time.

Now, perhaps, he was on the brink of finding his answers.

Jessica didn't respond. Instead, she turned away abruptly and moved over to the kitchen window, staring out at the rolling hills beyond.

'Talk to me, Jess,' he urged. 'What's wrong?'

'I'm so sorry, Ryan,' she said in a small voice. 'It's gone.'

Drake could barely process what he was hearing. 'What?'

'I burned it,' she admitted.

'Why would you do that?'

She turned reluctantly to face her brother. 'Like I said, I thought you were dead. I made myself believe it. The letter was the last thing you gave to me, the last reminder I had of you. Burning it was my way of… letting you go.'

Drake slumped back in his chair, defeated.

'I never imagined you'd come looking for it,' his sister said, trying hard to explain herself. 'I thought it was over. I thought you were gone.'

Drake barely heard her words.

'Then this was all for nothing,' he said quietly.

The key and the letter were both needed to decipher his mother's final message. Without one, the other was useless.

He felt her hand on his, could hear the pain and regret in her voice when she spoke. 'I'm so sorry, Ryan.'

Drake shook his head. 'It's not your fault,' he finally conceded. 'I've asked enough of you already. This one was on me.'

'But without the letter… what will you do now?'

Drake didn't answer for a while. Then, suddenly, he rose to his feet. 'Is Dad's car still in the garage?'

Jessica frowned, caught off guard by the question. 'Well, yeah…'

He nodded. 'Come with me.'

Chapter 2

Abbottabad, Pakistan

Bashir Shirani ascended the house's steep internal staircase with slow and deliberate care, the cups and pot of tea on his tray rattling slightly with each step.

The Master, the man around whom the entire household revolved, was a creature of routine for whom any change or delay was greatly aggravating. And, as the newest member of the staff assigned to attend him, the last thing Shirani wished was to incur his displeasure.

Hearing rapid footsteps and laughter below, the young man glanced over his shoulder as two boys charged along the short corridor at the base of the stairs, shouting and laughing as they rushed outside to play in the courtyard. The Master had fathered upwards of twenty children in his life, nine of whom resided in this compound. Many were young and boisterous, and not above playing pranks on their father's servants.

Fortunately, they were more intent on their own games than harassing him today, and he gratefully resumed his climb.

The top two floors of the main house were a private space reserved for the Master and his large family, though he would frequently hold meetings with his entourage there too. As Shirani reached the top of the stairs, he heard women's voices in one of the rooms beyond. It sounded like two of the Master's wives – he had three in all – engaged in some domestic discussion. He thought it might be Siham and Khairiah, since they had been with him the longest and tended to spend more time together.

His suspicions were confirmed when he entered the main living space on the top floor. Siham and Khairiah were there, talking softly as they laid out freshly laundered bedsheets, practising the same mundane routine they had performed thousands of times before.

Shirani admired them in a way. They had been with the Master more than half his life, travelling the world with him, remaining loyal and steadfast no matter the difficulties and dangers. Their lives had been neither short nor peaceful – a fact that was plain to see in their lined faces and greying hair. And yet they found a way to go on, to do what was expected of them.

'*As-salāmuʿalaykum,*' Shirani said, bowing in respect to the pair.

In Islamic culture, women were expected to be modest and deferential to men, especially in public. But within the confines of their own home it was a different matter. Men might have ruled the family, but it was generally accepted that women ruled the home. And nowhere was that more apparent than here in *Waziristan Haveli.*

'*Waʿalaykumu s-salām,*' Khairiah said, giving him the traditional response.

'I have brought tea, if he wishes it.'

Shirani had been explicitly instructed not to presume anything of the Master. Meals and refreshments were to be offered or suggested, but never in a way that implied obligation. To do so would be seen as highly disrespectful.

Khairiah nodded without much interest and gestured to the doorway opposite, which led into the Master's private chamber.

'He is in there.'

Approaching the door, Shirani paused to compose himself, then knocked lightly.

'Come,' a soft male voice called.

Opening the door, Shirani stepped inside.

The room beyond was small, sparsely furnished but cluttered with haphazardly installed electronic gear. There was nothing in the way of decoration or frivolity. The Master eschewed luxuries of any kind, despite his wealthy and privileged upbringing, preferring a simple and austere existence.

His personal workspace was, like much of the rest of the house, dimly lit by artificial lights. There was only one small window, and it remained firmly closed and shuttered.

This modest space was the Master's inner sanctum, functioning as a study, office, meeting room and occasional recording studio, where he would dictate messages to his followers. Shirani himself had never witnessed this, but he had heard rumours that such endeavours were fraught with difficulty. Neither a charismatic personality nor an accomplished orator, the Master delivered his abbreviated messages haltingly into the camera, pausing frequently, stumbling over his words and sometimes losing his train of thought, often requiring many takes before he was satisfied with the result.

Now he was seated on a low chair at the centre of this haphazard workspace, a blanket draped over his shoulders, his attention focussed on the old-fashioned TV set in the corner. The compound had no phone lines or internet access, but it did have satellite TV reception. The unit was tuned to the Al Jazeera news network, covering the unfolding civil war in Libya.

'As-salāmu'alaykum,' Shirani began, opening with the traditional greeting. He paused, waiting for a response.

There was none. The Master carried on with his viewing, apparently uninterested in the new arrival.

'I have brought tea, Master,' he ventured. 'If it would please you.'

Only then did he finally garner a response.

'Remarkable, isn't it?' the Master murmured, his voice soft and quiet, almost weak.

Shirani frowned. 'Master?'

The blanket stirred, the head turned as the Master looked at him. Shirani took in the familiar visage; the face seen on countless TV screens, websites and posters all across the world. The long prominent nose, the dark, deep-set eyes, the high forehead, the thick beard.

A man that most people in the Western world would gladly see dead.

And yet Shirani wondered how many of those people would even recognise the man seated before him now. The beard and hair had long since turned grey – he was still vain enough to dye it for his TV recordings – the eyes and cheeks were sunken, the face and brow deeply lined. Always tall and slender, he had lost weight during his self-imposed captivity and looked pale and sickly. Hunted and hated for almost a decade, the Master was a man old and frail before his time.

'This business in Libya,' he said, gesturing to the TV, which showed images of the embattled dictator Colonel Gaddafi addressing a crowd in Tripoli. 'Can you believe, that old fool actually blames *me* for the revolution in his country? He says I have armed his country's young people with guns and drugs, and turned them against him. Ha!' he snorted in grim amusement. 'What do you think of that, boy?'

Shirani resisted the urge to swallow, to shrink back from his penetrating stare. Suddenly the Master didn't look like a frail old man huddled beneath a blanket. He looked like the powerful, imposing figure who had fought the Soviets in Afghanistan, masterminded the attacks that had shattered American confidence and arrogance forever, and led a global jihad against Western imperialism for over a decade.

This man now wanted to know what *he* thought.

'I think the problems in Libya are of their own making,' he said carefully.

'Exactly, boy. Exactly,' the Master said as he sank back in his chair, satisfied with that answer. 'Gaddafi is too busy with his whoring and vanity to even notice his own people. And to think, such a man dares to call himself a Muslim.' The fire seemed to leap up behind his eyes in that moment. 'A fool. He has dug his own grave, and soon he will lie in it, I think.'

He paused, as if the tirade had left him weary, then looked at the tray in Shirani's hands. 'You've brought tea, then?'

'I have, Master.'

He nodded. 'Good, good. Then let us drink it before it grows cold.'

Setting down the tray on a small table beside his chair, Shirani poured a cup. His hand trembled a little as he worked; something that didn't go unnoticed.

'You're nervous, boy?'

Shirani avoided his gaze. 'It is… a great honour to be in your presence.'

'And you're worried I'll have you killed if you say the wrong thing?'

Shirani glanced at him in fright. But the dark eyes didn't seem so intense or penetrating now. There was a flicker of warmth and amusement in them.

'Though I may have to do something if you don't stop pouring.'

Shirani looked down and was shocked to see tea spilling over the rim of the cup. With a gasp of dismay, he pulled the pot away.

'Apologies, Master,' he gasped, bowing in supplication. 'Forgive me.'

'There is nothing to forgive,' the Master assured him. 'I'm an old man with little to do. I must take my fun where I can find it.'

He raised the overfull cup and took a sip, nodding appreciatively.

'It is good.'

'I'm glad it pleases you, Master.' Shirani hesitated. 'Is there anything else?'

The older man smiled and shook his head. 'I have put you through enough for one day, I think. You can go now.'

Shirani bowed again and was gratefully retreating from the room when the Master spoke up again.

'What is your name, boy?'

'Shirani. Bashir Shirani.'

'Shirani.' He thought on that. 'A good Pashtun name. From Khost, yes?'

'Yes,' Shirani said, surprised.

The Master nodded. 'Good fighters from Khost. I knew many during the war. They died like men.'

Saying nothing further, he turned his attention back to the TV and settled himself in his chair.

–

What neither man knew at that moment was that the area was being covertly observed. Cruising about 30,000 feet overhead at just under 200mph, was a single MQ-9 Reaper unmanned drone.

A pair of bulky 500-pound Paveway II laser-guided bombs hung from the wing pylons, ready to be deployed at the press of a button, and accurate enough to drop down the shaft of a well. Each one contained enough explosive power to reduce the fortified house to a heap of smouldering rubble.

And yet the aircraft's pilot, Josh Irvine, seated in an air-conditioned ground control centre hundreds of miles away at Bagram Air Base in Afghanistan, made no attempt to deploy this ordinance. Instead he leaned back a little in his chair, taking a sip of coffee from the steaming mug beside him as he surveyed the feeds from the drone's sophisticated Multi-Spectral Targeting System.

His job was not only to pilot the Reaper, but also to diligently record everything that it saw. And what it saw painted an interesting picture. Routine, they had soon come to realise, was of great importance there. Someone always emerged from the house at the same time each day, always bearing an empty tea tray. The man they were serving was clearly a creature of habit.

Irvine could almost imagine him at that moment, sipping his drink, believing himself safe inside his concrete prison. He glanced at the control column mounted in the centre of his drone terminal. The Reaper was orbiting the target area on autopilot, its sophisticated package of cameras and sensors constantly readjusting themselves to offer the best possible view. But weapons deployment had to be done manually. No computer would ever be entrusted with that task.

It would be so easy, he thought. A single button press, and 1000 pounds of high explosive would plummet through the air towards that place. It would take just under 40 seconds for the bombs to hit their target.

Flight Officer Josh Irvine could go down in history as the man who killed Osama Bin Laden.

Enough, he thought, taking another sip of coffee. Dwelling too long on such tempting possibilities was dangerous for a man in his position. His job was to observe and record only. No way would they stake something like this on a smart bomb that would leave nothing recognisable to identify. The killing, when it came, would be up close and personal.

And it was coming. He could sense it.

Chapter 3

Washington DC – June 20th, 1989

It was a warm, hazy summer evening in the capital as Marcus Cain drove east on Constitution Avenue. Glancing left, he was just able to make out the distant columns and gables of the White House, and caught himself wondering what might be going on within that great building, what matters of State and diplomacy were being discussed.

As the new head of the CIA's highly classified Special Activities Division, Cain knew better than most the power and danger of the secrets his country harboured, few of which ever crossed the desk of the president. Some things were too dangerous to entrust to so fleeting a holder of office.

Cain, however, had other business in DC tonight. The summons had been simple and direct, giving him only a location, date and time. He had known it would happen, of course. If you make a deal with the devil, then sooner or later he's going to collect.

Arriving at the designated meeting place, Cain had to admit he was perplexed by the choice of venue. Clandestine meetings were normally conducted in underground parking lots, beneath highway overpasses or in remote woodland, far from prying eyes. Not in distinguished-looking town houses barely a mile from the White House.

Parking up, he took a moment to survey the exterior, noting the subtle yet elegant architecture, the mirrored upper windows, the doorway that was larger and more imposing than normal.

This place wasn't a home.

Approaching the door, he found the intercom beside it and pressed the buzzer.

'Good evening,' a brisk and efficient female voice announced. 'May I take your name?'

'Marcus Cain,' he replied. 'I'm expected.'

There was a pause, then, 'Of course. Please come inside.'

There was a buzz and a click as the door was electronically unlocked. Cain took a moment to steel himself, wondering what he might encounter, before passing inside.

He entered a world of wood panelled walls, potted tropical plants, tasteful artwork and antique furniture that looked like it cost more than his apartment. It wasn't hard to see what this place really was – a private member's club. The kind of place specifically designed to be innocuous and unobtrusive from the outside.

Places like this existed all across the US, especially in the older cities on the East Coast, but Cain had never actually been inside one. He wasn't rich enough, important enough, or well bred enough to obtain membership.

'Welcome to L'infini, Mr Cain.'

Cain glanced over at the attractive blonde woman positioned behind a reception desk. She was smiling at him, but it was a polite, professional kind of smile. Her gaze, on the other hand, was shrewd and calculating.

'This is your first time with us?'

'That's right,' he acknowledged, his tone guarded. 'I have a meeting arranged.'

'Of course. Please, wait here and someone will be along to escort you.'

'I can make my own way.'

The young woman opened her mouth to respond, but she was interrupted by another voice coming from the high arched entrance to the dining area.

'Marcus. Good of you to come.'

Cain turned to face this new arrival, quickly taking in his appearance. He looked to be in his mid-forties, of average height, neither athletic nor overweight. His light brown hair, just starting to thin on top, was combed back from a high forehead and a thin, almost delicate face that showed its age quicker than it should have. Few could have called the man handsome, but his smile was confident and relaxed as he stepped forward to shake Cain's hand.

'Hope I didn't keep you waiting long?'

'Not at all,' Cain said as he shook it. 'I… don't believe we've met?'

'I don't believe we have,' the man agreed. 'I'm James.'

'Just James, huh?'

'Just James. I've always preferred first names. Identity without expectation.' He smiled again, the matter apparently settled. 'Anyway, I imagine you have questions for me.'

'You imagine correctly.'

He gestured back the way he'd come. 'Follow me, and we'll talk.'

James led him through what looked to be the restaurant area of the club. The man's straight back and precise walk put Cain in mind of some aristocratic lord, used to conducting himself with discipline and dignity.

The dining area was alive with the hum of conversation, the clink of glasses and cutlery. Ornate pillars of Italian marble rose to a vaulted ceiling overhead, from which a trio of elaborate chandeliers were suspended. Scanning the faces as they passed, Cain recognised a couple of congressmen, a senator and even a US ambassador.

'Quite the place you've got here, James,' Cain said as his host led him up a short flight of steps. 'Seems I'm in good company.'

'Membership of L'infini is… quite selective. Privacy and discretion are hard to come by these days.'

Presently he was conducted into a private saloon. The decor was just as opulent and tasteful as in the main restaurant, and the drinks bar would have put many professional cocktail lounges to shame. A place for the elite amongst the elite.

'You asked for this meeting,' he said, turning towards his host. 'Here I am. Now what can I do for you?'

'You can relax and have a drink, Marcus,' another voice advised. 'This isn't an interrogation. Let's not treat it like one.'

Cain spun around to see a woman emerge from a doorway on the other side of the room. Tall, shapely, and wearing a slender black evening dress that was entirely in keeping with her elegant surroundings, she was smiling at him with that same knowing, dangerously disarming smile she'd flashed the first night they'd met.

Freya Shaw. The woman who had appeared in his life without warning, with an offer he couldn't refuse. An offer that had changed everything.

'Thank you for showing him in, James,' she said, nodding to Cain's escort.

'Had a feeling you'd turn up again,' Cain said, quickly recovering his poise.

That disarming smile was still there as she sauntered over, a subtle but inviting sway in her hips. Whatever his misgivings, one thing Cain couldn't deny about Freya was that she was a strikingly attractive woman. Doubtless she was well aware of that fact too, and used it to her advantage.

'Like the proverbial bad penny?'

'You said it, not me.'

She halted just a little closer than necessary, her lips slightly parted as she looked him in the eye. He could smell her perfume, even fancied he could feel the faint warmth of her body.

'I'm not as bad as you think… unless I have to be.' There was a dangerous flicker in her eyes. 'Now tell me, what will you have to drink?'

'I'm on the clock.'

'Oh, come on, now,' she said, reaching up and gently straightening his collar. 'You wouldn't make me drink alone, would you?'

'Bourbon, on the rocks,' he finally said.

Her smile returned. 'Make that two, James.'

James, who had taken up position behind the bar, perused the bottles before selecting a bottle of Woodford Reserve cask strength, and pouring two glasses over ice.

'Don't you think we ought to do this in private?' Cain suggested as James handed the two glasses to Shaw. 'No offence, James.'

'None taken, Marcus.'

'I'd trust James with my life,' she explained. 'I assure you, we can speak freely here.'

She held out a glass to him, and reluctantly he took it.

'In that case, what do you want?' Cain asked. 'I presume you didn't bring me here for dinner and dancing.'

'And if I did?'

'I'm not much of a dancer.'

She pouted in mock disappointment. 'Shame, really. I am.'

'Enough. Why am I here?'

'Talk to me about Anya,' Shaw prompted him.

Anya. The young woman he'd recruited into the Agency, who had fought and risked her life in Afghanistan, who had captivated him in a way he never could have expected. The woman who harboured a destructive secret that had very nearly gotten them both killed.

'What about her?'

'What's her status as an operative?' Shaw asked, putting a slight pause between each word.

'She's… recovering.'

After being captured, interrogated and brutally tortured by the Soviets, then finally escaping over the border into Pakistan in appalling conditions, Anya should have died. She very nearly had, in fact. Only her innate toughness and iron will to survive had kept her going.

'But she's not back on active duty, is she?' Shaw pressed.

They both knew the answer to that. Anya had been largely absent from the Agency since her return to the US, reporting only reluctantly for psychological and physical evaluations.

23

'She went through a lot. It takes time.'

'She's gun-shy,' Shaw said, her tone growing colder and more business-like. 'That's the expression they use in your line of work, isn't it? She took a hit, and now she's afraid. A soldier who won't fight isn't much of a soldier at all.'

'And what would you know about being a soldier?' he said. 'When was the last time you risked your life for something?'

If he'd been hoping to rattle her with that forceful censure, he was to be disappointed. Shaw remained unmoved.

'There are many ways to fight. Not all involve guns,' she said cryptically. 'Either way, I have the perfect job to get Anya back into the swing of things.' She retrieved a folder from the end of the bar and presented it to him. 'This picture was taken in Ukraine two days ago. Recognise this man?'

Cain studied the black and white photograph. It was a man in his early forties, taken long-range but clearly recognisable all the same. Cain knew every member of Anya's unit as if they were his own family.

'Luka,' he said quietly. The former leader of Anya's task force, who had disappeared after the unit's disastrous ambush in Afghanistan. 'How did you get this?'

'We can find almost anyone.' Shaw explained, enjoying the moment. 'This man traded Anya and her unit in exchange for amnesty from the Soviets. He's a loose end, and who better to tie it off than Anya?'

'They were close, those two,' Cain warned her. Luka had been like a brother to Anya. 'You're asking her to kill a man she fought beside.'

'I'm asking her to punish the traitor who sold them out,' Shaw corrected him. 'What better way is there to exorcise those demons?'

Cain didn't answer that. This was a test. A test of loyalty, both for Anya and himself.

'Get her onboard with this, Marcus,' Shaw commanded him. 'Get her onboard and back into the field where she belongs.'

'What if I can't?'

Shaw's mouth twitched in a half smile as she considered her response. 'James, take your gun and point it at Mr Cain's head.'

In a flash, James had drawn a weapon from inside his suit jacket, and trained it on Cain as casually as if he were pointing a remote at a TV.

'What do you think you're doing?' Cain demanded. Having no sidearm of his own, there was little he could do to defend himself.

'Making a point,' Shaw replied, looking him hard in the eye. For all her sleek beauty, there was a core of cold steel within her. 'Do you know what defines James most of all? Loyalty. If I asked him to pull the trigger right now, he'd do it in a heartbeat and pour me another drink without batting an eyelash.' She glanced over at him. 'Isn't that right, James?'

'Say the word,' James replied. 'No offence, Marcus.'

'Let me make this perfectly clear,' Shaw went on. 'We want Anya's unit playing for our team. But they won't fight without her, and she won't fight without you. If you can't handle her, then... well, there's really not much point in keeping you around, is there?'

If Cain harboured any lingering doubts about how ruthless Freya Shaw could be, they vanished in that moment. She would order his death without hesitation or remorse.

'This how you always conduct your "business"?' he asked scathingly.

'I prefer my relationships to be mutually beneficial. But when a point needs to be made, I prefer to make it once only.'

Cain drained his bourbon, glaring at her the whole time.

'I'll talk to her.'

Shaw's smile returned, languid and disarming as ever.

'I knew you'd understand, Marcus.'

Washington DC – February 27th, 2011

Located on a narrow finger of land jutting out from the north bank of the Potomac, with the muddy sweep of the river on one side and the choppy expanse of the Tidal Basin on the other, the Franklin Delano Roosevelt Memorial certainly didn't enjoy the most auspicious of settings. Most tourists preferred to concentrate on more iconic and easily accessible sites along the National Mall, and thus the monument to the 32nd president of the United States saw relatively few visitors.

This state of affairs was compounded by the unfavourable weather today, which was cold and breezy, the steel-grey sky threatening rain. The leafless trees swayed and rattled in the fitful wind.

A shame really, Marcus Cain thought to himself. Compared to the overbearing, pretentious grandeur of most of DC's government buildings and towering monuments, there was a calming, understated elegance to the tumbling, man-made waterfalls and rough-hewn stone blocks that comprised the memorial's four outdoor 'rooms' – each one symbolising a different era of Roosevelt's long career in public service.

Halting opposite the stone statue of FDR, who was seated to disguise the paralysis that had blighted much of his later life, Cain found himself reflecting on the quote engraved in the wall beside him.

They (who) seek to establish systems of government based on the regimentation of all human beings by a handful of individual rulers… call this a new order. It is not new and it is not order.

How prescient those words seemed now, Cain thought to himself.

The click of shoes on the granite flagstones told him that someone was approaching. Cain didn't look around. He didn't have to.

His name was Richard Starke, the director of the National Security Agency. Cain's main point of contact with the Circle for almost twenty years. The man who currently held the keys to his ascension to the organisation's highest level.

It had been Starke's idea to meet here, eschewing their usual meeting place in the remote parkland far outside the city. Today was going to be different, Cain knew. The change of venue signalled a change of circumstances, for both of them.

'Here's what's going to happen,' Starke said without preamble. 'Later today, you're going to receive a call from the director of National Intelligence, notifying you that he's officially recommending your name to the president as permanent CIA director.'

Cain could feel his heart beating faster with every word.

'About thirty minutes later, you'll take a call from the White House. The president will confirm that he'll be tabling a motion in the Senate to begin confirmation proceedings. He'll congratulate you. You'll act humble and ask if he's sure he wants to go with you. He'll assure you that you're his guy, and that he's confident he'll get the Senate votes he needs to have you confirmed. Then he'll end by thanking you for your years of service. You'll say you're honoured, that you'll endeavour to uphold the office of director, and then you'll politely shut your mouth and wait for him to hang up.'

Having finished his terse set of instructions, the NSA director turned to regard the man standing beside him.

'Is this in any way unclear?'

'I think I can manage that,' Cain said, keeping his tone perfectly neutral. He was well aware that his promotion to permanent director was against this man's wishes. And as much as he'd forced Starke to bend to his will, the man remained a formidable enemy. It would not do to gloat on the eve of his greatest triumph.

'Good.' Starke paused before adding, 'You understand of course that all of this is predicated on you delivering on your promise?'

'I do.'

'Because if your target were to escape, you'd find the president's support would disappear along with him.'

'He's not going to escape, Richard,' Cain promised. He'd make sure of it – even if he had to travel to Pakistan to oversee Bin Laden's capture personally. 'Our intel is solid.'

Starke exhaled slowly, his breath misting in the cool air as he looked out across the Tidal Basin to the towering columns of the Lincoln Memorial. A perimeter of security operatives watched over the two men, far enough away that they could talk without fear of being overheard.

'This will be our last meeting, Marcus.'

Cain looked at him then, a little taken aback by the finality of that statement. He could sense the air of bitterness and resentment in the normally stoic man. For the better part of two decades, Starke had been his conduit to the Circle. His one and only means of communication with the still-unknown group that lay at the very top of the pyramid. Now that he was being removed, it could mean only one thing.

'So who will I be working with?'

'The next time you're contacted, it'll be directly.'

Cain actually let out a breath as his words sank in. This was it. After more than two decades of carrying out their wishes, fulfilling their directives, fighting their battles, he was finally going to meet the leaders of the Circle face to face.

'When?'

'You'll be given instructions when the time comes,' Starke explained cryptically.

Cain sensed, however, that Starke wasn't withholding information out of choice; he was merely repeating what he'd been told. This moment represented a seismic shift in power and authority between the two men. Cain's influence was ascendant, while Starke was being forced to move aside and make way for him.

'I suggest you don't arrive late for the meeting.'

'When have you ever known me to be late, Richard?'

Starke didn't respond to that, and nor did Cain expect him to. Instead he pulled up the collar of his coat and glanced around, preparing to leave.

'I guess this is where we go our separate ways.'

For all the times they'd met and talked over the past two decades, there was little about Richard Starke that he found personally appealing. All things considered, he wouldn't be sad to see the back of him. However, this was still the end of a long relationship. Sensing the gravity and significance of the moment, Cain extended a hand.

'I'll see you around,' he said, unwilling to give him anything more meaningful.

'Likewise.' Reaching out, Starke took his hand. But rather than letting go, he tightened his grip and leaned in slightly. 'I've never been one to offer advice, but I'll give you some for free today. Be careful of loose ends.'

Cain raised an eyebrow, surprised by the intensity of the man's expression. 'Loose ends?'

'Drake and Anya. You never did account for them.'

'Like I told you, they're gone,' Cain said, quickly recovering his poise. 'Buried under a mountain in Afghanistan. Nobody will ever find them.'

And yet despite his confident words, a kernel of doubt remained in the acting CIA director. A troubling question that had gone unanswered.

Starke held his eye for several seconds – an uncharacteristically direct act for such a taciturn man – before releasing his grip.

'Well, like I say: be careful of loose ends. They have a habit of coming back to bite you.' With that final warning, he turned and began to walk away. 'Goodbye, Marcus. And good luck to you.'

'I don't need luck anymore,' Cain said under his breath, turning his attention back to the memorial before him. He remained there for some time, neither moving nor speaking, his thoughts as dark and troubled as the brooding sky overhead.

Finally reaching a decision, he fished a cell phone from his coat pocket and dialled. It didn't take long for his contact to answer.

'Hawkins.'

'Jason, I've got a job for you,' Cain began. 'I need you to pay a visit to an old friend.'

Chapter 4

North Wales, UK

Drake had lost his father many years ago. Since then, most of his possessions had been sold off or given away. But, unknown to either of his children, their mother had retained one item belonging to him. Something she had kept and carefully maintained for years. A gift, perhaps a peace offering, for her son that she'd never been permitted to give him in life.

And here it sat, beneath a dust sheet in the house's solid stone-built garage: a sleek, brooding shape beneath the covering. A slumbering beast waiting to awaken once more.

Grasping the cover, Drake whipped it away, revealing the graceful, elegant form of a classic 1967 Austin-Healey 3000 sports car, its dark green paintwork gleaming flawlessly in the electric lights overhead.

Jessica had never been much of a car enthusiast herself, yet even she could appreciate the machine sitting silently before them. An object so inextricably linked to their father that it seemed to be imbued with his very essence. She could still picture him seated behind the wheel, his eyes alive with boyish delight as he fired up the engine.

Beside her, she felt sure her brother was entertaining similar thoughts. Compared to their aloof and distant mother, Ryan's relationship with his father had been fiery and tumultuous. Two very different men whose personalities never quite aligned, whose lives went in very different directions.

Stepping forward, Drake reached out and gently, almost reverently ran his hand along the bodywork, tracing the flared line of the wheel arch. His back was to Jessica. She couldn't see his expression, but she didn't need to.

'It's beautiful,' Jessica said, genuinely meaning it.

Then, to her surprise, Drake strode over to the garage's double doors, unbolted them and hauled them open, allowing weak afternoon sunlight to flood in.

She frowned. 'What are you doing?'

'Cars are meant to be driven,' he said, grasping the windshield and leaping lightly into the driver's seat. He looked up at her then and, just for a second, she saw a shadow of the man who'd raised him. 'Don't you want to try it? Just once?'

'Ryan, I...' she began to protest but trailed off. There were probably a hundred reasons why this was a bad idea, but right then, she couldn't name a single one.

'Trust me, Jess.'

She sighed, resigning herself to the inevitable. 'I know I'm going to regret this.'

Gripping the door sill, she hoisted herself up and over, settling into the passenger seat with a little less grace than Drake had.

'Might want to practise that one,' he advised with a wry smile.

Jessica's retort was a short, hard punch to the shoulder, delivered with enough force to remind him that she might be his younger sister, but she wasn't going to be mocked. 'Next one's aimed at your mouth.'

Grinning, Drake turned the ignition over. The old starter motor whined and strained, the engine turning sluggishly as it tried to fire. It caught once, struggled, faltered, then gave a cough and suddenly roared into life as oil and fuel began to flow freely again and old machinery rumbled back into action. The engine sounded rough and rattling for the first few seconds, and Jessica held her breath. But, to her surprise, it quickly settled down, the venerable machinery finding its rhythm again.

'You ready?' he asked.

Jessica glanced at her brother. 'I've—'

Before she could finish, he dropped it into first gear and stomped on the gas. The sports car rocketed forward, straight down her driveway and onto the narrow road beyond, the engine peaking and receding as Drake cycled through the gears. Chill wind whipped past her face, tugging at her hair as the speed climbed steadily.

40mph, 50mph...

The chassis strained beneath them, the engine roaring and snarling like a living thing as Drake pushed it hard.

'Jesus!' she cried out, gripping the door handle as Drake swung hard left, following the winding country road. The tyres skidded and screeched and bit into the tarmac, tenuously maintaining their grip. Stone walls and fences whipped by frighteningly fast on both sides.

'You're going to get us killed, you bloody maniac!' Jessica said, having to shout to be heard above the roar of the engine and the wind.

'Just getting a feel for it!' Drake called back, grinning just like their father had done. 'It's been a while!'

'Is that supposed to reassure me?'

'Not really.'

The winding country roads that traversed this region were all but deserted at this time of year, giving Drake free rein to push the powerful old sports car as hard as he wished. And push it he did, tearing through narrow turns and opening it up on the straights, unleashing the car's full power.

Despite her reservations, even Jessica had to admit there was something intoxicating about it. The roar of the wind, the throaty growl of the engine, the vibration of the machinery straining and labouring beneath them, the barely constrained power propelling them onward.

Drake seemed to have a sixth sense of just how hard to push it, how fast to take each corner, how close the wheels were to losing their grip. He took it right to the brink, pushing the car to the limits of its performance, and deep down she understood why.

She didn't try to intervene: this was something he needed to do.

They drove for some time, heading west, away from the mountains and valleys of Jessica's home, riding in virtual silence. It was too loud to converse much, and Jessica sensed this wasn't the right time.

Drake finally pulled over at a small, deserted parking lot, situated on a headland overlooking a broad sweep of sandy beach below. Beyond it lay the grey-green waters of the Irish Sea, shimmering in the late-afternoon sun. A cold breeze carried the sharp tang of sea salt and the intermittent crash of breaking waves.

Shutting down the engine, Drake sighed and looked out across the sea.

'You know how many times I wanted to do that?' he asked. 'Dad never would let me.'

'Can you blame him?' Jessica retorted. 'If he'd seen the way you drive, he would have kicked your arse.'

Her brother smiled, but it was tinged with sadness.

'I've made mistakes, Jess,' he finally said. 'A lot of them.'

'We all have.'

He shook his head slowly. 'Not like mine.'

Jessica listened in silence while Drake laid it all out. Everything that had happened since they last parted ways: the aborted mission to apprehend Marcus Cain in Pakistan, his team's ambush and capture, the desperate plan by Anya and a few others to bring about their rescue. He even told her of his growing mental instability, culminating in a deadly confrontation in Afghanistan just a few weeks earlier, where he'd learned the buried truth of his own past.

By the time he'd finished his astounding and harrowing tale, the sun was settling on the horizon, its fiery glow setting the sea and clouds ablaze.

'My God…' Jessica finally muttered, shaking her head in shock.

Even in her wildest imaginings, she could never have foreseen such a chain of events playing out for her brother. She could only guess at how he must have been feeling now, knowing the things he had done to get here.

'Like I said, I've made mistakes. The kind you don't come back from,' he acknowledged grimly. 'I wouldn't blame you if you felt differently about me now, Jess. I *am* different. I'm not the man you used to know.'

Jessica lowered her head, unable to look at him. 'I'm sorry.'

Drake swallowed but nodded, accepting it as one accepts all bad news they've long expected. He didn't deserve forgiveness and under-standing, from her or anyone else. On balance, he imagined the scales were now weighted pretty heavily against him.

'You don't have to be sorry. I understand, and… I don't blame you,' he promised her. 'No one could expect you to live with something like this.'

He reached for the ignition key, deciding they ought to start back.

'No,' she said suddenly.

Drake stopped, his hand on the key.

Tentatively, Jessica put her hand on his arm. 'Look at me, Ryan.'

He did, however reluctantly.

'I'm sorry for what you've been through,' she whispered. 'I… I can't imagine what it must have been like. To lose people, to be forced to make those choices, to not trust your own mind…' She trailed off, her voice strained and her eyes glistening. 'But... it doesn't change a thing. Whatever you were forced to do, you're still my brother. I love you, and I *know* you. I've always known you. I know you're a good man.'

Drake didn't say anything to that. He simply leaned over and pulled her close, hugging her tight the same way she'd held him when he'd turned up on her doorstep earlier in the day. When he let go at last, Jessica leaned back in her seat and turned her gaze out to sea.

'As for the letter, maybe... I don't know, maybe it's better that it's gone?' she suggested tentatively. 'Maybe it's time to let this one go.'

She could almost feel the darkening of Drake's expression, the tension that rose in him as he wrestled with his failure, wondering at what might have been. The mystery he would never solve, the answers he would never find.

'You're right,' he said quietly, conceding to it at last. 'This has gone on long enough. It has to end sometime.'

Jessica let out the breath she'd been holding, feeling the dark mood departing as if carried away by the cold breeze. Reluctant he might have been, but her brother had finally laid aside the burden he'd been carrying for the past two years.

'Thank you,' she whispered, resting her hand on his. Then, wishing to move past the difficult moment, she added in a brighter voice, 'Now can we get the hell out of here? I'm bloody freezing!'

Drake laughed then. A genuine, heartfelt laugh as he fired the engine back into life and pulled out of the parking lot.

It was almost dark by the time they made it back, and not a moment too soon by the looks of things. The first fat, heavy flakes of snow were beginning to fall as they pulled into her driveway.

Today had been one of the most foolish, most ill-conceived trips Jessica could recall making in a very long time. But she didn't care one bit. They'd both needed it. And even if her hands and feet were numb and her face was stinging, she'd enjoyed it.

'It's getting late,' Drake said as he bolted the garage doors closed, casting a quick look at the worsening snowfall. 'I should get going.'

'You must be kidding,' Jessica said, leading the way back towards the house. 'The roads around here are a nightmare once the snow starts. Stay for the night, at least until the weather improves.'

Drake glanced outside again. Having endured SAS Selection in these very mountains and valleys, he was all too aware of how quickly the weather could deteriorate. He'd never forget one particularly grim march along an exposed mountain ridge, when a sudden powerful gust had knocked every one of them over like bowling pins, including the directing staff.

However, that didn't mean staying here was a safe alternative. Drake was, as far as the CIA was concerned, officially dead – killed during a raid in Afghanistan several weeks ago. In theory at least, the international manhunt for him was over, and with it any lingering surveillance on his sister.

That didn't mean it was true, though.

'It could be dangerous,' he warned. 'People might be looking for me.'

'I know.' He saw a sly smile then, a mischievous gleam in her eye. The kind he'd given her earlier to get her in the car. 'But you know what? Fuck them.'

Drake couldn't help but smile. 'Fuck them, eh?'

'Yeah, fuck them,' she repeated, warming to the idea. There was a defiant, recalcitrant side to Jessica's nature that she didn't often show, especially as she'd grown into adulthood. But it was there all the same, and today's events had clearly awoken it. 'I've spent long enough being afraid of those arseholes. I think I deserve a night off. And so do you.'

Drake rubbed his jaw, weighing up the choice. Jessica, however, seemed to have made up her mind already.

'I don't know about you, but I haven't eaten a thing all day,' she said, turning away and heading for the front door. 'God knows, you look like you could use a decent meal.'

'Yeah? Who's making it?' Drake called after her.

'Piss off, I'm better than you,' she retorted. 'And I've got a bloody excellent bottle of merlot.'

Drake couldn't help but grin as he followed her. 'Now you've got my interest.'

The prospect of a hot meal, a good drink and the chance to reconnect with the sister he hadn't seen in two years was enough to melt through his reluctance. And more than that, he could feel the change in the air between them. The tension and distance seemed to have dissipated now, banter and playful insults quickly taking the place of sombre reflection and painful revelation.

Tomorrow Drake would have to begin again, finding a new way forward without the answers he'd come for. But for tonight at least, they were simply brother and sister. And that was enough.

Chapter 5

Drake awoke to a different world. The snow had continued unabated throughout the night, leaving the surrounding fields enshrouded in a sparkling blanket of soft whiteness, all laid out beneath a crisp blue morning sky.

The sun was just peeking over the horizon when he emerged from the house, trudging uphill through the snow. What he was about to do, he didn't want Jessica to overhear. In any case, the cell phone reception was notoriously patchy in the Welsh valleys, forcing him to seek higher ground.

He made it about 300 metres from the house before a couple of signal bars appeared on his phone.

It was about six a.m. here, making it late evening in his contact's part of the world. Knowing her as he did, he guessed it would be a few hours yet before she turned in. He just hoped she wasn't too intoxicated.

The phone rang for a good ten seconds before she finally picked up. Drake didn't speak right away, instead waiting while the phone's custom-built encryption software did its thing, establishing a secure connection with the other unit.

'Ryan, how's it going there?' Keira Frost asked. Drake could hear music and loud conversation in the background, confirming his suspicions that Frost had been hitting the bars. 'Did you find what you were looking for?'

'It was a bust, Keira,' he informed her. No sense in sugar coating it. 'The letter's gone. Jessica destroyed it.'

'Fuck…' It wasn't exactly poetry, but it effectively summed up his opinion on the matter. 'What will you do now?'

'This is a dead end. Nothing more I can do here.'

'I'm sorry, man. I know you had a lot riding on this.'

'Don't be. Maybe some things are better left alone,' he acknowledged. 'Anyway, that's not why I'm calling. I need you to do something for me.'

'Had a feeling you would,' she said cynically.

'I need you to find Anya for me,' Drake stated. 'Whatever it takes, whatever resources you need, make it happen.'

'Ryan…'

'No arguments, Keira.'

'Listen, Anya doesn't *want* to be found,' Frost warned him. 'You said yourself, some things are better left alone.'

'A lot of people don't want to be found. It's never stopped us before.'

'You're not hearing me. If Anya doesn't want to be found, she won't be. She'll go off the grid, disappear. Even I can't find someone like that.'

'It's not just her you're looking for,' Drake reminded her.

Frost hesitated, sensing what he was getting at. Anya might have gone dark, but she'd taken a member of the team with her. A man who almost certainly wouldn't live off the grid. If they could find him, it might lead them to Anya.

'It might be possible,' she conceded reluctantly. 'But I stress the word "might". He's good at what he does. It won't be easy.'

'It never is, but you're just as good as him. I know you can do this.'

'Fuck off,' she bit back. 'I don't need a bullshit pep talk.'

'So you'll do it?' he coaxed.

'It'll take time.'

'I've got plenty of *that*.'

Frost sighed, bowing to the inevitable. 'Say, through some miracle, you find her. What good do you think it'll do? She left for a reason, Ryan. She's not going to help us.'

Drake thought for a moment about the woman he was searching for. Anya – angry, betrayed, vengeful, lethal. A woman with nothing left to lose.

'It's not us I'm worried about,' Drake commented darkly. 'It's her.'

Part Two

Something to Strive For

Nothing is such a heavy burden as a secret.

French Proverb

Chapter 6

Marcus Cain was out of breath, sporting a dozen angry red mosquito bites and perspiring in the hot afternoon sun by the time he reached his destination. He'd been obliged to abandon his car several miles back when the old logging track – optimistically called a road – finally gave out.

It had been a long hike uphill to get here, following a game trail through the heavily forested foothills of the Blue Ridge Mountains as the temperature rose along with the sun.

Yet here he was, at one of the most isolated homesteads he'd ever visited. No phone line, no power or water, no road access. Nobody could enter or leave this place in a hurry, that was for sure. And that was exactly how the owner wanted it. A good defensive position that could only be approached on foot.

It certainly wasn't much to look at: a simple log cabin, constructed from rough, sawn timbers, its roof densely covered with moss. Perhaps an old hunting lodge or forestry outpost, repaired and repurposed.

As for the owner, there was no sign.

'Anya!' he called out, approaching the front porch. 'It's Marcus. I came here to talk.'

No response. It seemed she was absent.

Cain paused to consider his options, wondering whether to wait for her to return, go out looking for her or abandon his mission altogether. The second option would likely prove futile. Anya had grown up in this kind of terrain, and he was quite certain she could disappear into it without a trace if she wished.

'You're getting sloppy, Marcus.'

Whirling around, Cain watched as a figure emerged from the foliage, seemingly coalescing into solid reality before his eyes. A woman, her face smeared with dirt to aid concealment, dressed in woodland camo gear that blended in perfectly with her surroundings. She was holding a powerful black hunting bow, an arrow notched and the string drawn back.

A deadly weapon, trained on him.

'You gonna use that?' Cain asked, standing his ground.

'I could,' Anya reminded him. 'Your laws give me the right to defend my property.'

She was testing him, trying to make him sweat. 'All I want is to talk.'

Anya held him in her sights for a few seconds, the bow creaking slightly under the strain, before finally easing the string and lowering the weapon.

'I've done enough hunting today,' she decided, reaching down for the pair of dead rabbits by her feet and slinging them over her shoulder.

Cain watched as she dumped her hunting spoils on a chopping block at the side of the cabin, before laying the bow carefully aside.

'How long were you following me?'

'Picked up your trail about a mile back,' she explained, unzipping her camouflage jacket. 'You are not hard to find.'

'You are,' he said, giving her a meaningful look. 'What's going on, Anya? Why are you out here, in the middle of nowhere?'

'I wanted to be alone. This place suits me well enough.'

Drawing her hunting knife, she used it to separate the two rabbits and went to work on the first one, gutting and skinning it with brisk, clinical efficiency.

'And how long do you plan on keeping this up?'

'Why do you ask?' She didn't look at him, her attention focussed on her grisly task.

'Because you're better than this,' Cain ventured. 'The Anya I know never backed down from a fight.'

Slamming the point of her knife into the chopping block with enough force to leave the weapon standing upright in the wood, she glared at him.

'Is that what the psychologists at Langley told you to say? Appeal to my sense of duty? Threaten me with a wasted life?' She gave him a wan, almost pitying smile. 'We have both played those games long enough to know better.'

'This isn't a game,' he said. 'It's a chance to come back.'

'Like a good little soldier?' she asked mockingly.

'Like the woman I used to know.'

'Goodbye, Marcus.' Yanking the knife free from the chopping block, she gathered up the remains of her kill and headed for the edge of the clearing.

'We found him.'

Those three words were enough to stop her in her tracks. Cain watched as the young woman slowly lowered her head, saw her shoulders slump as she exhaled, saw the muscles and tendons in her forearm tense as she tightened her grip on the knife.

'Luka. He's in Ukraine.' Cain approached her warily. 'He sold out your unit, in exchange for amnesty from the Soviets.'

Anya didn't turn around right away, and Cain didn't reach out to her. He knew she wouldn't stand for it. Instead, he waited. Waited for her to compose herself.

Only when she trusted herself to face him did she turn.

'You're certain?' she asked, looking – hoping – for any trace of doubt.

Cain nodded. 'I read the whole dossier. He'd been in contact with them for weeks. He gave them everything: deployment patterns, radio frequencies, the works.' Reaching into the satchel he'd brought with him, he opened the file at the surveillance picture of Anya's former comrade and held it out to her. 'I wish it hadn't come to this.'

He saw the muscles in her throat tighten. 'What are you asking of me?'

'Luka has to answer for what he did,' Cain said quietly. 'One way or another, he will.'

'You want me to kill one of my brothers?'

'The man betrayed you.'

'The man fought with me, trained with me, bled with me,' she replied heatedly.

'Look, I can't tell you what to do. I came here to give you a choice, nothing more.' He paused. 'But before you decide, you should know they're offering you command of Task Force Black.'

It wasn't often that he saw surprise written so plainly on Anya's face. 'Command?'

'The men are loyal to you, and only you. After what you did in Afghanistan, they won't fight without you.' Cain allowed that admission to sink in, studying her reactions carefully. He sensed the flicker of pride and emotion his words had stirred up.

That was her weakness, he knew. The devotion she felt towards the men she'd fought beside. She'd struggled so hard, given up so much to win their acceptance. The news that she now had their respect, their loyalty, weakened her resolve.

'They need you now,' Cain said softly. 'And I think... maybe you need them.'

Slowly Anya reached out and took the dossier from him, her fingers leaving bloody smears on Luka's photograph. She stared at it for a time before lifting her head to meet Cain's expectant gaze.

'These don't sound like your words, Marcus.'

'What does that mean?'

'Freya.' The young woman sighed. 'She sent you here, didn't she?'

Cain knew that any attempt at deception now would be unwise, perhaps even lethal. 'She helped me when no one else would. The men she works for... they could help us make a real difference, just like we always wanted.'

Anya didn't answer him right away. But she gave him a look of sadness, almost pity, as if his words were a delusion that only she could see through. As if she could already see the path that lay ahead.

'You still don't see it, do you? They will use us until there is nothing left,' Anya said. 'They will be the end of you... and me.'

Despite the hot afternoon sun, Cain felt a chill of foreboding run through him. Anya's words weren't spoken in anger or frustration, but instead with a kind of weary acceptance, as if she'd already resigned herself to the dark future that lay ahead.

'I won't let that happen,' he argued defiantly. 'Ever.'

She handed him back the dossier, now marked by her bloody fingerprints.

'I'll come back, Marcus,' she said quietly. But when he tried to take it, she held on firmly. 'Not for you, or for her, but for my brothers. They are all that matters to me now.'

Cain held her gaze. The fire was back, burning fiercely behind those icy blue eyes of hers. A fire that had no warmth left for him.

Tel Aviv, Israel – April 24th, 2011

It was a warm, balmy evening in Tel Aviv, the heat of the day lingering long after the sun had set. A meagre offshore breeze sighed in from the Mediterranean, stirring the palm fronds that lined the roads as the pace of the city slowed for the night.

Chanan Russo certainly felt like slowing down as he pulled to a stop outside his home, waiting while the building's security gate trundled open.

An unassuming man of sixty-five years, he was reluctantly coming to terms with the fact that time was running against him. He felt stiff and weary when he rose each morning, waking often during the night to use the bathroom. His body, once lean and fit during his days in the Israeli Defence Force, was growing soft and weak.

He was, as much as he hated the fact, growing old.

And yet, he still had responsibilities. As a senior case officer for the Mossad – Israel's elite and much-feared intelligence agency – the demands of his work did not relent. His country had many enemies, both at home and abroad, and they had no regard for an old man nearing the end of his career.

Parking in the car port at the side of his house, he killed the engine and stepped out into the warm evening air. He inhaled, smelling the scent of juniper trees from his neighbour's garden. He'd always found the smell strangely comforting.

The house was in darkness as he entered, silent and empty since his wife's death nine years earlier. He didn't think he would ever quite get used to it.

This time, though, something was different. Tonight, the house wasn't quite as still as it should be. Tonight, it wasn't empty.

Instinctively, his hand went to the 9mm IWI Jericho pistol holstered at his hip.

'Stop.'

Russo froze, struck not just by the command, but by the voice that had delivered it. A woman's voice.

A switch was flicked, and suddenly the hallway blazed with light, revealing his assailant. A woman holding a silenced automatic trained on his centre mass. A woman he recognised.

Russo let out a sigh then. He had been waiting for this day for four years.

'I imagined you would find your way here,' he said, speaking English. He knew she understood Hebrew, but was not fluent enough in the language to properly converse.

Ignoring his words, Anya gestured to the weapon he had come so close to drawing. 'Take the gun out and place it on the floor. Then slide it towards me.'

Russo did as she asked, laying the Jericho on the tiled floor and giving it a kick with his foot to slide it towards her.

'Now close the front door,' she instructed. 'Don't even think about running.'

Russo might have laughed under other circumstances. At his age, he wasn't exactly quick on his feet.

Again, he did as she asked, closing the door to the outside world. As he did so, he caught the scent of juniper bushes before turning to face her once more.

She had aged since the last time they'd met. Still a strikingly beautiful woman, it was nonetheless obvious that the past eight years left their mark on her. There were lines around her mouth and eyes that hadn't been there before, a hardness to her features, a light of vengeance in her eyes.

Yes, Chanan Russo knew exactly why Anya was here tonight.

Bending down, she picked up his weapon, then gestured to the living room off the main hall. 'In there. On the couch. Keep your hands where I can see them.'

He knew better than to do anything except comply, stepping through the arched doorway and settling himself on the couch. Anya lowered herself into a chair opposite, keeping him covered.

'I am unarmed,' he said. 'Tell me what you want.'

He saw a flicker of something behind those blue eyes of hers then. Anger, fury, pain.

'What I want,' she repeated, before taking a long, slow breath. 'In 2003, you brokered a meeting between myself and an Iraqi defector who identified himself by the code name Typhoon.'

She was speaking coldly, clinically, as if delivering an official debriefing.

'I did.'

Anya nodded slowly. 'En route to that meeting, I was ambushed and captured by a Russian assault team.' She paused before continuing. 'Someone told them where I would be. Neither myself nor Typhoon wanted the meeting to fail. That leaves only one possibility, Chanan.'

Russo closed his eyes and sighed. In addition to her lethal assassination skills, he was well aware of Anya's uncanny ability to detect deception in others. The little cues and tics that went unnoticed by most people were as clear as day to her. Even trained intelligence agents had struggled to defeat it.

'Yes,' he said at length. 'It was me.'

Anya didn't react to his admission at all. Her expression was cold, emotionless, utterly focussed on him.

'Go on.'

'I was approached by a group of men who knew I'd been in contact with you. They knew you had used me as a broker for the meeting, and they wanted to know where it was happening.'

'Russians?'

Russo shook his head. 'No. Pakistani intelligence agents.'

That was when her mask began to slip. He heard an exhalation of breath, saw her focus waver for a moment as his revelation sank in.

'You're lying,' she spat.

'Am I?' he asked. 'Look at me, Anya. You tell me if I'm lying.'

'It makes no sense.'

'And yet it is the truth.'

Her tension was almost palpable now. 'Whose orders were they acting on?'

Russo couldn't help but feel a touch of sympathy for this woman, who had given up so much for men who appreciated it so little.

'I don't know.'

There was a flash from the silenced weapon, a muted thump, and an explosion of wood fragments and tattered cloth beside him. Russo flinched instinctively, feeling the sting of splinters in his arm and neck.

'Think hard.'

'I think I heard one of them mention a name. Vizur.'

The sudden widening of her eyes told him this name was familiar to her. 'You are certain of this?'

'As certain as I can be.' He leaned forward a little. 'Who is he?'

Anya didn't respond. There was a haunted, devastated look in her eyes.

Russo felt compelled to offer her something. 'I know how little this will mean to you, but… I am sorry for what happened.'

'You're sorry,' she repeated distantly. 'I spent four years in solitary confinement, Chanan. A place so far from the light that I forgot what it even felt like. The things they did to me…'

She trailed off, perhaps not trusting herself to say more. It was painfully clear to him that she had been broken in ways that could never be fixed.

Russo chewed his lip, deciding she was owed an explanation. 'The day those men paid a visit to me, they brought a laptop computer with them. They sat me down where you are sitting right now, and they showed me a live video feed of my daughter and grandson in the park. They made it clear that if I didn't give them what they wanted, my family would be dead within an hour. They would make it last the full sixty minutes, and they would make me watch every moment.'

He closed his eyes, thinking back to that terrible afternoon. The fear, the horror, the impotent rage.

'So I did it. I gave up your life to save theirs, Anya. And I did it without regret or hesitation. Because they deserved to live. They are good people, and we are not. We made the choice to be what we are.'

'I was good once,' she said in a small, pensive voice.

Russo didn't respond. He just watched as she rose slowly from the chair; the same chair from which he had betrayed her.

'You know what has to happen.'

Swallowing, Russo looked her in the eye and nodded. He'd known from the first moment he laid eyes on her. Perhaps he'd known since the news reached him that she had escaped from Russian custody.

'You know they will come after you,' he warned her. 'Mossad will not rest until you are dead.'

'I know.'

Standing up, Russo calmly straightened his tie. He couldn't really say why he did it, but it felt appropriate somehow. To die on his feet, facing it down as a man should.

'I'm ready.'

There was no formality, no final words of forgiveness or apology from her. Just two quick flashes, two heavy thuds as the rounds slammed into his chest. He went down, falling backwards onto the couch, his blood soaking into the fabric.

The last thing he saw as his vision faded was Anya, lowering the weapon and turning away. He caught himself wondering, in a distant sort of way, where she would go next, what she would do with this knowledge, and how many more men would die before she was finished.

Then those thoughts vanished, and Russo knew no more.

Chapter 7

Oxford – April 25th

It had been a fruitless and largely frustrating couple of months for Drake, chasing leads that ultimately went nowhere, and accomplishing little except to waste time and resources. Frost's worldwide search for Anya had yielded only occasional scraps of information; tiny hints to her movements that arrived far too late for him to act on. She was a ghost, moving across the world unseen and unheard.

But she was alive. That much was certain. And knowing her as he did, it was unlikely she'd walk away from whatever she was planning. It was only a matter of time before she made her move.

The call came through on a rainy Wednesday afternoon, while Drake was jogging along a path beside the River Thames as it wound its way through the heart of the ancient city. A call from Frost.

'What have you got?' he asked, trying to quieten his breathing.

Straight away Frost's tone made it clear this was different. Something had happened. Something big.

'A Mossad agent was assassinated in Tel Aviv last night,' she began. 'Intelligence services are shitting themselves over it, blaming everyone from the Palestinians to the Iranians. But witnesses reported seeing a woman leaving the scene around the time of the killing. A woman with blonde hair.'

A chill ran through him then, quickening his already pumping heart. 'What was the agent's name?'

'Russo. Chanan Russo.'

In an instant, Drake's mind flashed back to a conversation with Anya four years earlier, as they'd tried to piece together the circumstances that had led to her imprisonment in a Russian jail.

'I made contact with him through a broker, and after that we communicated through anonymous email accounts.'

46

'Who was the broker?' Drake asked.

'An Israeli Mossad agent named Russo. I had worked with him before, and he had contacts throughout the Iraqi government.' She shook her head. 'But I will not approach him again. He has close ties with the Agency.'

'Shit,' he said under his breath, the pieces falling together in his mind.

'You know him?'

'Russo brokered the meeting Anya was supposed to go to eight years ago,' Drake explained. 'She never made it.'

'You think he sold her out?'

'*She* obviously does.'

Drake shook his head, realising the magnitude of the decision Anya had just made. By taking out Russo, she had effectively broadcasted her presence to Cain and the Agency. They would have to know she was still alive now.

And if they knew Anya was alive, they knew he was too. The anonymity he'd enjoyed over the past couple of months had just vanished.

'I have to go,' he said, his mind racing. 'If they know I'm still alive, they'll come for Jess…'

North Wales, UK

Jessica was in a buoyant mood as she made her way downstairs, moving with the kind of spring in her step that she hadn't enjoyed in a long time. The long cold and darkness of winter were receding at last, the days growing noticeably longer as the world around her returned to life.

Making her way through to the small, comfortable workspace that served as her home office, she switched on her computer, intending to tackle the steadily growing list of emails. For obvious reasons, she had kept a low profile over the past few years, both professionally and personally, but that too was changing.

With Drake officially considered dead, the shadow that had loomed over her for the past few years had receded. Already she had begun making plans to end her self-imposed isolation and return to the real world – re-establishing contact with former business associates, feeling them out for job opportunities, speaking with estate agents and lawyers, looking at places to relocate.

She felt as if her life was starting afresh, and it was a good feeling. She was planning to tell her brother the next time he came to check in on her, and had even bought a bottle of his favourite whisky to celebrate.

She was just about to get started on her work when the doorbell rang.

Jessica glanced up. She didn't get many visitors. But there was always the possibility of a lost delivery driver or hiking party that had strayed off course in the twisting valleys.

Rising from the desk, she opened a drawer and fished out a little metal cylinder that she always kept there, popping it in the back pocket of her jeans out of habit.

The doorbell rang again as she strode through the hallway, unlatched the door and allowed it to open a few inches on its security chain.

The man facing her was about forty years old, short and stocky, the thinning remains of his hair closely cropped. He was wearing the dark blue coveralls and work boots of an engineer. Parked in the driveway behind him was a utility van.

'Morning,' he said cheerfully, glancing down at the tablet PC he was carrying. 'Mrs… Drake, is it?'

'*Ms* Drake,' Jessica corrected him. 'Can I help you?'

'Actually, yes. My name's Gareth Thomas,' he said, holding up an ID card. 'We've had some complaints about power outages in the area. Have you had any issues with your supply?'

'Not really.'

'Ah, good,' he said, clearly relieved. 'Well, not good, but it's a start. Would you mind if I check your mains box, just to get a reading?'

Jessica thought about it for a moment, her natural wariness vying with her desire to get it over with so she could resume her work. She was about to speak when her cell phone started ringing in the kitchen, distracting her. One of the few people who had her number was Ryan.

'Ms Drake, I really would like to get this done so I can move on,' the engineer said. He was smiling at her, but it didn't seem quite so cheerful now. There was a harder, more impatient undertone in his voice that immediately set her on edge.

'Actually, do you mind if I take this call first?' she said, pushing the door shut.

But quick as a flash, he jammed his heavy work boot in the gap, preventing her from closing it. Her eyes flashed up to his, meeting a steely, ruthless gaze.

'I insist,' he snarled as he brought up a pair of bolt cutters and snipped the security chain like a gardener pruning stray branches. With nothing to impede the door, a single hard shove with his considerable weight sent Jessica reeling backwards into the wall opposite with bruising force.

The world seemed to go into slow motion as he advanced through the doorway, the dark glint of a weapon in his hand, the long barrel of a silencer swinging up towards her. The amiable, apologetic face was gone now, transformed into a look of cold, calculating aggression.

There had been a time, several years earlier, when a situation not unlike this had befallen Jessica. When armed men had quickly and easily subdued her before bundling her into a waiting van. She'd barely even tried to fight back as shock and fear took over, like some animal caught in the headlights, unable to move, unable to think.

But that had been a different time, and she'd been a different person; naïve and unprepared. Not today.

Jessica went straight for him, closing the gap as fast as her legs would carry her. A mixture of self-defence training, instinct and sudden, raw fury had taken over. She didn't know who this man was, what he wanted from her or why, but it didn't matter.

The self-defence instructors she'd trained with had taught her some very valuable lessons about taking on an armed opponent. De-escalate if possible, retreat if necessary, and fight if essential. But if you're going to fight, go at it with everything you have. Hold nothing back.

Reaching into her back pocket, she whipped out the miniature can of pepper spray she'd put there, took aim and fired it straight into his face. She saw a momentary flicker of surprise before his eyes suddenly squeezed shut and his face contorted in agony. Jessica could feel the potent fumes stinging her eyes.

There was a sudden flash, and she heard a muted thump that reverberated off the walls, followed by the crash of splintering wood as a stray round punched through a nearby door. He was firing blind, but there was a good chance he might score a hit anyway.

Discarding the canister of pepper spray, Jessica swept her left arm up and drove it into his wrist. The impact painfully jarred the bones in her own arm, the vibrations shivering all the way up to her shoulder, but it didn't matter. What mattered was wrapping her other hand over the top of the weapon and pushing downward with all the force she could command.

The bones of the human wrist are not designed to cope with that kind of lateral pressure, and suddenly he was presented with a very clear choice: release the weapon, or watch as his radius and ulna bones snapped like twigs. He went for the former option, allowing her to wrench it from his grasp.

Jessica stayed right on him, delivering a savage kick to the groin that dropped him to his knees. Realising the danger he was in, he swung his fists left and right, before Jessica swung the butt of the gun against the side of his head. A dull, fleshy thump rang out as steel met skull.

It took two hard strikes to drop him, and she'd scarcely delivered the second one before she heard shouting outside. Glancing out the open door, she saw that the van doors had flown open and two more men were rushing towards the house, both armed.

Heart pounding with a mixture of anger, adrenaline and primal fear, Jessica tore down the hallway to the kitchen. She'd barely slammed the door shut behind her and wedged a chair against the handle when she heard footsteps and shouts in the hallway.

With great effort, Jessica forced back the mounting panic as she looked around the room, trying to stay logical and clear-headed. She was facing a larger force of armed professionals. She had been lucky and caught the first man off guard, but fighting his companions wasn't an option.

She needed another way out.

Her attention snapped to the alarm unit mounted on the wall nearby. She'd had one installed in every room, so she could trigger it from any part of the house. Leaping forward, she hit the panic button, and straight away the loud electronic wail of the exterior alarm began to blare out.

This done, she turned her attention to the weapon in her right hand. It was a Heckler & Koch automatic, its solid frame rendered even heavier by the bulky suppressor attached to the barrel. She didn't know the calibre, and nor did she care at that moment. It was loaded, and the safety was off.

Taking aim at the door, she squeezed the trigger three times, firing blind into the hallway beyond. The recoil was more powerful than she'd expected, and the thud of the subsonic rounds seemed to resonate up her arm. Nonetheless, the wood splintered and shattered as the rounds punched straight through, and over the sound of the alarm she heard a warning shout from the hallway.

'Contact! Contact!'

On the other side of the door, two operatives in tactical body armour had flattened themselves against the walls to avoid the random gunfire. Their Kevlar vests would protect them from direct hits, but there was always a chance that a lucky shot would strike an unprotected limb.

Already, one of their number was lying sprawled on the floor, groaning in pain. One untrained civilian should have been an easy snatch and grab. Now they were quickly becoming embroiled in a full-scale house assault against a target that they needed to capture alive. Worse, the deafening noise of the alarm rendered verbal and radio communication impossible.

Still, they had the advantage of training, firepower and numbers – three factors they were ready and eager to make use of.

The operative on the right unhooked a flashbang grenade from his webbing, pulled the pin and advanced on the door while his companion covered him. Exchanging a brief glance with his comrade, he silently counted down.

Three, two, one...

Allowing the fly-off handle to detach, he kicked the kitchen door open, shattering the chair wedged against it, and tossed the weapon inside. A second later, the house trembled with a concussive boom as the stun grenade detonated.

Both men were through the door in moments, their weapons sweeping the room, expecting to find their target blinded and incapacitated. Easy pickings.

The room was deserted.

'Clear!'

'Clear! Where is she?'

The back door was still locked and secured. Anyway, that entrance was covered by a third man outside. If she'd tried to make a break for it, he would have spotted her.

It was only when one of them glanced down at the floor that he noticed a rug had been moved, as if hastily thrown aside. And there, set flush into the floorboards, was a small wooden trapdoor.

Rushing forward, his comrade grasped the handle and yanked the door upward. What he failed to notice was the thin, barely visible tripwire attached to the door, or the sawn-off shotgun fixed to the wall in the shadows beneath it, its twin barrels pointing upward.

He certainly did notice it, however, when the weapon discharged two shells of buckshot directly into his chest with an almighty crack, the impact knocking him backwards so that he landed in a sprawl several feet away. His vest had barely saved him from what would otherwise have been a lethal hail of close-range projectiles, but the force of the gunshot had bruised his ribs and knocked the air from his lungs.

'Shit!' the other operative hissed, reaching for his radio as his comrade struggled to get up. 'All units, be advised we have a hidden exit in the kitchen floor. Target may be outside the perimeter. Get me eyes on, now!'

He'd barely issued his terse command before the sound of an engine firing up drew his attention outside. The noise was high-pitched and rough, not a car engine but something smaller and lighter. He rushed over to the broken kitchen windows just in time to see a dirt bike go rocketing out of a stone outbuilding nearby, with his target bent low over the handlebars.

Taking hasty aim, he opened fire through the broken glass, spraying a burst of submachine gun rounds at the fast-moving vehicle, hoping to puncture a tyre or disable the engine. But the shots just churned up clods of wet earth several feet behind his target.

And then, in a flash, she had disappeared beyond his line of sight.

'Be advised, target is on the move,' he snapped into his radio, throwing open the back door and rushing outside. 'Heading north-east towards the woods. All units, move to intercept!'

Jessica was oblivious to the frantic orders being issued in her wake as she twisted the throttle hard, urging the bike down the grassy slope away from the house at dangerously high speed. Water splattered her face, soaking the long hair that streamed behind her in the rushing wind.

Swinging the handlebars hard right, she eased off the throttle and leaned her weight to one side while the bike sliced through the turn, before giving it full power again. The rear tyre spun and clawed at the wet ground, throwing up clumps of mud and torn grass, but somehow she managed to hold the fishtailing bike under control.

At any moment she expected more gunfire to erupt behind her, but no such thing happened. The house receded into the distance, alarm still blaring, though she didn't ease up for a second or dare to look over her shoulder.

It would be easy to blockade the few roads in and out of this area, rendering escape by car impossible. Jessica had long been aware of this, hence her investment in a small, lightweight trail bike designed to cope with difficult terrain. Not exactly her style, but after considerable trial and error, she was confident enough to handle the temperamental machine.

More importantly, she knew this place like the back of her hand. She knew the hidden trails and half-forgotten tracks that wound through these mountains and valleys.

And how to exploit them.

A small river, swollen by spring rains and meltwater, wound its way down the valley, its progress mirrored by a narrow footpath. Used infrequently by hikers on their way to the nearby peaks, and only haphazardly maintained, it was hardly a smooth highway, but it was passable. The slopes around it were crowded with trees that had flourished in the sheltered ground, providing ample cover.

Forcing herself to ease off the throttle as she negotiated the steep slope, wildly dodging trees and bushes as she went, Jessica was forced to lean heavily on the brakes. But as soon as her wheels touched down on the hard-packed surface, she gave it everything she had. The 50cc engine growled as the lightweight vehicle shot down the path in a spray of mud and exhaust fumes.

This path ran for several miles more south–east, following the river until it emptied into a larger watercourse. There was also a small village at this confluence, built beside an ancient stone bridge that forded the fast-moving river. An obvious ambush point for her pursuers. Fortunately, Jessica knew of other points where the path branched off, allowing her to circumvent this bottleneck.

The automatic she'd stolen back at the house was a hard, solid shape digging painfully into her side, but she didn't consider discarding it. It was her only usable weapon for the time being, and if push came to shove, she would use it to shove hard. No way was she going to meekly capitulate like she'd done before.

Reaching up, Jessica pushed back a lock of sodden hair from her eyes. Those men must have been looking for Ryan, but how did they know he'd been there? Why come now, after all this time?

One way or another she had to warn him.

Her phone was in her pocket, hastily snatched from the kitchen table. Rising out of the seat long enough to yank it free, she speed-dialled Ryan's number.

Sure enough, it rang out only twice before Drake's voice came on the line.

'Jess, are you okay?' he asked, his concern obvious. Had he already known she was in danger?

Holding the unstable bike steady with one hand and pressing the phone against her ear with the other, Jessica practically shouted into the device.

'Ryan, listen to me. I—'

Before she could say another word, the bike was jerked to a sudden, violent halt, the momentum launching her right over the handlebars. For a sickening, terrifying moment, Jessica was airborne, the world spinning around her as she tumbled helplessly through the air.

She barely had the presence of mind to tuck her head in as the ground rushed up to meet her like a giant rocky fist. And suddenly she was skidding and rolling along the path, sharp stones tearing at her skin and jarring impacts bruising the flesh and muscles beneath.

When she finally rolled to a stop, battered and bleeding, her vision blurry, she was about 20 yards further down the path. She could hear the bike engine chugging away, still valiantly running despite the collision.

Through the fog of pain and confusion, a single question leapt into her mind: what the hell had just happened?

Wincing in pain, she struggled to sit up, managed to turn and look back at the scene of the crash. That was when she saw the length of cable strung between two sturdy trees, right across the path. Strong enough to stop a lightweight dirt bike in its tracks.

Instantly Jessica felt a surge of fear. Someone was waiting here for her.

'Well, well,' a female voice mocked her. 'Gutsy move, lady. Guess you're not as much of a pussy as your brother.'

Turning, Jessica watched as its owner emerged from cover. A woman, no more than thirty years old, with short blonde hair and a slender, almost delicate build. She was wearing body armour over civilian clothes, yet she appeared to be unarmed.

She smiled. A cold, malicious smile.

'Why don't you make this easy on us both and surrender, huh?'

Jessica had no intention of surrendering, peacefully or otherwise.

Something was still digging painfully into her side. It was the pistol, shoved into the belt of her jeans. Somehow it had stayed with her in the crash.

Without hesitation, Jessica went for it. The young woman saw her move and rushed straight at her with frightening speed as Jessica yanked the gun free and rose up to her knees, bringing the weapon to bear. She had never shot a person before, but she wouldn't hesitate to do so now. It was kill or be killed.

Reaching up with an awkward, unpractised move, she flicked the safety catch off. It took less than a second, her forefinger already tightening on the trigger. But just as she did so, the young woman leapt in with a perfectly placed kick, knocking the gun clean out of her hand.

Stunned by the speed and ferocity of the attack, Jessica tried to lash out with a strike to the midsection. A good hard strike to the sternum would drop her like a brick. This woman might have been fast, but she was smaller and weaker than Jessica. She could take her.

But her opponent easily deflected the attempted blow and countered with another brutally efficient kick that sent Jessica sprawling backwards. Injured and disoriented, she was completely outmatched, and in no condition to go on the offensive again.

Coughing and gasping for air, Jessica opened her eyes to see something brightly illuminated on the ground close by. Her phone, the screen cracked but still functional. Showing an active line.

If they got their hands on the phone, they would trace the call and use it to locate Ryan. She couldn't let that happen. Raising herself up with infinite effort, she began to crawl towards the device.

The mysterious female operative seemed to mistake this as a feeble bid to escape, and smiled in amusement.

'That all you've got? Goddamn, at least make me work for it,' she taunted, circling her like a shark waiting to strike. 'Guess you're not so different from your brother, after all.'

With a final desperate effort, Jessica lurched forward, snatched up the phone and tossed it into the river just as a boot came in against the side of her head, and an explosion of darkness enveloped her.

Chapter 8

Jessica awoke to jolting movement, the muted rumble of a vehicle engine and the steady patter of raindrops on a windshield.

She was hurt. The violent collision that had thrown her from the bike, combined with the brutal beating she'd taken, had left her with myriad cuts and bruises. She didn't think she'd broken bones, but her jaw throbbed where she'd been struck, and even small movements tore at the congealed blood that had stuck her clothes to her skin.

Opening her eyes, she was able to discern the interior of a car, probably an SUV judging by the size and layout. Night had fallen. It was dark beyond the tinted windows, but she made out stands of densely packed fir trees lit by their headlight beams. A second vehicle led the way up front, visible as a vague blur through the rain-covered windshield. She had no idea where they were. She didn't recognise the road or the terrain, but it was clearly a remote spot.

She inhaled, catching the distinctive aroma of tobacco smoke.

'Hey, there she is,' a jeering and by now familiar voice remarked. 'Shit, I was starting to think I'd hit you a little too hard. Don't die on me just yet.'

The woman who had beaten her unconscious was positioned opposite, in one of the rear-facing seats. Dressed in civilian clothes, with her body armour removed and a cigarette in hand, she was a picture of relaxed confidence. And she was still smiling that malicious, mocking smile.

Without hesitation, Jessica lunged for her enemy, only to find herself jerked painfully backwards. A pair of steel handcuffs bit into her wrists, secured to one of the car's Isofix points and preventing her moving more than a few inches.

'Wouldn't try that, if I were you.' Reaching into her jacket, the woman produced a small handheld taser unit and waved it under Jessica's nose. 'Our orders were to bring you in alive. That's a pretty broad definition, though.'

Alive, Jessica's mind echoed, temporarily forgetting her perilous situation.

'Never got the chance to introduce myself,' she went on, enjoying herself. 'My name's Riley. I'd shake your hand but, you know...'

'What do you want with me?' Jessica demanded.

'Shit, you must be dumber than I thought.' The young woman leaned closer. 'We want your brother. We know he's still alive, and you're going to tell us where he is.'

'How the hell should I know?' she asked, feigning ignorance. 'I haven't heard from him in years.'

Riley took a long, thoughtful drag on her cigarette before exhaling into Jessica's face. 'Want to know what gave you away?' she asked. 'It was your grocery bill.'

Seeing the dawning realisation in Jessica's eyes, she carried on. 'See, we don't need eyes on your house to keep tabs on you, Jessica. You'd be amazed what you can learn about someone just by following their electronic trail. We can read their emails, filter their search history...' She gave a sly smile. 'Even their porn habits. You wouldn't believe the kinky shit your average congressman searches for.'

Jessica looked away, refusing to meet her gaze.

'You know what the clincher was in your case?' She paused, and Jessica heard the faint hiss and crackle of smouldering tobacco as she took another drag. 'The whisky.'

Jessica's heart sank in that moment. She knew exactly the mistake she'd made. Looking back on it now, she couldn't believe how foolish she'd been.

'Talisker – Ryan's favourite brand. In the past three years, you've never purchased a single bottle of the stuff.'

Jessica glared at her. 'I want a lawyer.'

The young woman stared back at her for a few seconds in tense, stony silence. Then abruptly she broke out into a fit of laughter, accompanied by chuckles from the two male operatives up front.

'Oh, sweetheart,' Riley finally said, wiping a tear from her eye. 'You really don't understand the kind of shit you're in, do you? There's no due process for terrorist suspects.'

'You can't just abduct people. My government will—'

'We *own* your government,' Riley interrupted. 'And even if we didn't, you really think we don't know how to make people disappear? Trust me, the only thing in *your* future is a black site in some country that most people couldn't find on a map, where you're gonna spend the remainder of your short-ass life. They'll torture and interrogate you until you'll wish you had more to give them. And when they're finally done, they'll take what's left of you out to some forest in the middle of nowhere and put a bullet through that pretty head of yours.'

Despite her anger, her hatred, her impotent frustration at being restrained, Jessica felt a tight knot of fear coil itself around her stomach. She didn't doubt for one second that this woman was speaking the truth.

'Of course, you could avoid all that by telling me what I want to know,' Riley said, addressing her almost conspiratorially. 'We both know you're going to give it up in the end, so why not make it easy on yourself, Jessica? Hell, play your cards right, you might even get to walk away from this.'

Jessica looked down in silence, as if torn about how to respond. Riley, sensing her wavering resolve, leaned forward expectantly. She'd interrogated enough people to know when one was about to break.

Then something happened that neither of them expected.

A sudden crash of rending metal jerked her attention to the road ahead, where a big, bulky flatbed truck had roared out of a fork in the road and slammed into the forward section of the lead SUV. But instead of slamming on his brakes, the driver of the truck kept his foot on the gas, propelling the crumpled vehicle towards the edge of the roadway, and the steep drop on the other side.

'Oh, shit!' their driver called out, stamping on the brakes.

Jessica saw the passenger door fly open as one of the SUV's occupants made a desperate attempt to bail out, before the rear end tipped over and the entire mass of buckled metal and human passengers disappeared over the edge. In a matter of seconds, half of their convoy had been wiped out.

'Get us out of here!' Riley commanded, her arrogant confidence vanishing now as it became obvious they'd been caught in an ambush.

The truck was blocking the way ahead, and the road was too narrow to make a turn. Throwing the SUV into reverse, their driver stomped on the gas, sending them fishtailing backwards in a spray of mud and loose gravel. But just as they were picking up speed, a resounding boom from somewhere in the woods behind seemed to rumble up through the chassis.

Twisting awkwardly in her seat, Jessica watched as one of the tall pine trees leaning in close to the road toppled over, smoke billowing from the shattered base, before crashing down across the road. She saw this, and so did the driver, but he was too late to stop them from reversing straight into this sudden, impassable barrier.

Jessica grunted as the SUV's tailgate crumpled under the impact, accompanied by the tinkle of shattering glass and buckling plastic. The sudden collision knocked Riley off balance, pitching her out of her seat and onto the floor.

She was just picking herself up when a figure leapt down from the truck's cabin up ahead; a masked man in dark clothing. Jessica watched him calmly advance to the driver's window, raise a weapon to his shoulder and take aim.

'Shit! Get down!' one of the operatives up front yelled.

A moment later, the side window disintegrated in a spray of broken glass, the staccato flash of the weapon's muzzle flare illuminating the gloom as their attacker triggered a long sustained burst on full automatic. The effect on the two operatives up front was devastating, both men jerking and writhing as rounds tore through their bodies, their blood splattering the inside of the windshield.

Restrained by the cuffs, Jessica could do nothing more than flatten herself on the rear seat, praying that a stray round didn't hit her.

Beside her, she saw the side door fly open as Riley bailed out, staying low to avoid the hail of incoming fire as she drew her sidearm and turned the weapon at their masked attacker.

Jessica's reaction was instinctive. Lashing out with both feet, she caught the woman squarely in the shoulder. The pistol barked once, the round ricocheting wildly off the car's metalwork as Riley lost her balance.

But rather than try to recover and open fire on her attacker, the young woman rolled backwards and leapt over the edge of the roadway, plunging into the dense undergrowth below just as another burst of gunfire chewed up the ground where she'd been standing.

Staring in amazement, Jessica watched as the lone ambusher ejected the spent magazine from his still-smoking weapon, slapped a fresh one home and strode over to the edge of the road, staring down the sights into the dense woodland below. Seeing no sign of his elusive target, he lowered the gun and turned towards the vehicle.

Jessica's heart swelled as he approached, realising Ryan had somehow caught up with them and come to her rescue, knowing he would pull the mask off and she'd see his familiar, comforting face.

'Are you all right?'

Jessica blinked in surprise. It wasn't the deep voice and English accent of her brother that addressed her then. This voice was female, and foreign.

'Are you injured?' she repeated.

'Who the fuck are you?' Jessica asked.

'Doesn't matter,' she replied, producing a standard-issue cop key and unlocking the cuffs. The moment she was free, Jessica spotted the portable taser that Riley had threatened her with earlier and snatched it up.

'Like hell it doesn't,' she hit back, brandishing the weapon. 'I've been shot at, kidnapped and interrogated already today. Why should I trust you?'

The woman stood still and silent, watching her as rain pattered down around her. Her face was obscured by the mask, leaving only her eyes exposed. They were locked on Jessica now.

'If I wanted to hurt you, we wouldn't be having this conversation.'

Jessica had to admit, she had a point there.

With this sobering warning delivered, the woman pointed in the direction Riley had disappeared. 'She'll call in reinforcements. If you want to stay alive, I suggest you follow me.'

'Where are you going?'

'Anywhere but here.'

The woman backed away, allowing Jessica to clamber out of the ruined vehicle. Her gaze was inevitably drawn to the dead operatives in front, and the gory mess painting the windshield.

'It was them or you. Don't feel bad for them.'

'I don't,' she said quietly.

'Good. Now help me with this.' She had moved around to the driver's side window, reaching in and hauling the steering wheel over so that the car was angled towards the road edge. 'Push now!'

Jessica guessed what she had in mind and took up position on the other side, straining to push with all the strength she could summon. The road beneath them was muddy, but the car was on flat ground, and once it began to creep forward under their combined efforts, it quickly gathered pace. Jessica's mysterious saviour kept her grip on the wheel until she was almost at the edge, letting go just as the car toppled and rolled down the steep embankment.

'Let's go!' the woman called out, not even bothering to watch the wreck tumble to the bottom of the gorge a hundred feet below.

Jessica followed as she returned to the flatbed truck, which was still parked across the road with its engine idling, and clambered up into the cab. One look around the interior, cluttered with Cardiff City football stickers and empty takeaway wrappers, was enough to confirm that this vehicle didn't belong to her saviour.

'You should buckle up,' the enigmatic new arrival warned, throwing the big truck into reverse.

'*Now* you're worried about safety?' Jessica said as the vehicle lurched backwards, turned and accelerated away from the scene.

Chapter 9

Gasping for breath, Riley reached up and managed to hook her arm around the low-lying branch that had partially toppled into the river. Fighting hard against the fast-flowing current, the young woman pulled and kicked, working her way along until at last her boots found purchase on the rocky riverbed and she was able to haul herself up onto dry land.

Her retreat downhill from the ambush site had been little more than an uncontrolled, headlong plunge down the steep muddy slope, through stands of sharp thorny bushes that tore at skin and clothes, avoiding rocks and tree trunks just waiting to break bones.

Riley was as nimble and agile as a professional gymnast, allowing her to avoid the worst of these potentially fatal obstacles, only to plunge into the freezing river that ran along the valley floor. The physical discomfort didn't concern her, but the sting of failure was far more telling.

Crouched low beside the gurgling watercourse, she forced her shivering muscles to stop, held her breath and listened, head cocked slightly as she strained to detect any sign of pursuit. Finding none, she rose to her feet, reached into her jacket pocket and fished out her cell phone. The screen was cracked, likely damaged during the fall, but the unit was waterproof and still operable. Forcing her chilled hands to work, she clumsily dialled a number and waited while the call connected.

'What's your sitrep?' Hawkins asked right away.

'The op's blown. Drake was ready for us.'

Silence greeted her for a second or so. 'What happened?'

'We were ambushed while exfilling,' Riley explained. 'The team's dead.'

'You're not,' Hawkins pointed out, his undertone of accusation clear.

Riley was wise enough not to rise to that one.

'What's their last known position?'

She had no idea. The rural Welsh landscape wasn't exactly home turf for her. In fact, she was rapidly coming to hate this cold, wet, bleak little country.

'Trace this signal. They hit us just west of here, can't have been more than a few minutes ago. They must still be in the area.'

'Fine. We'll vector in air assets and ground units.'

'We'll need a clean-up crew too,' Riley added. She knew the deaths of her team would mean little to Hawkins, but the loss of resources and the potential for exposure was a danger that had to be contained.

'Get yourself to extraction point Bravo.'

'I can help,' she protested. Right now, she wanted nothing more than to grab a weapon and hunt Drake and his sister down like animals.

'You can help by getting to the evac point,' Hawkins cut in sharply. 'We've had enough fuck-ups already tonight. I don't need more.'

Riley gritted her teeth. 'Copy that.'

The line went dead. Lowering the phone, the young woman let out a slow breath, then drew back her arm and hurled it against a nearby rock. The device shattered with the tinkle of broken glass, though it did little to alleviate her burning anger.

This wasn't over, she told herself. It would end only when Drake died by her hand.

–

Jessica leaned back in her seat, relishing the hot air blasting from the truck's heating system. The initial surge of fear and adrenaline that her body had produced during the ambush was thinning, and she felt dreadfully weary all of a sudden. She fancied she might have been able to nod off if it weren't for her companion's haphazard driving.

She pushed the big clumsy utility vehicle hard, manoeuvring it like a sports car. The engine roared as they tore down the remote road, tyres skidding and clawing at the ground as she fought with the heavy steering, sometimes coming perilously close to the unfenced road edge.

'Don't you think we should slow down a little?' Jessica suggested, tensing as a low-hanging branch slammed against the side window.

'Not if you want to get out of this,' the woman replied. 'They'll vector in air assets with thermal imaging to track us. Our only chance is to get beyond the perimeter before they start their sweep.'

Jessica craned her neck to look up, imagining aircraft sweeping in to take them out. 'All that just for me?'

'Not you,' her companion stated. 'It's your brother they want. You're just leverage.'

'You really know how to make a girl feel special.'

'I'm here to keep you alive, not to stroke your ego.'

Jessica bit her tongue, opting not to take the bait. 'I need a phone.'

'Not yet.'

'I have to warn Ryan. If he goes there—'

'He won't,' she stated simply, as if it were an incontrovertible fact. 'Ryan's at least a hundred miles from here.'

'How exactly do you know that?'

No answer.

'You're Anya, aren't you?' she said, taking an educated guess. 'You're the one he's been looking for. You've been here this whole time, right under our noses.'

Again, there was no response. Sensing she wasn't going to get anything more from her enigmatic companion for the time being, Jessica rubbed her arms and focussed on trying to get warm and dry.

They carried on at high speed for a good twenty minutes, gradually joining more substantial roads until at last they stopped at a roadside services area. Alongside the usual fuelling stations and 24-hour fast food outlets, Jessica spotted a small chain hotel.

'This is where you get out,' her companion informed her. Reaching into her jacket, she held out a keycard emblazoned with the hotel's corporate logo. 'Go to room twenty-six. You'll find some money, a phone and a set of clean clothes.'

Jessica frowned. 'That's it?'

'That's it.'

'What about you? Where will you go?'

'Don't worry about me.' Jessica thought she detected a forlorn note in her voice.

Taking the keycard, she looked back at her masked companion. 'Come with me, Anya,' she said. 'If they really are after us, we should stick together.'

She shook her head. 'Ryan wouldn't want to see me.'

Jessica sighed but nodded, conceding defeat. She was about to leave, but hesitated after opening the door. 'Look, for what it's worth… thank you. For what you did. I wish I could repay you.'

'Stay alive. That's good enough.' She looked poised to say more, but instead pointed at the hotel. 'Now go.'

Chapter 10

Vienna, Austria – July 19th, 1989

Cain heard the sounds of cheering and applause long before he reached his destination. Ascending a short flight of steps onto an expansive viewing platform, he paused briefly to take in the dazzling spectacle laid out before him.

Sunlight flooded into the hall from great windows set into the arched ceiling, the glow of natural light magnified and reflected off pristine white walls inlaid with intricate stone pillars, sculptures and carvings. Ornate crystal chandeliers hung down, though their illumination was hardly required.

It reminded him of a cathedral, or some grand palace or museum. But it was no such thing. The purpose of this place was evident as he peered over the balustrade.

Far below, on a hard-packed dirt floor that appeared at odds with the opulent surroundings, a group of five snowy-white horses were being ridden by men in extravagant formal uniforms, performing a series of complex turns and jumps, even rearing up on their hind legs and appearing to 'walk'. They moved with the rigid precision of soldiers on a parade ground.

Cain was no equine enthusiast, but even he could appreciate the training and dedication on display: the famous Lipizzaner stallions, widely regarded as the most highly trained horses in the world.

If nothing else, he had to admire his contact's flair for the dramatic. But then, that was something he was coming to appreciate about Freya Shaw – she did nothing in half measures.

'Remarkable, aren't they?'

Cain didn't need to look to know that James had slipped in by his side. Freya's faithful assistant and bodyguard. He was looking down in approval at the display below.

'I've always considered them a perfect example.'

'Of what?' Cain asked.

'The power of obedience.'

Another ripple of applause travelled through the spectators as one of the stallions reared up and walked backwards, front legs kicking out.

'Depends on your perspective,' Cain replied without looking at him. 'You see obedience. I see horses that have been broken.'

He heard a faint chuckle. 'To each their own.'

Cain hadn't come here to verbally spar with Freya's lackey. 'I've got places to be. Where is she?'

'Walk with me,' James said, unconcerned with Cain's sharp tone.

He led the way across the wide balcony, conducting Cain to a more secluded section of the viewing gallery. Freya was waiting for him, observing the display below with mild interest. She was dressed more conservatively than she had been at their last meeting, eschewing the evening gown in favour of charcoal grey trousers with a blouse and matching jacket.

Reaching into his pocket, Cain laid something on the stone baluster beside her. A set of dog tags, still on their chain. Stained with dried blood.

He saw her eyes flick to the gory trinket, the faint smile at the corner of her mouth.

'Well done, Marcus.'

'Anya did her job, just like you asked,' Cain replied. Anya, the good soldier, still doing her duty, risking her life for people who neither knew her nor cared about her.

Indeed, Anya was the whole reason he'd come to Austria. The guard towers and electric fences that had covered the border between Austria and Hungary had recently been dismantled, allowing tourists, refugees and in this case, CIA assassins, to flood across the mostly unguarded border from East to West.

Anya had returned to the US embassy only yesterday, grim-faced and subdued, bearing the evidence of her successful mission. And Cain had been there to confirm it.

Turning towards him, Freya's smile broadened.

'Now that... business is out of the way, I think it's time you and I talked about the future.'

'Specifically?'

She nodded towards the exit. 'You'll have noticed a lot of East German cars on the roads around Vienna, yes?'

That was an understatement. Everywhere Cain looked on the drive here, he'd seen the distinctive boxy chassis of Trabants and Ladas, most of them in poor condition. People from all over the Eastern Bloc were surging into Western Europe, fleeing a collapsing regime.

Cain leaned in closer. 'What do you want, Freya?'

'The same thing as you – peace in our time. So do the men I work for,' she explained. 'The only difference is how we go about it.'

'That difference being?'

'Your friends in the CIA and the Pentagon see only the problems that are presented to them. An invading army to be defeated in Afghanistan, for example. What's the saying? If all you have is a hammer, then everything looks like a nail?'

'We had a job to do, and we did it,' he reminded her, in no mood to be lectured.

'Actually, Anya and her unit did it. And they did it exceptionally well.' There was a faint trace of mockery in her voice when she said this. 'But as brave as they were, there were limits to what they could accomplish. A country defeated from the outside will only become harder and more determined to rise up again. To truly defeat your enemy, you have to dismantle their will to resist. You have to beat them from the inside.'

She glanced down at the Lipizzaner stallions, so dutifully performing for the crowd below. Not one of them dared show disobedience; such thoughts had long since been drilled out of them.

'You have to break them.'

He could see no reason to dispute that assessment. 'I'm listening.'

'The Soviet Union is on the verge of collapse. They're out of money, out of troops, out of time. The Iron Curtain, the Eastern Bloc... all of it is balanced on a knife edge. One little push at the right time and place is all it would take.'

Weakened and demoralised by their humiliating retreat from Afghanistan, there was little appetite in the Soviet military for further conflict. Meanwhile, a dire economic situation had been compounded by devastating accidents like the nuclear meltdown at Chernobyl. Worst of all, Gorbachev's policies of Glasnost and Perestroika, intended to ease the growing pressure for political reform, had instead opened the floodgates for even greater demands.

'Imagine it for a second. No more Berlin Wall, no more missiles, no more proxy wars. The world you and I grew up in, the world as it's been since the Second World War, is going to disappear. Who do you think is going to shape the new one? Politicians worried about the next election cycle? Intelligence agencies weighed down by endless committees and congressional oversight?'

She shook her head.

'That's where we come in. My organisation represents a different way of thinking – one that isn't caught up in political point scoring or held back by fear and hesitation. Imagine clearly understanding the root cause of a problem *and being able to take swift and decisive action to fix it. With nobody standing in your way.'*

None of this was news to Cain, of course. And yet, listening to her speak in that moment, hearing the passion and excitement in her voice as she shared her grand aspirations of reshaping the world, Cain couldn't help but feel drawn to her. Not just the woman, but what she represented.

That same fire had once burned in him: the desire to have a real impact on the world, to leave it in a better state than how he'd found it. He saw that opportunity in Freya far more clearly than he ever had with the CIA. She was a gateway to a new world. A world of limitless potential, unbounded by shifting public opinion, wavering politicians or petty tribalistic concerns.

This woman standing before him seemed to understand that need in a way no one else ever had. Certainly not Carpenter, the career military man who had first drawn Cain into this, now obsessed with enhancing his own prestige, or the increasingly corporate and risk-averse leadership of the CIA.

Not even Anya, for all her undeniable abilities. He understood more clearly now the fundamental limitation of her world view, her inability to see beyond her own experiences, to embrace the larger and more complex picture. Set against a woman of Freya's calibre, she seemed painfully young and naïve.

'We have a chance here, Marcus. To make our own history, redraw the map of the world forever. That's what we are, that's why we exist. We don't just want to change this world, we want to remake it into something better.'

He couldn't rightly say how she'd done it, but somehow she had cut right to the core of who he was, perfectly articulating everything he wanted his life to mean.

How could he refuse such an offer?

'All right,' he finally said. 'I'm in.'

Freya's smile was radiant. Radiant and victorious.

'Then we have a lot of work to do.'

Washington DC – April 25th, 2011

The Hart Senate Office Building was a far cry from the neoclassical faux grandeur of many of DC's better-known government buildings. A stark, square concrete edifice laid down in the 1970s, it was a utilitarian office space designed to be functional rather than decorative.

It was also the place where Marcus Cain's political fate would be decided.

Starke's prediction a couple of months back had proven to be accurate almost to the minute. Cain had barely returned to his office before he was called by the director of National Intelligence, advising that he had been recommended to the president for promotion to permanent director of the CIA.

Not long after, the president himself had called to congratulate him on the recommendation, his voice smooth and his words measured and carefully chosen, as they often were. Cain had done his part, agreeing where it was expected, offering assurances where they were required and even laughing at a few jokes where necessary.

But what was happening now was no laughing matter. As with any directorial appointment, he still had to face several days of interviews by the Select Committee on Intelligence – the governing body of experienced legislators assigned to oversee and approve the work of the US intelligence services. It was the job of this committee to probe and test him, to ask difficult questions of his career, background, political views and even his personal life, ensuring he was fit to hold the office of director. In the end, his appointment was decided by a simple majority vote.

He had been assured by Starke that enough of the committee was under the Circle's influence to get him through the confirmation vote, but they didn't control every single one of them. There was always a chance that a hostile senator would throw him a curve ball. And as Cain had learned from a long career in this political minefield, nothing in DC was ever guaranteed until the votes were cast and counted.

He was jolted out of these thoughts by the buzz of his cell phone.

'Make it quick, Jason,' he said as he headed towards the hearing chamber, the building's massive central atrium on his right. 'I'm due to appear in ten minutes.'

'Your hunch was right. Drake's still alive.'

Cain's steps faltered. 'You're sure?'

'We had strong evidence he'd made contact with his sister over the past few weeks, so we sent in a team to interrogate her. They got ambushed while exfilling.'

'Casualties?'

'Some.' He didn't sound particularly concerned. 'A clean-up crew's already taken care of it. We haven't been compromised.'

Cain's jaw tightened. Starke's warning about leaving loose ends untied rose unbidden to his mind. And Ryan Drake was a loose end that had troubled him for a long time now. Despite everything thrown at him, the man simply refused to die.

'Where are they now?'

'We're working on it.'

This was the very last thing Cain needed, with his confirmation vote just days away. He couldn't afford to fail now. Not after everything he'd done to get here.

'I want this finished, Jason,' he said, speaking slowly and clearly so there could be no doubt or question. 'Once and for all. Whatever it takes.'

'It could get messy,' Hawkins warned him. 'Drake won't go down without a fight.'

'I said whatever it takes. You don't come back until it's done. Do you understand?'

Hawkins was silent for a second or two. 'I do.'

'Good. Now get on it.'

Shutting down the phone, Cain closed his eyes, took a slow breath to focus his mind, then resumed his walk towards the main hearing chamber.

Chapter 11

North Wales, UK

'It was Cain. He sent them there,' Jessica explained, leaning over a chair as Drake applied a dressing to the bloody graze across her shoulder. 'They were planning to use me to get to you.'

Finding the room exactly as described, she had used the burner phone to put a call through to her brother, warning him not to go to the house and giving him her location. A couple of hours later, he was with her.

The first priority had been to clean her up and tend to her injuries. Jessica had discarded her sodden clothing on arrival, showered and changed, though she'd been quietly shocked by the mess when she saw her own reflection.

'Goddamn it,' Drake said under his breath.

'I should have been more careful,' she said, filled with self-recrimination. 'I should have known they'd be keeping tabs on me. I told myself I'd never let something like that happen to me again.'

'It's not your fault, Jess. It's mine.'

'How?'

'Anya,' he explained. 'She took out an Israeli Mossad agent yesterday.'

Jessica frowned. 'I don't understand. What does that have to do with me?'

'Killing him was proof that she didn't die in Afghanistan. And if they know Anya's alive, it's a fair bet I am, too. It was only a matter of time until Cain came after you.' Drake shook his head, knowing they could play the blame game for hours and achieve nothing of value. 'Tell me what happened.'

He listened while Jessica related the story of the attack on her house, her desperate escape attempt and subsequent capture.

'They told me they were going to take me away forever. Torture me, kill me...' Her voice grew strained, 'That's when *she* showed up.'

'She?'

'I never saw her face. But she was waiting for them. She took out their convoy, got me to safety. She's the only reason I'm not dead or captured.'

Drake leaned back, stunned by what he was hearing. There were other female operatives he knew of, such as Frost or Mitchell, but they were both accounted for. They wouldn't have come here without notifying him.

Based on her story, the only logical conclusion he could draw was that Anya had travelled to the UK after taking out that Mossad agent. But if so, why? Was she hoping to make contact with Drake? Or was there another motive at play?

'Did she say where she was going? What she would do next?'

'Nothing. She told me to contact you and stay safe, then she left.'

Drake was silent as he considered this, his expression dark, his thoughts in turmoil.

'It's her, isn't it?' Jessica asked. 'Anya.'

'I don't know.'

'I think you do. You're like magnets, you keep pulling each other back. Maybe she realised it before you did.'

'Let's focus on what we know for now,' he said tersely. 'We know they're after me. We know they had you under surveillance. And we know they'll try to follow this up before they lose us again. That means we can't stay here long.'

Today's events proved the manhunt for Drake was back in full force. They knew he was alive, and they knew Jessica had been in contact with him. In the space of a single day, they had both become wanted fugitives again.

It seemed that Jessica was entertaining similar thoughts.

'I can't go back there, can I?'

When Drake didn't respond, she turned around to look at him. There was a sad, lost look in her bright green eyes.

'My home. My old life. They'll be hunting for me now, too.'

'We'll figure this out,' he promised her, squeezing her hand. 'But we'll have to leave the UK for a while. It's too hot here, and there's no reason to stay now.'

Drake's mind was already racing ahead, considering his options, trying not to acknowledge that they were growing perilously slim. He was running low on resources, allies, places to hide. His world was shrinking, while his enemies were growing stronger and more numerous.

'Ryan...'

He stopped, struck by her sudden change of tone. She sounded hesitant and afraid now. What could she possibly say that was worse than today's events?

'There's something I have to tell you,' she said. 'But I'm scared. I don't know what you'll think of me.'

'Jess, you almost got killed today because of me. Why would I be angry with you?'

Jessica sighed and looked down at her hands, searching for the right words. He didn't press her, just gave her the time she needed.

'You came back here because you were looking for something,' she said at length. 'Something I told you was lost.'

Drake could feel his heartrate rising. 'That's right.'

When she looked up again, he could see the pain and guilt etched on her face. 'I lied to you, Ryan. The letter wasn't destroyed. I know exactly where it is.'

–

Having made her way to the extraction point by hiking through several miles of rough terrain, Riley had eventually been picked up and brought to a nearby safe house.

She was just lighting up a cigarette when the door opened and the menacing form of Hawkins entered.

'Give us the room, please,' he instructed the other operative keeping watch.

The man knew better than to argue, quickly departing and closing the door behind him. Riley avoided eye contact as the big man paced slowly and thoughtfully across the room. She could practically feel the anger radiating from him and, despite herself, she was afraid.

She had good reason to be.

'Talk to me,' he said gently.

Riley took a drag. 'There's not much to say. We picked up his sister as instructed. Drake laid an ambush for us. My team died.'

'And you're sure it was Drake,' Hawkins coaxed. 'You saw his face.'

Riley frowned, thinking back to the chaotic firefight. 'He was wearing a mask, but it had to be him. Who else could have pulled off shit like this?'

'That's a good question.'

She felt his hands on her shoulders, gentle and soothing. Then suddenly they clamped around her throat in a vice-like grip, lifting her right out of the chair and shoving her backward. She let out a startled gasp as Hawkins pinned her against the wall.

'Seems to me, you don't know much of anything tonight.' His cold blue eyes flashed dangerously. 'So tell me, what am I to do with you?'

To try to fight back would be suicidal. Hawkins was twice her size and many times her strength. Likewise, begging for mercy and forgiveness would only engender disgust.

Instead she took a different path, allowing her body to relax, to become soft and malleable in his hands. Her lips parted a little, her eyes widening. She tilted her face up towards his, moving her hips closer to him as she let out a soft moan. In a matter of seconds her whole demeanour seemed to have changed, becoming subtly enticing, alluring, arousing.

'I think you know what you want to do with me,' she whispered.

She saw a smile flicker across that rugged, cruel face. He knew the dangerous game she was playing, but he didn't reject it. Danger was something that had always appealed to him.

Riley closed her eyes as she pressed herself against him, feeling his sudden need, feeling his grip on her neck slacken a little. Hawkins was like a gun with a hair trigger – one had to handle him with great care.

Yes, she knew what he wanted to do with her all right.

Chapter 12

'Say that again,' Drake prompted his sister. He needed to hear it from her again. Needed to be sure.

'I lied to you,' she said, practically forcing the words out. 'I told you I'd destroyed the letter, but I didn't.'

'Why?'

'Why?' she echoed, giving a bitter, sardonic laugh. 'Because I've seen you risk your life time and again, Ryan. I've seen you gamble and lose everything and everyone you cared about. And for what? Where has it all gotten you?'

Drake had no answer for her, and she didn't expect one.

'I knew you'd risk everything to get to the truth, no matter where it led you. I wanted you to give it up, leave it all behind. The whole fucking horrible mess. Just for once, I wanted you to think of yourself. So I lied, thinking it was... better for you.' She looked down, her shoulders slumped miserably. 'But it wasn't for you. Not really. I suppose I lied to myself about that as well. It was for me. Because I couldn't stand to see you leave again, knowing you might never come back.' She sniffed, wiping her eyes. 'I'm sorry, Ryan. I really am.'

Drake sighed and sat down beside her. He supposed another man might have been furious that she'd deceived him and wasted his time. But no such emotion stirred in him, because he understood why she'd done it.

'It's all right,' he whispered, putting an arm around her. 'I understand. It wasn't fair to put you in that position.'

He felt some of the tension leave her then, knowing he at least forgave her. But she didn't look any happier. 'But it doesn't change anything, does it? You're still going after it.'

She knew the answer as well as he did.

'I don't have much choice. This could be my last chance.' Pulling away a little, he gripped his sister by the arms and looked her in the eye. 'Where's the letter?'

The docklands area of Liverpool was one of the biggest in the country, handling tens of millions of tonnes of shipping every year, from oil tankers and mighty Supermax cargo haulers to luxury cruise liners.

Stepping out of the car, Drake paused to stare in awe at the towering hull of a massive cargo hauler, its decks stacked high with multi-coloured containers that resembled enormous Lego bricks. Floodlit cranes worked tirelessly to offload them along the dockside, waiting for trucks and trains to haul them off.

However, their errand here tonight had nothing to do with shipping.

'Lead the way,' he said, following Jessica towards the self-storage facility ahead; a warehouse nestled amongst the silos, office blocks and container yards that crowded the dock facility. A sign on the front proudly proclaimed that it was fully secured and open 24/7. Access was via a numeric key panel.

'Why here?' Drake asked as Jessica punched in the code. Fortunately it was late at night and, although the docks themselves were still a hive of activity, the industrial parks around them would be quiet for several hours yet.

'I always had a feeling something like this might happen,' she explained. 'The house was too exposed. I needed a place no one else knew about. So I hired a locker under a fake name, and hid most of Mum's stuff there. Including the letter.'

'Smart,' he acknowledged.

She glanced up at her brother. 'I have my moments.'

The door buzzed open. A night watchman in the nearby security booth glanced up, nodding at them without much interest. Drake was careful to keep his head down and his face away from the security cameras overhead.

Making their way down the rows of identical roller doors, Jessica came to a stop outside one and went to work on the key panel. Drake was impressed by her foresight of using a facility with access codes rather than physical keys that could be lost or misplaced.

With a single crisp beep, the magnetic lock disengaged, allowing Drake to haul the steel shutter up.

The space beyond was about three metres deep and perhaps two metres wide. The walls were plain cinderblock, unpainted and unadorned save for a single light fixture. Jessica flicked it on, illuminating piles of dusty cardboard boxes of varying shapes and sizes, neatly stacked against the far wall. There must have been a couple of dozen at least, containing the personal effects and paperwork their mother had accumulated over a span of decades.

'This could take a while,' Drake said as he surveyed the formidable horde. The chances of making a quick getaway seemed to be fading rapidly.

'Not if you put some thought into it,' Jessica replied, moving forward and scanning the labels on top of each box, selecting one in particular. In a matter of seconds, she'd found what she was looking for, and held up the handwritten letter.

Drake eyed her suspiciously. 'You are *far* too organised to be my sister.'

'Someone in the family had to be. Anyway, I had a lot of time on my hands.'

Letting that one go, Drake took the letter from her and unfolded it.

'So what happens now?' Jessica asked as she closed the steel shutter behind them, giving them a measure of privacy.

'Now we find out if my hunch pays off,' Drake replied, laying the letter on top of the piled-up boxes. Its paper was creased and slightly yellowed now, but the writing was still clearly legible.

Drake laid the key down beside it. The two pieces of the puzzle finally reunited.

Both of them paused for a moment to read the short message.

Ryan,

If you're reading this, then I pray it's because Jessica brought you here. It saddens me greatly that I was never able to do it myself, and that was my failing. I let you down, Ryan. In many ways.

I wasn't the mother you deserved. I couldn't be there for you the way I wanted to be, or tell you the things I wanted to, but never for a moment blame yourself. It was my fault – all of it. I don't expect you to forgive me, but perhaps in the end, you might understand.

I wish there was a way for me to explain everything that's happened, everything I did and everything I tried to do, but this isn't something I can tell you. The only way is to show you, and let you judge for yourself.

Always yours,

Freya

'She loved you, Ryan,' Jessica said quietly. 'Even if she didn't always say it.'

Drake didn't meet her gaze. 'Let's just get it done, yeah?'

He produced a pen and began noting down the numbers etched into the side of the key. In all, there were four sets of three, forming a grouping of sorts. Clearly it was some kind of code, though the meaning and intent were lost on her.

'Are you going to tell me what I'm looking at?'

'Ever heard of a grille cipher?' he asked as he finished up.

'Do I look like a cryptographer to you?'

Drake grunted. 'It was invented in the sixteenth century by some Italian bloke named Cardano, who came up with a way to hide coded messages inside chunks of plain text. The grille was just a piece of paper with holes punched in it. All you had to do was hold the grille over the original message and make a note of the letters in the holes. So simple even I can do it.'

'But we don't have a grille,' Jessica pointed out.

'No, but we've got the next best thing.' He indicated the first stream of numbers – 1, 2, 1, 1. 'Each number group represents a letter placement in the message. Paragraph, line, word, letter.'

Frowning, Jessica followed this guide on their mother's letter, arriving on the letter M.

'M,' she repeated. 'Okay, what about the others?'

1, 2, 2, 2 – R

1, 2, 11, 6 – F

2, 1, 11, 1 – F

'What the hell is MRFF?' Jessica asked, perplexed and disappointed. She had expected something more explicit. 'Maybe we made a mistake?'

Drake shook his head. 'There's no mistake. I checked it twice.'

'But this doesn't tell us anything. What's the point in leaving us a coded message if we don't understand the bloody thing?' She was quiet for a few seconds. 'Give me your phone, Ryan.'

Bringing up a Google search on the device, she went to work. Amongst the thousands of search results, she found a medical research fund established by the Australian government, a civil liberties group advocating for religious freedom in the military, and a materials recovery firm to name but a few. None of them relevant to them or their mother.

She shook her head, handing back the device in defeat. 'No joy there.'

Drake, however, had not been idle during her search. He'd been quietly mulling over everything he knew about his mother, her situation and her possible thought process when encoding her message.

'She would have to assume this letter could fall into the wrong hands. People with resources and decryption skills. Sooner or later they could make the same connection I did and decipher the message.'

'So?'

'So... whatever this means, it was intended for me alone.' He frowned. 'Something only I would recognise.'

'Great. Like what?'

Suddenly Drake snatched up the letter and the key, opened the box on which they were resting and started rifling through the contents. It contained a vast assortment of printed stationery – old legal documents, property deeds, invoices and countless other bits of bureaucratic paraphernalia that a person accumulates in their life. It had all belonged to their mother and, by the looks of things, had remained undisturbed since her death.

'Care to explain what you're looking for?' Jessica asked as Drake pulled off another lid, tossed it aside and rifled through the contents.

'You were still young when Dad died,' he said absently as he searched. 'No, this stuff's too recent.'

'I was. Continue.'

'So you probably don't remember who handled all the legal stuff. Wills, inheritance, that kind of thing?'

His sister frowned. 'Mum dealt with that. I suppose she had her own lawyer handle the paperwork.'

Their parents had long since divorced by the time their father passed away, but as the legal guardian of his children, Freya had stepped in to settle his affairs.

'She did,' he agreed, opening another box. 'A family lawyer, in fact. Been with us for as long as I can remember. His name was... Fitzgibbons. Frederick Fitzgibbons.'

'Quite a mouthful.'

'You're not kidding.' Drake's eyes lit up as he found what he was looking for. 'Imagine being a lawyer and having to sign that fucking name a hundred times a day. So he didn't. He abbreviated it.'

Snatching up an old piece of legal correspondence, he held it up for inspection. Beneath the paragraphs of boilerplate legalese, a simple signature had been hastily scrawled.

Sincerely,
   FF

'FF.' Jessica's eyes snapped up from the document to the man holding it. 'Bloody hell.'

'Mr Frederick Fitzgibbons,' Drake announced. 'That's where she wanted me to go. That's where I'll find my answers.'

His sister looked at him, surprised and impressed. 'And to think, you were always shit at puzzles.'

'You're not the only one in the family with brains,' he replied, quickly scanning the letter heading for a reply address. 'Looks like Fitzgibbons' office is in central London.'

Already he was computing the journey that lay ahead, considering the risks and possibilities. Getting to Fitzgibbons' office would be easy. Getting there undetected would prove more challenging.

Jessica glanced up at him, a smile forming. 'What are we waiting for?'

Chapter 13

Seventeen, eighteen, nineteen…

Arms straining with the effort, fingers closed around the overhead bar in a white-knuckle grip, Anya hauled her body up, forcing her burning, weary muscles to comply. A trickle of sweat ran down between her shoulder blades as she repeated the demanding movement, the freshly healed scar tissue across her back still a little raw and sensitive.

Twenty, twenty-one, twenty-two…

The US Marine Corps considered twenty pulls-ups to be the ideal standard in their combat fitness tests, but the unit in which Anya served expected even more than that. No allowances had been made because of her sex, and while it had certainly made life difficult for her, she understood the simple, pragmatic logic of it. No leniency was asked for or given.

So she had fought and trained even harder than the others, forcing herself to exceed her physical limitations through sheer willpower and stubborn determination.

Twenty-three, twenty-four…

Her arms were trembling now, the muscles aching as acids began to build up inside the fibres, her body warning her it was approaching the limits of what it could do. Like a car engine pushed to the redline.

Twenty-five…

Her pulse was pounding in her ears as she gritted her teeth, willing her arms to raise the rest of her body up. She made it about halfway before her strength gave out, hanging there for a second or so through sheer resilience, before finally conceding defeat and allowing herself to drop to the floor.

Trying to settle her breathing, she looked down at her hands, slowly clenching and unclenching the fingers, watching as the tendons and ligaments in her forearms grew as taut as steel wires before easing off.

There was no question that she still possessed a lean and robust physique. She imagined she would even be considered physically powerful by many. But *she felt the difference, the subtle yet inescapable reality that she was not quite what she'd once been. She was diminished somehow, reduced.*

And of course, there was the change she couldn't see, confirmed during a terse and perfunctory doctor's visit a few months earlier. The knowledge that she would never be able to carry life within her, that she would never have children of her own.

She had tried to tell herself it was a blessing, that the life she'd chosen left no room for such fantasies. But it had been cold comfort, both then and now. The knowledge that something had been taken away from her. Something no amount of training could never get back. A doorway that might have led her down a new path in life had been slammed shut forever.

She closed her eyes and exhaled, carefully considering whether she ought to act on the sudden upwelling of anger and injustice that seethed inside her.

'Damn it!' she shouted in her native Lithuanian as she drew back her fist and slammed it into the plasterboard wall before her. The brittle material gave way under the blow, leaving a crumbling, fist-sized dent.

Anya swallowed and let out a breath, trying to ignore the ache in her hand and the twinge of embarrassment her outburst had provoked.

'You're wasting your time, you know.'

Spinning around, Anya was surprised to find someone had approached without her knowledge, moving swiftly and silently across the padded floor of the gymnasium. A woman she recognised from their one and only meeting six months earlier.

'Don't get me wrong,' Freya Shaw continued, amused by Anya's discomfort. 'I admire your dedication. And the tough female soldier routine is just... delightful. But that's one fight you'll never win.'

'How did you get in here?' Anya demanded, both irritated and a little unnerved by the intrusion. Camp Peary was a high security military facility, designed for special forces units and CIA field teams to train and prepare for active operations.

It was not the kind of place a civilian could simply walk into.

Shaw didn't answer this, though Anya saw a flicker of a smile as the older woman moved slowly around her. Sleek and elegant, well dressed and perfectly groomed, she was everything Anya wasn't; a fact that both women were acutely aware of in that moment.

'It doesn't matter how many weights you lift or how far you run. You'll never be as big or as powerful as they are,' she explained patiently. 'You're simply not built for it, Anya. And the harder you try to overcome that, the harder reality will push back against you.'

Anya's hands curled into fists as she glared at Shaw. This arrogant, manipulative woman who dared to lecture her on what she was and wasn't capable of.

'I have made it this far,' she pointed out. 'Many people like you have tried to stop me, or tell me I couldn't. But here I am.'

'Here you are indeed,' Shaw agreed. 'That tells me two things about you. You're resilient, and short-sighted. One of those makes you an asset, the other a liability.'

Anya could feel her heart rate increasing as Shaw's words seeped into her mind like poison, somehow cutting to the very core of her psyche. Seeking a distraction, she bent down and picked up her bottle of water.

'I came here today to find out which of those qualities is stronger in you. Whether I can make you into something useful, or whether you'll always be just a dumb "valstietis" who wants to play soldiers...'

Anya stiffened at the vulgar insult in her native language. She'd heard more than enough. Smashing the glass bottle against the nearby exercise frame, she whirled around and brought the jagged end up against Shaw's throat.

Shaw didn't flinch, didn't move a muscle as Anya held the improvised weapon barely an inch from the vulnerable skin.

'This "girl" has killed people smarter and stronger than you,' Anya hissed. 'Say the wrong thing and we will find out how much of liability I really am.'

Anya had killed plenty of men up close and personal before, but never a woman. Not that she had any unique compassion or loyalty towards her own sex, just that the opportunity had never presented itself. The thought even crossed her mind that it would be interesting to see if they died any differently.

But far from being afraid, as she rightly should have, Shaw met her baleful gaze with a look of cool, detached satisfaction, as if she'd made a point in some academic debate.

'I suppose I should add "easily provoked" to the list.'

Anya brought the jagged edge of the bottle closer so that it touched the skin right around her carotid artery. She knew just the right angle and amount of force to use, and that if she did so, Shaw would be dead in under a minute.

'Do you think this is a game, Freya Shaw? Shall we play together, you and I?'

'That's one way to look at it,' Shaw replied. 'That being the case, you ought to think more than one move ahead. For example, you could kill me right now—'

'Give me a reason not to.'

'If you did, the two snipers covering this gym hall from the overhead windows would drop you before you'd taken three paces.'

Anya held her stare for a second or two before glancing up at the building's windows. Sure enough, she saw at least one figure crouched down beside a window that had been opened to let fresh air in, saw the long barrel of a rifle trained on her.

'Planning and foresight. You can't take my life without sacrificing your own. So here we are — stalemate.' Shaw's expression took on a harder, more commanding look. 'Now take that thing away from my throat before I lose my patience.'

Anya stubbornly kept it there for a few more seconds, hoping to make her sweat, hoping to ruffle that infuriatingly flawless composure. When it became apparent that it wasn't going to happen, she finally lowered the broken bottle and withdrew a few steps.

'Good girl.' Shaw looked as if nothing remotely unusual had just happened. 'Now, there's another reason I came here today.'

'What?'

'I like you, Anya.'

Anya snorted in amusement. 'If you must lie, at least make it believable.'

'I'm serious. You have intelligence, courage and determination. I know what you went through in Afghanistan.' At a sharp look from Anya, she held up a hand. 'Relax. Something like that would have broken most people, man or woman. But you made it out. More importantly, you had the courage to get back in the game.'

A flicker of an ironic smile showed at the corner of her mouth.

'And as I just discovered, you haven't lost your fire.'

Anya closed her eyes and sighed as the truth dawned on her. 'This was a test.'

It was becoming apparent that Freya was always thinking ahead. Everything she did, every seemingly inconsequential action or conversation, served a higher purpose.

'Now you're starting to understand.' Taking a step forward, Shaw nodded at Anya's body, lean and fit after her strenuous workout. 'You've developed this as much as you can.' Then she held a finger up and lightly tapped her temple. 'But this… this is far more dangerous.'

Anya looked at her closely, trying to discern the woman's intent. Normally she could read people with ease, but with Shaw she found herself unaccountably lost.

'When people look at us, they see weakness. And who can blame them, really? We're smaller than them, softer, less aggressive. We can't run as fast, lift as heavy or hit as hard as they can. From the moment we're born, we're at a disadvantage. They know this, and in our most honest moments, so do we.'

Anya bristled visibly at this statement. She had been told similar things for much of her life, and hearing it coming from a woman did little to improve her mood.

'But don't you see, Anya? That's not a handicap at all; it's our greatest advantage. We'll always be ignored, overlooked, underestimated. No one sees us a threat, so no one sees us coming. We don't fight against that, we use it.'

Anya was listening to her now, but not with the casual disdain and irritation she had felt before. Now she was really listening. Somehow, Shaw seemed to have seen right through her, laid bare her own fears, insecurities, hopes and grievances.

'What do you want from me?'

'You've spent the past five years playing their game. You played well, but it will always be their game, their rules. That's the kind of game you never win.'

Shaw's expression changed in that moment. The mask of confidence and composure slipped a little. And Anya suddenly understood that Shaw had been in the same position, had fought the same battles long before herself. She had made those same mistakes, but she had learned from them.

'But what if I showed you how to change the rules of the game? What if you were able to be the person you're supposed to be, instead of breaking yourself trying to fit someone else's mould?'

'And what am I supposed to be?' Anya asked, wary of flattery and empty promises.

'You're supposed to be better,' Shaw said firmly. 'Better than us, better than me. You're supposed to be the future. With my help, I think you can be just that. If you trust me.'

Anya scrutinised her closely, seeking some hidden tell, some insidious sign of deception, and yet finding none. As best she could tell, Shaw's offer and her intentions appeared to be sincere. And after everything she had been through in the past year, everything she had lost and sacrificed for someone else's cause, it would be a lie to say she wasn't tempted by it.

'For most of my life, I have been other people's pawn. I won't be one for you.'

At this, Shaw smiled. Not a devious or malicious smile, but a smile of acknowledgement. And, perhaps, a touch of respect.

'Anya, by the time I'm finished, you won't be a pawn. You'll be a queen.'

An uneasy quiet hung over the ancient city of Jerusalem, the crescent moon rising over a cityscape of antiquated stone buildings, narrow cobbled streets lined with acacia trees, secluded courtyards and back alleys. There was a tense stillness in the air, an unspoken sense of anticipation in a city that had known little else but war and conflict throughout its long history.

Fraught with tension and division it might have been, but people still flocked from all over the world to visit the place. American Jews revisiting their ancestral homeland, Muslims on pilgrimage to the mosque on Temple Mount, tourists from scores of countries there to experience the sights and learn the history.

For all of these reasons, Jerusalem had a vibrant night life, with restaurants, bars, cafes and underground nightclubs flourishing in streets and districts that had stood for millennia.

In short, it was a perfect place for a white woman who'd assassinated a high-ranking Mossad officer just days earlier to disappear. And it was in one of these busy underground bars that Anya found herself, seated in a corner with her back to the wall, an empty glass of vodka in front of her. Normally she wasn't a big drinker, preferring to keep a clear head, but tonight was different.

She felt troubled and restless after her mission in Tel Aviv two days ago, brooding on what she'd learned from Russo. The name Vizur could only refer to Vizur Qalat, a Pakistani intelligence officer that Cain had met with last year to broker a clandestine intel-sharing deal. Why would this man have ordered her capture? She had never even met him, to the best of her knowledge.

The deeper she dug, the more questions she came away with. And yet she was determined to keep going. Whatever scheme Qalat and his accomplices had concocted, it had resulted in the destruction of her unit and four long years in a Siberian prison. That was something which couldn't go unanswered.

This would be her final mission. Not for a flag, a country, an ideology or a secret organisation, but for herself. As for what came after, she didn't know. Perhaps there wouldn't even be an After.

She glanced up as the bartender wandered over, a bottle of vodka in his meaty hands. He was a bear of a man, well over 6 feet tall and 300 pounds of fat and muscle, but his imposing appearance was belied by his cheerful, gentle demeanour.

'You want one more?'

Giving him a weak smile, Anya held a hand over her glass. A couple of vodkas had helped take the edge off, but she couldn't afford to overdo it.

Nodding understanding, the bar owner moved off to tend to other customers. But as he did so, Anya happened to catch another man's eye, seated at the far end of the bar. She caught the interest in his expression as he stood up to approach.

Anya's hand slid beneath the table, gently thumbing off the safety on her weapon as she looked him up and down. He was about her age, she judged. Average height for a man, but in good shape, no fat on him. Sandy brown hair, medium length. Bright blue eyes, rugged features that bordered on handsome, and a tanned, weathered complexion. He was wearing a loose cotton shirt, worn jeans and dusty desert boots that looked like they'd seen decent use.

'Forgive the intrusion, but it breaks my heart to see a beautiful woman drinking alone.' His accent was British. Smooth and well spoken. There was a glimmer of attraction in his eyes.

'I'm not drinking,' Anya pointed out, nodding to her empty glass. She had little desire for company tonight, and certainly not the romantic kind.

'But you *are* beautiful, and alone,' he replied. 'Perhaps I can help with that.'

He slid into to a chair opposite without waiting for permission. Seeing the new arrival, the bartender came over to take his order.

Ordering a beer for himself, he added, 'And a vodka for the lady. Stumbras, wasn't it?'

'You are very forward,' Anya remarked as the bartender fetched their drinks, both irritated by his presumptuous move and just a little impressed. Plenty of men feigned aggressive confidence, but this one was of a different sort.

He shrugged. 'When I see something I like, I go after it. Life's too short not to. Don't you agree?'

'It depends what you go after,' Anya replied. 'Not everything is as it seems.'

'That's true, but isn't that what makes people so interesting? Everyone has a story to tell.' He took a sip of his beer. 'Your accent, for example. Lithuanian, if I'm not mistaken?'

Anya's brows rose in surprise, which prompted an amused laugh.

'The way you stress the Rs and the Ls. A dead giveaway. Of course, it's softer in your case, with a hint of East Coast American too, I think. I assume you grew up in Lithuania before moving to the West.'

'You assume a lot.'

'Feel free to correct me if I'm wrong.'

Anya said nothing to that, which prompted a wry smile.

'In my line of work, details count. One learns to pay attention to them.'

Anya tilted her head. 'And what would that be?'

'I'm a journalist.' He paused before adding, 'Freelance, you might say. The name's Blake. Carter Blake.'

She'd heard enough. Of all the people she might socialise with, an investigative journalist who already knew more about her than she was comfortable with wasn't one of them. Downing her vodka, Anya set it down on the table.

'Thank you for the drink, Blake,' she said, standing up. 'I hope you find a good story of your own.'

She saw a flicker of disappointment, though he tipped his beer to her. 'Likewise.'

Ascending the stairs into the cool night air, Anya glanced around to get her bearings. She was in the Old Town, the historic centre of the city. About half a mile away, the weathered stone walls, soaring towers and the great plateau of Temple Mount were starkly lit from below by floodlights. And in the midst of it all, the gold-plated Dome of the Rock.

The Mount was the focal point of multiple religions, a symbol of the endless conflict that had stained the ancient ground of Israel for millennia. Everyone from the Romans to the Persians, the Crusaders and the Knights Templar, and even the Ottomans and the British had conquered and fought over this place, successive empires rising and falling with the tides of history.

Pulling on a shawl to cover her hair, she set out eastward through the complex labyrinth of cobbled streets and alleyways. Her head was down but her eyes were alert, her posture relaxed but ready, her hands thrust in the pockets of her jacket.

She turned left off the bustling main street, taking a side alley heading north. The old buildings loomed over her, nearly blotting out her view of the stars overhead. Away from the lights and activity of the main thoroughfare, her senses began to sharpen.

It wasn't long before she detected the sound of footsteps behind her. Not running, but keeping pace with her.

Reaching an intersection of several alleys and small roads, she turned sharply right and picked up her pace. The footsteps followed. Two sets, moving fast but steady.

She turned right again at the next intersection, passing through an arched wall into a small courtyard beyond. It was overlooked by darkened sandstone buildings, their windows firmly shuttered.

Just as she'd expected, a welcoming committee was waiting for her.

Anya halted, facing the two men on the opposite side of the courtyard. Both were tall and well built, one black and the other Hispanic. Both were dressed in loose shirts and jackets. The kind of clothes in which one could easily conceal weapons.

Both were watching her with dark, wary eyes.

'Should have stayed for that drink,' a voice remarked from behind.

Anya didn't need to turn around to know that Blake had followed her from the bar.

'Who sent you?' she asked quietly, backing towards one corner of the courtyard as the ring closed around her. 'Mossad? The CIA?'

Her eyes flicked to each man in turn, taking note of their stances and weapons. The two men in front were armed with tasers – X26 police-issue units. Non-lethal, intended only to incapacitate her.

The other two were packing automatics. One was a Glock 22, the other was possibly a Sig Sauer P220, though she couldn't be sure in the dim light. Both had suppressors fitted.

'Nothing as grand as that, I'm afraid. There's ten million dollars on your head. A man could retire with that kind of money. Now get those hands up where I can see them, please.'

Anya let out a snort of disgust. 'You're bounty hunters.'

A ripple of laughter passed through the four men covering her.

'If you want to call it that,' Blake confirmed. 'It's nothing personal, just business.'

'You don't have to do this, Blake,' Anya implored him. She still had her hands firmly in her pockets. 'You can still walk away.'

Unknown to them, her hand was closed around the heavy metal sphere in her pocket, her thumb working against the pin until she felt it snap free.

'That's not how this story plays out, I'm afraid.' His voice took on a harder edge. 'Now show me those hands.'

'You mean this hand?' Anya asked, holding out the grenade she was clutching, the pin now dangling from her thumb. Half a second later, she released her grip on the fly-off handle, and hurled the weapon at them.

She saw them flinch slightly, one or two backing away, but Blake stood his ground. His silent reassurance steadied the others, and they held the line, keeping her covered.

'Nice try,' Blake scoffed, amused by her attempted deception. 'But we both know the grenade isn't live.'

Ignoring his mocking tone, Anya tensed up, readying herself for what was coming.

There was a loud pop like a firecracker followed by an eruption of dense white smoke as the grenade burst apart, engulfing the courtyard in a blinding chemical haze.

'Shit, we're blind!' a voice cried out.

'Fire! Fire!' another yelled, accompanied by the dull, heavy thud of a suppressed weapon as he emptied rounds into the smoke, aiming at Anya's last known location.

But she was no longer there, having leapt aside and rolled into a crouch. The world seemed to go into slow motion as she reached down, yanked her silenced Colt 1911 handgun from inside her jacket and darted towards the source of the first shout.

A shadowy figure emerged from the gloom. She thought it might be the Hispanic man, judging by the general height and build.

She took aim at his head and squeezed the trigger. Her weapon spat out two shots, the suppressor thudding with each one. The first missed as he saw her coming and tried to duck aside, but the second caught him just behind the ear, blowing away the rear portion of his skull.

No need to follow that one up. He'd be dead before he hit the ground.

One down.

The black man must have heard the sounds of suppressed gunfire, because she heard the sudden pop as a compressed gas canister was expended and was aware of something whizzing over her head. The twin prongs of a taser, the conducting wires trailing back towards its source.

It couldn't have been easier. Using the wires as a guide, she put two rounds straight into his face, crumpling the front of his head into a wet pulpy mass of shattered bone and bloody flesh. She heard a muffled, gurgling cry as he staggered backwards, clawing at what was left of his face.

Two down.

But the smoke was beginning to clear now as the cloud dispersed. 'Contact!' came a shout from her left.

Closing the last few steps between her and the man she'd shot in the face, she grabbed him by the jacket and shoved him in front of her just as a trio of suppressed shots rang out. She could feel his muscular body jerking and shuddering as the rounds tore into his torso, but it didn't matter now. He'd served his purpose.

Even as her human shield fell, Anya raised her weapon, sighted the muzzle flash and opened fire, putting two rounds into her next target's centre mass, one of which passed straight through his forearm before shattering his ribcage. A third shot to the forehead dropped him.

Three down.

Hearing the faint click of a weapon being raised behind, Anya reacted instinctively, spinning around and allowing herself to drop like a stone as she brought her gun around to face Blake. He had dropped into a crouch to avoid the stray rounds flying in all directions. In the instant before she squeezed the trigger, she saw his rugged, handsome face twisted in anger.

Both combatants fired at the same instant, their silenced weapons thumping as they discharged. Anya felt a sting at her shoulder as she landed hard on the dusty ground, while Blake was kicked suddenly backwards, a cloud of red mist exiting from his back.

Reaching up, Anya felt warm, wet blood on her hand. She moved her arm and flexed the fingers experimentally, checking for tendon or nerve damage. Everything seemed to work. It was a flesh wound only.

The pain hadn't quite reached her yet, but she knew it would come.

Her weapon was dry. Picking herself up, she ejected the spent mag from the M1911, fished a fresh one from her jacket and pressed it home; an action she'd repeated so many times that it was almost as natural as breathing.

Blake was lying sprawled on his back, writhing and twisting to little effect, frothy foam leaking from the hole in his chest. Kicking his gun away, Anya looked down at him with something akin to pity.

'I told you to walk away,' she said, angry with him for what she'd been forced to do.

Blake tried to say something in his response, but all that came forth was a gasping, rattling wheeze. The sound of a dying man.

She saw that knowledge, the fear in his eyes.

'Speaking of stories,' she said as she raised her weapon. 'This is where yours ends.'

Two more rounds to the chest ended his struggle.

Four down.

Chapter 14

London, UK

One thing that never ceased to amaze Drake about the nation's capital was the frantic pace of expansion and development. London had effectively become the world's largest building site in the past twenty years. Everywhere he looked, cranes, gantries and the steel skeletons of new office blocks and high-rise skyscrapers soared into the evening sky.

It was a city of jarring contrasts. Rows of ornate Victorian and Edwardian town houses and public buildings stood next to brutalist concrete monoliths thrown up in the Sixties and Seventies, which were in turn being supplanted by a new generation of ultramodern steel and glass towers.

People, cultures and religions from all corners of the globe crammed together into one space. A place where past, present and future collided in a vibrant mess that was as fascinating and unique as it was overwhelming.

Today, however, Drake's mind was less on his surroundings, and more on the meeting that lay ahead. After calling Fitzgibbons' office and requesting a meeting, his secretary had agreed that he would see them at five p.m.

Which was just as well, because by that point Drake had already boarded a train from Liverpool to London Euston station with Jessica in tow. Trying to drive in central London was, as he knew from experience, an exercise in futility. It would also mean passing innumerable traffic cameras that he was keen to avoid.

The train was the most direct option, though it too was not without risks. He had been careful to choose a seat that wasn't directly covered by the train's internal cameras, keeping his head down as he moved around.

Now that they were approaching the station, Drake glanced at his sister seated opposite, concerned both for her state of mind and the risk she posed. Jessica had grown quiet once the rolling fields and small villages of the English countryside gave way to the grey high-rises of the London cityscape, dotted with the orange glow of lights against a heavy overcast sky.

She was staring forlornly out the rain-spattered window at the shops, bars, restaurants and pedestrians sliding by as the train reduced speed, but she wasn't really seeing any of it. Drake could guess what was on her mind.

'Been a while, hasn't it?' he said quietly.

She sat up straighter, stirred from her reverie. 'Since the divorce, you mean?' she replied with a bleak half-smile. 'Yeah, it's been a while.'

Her experiences several years ago had wrought a profound change on Jessica's life. Once happily married, lively and sociable, she had become angry, troubled and withdrawn. The impact on her marriage was as inevitable as it was painful.

'I'm sorry, Jess,' he said, well aware of how inadequate those words must have sounded. Whether intended or not, the war he'd become embroiled in hadn't just impacted his own life. Too many innocent people had been caught in the crossfire.

Jessica didn't respond, staring out the window in contemplative silence.

The train's intercom pinged and the tinny, automated voice announced they were approaching their final destination.

'This is it,' Drake said, glad of the reprieve. 'Remember what I told you. Head down, no sudden moves.'

They disembarked, merging with the thousands of other commuters streaming towards the doors at the south end of the terminus, and out into the noise and bustle of central London.

Traffic surged along the main drag opposite, cars jostling for position as double decker busses lumbered by, while bikes, mopeds and cyclists zipped in between. Several buildings in the vicinity were festooned with scaffolding, the rumble of machinery and the rattle of jackhammers emanating from within. Rain was already pattering down from the leaden sky.

Still, the inclement weather worked to their advantage. 'Hoods up,' Drake instructed.

London was notorious for its high-density CCTV coverage. If MI5 became aware of their presence here, it would only be a matter of minutes before the sighting was forwarded to the CIA. Then the game would be up.

Getting his bearings, Drake pointed west. 'This way. Let's go.'

Fitzgibbons' office was barely half a mile from Euston station. An easy ten-minute walk under normal circumstances.

They set off together, moving through the throngs of pedestrians, Drake with his hands in his pockets and his head down. Just another anonymous commuter on his way home.

Drake was accustomed to operating in urban environments like this, appearing relaxed and disinterested while maintaining tight situational awareness. Jessica, however, was a different prospect. She looked tense and distracted.

This was bad news. People have an innate ability to sense fear and discomfort in others, born from the base, primal instincts that had kept their prehistoric ancestors alive. Just like gazelle on the African plains, if one of the herd tenses up, the others will become wary too.

'Take it easy,' he advised, his voice low. 'Slow it down.'

'Worry about yourself, Ryan,' she snapped back.

Nonetheless, she seemed to compose herself as Drake turned south at a big intersection just east of Regent's Park. Despite his sister's unease, they were making good progress. That is, until they heard the wail of a police siren heading in their direction.

Drake saw Jessica stiffen up. He could imagine the questions and fears tumbling through her head at that moment. Had they been discovered? Could they escape? Which way should they run? Would they have to fight their way out?

Drake could see the blue flashing glow approaching fast, yet he felt little immediate concern. If they had indeed been spotted, it wouldn't be a local police unit that was dispatched to take them down.

'Relax. It's not for us,' he assured her over the growing clamour.

Sure enough, a police van sped past and roared through the next intersection, traffic awkwardly parting to make way for it. Drake let out a relieved breath and turned his attention back to his sister.

She too had turned away from the road, rattled by the close call and eager to move away from the scene. Unfortunately, her haste to get going carried her straight into the path of a plump, middle-aged woman who was walking fast in the opposite direction, head down and eyes glued to her phone.

The collision happened before Drake could intervene, the woman losing her grip on the phone, which clattered to the ground. At the same time, Jessica drew away suddenly, her hood falling back and her hand going instinctively to her back pocket.

'Oh, shit!' she snapped, glaring at Jessica with obvious irritation. People nearby had slowed down, watching the encounter with mild interest.

'I… I'm sorry. I didn't see you,' Jessica stammered, recovering herself and bending down to retrieve the device.

'It's fine! Just leave it.' Before she could act, the woman had swooped down and snatched it up, wiping spots of water from the casing and quickly inspecting the screen for damage.

'I can pay if it's damaged—' Jessica offered.

'I said it's fine,' the woman repeated irritably. She paused before adding, 'Try looking where you're going in future.'

'It's okay,' Drake said, quickly inserting himself between them and steering Jessica away from the scene. 'It was an accident, that's all. No harm done.'

Casting a final look of annoyance at them, the woman continued on her way. The other bystanders who had slowed to watch were likewise dispersing. Little accidents and misunderstandings like this were common in a crowded city, and most of them would have forgotten about it in a matter of minutes.

Drake, however, had seen something in the seconds after the collision; something that had gone unnoticed by everyone else. He knew what Jessica had been reaching for.

'Put your hood back up,' he said quietly, his voice carrying a harder undertone of command.

'I'm fine,' Jessica protested as he led her forcefully into the narrow side alley used for deliveries. 'I said I'm fine!'

Saying nothing, Drake reached behind her and snatched out the item hidden in her back pocket. 'Hey! What are you doing?'

'You tell me,' Drake replied, holding up the dark metal switchblade she'd been carrying. 'What the hell is this, Jess?'

'Protection. What do you think?'

'Use your head, for Christ's sake. You get caught with a knife here, you're fucked.'

With firearms being difficult to procure in the UK, knife crime had become an epidemic in big cities. As a result, the police didn't mess around when it came to illegal carrying. Anyone caught would be arrested and charged on the spot.

Jessica eyed him shrewdly. 'And you expect me to believe for one second that *you're* unarmed?'

Of course he wasn't. Drake rarely went anywhere without a weapon now.

'That's different.'

'Why?'

'This is what I do. It's my world.' He shook his head. 'Not yours.'

'Oh, spare me the protective big brother routine,' she scoffed. 'You weren't there when they took me four years ago, and you weren't there when they came for me yesterday.'

Drake felt like he'd been punched in the guts. The anger and betrayal in her voice was obvious, and worse, entirely justified.

'I'm here now, Jess. I'm not going anywhere,' he said, speaking more softly now.

'It's not enough, Ryan. Not anymore.'

She held out her hand, waiting for him to return the weapon.

He didn't. Instead he slipped it into his own pocket.

'Let's be clear about one thing,' he said. 'We do things *my way*. You follow my lead, do what I say, and you stay alive. That's how this has to play out.' Turning away, he headed back towards the main drag nearby. 'Let's go.'

'What if you're not enough?' Jessica called after him.

Drake halted briefly but didn't turn around.

'I will be.'

He heard Jessica swear under her breath, then the sound of her footsteps splashing through the puddles towards him.

Caught up as they were in their fraught exchange, neither of them had noticed the overhead security camera covering the entrance to the street.

Chapter 15

GCHQ, Cheltenham

Senior intel analyst Wilson Hager yawned and stretched at his terminal – one of many in the operations centre of the Doughnut, GCHQ's famous headquarters building – then opened the next batch of referrals from the automated facial recognition system. It had been a busy shift, with no sign of slowing down.

He was contemplating going to fetch a coffee when his terminal pinged with a new request. This one was red-flagged as high priority.

Quickly setting aside his other workload, he opened it up and scanned the contents.

> Subject – Jessica Drake
> Sex – Female
> Age – 35
> Ethnicity – Caucasian
> Status – Known associate of Tier 1 Wanted Subject

Hager felt a little jolt of adrenaline at this news. Tier 1 was the highest level of interest, reserved for international criminals, terrorists and known foreign intelligence operatives.

When Jessica Drake had thrown back her hood on that rain-soaked street in central London, her face had automatically been captured by the CCTV camera overlooking the street and downloaded to the GCHQ servers. The service's powerful artificial intelligence, churning through terabytes of data every second, had identified her particular arrangement of facial features and triggered a database match in just 113.56 seconds.

Opening the image of Jessica, Hager first ran it through a diagnostic tool designed to be more thorough than the standard AI sweep.

It delivered a 98.2 per cent match.

Next, Hager set the most recent file photo of the subject alongside the CCTV image and compared them himself, noting similarities in bone structure, skin tone, and facial composition. He marked the tag as Verified.

This done, he opened a link to the original video file so he could review it in context. The jerky footage showed the subject walking against the flow of pedestrian traffic, distracted by a passing police van and colliding with a passing civilian. Advancing the video through the encounter, he watched as she left the scene with a second individual.

A man.

A man who steered her into a nearby service alley, presumably to speak in private. But his actions allowed Hager to snap a partial image of his face and run it through facial recognition. The system came back with a 77.4 per cent probability match.

> Tier 1 Suspect Match: Identity Classified – Contact your
> administrator immediately

No sooner had he scanned this result than his desk phone started ringing. It was coming from his immediate superior, Oliver Pendleton.

Hager snatched up the unit. 'Hager.'

'Wilson, it's Oliver. I've just had a Tier One alert flagged from your terminal,' he began, his voice sharp and clinical. 'How long ago was the image captured?'

'Erm…' Hager checked the time stamps. 'About five minutes ago in central London.'

'Get a track on the suspect's current location. We need to know exactly where he is.'

'Sir, it would help if I had an ID—'

'Just get on it, Hager,' Pendleton snapped.

London, UK

Eager to reach their destination without further mishap, Drake forged ahead, scanning the street signs overhead until at last he spotted the one he was looking for and turned into it: Middleton Place.

Too narrow to accommodate cars, it looked more like a pedestrian crosswalk between the busy roads at either end. The result was a tight and rather gloomy street about 50 yards long, mostly cramped flats, with a few small businesses peppered about.

Music and light spilled from an old-fashioned-looking pub on the corner, small knots of men standing outside smoking and talking. Much as Drake could have murdered a pint, he had other business to attend to.

And that business lay about halfway along the narrow street.

'You sure this is the place?' Jessica asked dubiously, staring up at the dreary edifice that stood before them. A product of nineteenth-century Victorian architecture, it was a narrow, two-storey building sandwiched uncomfortably between larger structures that loomed over it like domineering big brothers. The stonework was weathered and darkened by decades of pollution, the paint peeling, the windows dirty and covered by cheap net curtains. A casual passer-by would be forgiven for thinking the place was long-defunct, but electric lights were dimly visible behind the tatty curtains.

'Pretty sure,' Drake said, pointing to a tarnished brass plaque by the door: *Fitzgibbons and Carter Legal Services*.

Their online searches had failed to yield anything substantive on this legal firm – no website or social media presence, no mentions in news articles, not even an entry in the local business directory. Whatever Fitzgibbons and Carter did for a living, they certainly didn't shout about it.

Drake ascended the worn steps and tried the door. Finding it locked, he pressed the intercom. There was no buzz, and no light indicating the unit was connected.

'Oh, bloody hell,' Jessica grumbled, stepping past and thumping the door hard.

Seconds ticked by as the rain pattered down and the cold wind gusted along the narrow street, carrying empty crisp packets and other pieces of drifting trash. The warm, lively pub was looking more appealing by the minute.

At last there came the crunch of a reluctant lock being turned, and the big door swung open to reveal what Drake assumed to be Mr Frederick Fitzgibbons.

With a lined and sagging face, watery eyes that had spent a lifetime scrutinising tedious legal documents and only a few wisps of uncertain white hair over his bald pate, Fitzgibbons must have been well into his seventies if he was a day.

He scrutinised Drake and his sister over the rims of his reading spectacles, eyeing them as if they might rob him at any moment. Which wasn't an entirely unfair assessment, given their appearance.

'Yes?' he said, his voice clipped and terse.

'The name's Drake. Ryan Drake. I'm here to see Mr Fitzgibbons.'

'Regarding?'

Reaching into his jacket, Drake produced the key given to him by his mother. 'I'm looking for something to stick this in, and I'm not too particular.'

Fitzgibbons' eyes opened wider. 'I see. You'd better come in, then.'

Stepping back, he allowed Drake and Jessica to enter before closing and locking the door behind them.

Chapter 16

GCHQ, Cheltenham

Hager looked up briefly from his terminal as floor manager Oliver Pendleton hurried over. A brusque, efficient man with dark hair and a neatly trimmed beard, he always seemed to run at 110 per cent, somehow making everyone around him feel inadequate no matter how hard they were working.

'What do you have, Wilson?' he asked, leaning forward to scrutinise his work.

'I've got a confirmed visual match on two persons of interest. Subject One is Jessica Drake, a thirty-five-year-old British female. Subject Two is a Tier One Person of Interest, no name or nationality.'

'Where are they now?'

Hager brought up the traffic surveillance camera and scanned the image before pointing to two individuals walking side by side, heads down and hoods up. 'There they are, heading west on Langham Street.'

'Where are they going?' Pendleton wondered aloud.

His answer wasn't long in presenting itself. The two figures turned left into a narrow side street.

'There,' Hager said, his excitement building. 'Middleton Place. It's a pedestrian street that runs between the two main roads.'

'Any cameras in there?'

'No public systems, but there may be private units we can access.'

'Okay. Get on it,' Pendleton said, turning away and quickly dialling a number on his cell phone: a direct line to the head of MI5.

'It's Pendleton, sir. We have him.'

–

The interior of *Fitzgibbons and Carter* was pretty much what Drake had expected. The main hallway had likely been an impressive foyer when this place was first constructed, with high ceilings, wood panelled walls, tiled floors and intricately carved cornice work. But time and neglect had rendered it a bleak, depressing place, the floor tiles cracked and missing in places, the carved woodwork obscured behind countless layers of paint. Cheap strip lighting provided illumination. The damp, musty smell peculiar to old buildings hung in the air.

'Thank you for agreeing to see us at short notice, Mr Fitzgibbons,' Jessica ventured. 'I imagine you're... erm, a busy man.'

'Not at all, Ms Drake. For an account like yours, there's always time.'

To their surprise, a curious change had come over Fitzgibbons. The bent back straightened out as he drew himself up, the frail and diminished body grew sprightly and firm, the wizened and careworn face relaxed. It was as if the man was growing younger before their very eyes.

'Ah, that's better,' he said, removing the reading spectacles before thrusting out a hand to Drake. 'Frederick Fitzgibbons at your service.'

Drake shook hands warily, surprised by the vigour of his grip. All was, apparently, not what it seemed with this man.

'Forgive the amateur theatrics, but one has to maintain appearances,' Fitzgibbons explained.

'Why, exactly?' Jessica asked.

The old lawyer gave her a patient smile. 'Anonymity, of course. It's one of the main reasons our clients use my organisation.' Sensing his words had done little to illuminate them, he beckoned for them to follow. 'I imagine you have a lot of questions. Please, follow me and I'll explain everything.'

With that, he hurried off with fast and purposeful strides. Left with little alternative, Drake and Jessica followed in his wake.

'What on earth is going on?' Jessica whispered.

'I don't know, but stick close,' Drake advised, watching their host warily.

Turning a corner, Fitzgibbons opened what looked like an old storage cupboard. Leaning in, he pulled on some hidden catch or lever, and suddenly the rear wall slid back, revealing an old-fashioned cage-style elevator. He pressed the button beside it, and there was a hum as the lift machinery went to work.

'I must say, it's a pleasure to finally meet you both. I'm just sorry it couldn't have been under happier circumstances.' He paused, nodding to Jessica. 'My condolences for the loss of your mother.'

'Thank you,' Jessica said, hesitating before adding, 'You mentioned something about "an account like yours". What did you mean?'

The elevator arrived with the crisp ping of a bell. Opening the cage, the old man gestured for them to enter. Warily they stepped inside, Jessica swallowing down an unpleasant feeling of claustrophobia. After pulling the cage shut, Fitzgibbons pressed the descend button.

'Your mother Freya was one of our most valued clients, Ms Drake,' he explained as the elevator slowly moved down its shaft. 'Her account included our full range of services.'

The elevator shuddered to a halt, allowing Fitzgibbons to open the cage once more. The plush, tastefully decorated and well-lit hallway stretching before them was a world away from the drab, cold and neglected building above.

They weren't alone here, either. A pair of men in suits, much younger and more heavily built than Fitzgibbons, flanked a set of double doors at the end of the corridor. Drake had been in enough secret facilities to recognise security men when he saw them.

'What is this place?' Jessica asked, staring around in awe.

'Consider it a… storage facility,' the old man said, escorting them towards the double doors. 'Our clients value two things – security and discretion. My organisation exists to provide both.'

His words might not have meant much to Jessica, but for Drake it was entirely different. Over the years he'd heard rumours about places like this, almost urban legends in his line of work. Safety deposit vaults for the world's richest and most notorious personalities. The kind of places that would store and handle just about anything (or anyone) for the right price, no questions asked.

'This is a shielded structure. Your mobile phones won't function down here,' he explained apologetically. 'A security precaution that I'm afraid we must insist upon.'

'For you, or us?' Drake asked.

'For all of us,' Fitzgibbons replied. 'As I said, discretion is a priority here.'

The security operatives opened the doors as they approached, permitting entry to a large, luxuriously appointed conference room beyond. A long table with rows of chairs along both sides occupied the central part of the room, facing a wall-mounted TV at the far end. A couple of additional couches and chairs had been positioned in various places around the room. The place reminded Drake of an old-fashioned gentlemen's club.

As the doors swung closed, Fitzgibbons let out a breath and clapped his hands.

'Well, thank you for indulging us. This can be an unusual place for first-time clients. Please don't take this as an insult, but we had begun to wonder if you would ever find us.'

'I get that a lot these days,' Drake said, giving his sister a look.

'Indeed. Well, your package is being retrieved from our vault as we speak.'

'Package?' Jessica chipped in.

'Your mother left the contents of her safety deposit box for you, to be presented on your arrival. You will of course need her personal security key to open it.'

'What do you know about her?' Drake asked.

'As I say, Ms Shaw was one of our most valued clients. Her account services included full access to any of our facilities worldwide, Asylum and Safe Passage agreements, and document and equipment procurement.'

'There are more places like this?' Jessica asked.

'Many more. Not all of them are as charming as our little establishment here in London, of course.'

Drake, however, was less interested in Fitzgibbons' international empire than he was in the woman who had led them here.

'Can you tell us what Freya was involved in? Who might have wanted her dead?'

At this, the old man shook his head sadly. 'Mr Drake, my organisation's policy is one of strict neutrality. We are… somewhat removed from matters of international politics, including our clients' occupations.'

Their brief discussion was interrupted by a polite knock at the door.

'But given that she left specific instructions for you to be granted entry, I daresay her safety deposit box might shed some light on things.'

The doors opened, and another man entered bearing a locked metal box. It was bulky, about the size of a large briefcase, with folded handles set into the sides to aid with carrying. Resting on top was a laptop computer.

Setting the box and the laptop down on the conference table, the man gave Fitzgibbons a curt nod and promptly departed.

'Most clients prefer to access their boxes in private, so unless you need anything else, I'll leave the two of you alone,' the facility manager announced. 'The door will be locked and guarded at all times. This room is soundproofed and free from electronic monitoring, so you can be assured of absolute privacy.' He pointed to an intercom set into the conference table. 'Please call if you need assistance, or you're ready to leave. Otherwise, the room is yours for as long as you need.'

Fitzgibbons excused himself, moving with the same brisk, efficient strides as before. The doors swung closed behind him, followed by a muted click as the locks were engaged.

No sooner had they been left alone than Jessica let out her breath and practically fell into one of the high-backed chairs.

'This may be the most surreal experience of my life. Coded letters, conspiracies, secret underground vaults…' she said, rubbing her temples. 'Seriously, is this the kind of thing you get up to when I'm not around?'

'Not really,' Drake admitted. He was in uncharted waters now, with no past knowledge he could make use of. All he had was the box in front of him.

'Well?' Jessica prompted. 'Are you going to open it?'

Drake looked down at the key that had so mystified him these past few years, so close now to fulfilling its purpose. It was a substantial weight in his hand, the significance of this moment somehow adding to its feeling of ominous weight.

'We're going to learn things about her today,' he warned his sister quietly. 'Things we won't be able to forget. You sure you want to do this?'

Rising slowly to her feet, Jessica looked at him. 'I didn't come all this way to turn back now.' Taking a deep breath, she gave a firm nod. 'I'm ready.'

Stepping forward, Drake inserted the distinctive three-bladed key into the armoured box, gripped it firmly and gave it a turn.

There was a muted click as the internal locking mechanism disengaged, and the top sprang open slightly. Drake swung the lid upwards, surprised both by its thickness and weight, at last revealing the contents.

Chapter 17

Standing by the window of the corner office that he'd requisitioned, Jason Hawkins took a sip of his coffee as he stared out across the London skyline. He'd never cared much for England. Shit weather, shit food and, if the burnt and bitter contents of his cup were anything to go by, shit coffee, too.

But here he was, on the top floor of the bizarre, pyramid-like fortress that served as the headquarters of MI6, situated at Vauxhall Cross on the south bank of the Thames. Cain had already seen to it that he was afforded every bit of clearance and cooperation he needed to go about his business.

The Brits clearly resented his presence here, not that he cared much. They were paper tigers, capable of doing little more than pissing and moaning about things they didn't like. The Agency owned them, and now Cain effectively owned the Agency. Which gave Hawkins all the authority he needed.

And what he wanted most of all was to find Ryan Drake and kill the son of a bitch. They'd played a long game of cat and mouse, and though Hawkins had come frustratingly close to ending it on several occasions, somehow Drake had eluded him.

But not for much longer. He couldn't explain it, but deep down he felt it. The pieces moving into their final positions.

The endgame.

His thoughts were intruded upon when the door to the office flew open and a young intelligence officer hurried in.

'I assume you never learned to knock?' Hawkins asked pointedly.

'Sorry, sir. But you said you wanted to be notified right away if we got a lead.' He held out a printed report. 'We have a confirmed sighting.'

Abandoning his coffee, Hawkins snatched the printed report and quickly scanned it, his excitement growing with each line. Drake had been sighted, right here in London. And even better, his sister was with him.

One thing he had to commend the Brits on was their surveillance capabilities. In many of the countries in which he'd operated, a man could disappear without difficulty. But not here. Here there were almost as many cameras as people; something Drake himself was doubtless aware of.

So why was he here? Why take the risk?

'How accurate is the facial match?'

'Accurate enough for GCHQ to flag it.'

'And how long ago was this taken?'

'About ten minutes.'

Hawkins turned away, looking out across the city as if his vision could somehow penetrate the hundreds of buildings that stood between them. If this match was accurate, then Drake was just a few miles away from him at this very moment.

'Put my team on alert. Tell them to be ready to deploy,' he instructed. 'You also have your own field teams, I assume?'

'We do, sir. Two rapid response teams on permanent standby. They can be anywhere in the city in under thirty minutes. Plus local armed police units.'

Hawkins smiled. 'Get them ready to move.'

'Which one?'

'All of them. Go now.'

As the young officer hurried away, Hawkins consulted the address where Drake was suspected of making entry. *Fitzgibbons and Carter Legal Services.* The name was familiar to him, though it took him a few seconds to recall why.

When he did, a slow smile began to form.

'Ryan, you clever son of a bitch,' he whispered. Now he knew why Drake had come here, why he'd taken the risk. Why he thought himself safe.

Vaults were considered the safest of safe houses, protected not only by physical security measures but also by a more subtle, yet far more formidable series of agreements and treaties amongst the major players in the intelligence world. They were like the Switzerland of the covert espionage game, their neutrality almost inviolable.

Breaking such an agreement could have serious consequences, but that wasn't his concern any longer. Cain had told him to use any and all measures to take down Drake, no matter the cost.

No matter the cost.

Chapter 18

'My God,' Jessica gasped as her eyes alighted on the contents of the box.

Drake didn't blame her. He was by now quite familiar with 'security blankets', as they were known, and recognised the contents right away. His sister, however, came from a different world.

The first and most obvious items were the stacks of money, wrapped and secured inside plastic Ziploc bags, each holding a significant quantity of different currencies, from US dollars to pounds and euros. Opening one, Drake guessed he was holding forty, maybe fifty thousand pounds.

He set the bundle aside. The money might prove useful in due course, but Freya hadn't brought him all this way just to pad out his bank account.

The next item was equally familiar. A Glock-17 automatic pistol, set within a foam-lined protective box. A box of 9mm shells and two spare magazines were packed beside it.

Money and a weapon were standard items in boxes like these, allowing the recipient easy access to the two most effective means of escaping trouble – fighting or bribery.

But it was the smallest item that interested him most. A USB memory stick, presumably containing data that she wanted him to see. It also explained why the laptop had been provided. Whatever was on that memory stick, it was why they were really here.

'What could be on it?' Jessica asked as he carefully removed it.

His attention turned towards the laptop. 'Let's find out.'

Inserting it into one of the spare ports, Drake waited while the machine accessed its contents. Moments later, a single video file became available. Clicking on it, Drake took a seat beside his sister and waited.

After a few seconds of blackness, the screen changed and he found himself staring at the face of his mother. Seeing her alive and well again brought a sudden chill to him. A message from beyond the grave, as it were.

He heard a sharp intake of breath by his side. He might have grown estranged from Freya over the years, but Jessica had remained close with her, unaware of the secrets she harboured. She'd felt loss and grief at her death. Drake just felt empty and cheated.

He pushed those thoughts aside as he scrutinised the video for important details. Judging by Freya's age and general appearance, this video had been made shortly before her death.

The background was also immediately familiar, since he had a plain view of the very same wood-panelled walls from where he was sitting.

'Ryan,' she began, and once more he felt a chill at the sound of her voice. 'If you're watching this, it means you understood my message.' She paused before adding, 'It also means that I'm dead.'

She said this without regret or emotion. It was a simple, matter-of-fact statement.

'I imagine you have a lot of questions for me. I'll do what I can to answer them truthfully now.'

Drake felt a hand, warm and soft, laid on top of his. His sister, preparing herself for what was coming, needing to feel his presence.

'And the truth, in my case, begins with a lie. My life, my career, almost everything you and your sister were told about me since childhood, was all a lie. I wasn't a journalist or a writer. I was an intelligence officer working for MI6, recruited not long after I finished university. I went on to serve as a field agent for six years.' She sighed. 'I suppose I was exactly the kind of person they were looking for – young, attractive, intelligent and... in my own way, eager for adventure. I became very good at what I did.'

Drake said nothing as he listened to this. Given her connection to the Circle, it wasn't surprising that other aspects of her life were shrouded in deception. But to hear her actually say it in such stark, precise terms was still a disconcerting experience.

'I couldn't tell anyone close to me, of course. Not even your father.' At this, Drake saw a flicker of genuine regret. 'Looking back on it, I should have realised a job like that doesn't leave much space for a marriage. I was trying to live in two different worlds, and I never could bridge the gap between them. That was my failure, not his.'

Drake found himself struggling to reconcile this ageing, regretful, apologetic woman on the screen with his own memories of a cold, distant, dismissive mother who always seemed to be somewhere else, always had something more important to do, always left early and came home late, if at all. Who always made him feel like an annoying hindrance, an inconvenience to be tolerated.

Suddenly he was seeing that woman in a very different light. He saw the forces that had been at work behind the scenes in her life, like a shadow looming over everything she did. How could you be expected to make decisions that could shatter or even end lives one day, and take your kids to the playpark without a care in the world the next?

As Drake knew from experience, few people found a way to reconcile those two vastly different worlds into one life.

'I won't pretend that I was always a good person, or that things always worked out for the best. You know as well as I do that our world doesn't operate like that. But I did the job because I believed in it. I believed I could do good with my life. Something meaningful.'

Her expression changed then, her mood darkening.

'Everything changed when I was assigned to head up an operation in Northern Ireland in 1983, working to infiltrate an IRA cell. An SAS officer named Faulkner lost his nerve and blew the operation, and two of our best assets were executed as a result.'

Drake felt himself tense up at the mention of that name. He knew David Faulkner all too well, just as he knew first-hand how dangerous and unstable the former SAS officer could be. Drake had shed no tears when the man had been killed a few years ago in Libya.

'Most of the blame fell on me.' A faint shrug of resignation. 'I was a senior intelligence officer, and a woman. There weren't many of us back then, and there were plenty who resented me for it. Plenty who wanted to see me take a fall. Well, they got their wish. I was reprimanded and demoted to a desk job. It was... made very clear that my career in the intelligence service wouldn't be going much further.

'That's when I was approached by a representative of a... new organisation – a joint effort between intelligence and military officers from many different countries, operating above and beyond the constraints of their own governments. An organisation that wasn't subject to the whims of politicians or changing government priorities. They were intended to be something different, something more powerful and permanent. And they wanted me to be a part of it. They had no name at the time, but they've been given lots of them over the years. You would know them best as the Circle.'

Indeed he did. And Drake wasn't surprised by the insidious manner in which they had recruited Freya, picking a talented intelligence officer whose career had been effectively derailed, and offering her a way out. A chance to restart an otherwise wasted life. The opportunity to make a difference again.

'I'd like to tell you that I saw him for what he was, that my loyalty wasn't for sale, but I can't. I've told enough lies already. The truth is… I accepted his offer,' his mother acknowledged, raising her chin a little as she said it. 'I did it because I wanted my life to mean something again, and I did it willingly. I agreed to work for the Circle.'

Drake leaned forward. As much as he'd been listening intently to every word, he sensed that what she'd said so far was merely setting the stage. It was what was about to come next that represented her real message.

'I had spent most of my career up to that point recruiting foreign assets. You could say I had a talent for reading people, understanding what they wanted and feared, and using that against them. The Circle recognised that too, and I was brought in to help recruit others to our cause – intelligence operatives, military officers, even diplomats and government officials. I became very good at bringing people in line.'

Another pause. Drake held his breath, waiting for what was coming.

'That's when a young CIA case officer came to our attention. A man named Marcus Cain.'

Chapter 19

The trio of black SUVs rocketed down the busy London street towards their target, blue lights flashing and engines roaring as the drivers leaned hard on the gas. Traffic parted before them like a river, with many vehicles forced to swerve and mount the kerb as they sped past.

Hawkins was unconcerned by the chaos in their wake. His mind was firmly fixed on the task ahead. He was under no illusions that it would be easy, for the man they were hunting was both dangerous and resourceful, but he was determined to make it happen.

'What's the status on the rapid response team?'

His communications specialist was hunched over a laptop, bracing himself as their driver swerved to avoid a bus. His radio earpiece was buzzing almost non-stop as various agencies and field teams worked to coordinate their efforts.

'They're en route now, ETA is just under ten minutes. Local police have alerted all officers in the vicinity. They're vectoring in now.'

'Have them keep their distance and form a perimeter,' Hawkins ordered. 'Drake spots uniformed PD, he'll bug out.'

'Copy that.'

'What do we know about the target building?' he asked next, eager to obtain every scrap of information he could. House assaults like this were normally planned days or even weeks in advance, giving them all the time in the world to learn every facet of the building they were assaulting.

'Two-storey town house, built at the turn of the century. Solid brick walls, access from the front and rear. No records of renovations or construction work.'

There wouldn't be, of course. Vaults were constructed under conditions of absolute secrecy, often requiring years of patient labour before they went active. Their strength lay in their anonymity rather than the physical security measures protecting them, though they, too, were often formidable.

'We need all entrances and exits locked down,' he instructed. 'Nobody leaves that area without us knowing.'

'GCHQ are all over it,' his comms expert confirmed. 'They're monitoring all surveillance feeds. If he tries to leave, we'll know.'

'What about air cover?'

'The Brits are vectoring in a police chopper as we speak, and the field teams have got unmanned drones that they can deploy.'

Hawkins held on tight as the driver cut in front of a van and stomped on the accelerator, ignoring the horn blasts in their wake. An idea had already come to him.

'Bring up the blueprints of any adjacent properties,' he instructed. 'Find me one with a basement.'

Chapter 20

Brother and sister sat silent and enraptured as their mother, her expression calm and her voice composed, laid out the details of her life.

'Marcus Cain had been a rising star in the CIA's Special Activities Division, but his career had fallen apart after a failed rescue operation in Afghanistan. The Circle could see the potential in him, though, and so could I. I recruited him, we saw to it that his career was restored and he rose quickly through the ranks. He was intelligent, highly motivated and ambitious. The kind of man the Circle had always found it easy to manipulate.'

She paused before going on, and Drake heard a faint exhalation. She was about to deliver bad news.

'The truth, though, is that he wasn't the one they really wanted. Cain was useful in his own way, but it was his asset that had the real potential. A woman Cain had almost thrown away his entire career for. A woman named Anya.'

Drake stiffened up as the name issued forth, the world seeming to slow down around him as he listened intently.

'She was a soldier unlike anything we'd seen before. She had no vanity or ambitions to exploit, she wouldn't be manipulated or coerced like so many others had been. The only person she would listen to was Marcus. He was the key to controlling her, and I was the key to controlling him. And when we got them working for us, it didn't take long for them to prove themselves.'

East Berlin, German Democratic Republic – October 25th, 1989

Otto Fischer took another drag on his cigarette, the tobacco glowing and hissing, then exhaled a cloud of grey smoke. The car's wipers swiped rhythmically at the rain as he drove home through the late-night streets of East Berlin, the heating vents blasting out warm air to ward off the late October chill.

The car itself was new: a recent delivery fresh off the assembly line. One of the advantages of his rank and position. Driving it always made him feel good, especially when he passed an old woman trudging along the sidewalk in a tatty-looking coat, hunched down against the rain and cold. People of her generation were no strangers to hardship and defeat, but not Fischer. He was part of a new breed of Germans; a younger generation unencumbered by the shame and failures of the past.

But he had another reason to feel good tonight.

He felt a hand, warm and soft, laid on his thigh, and glanced at the pretty young blonde beside him. He saw the shy, almost girlish smile, the shining attraction in her blue eyes, and felt his pulse quicken at the thought of spending the night with her.

He'd met her at one of the beer halls he drifted into after a particularly long work day, soothing his worries with a few drinks. Then he'd spotted a tall, attractive young woman with a demure smile and eyes that kept catching his.

Emboldened by the liquor in his blood, it hadn't taken him long to approach and strike up a conversation, learning that her name was Annika, she was Lithuanian by birth, and she'd come to East Germany to study medicine. She was supposed to have met one of her fellow students for drinks that evening but, much to her disappointment, he hadn't shown up.

His loss, Fischer thought with a grin.

A few drinks later, and her shyness had given way to a lively personality, an infectious laugh and a radiant smile that was enough to attract the attention of more than a few men nearby, some of whom were already out with their supposed sweethearts.

Fischer knew well enough how easy it was to capture the imagination of young and impressionable women like Annika, especially ones from rural backwaters like the Baltic states. Country girls, used to the coarse talk and fumbling advances of men who had never travelled beyond their own province.

Soon enough they were on the way back to his apartment. Fischer was looking forward to fucking the pretty blonde who so many others had watched with envious eyes, just as he enjoyed driving in the warmth of his car while others endured the cold.

'Are we close?' she asked, an edge of breathless excitement and nervousness in her voice. She wasn't used to doing this sort of thing.

'We're close,' he assured her.

Her hand strayed a little higher up his leg. 'I'm looking forward to seeing it.'

Fischer's apartment block was an elaborately styled building of Prussian design, rebuilt and renovated after the war, instead of the cheap concrete slabs that had been hastily thrown up everywhere else. A place reserved for men of consequence.

Parking on the street nearby, he led her inside, the two of them running hand-in-hand to escape the rain. In moments they were in the elevator, heading up to the top floor.

'I've never seen a place like this,' she said, visibly impressed. 'It's beautiful.'

'One of the advantages of my job,' Fischer replied vaguely, his hand travelling down her back to squeeze her buttocks as the doors pinged open. 'Come, I'll show you the rest.'

Unlocking the door to his spacious apartment, whose windows permitted views across the Wall into the brightly lit West Berlin cityscape, he led the young woman inside, eager to be alone with her.

'Take your coat off and I'll—'

His sentence was cut short by a grunt of pain as something hard slammed between his shoulder blades, followed by a sharp kick to the back of his knee that buckled his leg. He went down, falling to his knees on the solid wood floor, his mind a whirl of confusion and pain and growing anger as he realised that Annika had attacked him.

'You bitch!' he growled as he spun to face her, fumbling inside his jacket for the Makarov service pistol he kept there. But even as he whipped the weapon out and turned it on her, he found his gun hand seized in a frighteningly strong grip that twisted his wrist back on itself.

Muscles and tendons screaming in sudden protest, his grip slackened and the gun was torn from his grasp. He saw something swing around towards him, felt a flash of light and an explosion of pain, and then blacked out.

When he awoke later, he was lying on his side on his bed, hands and feet bound painfully tight behind his back. A few experimental movements confirmed that his bonds were both strong and securely fastened. Something had been rammed into his mouth and secured with tape, preventing him from emitting anything beyond a muffled groan.

His heart rate soared, a sheen of sweat dampening his skin as his eyes flicked back and forth, unable to see much in the gloom. He heard the click of a light switch, and blinked as Annika walked into view.

Only this was a very different Annika from the shy, demure student he'd met at the bar earlier. This woman was hard and cold, her merciless gaze fixed on him as she sat down on the edge of the bed, watching him in silence for a few moments.

'You're wondering if I'm going to kill you,' she began matter-of-factly. 'Well, don't worry, Otto. No matter what happens tonight, I'm not.'

Fischer flinched as she reached into her pocket and drew out a small but wickedly sharp-looking knife, holding it up so that he had a good view of the blade.

'What I'm going to do instead is sever your spinal cord between the fourth and fifth vertebrae, leaving the major arteries untouched. You'll still be able to breathe and speak, but that's all you'll be able to do from this point onward. You'll be permanently paralysed from the neck down, you'll need people to feed and wash and look after every aspect of your life. Oh, and going by past experiences, you'll probably soil yourself. But that is something you'll certainly have to get used to.'

Fischer saw a sudden terrifying image of his future playing out before his eyes. A future of dirty hospitals, disinterested nurses, pitiful visits from his former friends and comrades. Bedsores and infections. Shitting and pissing into plastic bags.

He shouted into the gag then, trying to plead for mercy as she leaned in towards him, rolling him over onto his front despite his frantic attempts to buck and kick.

'At least it will be relatively painless,' she said, pressing the blade into his neck.

Fischer let out a tortured howl of terror and impotent fury that emerged only as a pitiful moan, squeezing his eyes shut and clenching his fists so hard that it hurt, waiting for the sudden numbness as the blade severed his nerve endings and rendered him a prisoner in his own body.

'Or we can make a deal,' she said quietly.

Fischer opened his eyes to find her face just inches from his.

'Would you like that, Otto?'

Frantically he nodded, not knowing or even caring what he was agreeing to.

'Good. A demonstration is scheduled to take place at Alexanderplatz on November fourth. The biggest protest march the GDR will ever see. You know of this, yes?'

Again he nodded. He was all too aware of the planned march, organised by East Berlin students and other activists demanding political freedom and civil liberties. For the past few weeks, the East German authorities had been debating how to handle it, whether to let the march go ahead or crack down on the organisers. Tomorrow they were scheduled to make a final decision.

'I imagine you do. As one of the most senior Stasi officials in the city, you'll be a key voice at tomorrow's meeting.'

Fischer's eyes were wide with fear and disbelief. How did she know all of this?

'You're going to recommend that the march be given permission to go ahead, Colonel Fischer. You're going to insist that trying to prevent it would only encourage further unrest, and that it should be allowed to proceed peacefully. You'll do this, because you know what will happen if you don't.'

Despite his terrifying situation, Fischer knew that such a decision could well end his career. The situation in East Berlin was precarious already, and the only thing holding it in check was the fear of government reprisal. A mass protest like this could push the GDR into open revolution. And it would all be because of him.

'I know what you're thinking, Otto,' she said, as if his thoughts were written plain on his face. 'You're thinking you could agree to the deal, then renege on your promise once you're safe. But know this. You'll never be safe from me, or the people I work for. No matter where you go, whether you change your name or even your face, I'll make it my mission to find you. And when I do...'

She held up the knife once again, bringing it in so close to his eye that he was sure the blade must touch the tender flesh.

'Well, believe me, it won't be painless next time. Do you understand me?'

Fischer didn't care to imagine the torture and mutilation this woman might be capable of inflicting before she finally departed, leaving him paralysed and ruined. Nor did he doubt that she would hunt him to the ends of the earth if he betrayed her.

Faced with such a horrific threat, the only thing he could do was nod.

'You will do what I say?'

Again he nodded, knowing it would likely mean the end of his career, and perhaps the GDR as a whole. Knowing all of this, and accepting it.

The knife was withdrawn, and he saw a flicker of a smile. Only it wasn't the shy, arousing, feminine smile of before. It was a cold smile of satisfaction.

'That's good, Otto. With luck, you'll never see me again.'

A few moments later, he felt a sharp prick in his neck. Not the bite of a knife blade, but the tiny insertion of a syringe followed by the flood of coldness as a powerful sedative was deposited in his bloodstream.

When he awoke from his drug-induced sleep the next morning, he was unbound and alone, as if nothing had ever happened. He would never see his sinister visitor again, except in the occasional nightmare.

'The Alexanderplatz rally was the biggest mass demonstration in East German history,' Freya explained. 'It was the spark that ignited the powder keg of East Berlin. Just like we planned. And... well, you know the rest.'

Less than two weeks later, the Berlin Wall, the symbol of Soviet occupation of Eastern Europe and the Cold War itself, would fall amidst euphoric celebrations. It would start a chain reaction of demonstrations and revolutions all across the continent, leading to country after country declaring independence. Barely two years later, the remnants of the USSR would dissolve altogether.

The simmering conflict and rivalry that had divided the world for almost half a century, sparked proxy wars all across the globe, cost millions of lives, bankrupted economies and almost dragged humanity into nuclear Armageddon, effectively ended in Berlin on a chilly November evening in 1989.

And the Circle had engineered all of it. The implications were so staggering that for a few seconds Drake simply tuned out, forgetting the recording as he fought to process it all.

But above all his speculation and shock and disbelief, one question rose to the forefront of his mind. Why hadn't she told him?

He blinked, his attention returning to the video.

'... like to say that was where it ended, that Marcus and I had achieved our objective and went our separate ways,' Freya went on. 'But the truth is, we began working more closely in the months and years that followed. There was so much to do. We'd created a new world, and it was our responsibility to set it on the right path.'

Again a faint sigh. The sigh of bad news.

'The more I came to know him and understand how he thought, the more I felt like he understood *me*. At times, it seemed almost like we shared the same mind, like there was nothing we couldn't do if we worked together. I'd never met a man like that before. And... I suppose what happened next was inevitable.'

Chapter 21

The lead SUV screeched to a halt at the entrance to Middleton Place, nearby pedestrians backing away in surprise and alarm as several men in dark military-style clothing and bulky combat vests leapt out and advanced into the narrow street beyond. They were soon joined by a similar team at the opposite end.

The street was locked down, armed operatives quickly converging on the target building from both ends. A third police unit was moving to blockade the rear exit, in case their targets tried to slip out that way.

'Alpha team in position,' Hawkins heard the voice of his secondary team leader crackle in his ear as he advanced. 'Moving in.'

'Copy that. Keep it tight,' he replied, eyes sweeping left and right to the shuttered shops and narrow town houses that overlooked the street.

A couple of drunken civilians emerging from the pub stopped to gawk at them, before a barked order from one of the team prompted them to retreat back inside.

'What have you got, aerial?' Hawkins spoke into his radio.

A pair of small, remotely piloted drones were hovering somewhere overhead, observing the target building and the surrounding streets. Such unmanned vehicles had come on in leaps and bounds over the past several years, allowing field teams to quickly and easily obtain an overhead view of a target area. This one even had night vision and thermal imaging cameras, allowing it to see through walls.

'The only heat blooms are coming from the ground floor,' the drone operator reported. 'The rest of the building looks unoccupied.'

'Copy that. All units, stand by to move in. Any activity at the rear entrance?'

'No movement here. We've got it locked down.'

As his first assault team took up position by the main door and his secondary team hurried to take up position, Hawkins paused to think about the man he'd come here to kill. Ryan Drake was here somewhere, perhaps just a few yards beneath his feet. A rat trapped in the underground maze that was soon to become his coffin.

With that thought fresh in his mind, Hawkins spoke a single terse command into his radio unit. 'Go!'

His lead operative was carrying a device affectionately known as a 'master key'. Essentially a compact but extremely powerful hydraulic bolt gun similar to those used to kill cattle, it was just as effective at taking out door-locking mechanisms.

A sudden explosive hiss was followed by the bang and crunch of metal and wood giving way beneath several thousand PSI of pressure. The ruined door was shoved open and the assault team piled in, weapons drawn and safeties off. They had orders to shoot to kill, and would make full use of this leeway.

The thump of footsteps was accompanied by a cacophonous bang as stun grenades were lobbed into dusty old offices. Stacks of yellowed old paper and broken glass were blown in all directions by the detonations.

'Go! Go!' one team member shouted, advancing inside the next room, weapon sweeping the shadows.

'Room clear!' another replied. 'Move up!'

On they went, moving quickly and efficiently from room to room, clearing each one in turn before advancing up to the second level, each time finding old offices filled with outdated equipment, and storage rooms that looked like they hadn't been touched in decades.

The one thing they didn't find was the man they'd come here to take down.

Chapter 22

Drake and Jessica were suddenly interrupted by a knock at the conference room door, snapping their attention away from the video. Drake paused playback just as Fitzgibbons strode in, his previously cool and composed demeanour gone.

'What's going on?' Drake demanded, sensing trouble.

'I apologise for the interruption,' Fitzgibbons explained. 'But I'm afraid your secret is out. The building upstairs is under attack.'

Jessica let out a gasp of dismay, clearly thinking the same thing as Drake. They were trapped down here with no means of escape.

'You said this place was secure,' Drake snapped.

Fitzgibbons fixed him with a sharp look. 'It *is* secure, I assure you. But the streets and roads around it are not. Our clients are responsible for their own safety outside our walls, and it would seem you were spotted.'

Drake's mind was already racing as he considered his options, though there were precious few. If the Security Service had discovered their location, they would certainly have the building under surveillance already. They couldn't sneak out, and trying to fight their way past armed field teams would be suicidal.

'It was me, wasn't it?' Jessica said grimly.

'You don't know that.'

She looked at him, her expression conveying the depth of her guilt and regret. 'Yes I do. They must have seen me when I bumped into that woman. If I'd been thinking clearly, none of this would be happening.'

Drake squeezed her arm, wishing he could offer more tangible reassurance, then turned his attention back to Fitzgibbons. Something about the man's demeanour told him their situation wasn't as hopeless as it seemed.

'There must be another way out of here.'

'As I said earlier, your mother's account includes a Safe Passage agreement.'

'Meaning?' Jessica asked.

'Come with me,' Fitzgibbons said, gesturing for them to follow him. 'I must ask you to be quick. There isn't much time.'

Jessica was already on her feet and making for the door. Drake yanked the memory stick from the laptop and slipped it in his pocket as he brought up the rear.

The tempo of the underground facility had changed considerably. Personnel were hurrying from room to room, moving quickly to lock the place down and, most likely, destroying any sensitive material before it could be captured.

Drake paid them little heed, concentrating on Fitzgibbons as he rounded a corner and halted near a section of wood-panelled wall. They watched as he stooped down and pressed a small section of decorative panelling near the floor.

There was a click as some hidden latch or bolt was disengaged, and suddenly the entire section of wall swung inwards, revealing an old-fashioned brick tunnel beyond, dimly illuminated by soft fluorescent strips running along the floor. Cold, stale air wafted in as Fitzgibbons stepped aside.

'This tunnel runs about a hundred yards,' he explained. 'At the end you'll find a stairwell. Climb it to reach a car garage, where a vehicle will be waiting for you. The keys are in the ignition.'

'What about you?' Jessica asked.

'I'll be safe here. This facility is well protected, and my organisation has some... influence over the security services,' Fitzgibbons said with a wry smile. 'Now go. Good luck to you both.'

Drake knew this was no time for debate. Instead he simply nodded, offering the elderly man silent acknowledgement and gratitude, still not sure what to think about him or the bizarre, secretive world he inhabited.

He felt inside his pocket, clutching the little plastic memory stick. Whatever else Freya had to tell them, it would have to wait until they were clear of this place.

Taking Jessica by the hand, he stepped into the tunnel as Fitzgibbons swung the door closed behind them, sealing them inside.

With his obligations fulfilled, Fitzgibbons turned away and began to march back towards the Vault's communications room, where he intended to put in a priority call to his superiors. The people he worked for possessed a degree of influence over the governments of most countries in which they operated, allowing them to call in favours from time to time.

Today was such a day.

'Mr Stevens!' he called out.

His chief security officer was by his side immediately.

'What's our situation?'

'Armed special forces teams are upstairs. They've breached the upper building, but that's as far as they've gone.'

'Are we in full lockdown?'

'Yes. The elevator is shut down and power switched to internal generators. There's no way in.'

'Good. Have the communications centre—'

Fitzgibbons was cut off by a sudden, violent explosion that knocked him off his feet. He landed hard on the carpeted floor, pain blazing from his old joints. Stunned and partially deafened, he opened his eyes but could see almost nothing, the corridor obscured by smoke and swirling dust.

'Mr Stevens,' he said, holding a handkerchief against his mouth to ward off the choking haze. There was no response from his security operative. 'Mr Stevens!'

Looking over, he saw the man lying sprawled on his side nearby, his head caved in by a piece of flying debris.

Vaguely, Fitzgibbons was aware of panicked shouts, accompanied by the chatter of automatic gunfire, and realised with alarm that the Vault had been breached. How had they found their way down here so quickly?

He was just struggling to his feet when a trio of figures emerged like ghosts from the smoke, the beams of their green laser sights tracking back and forth before coming to rest on him.

'Freeze! Don't move!' one of them shouted, his voice muffled by the gas mask he was wearing.

Fitzgibbons raised his hands to show he was unarmed, watching as the largest of the three operatives lowered his weapon and stepped forward. Reaching up, he loosened the strap on his mask and pulled it away, revealing a hard, rugged face that might have been considered handsome. The only blemish was a faintly visible scar down one side.

Jason Hawkins looked down at the old man kneeling before him, feeling a moment of satisfaction at how quickly his team had breached this place. As it turned out, it was the nearby pub that had proven to be their way in; more specifically, the deep cellar beneath it. A few shaped charges placed along the wall had been all it took to blast their way in here.

'You're the Vault manager?'

'I am,' the old man answered.

'Good. Answer my questions and maybe I'll let you live. Where are they?'

'I haven't a clue what you're talking about.'

Hawkins smiled faintly and raised his weapon. 'I'm not in a patient mood, old man.'

Fitzgibbons looked up him defiantly. 'You have no idea what you've done today,' he said, his voice conveying a confidence and authority that was boldly independent of his situation. 'This is an act of war. Believe me, *young man*, the people I represent—'

He was abruptly silenced when Hawkins took aim and put a single 5.56mm round through his forehead. As the dead man fell backwards in a heap, Hawkins shot him a contemptuous look.

'War's over,' he said with a malicious smile. The Vaults and the people who operated them were a relic of a different world. As far as he was concerned, it was high time for a change.

Lowering his weapon, he turned away to his two teammates.

'He was stalling us,' he decided. 'There must be another way out. Find it, and warn our ground and air assets to be on the lookout. In the meantime, I want to know what Drake came here for. Go!'

–

Drake was ascending a narrow spiral staircase, his Browning automatic clutched tight in one hand, Jessica's hand in the other, their footfall on the metal steps echoing off the walls as they climbed.

'I'm sorry, Ryan,' Jessica whispered. 'If I hadn't fucked up—'

'Save it,' he interrupted. Self-pity wasn't going to help them. 'Right now, getting out of here is our only priority.'

She didn't say anything to that. Rounding the final turn of the staircase, they encountered a steel door; heavy-duty and designed to withstand assault. Reaching out, Drake gripped the handle, preparing himself for what lay beyond.

'What if they're waiting for us?' Jessica whispered.

Drake thought about it for barely a second.

'Stay close to me,' he replied, unlatching the door and swinging it open.

Rather than massed police officers or shadowy government agents, they found instead a simple, nondescript car garage starkly lit by cheap strip lighting. No windows, no tools or shelves or any of the clutter one would find in a normal building like this.

A sleek black BMW saloon sat in the centre of the room, its windows tinted to conceal the interior. Opening the driver's door, Drake found the key fob on the seat.

'Get the doors,' Drake said, slipping into the vehicle and pressing the ignition button. The engine fired up first time, growly with smooth, refined power.

Jessica hurried over to the main doors and hit the automatic winch control. As they trundled upward, she leapt in beside Drake.

'Are we going to make it out of this?'

Drake's only answer was to step on the gas. In moments, the luxury car sped out of its garage and onto the road outside, accelerating away from the scene.

Chapter 23

'Talk to me, Sanchez,' Hawkins barked into his radio as he emerged into the street, ignoring the strobe-like flash of blue lights and the crowds of onlookers behind police barricades, their smartphones recording everything. He had pulled on a balaclava to hide his face.

Smoke billowed up from the basement of the pub, leaking through windows damaged by the blast. The clean-up operation was going to be quite an undertaking, but that was for someone else to worry about.

Hawkins' only remit was to find Drake, no matter the cost.

'Air assets are on the case, sir,' the voice of his communications specialist crackled in his ear. 'GCHQ are working every camera in a half mile radius.'

'Fuck that, they'll never narrow it down fast enough,' he said, striding towards the SUV that Sanchez was operating out of. Away from prying eyes now, he ripped off the cloying balaclava and fixed his comms specialist with a hard look.

'Their exit would have to be underground,' he decided. 'Something to get them outside a police perimeter.'

'A tunnel,' Sanchez agreed.

The entrance to such an escape route would be well hidden to prevent discovery. Locating such a concealed portal could take days, and Hawkins had no time to waste. Every second that passed was a second wasted.

'Pull up a schematic of the area and look for underground construction. Sewers, subways, anything that could have been accessed from the Vault.'

Sanchez was hard at work on his computer, sifting through the reams of data streaming in. London in the twenty-first century sat atop a complex warren of old tunnels, disused sewers and abandoned subway and maintenance lines, many laid down before Hawkins' grandparents had walked the earth. Some had never even been cata-logued, discovered only when the foundations of newer buildings were being excavated.

'Seconds count, Sanchez,' Hawkins warned.

'Working on it.'

He didn't look up, utterly focussed on his task as he scrawled through subterranean blueprints and ordinance survey maps. Then his face lit up.

'I've got something!' Turning the laptop around, he indicated a tunnel that bisected the street they were now on, running almost directly beneath the Vault. 'Looks like a section of access tunnel for a planned subway station just east of here. The station never opened and the tunnel was sealed off.'

A smile began to spread across Hawkins' face. The smile of a predator closing in on its prey. 'Find where that tunnel terminates and get GCHQ on it now.'

–

Drake and Jessica were hurtling eastbound on the main drag, cutting left and right to gain ground in the heavy traffic. Their hastily chosen course was taking them out of Fitzrovia and into the Farringdon district of the city. Drake was hoping to reach the comparatively downmarket and crowded East End of London, with its sprawling docklands and loosely policed council estates. The kind of place they could disappear.

Drake was well aware that speeding might attract police attention, but the need to put as much distance as possible between them and the besieged Vault was even more urgent. The force hunting them had access to the full apparatus of the UK security services. It was by no means certain they would escape it.

'Where are we heading?' Jessica asked, clutching the overhead handle as Drake swung them hard right, cutting across an intersection and narrowly missing a delivery van.

'Anywhere that isn't here,' he replied, though he was obliged to lean hard on the brakes when traffic in both lanes slowed, blocking the road with a river of red lights.

One thing that no amount of determination or driving ability could overcome was the perils of central London traffic.

'We've got him!' Sanchez declared.

Hawkins looked up. 'Talk to me.'

'GCHQ just called it in. A black BMW was spotted leaving a parking garage right above the termination point of the tunnel. They're backtracking camera footage right now, but the vehicle was confirmed heading east.'

'How long ago?'

'Three, maybe four minutes.'

'Vector in all available air and ground assets, and coordinate with GCHQ. I want that son of a bitch boxed in.' With his instructions issued, he leaned in to speak with the operative behind the wheel. 'Get us moving! We're going after him now.'

–

Drake saw the distant flicker of blue lights in his rear-view mirror. There could be little doubt that they were for him. Whether through bad luck or bad judgement, they'd been spotted. The net was closing in, and their options were narrowing by the second.

Jessica had seen it too and reached the same conclusion.

'Ryan…'

'I know.'

'They're coming this way.'

'I know!'

To sit here motionless would be suicide, while their chances of escaping on foot were virtually zero. They had to find another way out. Considering the situation for a second or so, Drake suddenly swung the wheel over and stomped hard on the accelerator, performing a high-speed U-turn into oncoming traffic.

'What the hell are you doing?' Jessica cried out, wincing at the horn blasts sounding behind them as Drake accelerated away.

'Getting us out of here.'

'You're taking us straight towards them! Are you insane?'

Spotting a one-way side street up ahead, he went for it without hesitation, turning hard left and disappearing from the main road with tyres screeching as they fought for purchase on the slick tarmac. He could feel the car's traction control system working hard to keep them from spinning out of control.

'You know that sign said No Entry, right?'

'Hadn't noticed,' he lied, barely scraping past a car heading in the opposite direction and ignoring the obscene gestures from the driver as he powered away.

–

'Target has changed course,' Sanchez reported, bracing himself as the SUV accelerated hard, making full use of their lights and sirens to part traffic in their way. 'Now heading south towards Waterloo Bridge.'

'Stay on him,' Hawkins commanded.

'We've got him on aerial,' the comms specialist confirmed. 'Choppers and drones have visual contact locked in. No way he's losing us now.'

'What about ground assets?'

'We've got police mobile units closing in from all sides. He's boxed in.'

Hawkins smiled. 'Time's up, Ryan.'

–

Knowing the main roads would be too busy to negotiate, Drake was forced to fall back on London's network of narrow residential streets, many of which were integrated into confusing one-way systems that he promptly ignored.

He was maintaining a generally south-east course, hoping to get out of the congested city centre and into the sprawling suburbs beyond, where CCTV was less concentrated and lighter traffic would allow him to gain speed.

But first he needed to lose their ground pursuers, who were closing in despite his best efforts.

'How are they still with us?' Jessica asked, glancing over her shoulder. 'There's no way they should be able to see us.'

'They've got us on aerial surveillance,' Drake admitted. 'No way to shake them off.'

Jessica craned her neck to survey the sky above them, but there were too many buildings and too much light pollution to see much.

'Then what do we do?'

Snatching his cell phone from his pocket, Drake punched in a number and waited for the call to connect. Fortunately, it was answered almost immediately.

'Frost.'

'Tell me you're at your computer,' Drake began, slowing only marginally before surging across a main road and into another side street beyond.

'Yeah. Why?'

'Listen carefully. I need you to—'

'Ryan!' Jessica shouted, bracing herself against the dashboard.

Drake slammed on the brakes as an SUV appeared at the end of the street, blocking their path. The BMW skidded to a halt as the other vehicle's door popped open and a man leapt out, a Heckler & Koch G36 assault rifle in hand. A man whose face was lit with malicious glee as he took aim.

Jason Hawkins.

'Get down!' Drake cried, pushing Jessica down into her seat as the assault rifle spat a short, vicious burst at them.

Drake tensed up as the stream of rounds impacted the windshield, expecting them to punch straight through and tear into him.

No such thing happened. Instead there was a tight series of hollow *thumps*, and Drake flinched as a trio of small cracks appeared in the glass. Beyond it, Hawkins' look of sudden confusion mirrored his own. It took him a second or so to realise the car had been reinforced with bulletproof glass.

Hesitating no longer, Drake threw it into first gear and stamped his foot on the accelerator. The powerful engine roared and the BMW rocketed forward, heading straight for the man standing dead ahead.

Hawkins opened fire on full automatic, aiming at the vehicle's engine block. Drake ignored the rounds now ricocheting wildly off the car's bodywork, striking buildings and parked cars as he cycled up through the gears, tearing towards his target.

'What are you doing?' Jessica yelled. 'You're going to crash!'

'Stay down!' he replied, his eyes locked on Hawkins as they closed in rapidly, their speed climbing with every second. He imagined the dull thump as they impacted, the crunch of bones shattering against steel, the agonised cry as the life was crushed out of his enemy.

The firing ceased as Hawkins' weapon ran dry. With no time to reload, he turned and leapt aside. At the same moment, Drake swung the wheel over, aiming for the rear end of the SUV blocking his way.

'Hold on!' he cried, bracing himself against the wheel.

An almighty bang, the crunch of buckling plastic and the tinkle of broken glass rang out as the front quarter of the BMW slammed into the rear of the SUV, spinning it aside like a downed bowling pin so that it collided with a parked car nearby.

Jerked painfully forward against his seatbelt, Drake managed to keep his foot on the accelerator, praying the BMW's drivetrain had survived the impact. Miraculously, the engine carried on running, and though the steering now felt distinctly heavier, the car seemed to be in running order.

Screeching around a corner at the end of the street, he powered away as fast as the damaged vehicle would allow.

'How the hell did we survive that?' Jessica asked, staring at the bullet-scarred windshield.

'They gave us a fucking good car,' Drake replied, feeling around for his cell phone on the floor at his feet. The call was still connected, and Frost was none too pleased about what she'd just heard.

'Ryan, talk to me, you son of a bitch!' her voice blared out of the phone's little speaker. 'What's going on?'

'Long story, bad news,' he replied, wedging it against his shoulder. 'Right now, I need your help.'

'Shit, what else is new?'

–

In their wake, Hawkins picked himself up from the trash-strewn gutter and surveyed the damaged SUV. The crash had spun it around and caved in the entire rear quarter, buckling the wheel and probably snapping the rear axle. The driver was rubbing his neck and struggling to get the door open.

Clenching his jaw in barely restrained frustration, he reached for his radio.

'Tell me you still have them on aerial.'

A couple of thousand feet overhead, an Airbus H135 lightweight chopper assigned to the National Police Air Service swung left in a wide arc to pursue the BMW. Its powerful downward-looking surveillance array was locked onto the target vehicle, automatically tracking and rotating to keep it in sight.

'Copy that,' the pilot responded. 'Air One has them in sight. Target now heading south towards Victoria Embankment.'

'I want all bridges in that area locked down,' Hawkins ordered.

With a top speed of 170mph, the H135 could easily outrun and outperform any ground vehicle in existence.

Visual tracking data from its cameras was being automatically downloaded to GCHQ, and cross-referenced against CCTV number-plate recognition on the ground, creating a digital web that had silently ensnared the fugitive vehicle.

A web which was closing inexorably around them.

–

Drake meanwhile was rocketing through the heart of the city, passing the ancient fortified walls of the Tower of London, the floodlit towers and elevated walkways of Tower Bridge, and the sleek, ultra-modern skyscrapers of Southwark beyond.

He paid these iconic landmarks no heed, pushing the car as hard as he dared, caring nothing for the stop signs or traffic in his way. Time was running out. If he was to put his plan into action, it would have to be now.

'I see lights up there,' Jessica said, spotting the flashing strobe lights of an aircraft shadowing them. 'They're following us.'

'Police chopper,' Drake replied, eyeing the temperature gauge on the dashboard. It was climbing rapidly. The crash had likely compromised the engine coolant system. It was only a matter of time before the whole thing seized up.

His cell phone was now on hands-free mode. 'Keira, we're almost there. Are you ready?'

'Give me a few minutes,' the young computer specialist replied testily, as she often did when working against the clock.

'We don't have a few minutes.'

'Well, fuck me. Would you like to swap places?'

'Gladly,' Drake snapped.

Entering a one-way road with liberal use of the horn, he sped through a junction in the shadows of a train station and turned hard right. Within moments, concrete retaining walls rose up on either side as the road descended.

'Christ, I hope this works,' Jessica whispered, bracing herself.

'Keira, I'm gonna lose signal in a few seconds,' Drake cautioned. 'It's now or never.'

There was no response. Up ahead, a massive brick portal rushed towards them.

'Keira, talk to me.'

Drake thought he might have heard the young woman's voice before their car disappeared into the tunnel and the signal cut out.

—

Though London is well known for the many bridges, old and new, criss-crossing the River Thames, there are in fact a number of tunnels bored deep beneath it. Most of them carry rail traffic for the city's Underground network, but a small number were intended for road users.

Including the Rotherhithe Tunnel, connecting the borough of Tower Hamlets with Southwark. Laid down more than a century earlier, when motor cars were only just beginning to appear, it had since become a busy route for commuters in the eastern districts.

Today it would become an escape route for Drake and his sister.

'Air One, target just entered Rotherhithe Tunnel, heading south,' the chopper pilot reported.

'Copy that,' Hawkins confirmed. 'Be ready to intercept on the south side.'

'Roger, Air One is en route.'

Banking left, the chopper circled towards the southern exit of the tunnel, which was disgorging a steady stream of traffic. Its infrared cameras were locked on, automatically cataloguing each vehicle as it appeared. And yet there was no sign of the BMW. The seconds ticked by, but still the car didn't emerge.

'Where is he, Air One?' Hawkins demanded. 'Give me a sitrep.'

'Air One, no sign of him. Standing by.'

'He should be there by now. What's going on?'

'Air One is on standby.'

Suddenly another voice crackled over the radio net. 'All units, this is command. We have a verified traffic cam sighting at the north end of the tunnel, heading east.'

'Say again, command?' the pilot requested.

'Cameras picked up the target vehicle at the north end of the tunnel.'

'Son of a bitch doubled back on us,' Hawkins snapped, realising Drake's attempted ploy. 'Move in, Air One. Do *not* lose him!'

'Roger, Air One is moving north.'

Banking hard, the aircraft roared back over the river, the surveillance package mounted beneath its airframe automatically reorienting itself, eagerly searching for a target.

Meanwhile on the ground, police units closed in from all sides, blocking off potential escape routes. The pilot took note of the flashing lights converging from multiple directions. The trap was sprung.

And yet, the one thing missing in all of this was the target vehicle itself. Bringing the aircraft into a hover about a thousand feet above the scene, the pilot scanned left and right, looking for the damaged black BMW and finding nothing which resembled it.

'You got anything?' he asked his co-pilot.

'No visual hits,' the man replied, urgently scanning. 'Where the hell is he?'

'Command, confirm target location.'

'We have a confirmed camera ping directly below you.'

'We're not seeing it. And there are ground units everywhere. Please advise.'

Confused silence greeted his urgent request.

—

A thousand feet below, a trio of police cruisers screeched to a halt at the busy road junction. Leaping out, the officers moved in with tasers at the ready, scanning the rows of cars that were now boxed in.

Frightened and confused drivers stared back at them, but the officers paid them little attention. They were looking for a damaged black BMW, and the fugitive behind the wheel.

Yet as they moved from car to car, their confusion and disbelief grew. There was a Ford, a Vauxhall and a pair of Volkswagens, ranging in colour from silver to red. But no BMW.

'What the fuck's going on?' one of the officers asked, glancing around in bewilderment. 'Why are we not seeing him?'

His colleague, a sergeant and the most senior officer on site, had the honour of calling it in. 'Unit Six here, we've got negative contact. Repeat, negative contact.'

'Confirm that, Six,' Command demanded. 'You should be right on top of him.'

'Confirmed. He's not here.'

Somehow, through some means that none of them could comprehend, their prey had slipped through the trap. It would be some time before they discovered the source of his deception, by which point Drake and his sister would be long gone.

Chapter 24

Five minutes earlier

As the BMW roared down the Rotherhithe Tunnel deep beneath the River Thames, the temperature gauge was at redline and wisps of steam were trailing from beneath the hood. Drake could feel over-heated components grinding against each other, the engine's steady rumble turning to a shuddering, rasping growl.

It didn't matter now. The car had gotten them as far as it needed to. Waiting until he was at the tunnel midpoint, Drake glanced over at his sister.

'You ready?'

Jessica nodded, bracing herself.

Drake jumped on the brakes, bringing the BMW to a screeching, shuddering halt amidst a cloud of steam and tyre smoke. The driver of the white Vauxhall Corsa tailing behind reacted instinctively, braking hard and leaning aggressively on his horn as he came to a stop just yards from the ailing BMW.

Opening his door, Drake leapt out and strode over to the Corsa's driver, who opened his window to yell at him.

'Oi! What you playing at, you prick?' the overweight thirty-something driver shouted. 'Almost ran into the back of you!'

Ignoring him, Drake drew his weapon and shoved it in the man's shocked face. 'Out of the car. Now.'

People can react in a variety of ways to situations like this, some-times with disastrous results, but most of the time they simply freeze up, paralysed by fear and disbelief. Drake used that moment of shock to his advantage, grabbing the driver by his T-shirt and hauling him out.

'Don't kill me! Please!' the man stammered, cowering against the tunnel wall.

'Fuck off,' Drake replied, leaping into the driver's seat and slamming the door shut. Jessica was waiting for him.

Saying nothing more, Drake threw the car into gear, rounded the crippled BMW and accelerated away.

'How do you know this is going to work?' Jessica asked as the road sloped upwards and the tunnel exit drew closer.

'I don't,' he admitted. 'But it's all we've got.'

'How reassuring.'

'No matter what happens, stay close to me. Okay?'

If all else failed, they would ditch the car and make a run for it, hoping to disappear into the hive of back alleys and side streets. He was under no illusions about their chances, but it was better than nothing.

He felt her hand on his arm as they approached the exit, concrete walls rushing past until suddenly the roof above them disappeared, revealing the vast night sky. A sky that looked mercifully clear of aircraft.

'It worked!' Jessica gasped, glancing around in amazement.

Drake's phone started ringing within moments.

'Good work, Keira. Didn't doubt you for a second.'

'You should have,' Frost replied, her annoyance obvious. 'That fucker went down to the wire.'

Though the tech specialist was unable to penetrate the formidable cyber defences around GCHQ, she had been able to target the far more vulnerable traffic camera system that was being used to pinpoint their movements. Feeding some dummy license plate hits into the system was enough to convince them that Drake had doubled back while out of visual contact, and was heading north once more.

'Next time I'll schedule something in the diary.'

'Very fucking funny. I suggest you make like the proverbial tree,' the young woman continued. 'It won't take them long to figure out what happened.'

'Copy that. We're out of here.'

Frost sighed. 'I'll expect a full explanation later, you know.'

'That could take a while,' Drake advised. 'I'll contact you once we're clear.'

'Bet your ass you will.'

As Drake ended the call, Jessica gave her brother a wry smile. 'Not bad, Ryan.'

'Save the champagne,' Drake warned her. 'We still have to get out of the city.'

Chapter 25

Jerusalem, Israel

Jerusalem's Old Town is a warren of ancient streets and buildings hemmed in by fortified walls erected millennia earlier to defend against invading armies. The result is a densely compressed ecosystem of houses, shops, restaurants, cafes and hotels quite unlike anywhere else on earth.

In one particular hotel room amongst this urban clutter, a young man sat hunched over his laptop computer, intently watching the decryption program it was busily running.

He was engaged in a fierce and contentious struggle, the course of which could change at any moment. A conflict waged not with swords or guns, but fought across the digital battlefield of cyberspace.

And his opponent tonight was a challenge indeed.

Someone had been surreptitiously probing for him online, sending out digital feelers that would search for his virtual presence, trying to discern his physical location. He'd been tagged somehow – some tiny vestige of a tracking program buried deep within his system registry, hiding far beyond any diagnostic tool or manual search.

At first, he'd been able to swat away these attacks for the petty irritations they were, but his adversary had been growing in both persistence and sophistication, learning from her mistakes and seeking out weaknesses.

And he was quite certain his adversary was female. Keira Frost, the fiery, abrasive young woman whose cockiness was, in his opinion, entirely unwarranted given her limited abilities.

Frustrated by her growing interference, Alex had decided to go on the offensive. Turning the tables against the would-be hunter, he had managed to trace her attacks back to their source, allowing him to deploy his full arsenal of hacking software. Once he'd broken in, he intended to drop a couple of the most destructive viruses available into her system.

It would take weeks before she could come after him again. By which time he'd have finished his work and disappeared, perhaps for good.

A prompt appeared on screen, advising him that the first layer of her firewall had been compromised. He smiled and gulped down the tepid remains of his coffee, waiting for the inevitable breakthrough.

Then something strange happened. A new window popped up in the centre of his screen. An encrypted chat window, with a single sentence.

WHY ARE YOU DOING THIS?

To say Alex was surprised would be an understatement. After weeks of surreptitiously hunting for him online, Frost was now reaching out to him directly, as if calling for a truce between two warring armies.

The question was, why?

Was it a genuine attempt to open a dialogue, or a desperate effort to buy herself time? Alex's fingers hovered over the keyboard as he debated what to do, whether to continue the attack, respond to her query, or break off altogether.

He had specific instructions not to engage with Drake or any member of his team. It was the absolute demand under which he was currently working, and one that he was extremely wary about disobeying. Because one thing his employer didn't tolerate was insubordination.

But did she have to know? Why was Frost reaching out to him? Was there some news she wanted to impart? Something Alex needed to know?

He was interrupted by a loud knock at the door, jarring him out of his thoughts.

This was a choice he would have to make another time. Hurriedly shutting down the computer, he reached for the Beretta 9mm automatic on the table beside it and checked the chamber, catching the glint of brass in the breech.

Alex could vaguely remember a time when the mere sight of a real firearm would have made him nervous, never mind the prospect of using it. That time was long past, and deep down he knew it would never return.

Shoving the weapon down the back of his jeans, he crossed the room and removed the chair he'd wedged against the door.

His heart was beating faster, as it always did at times like these. Every new day was a risk, every knock on the door could be the last. Gripping the weapon, he unlocked the door and allowed it to swing open on the chain.

The woman facing him was tall, standing almost eye-to-eye with him. In her early forties, blonde haired, with Nordic features and sharp, intense blue eyes.

Anya.

'You alone?' he asked, unable to see more than a few inches to either side.

'No.'

Alex relaxed. Had she said yes, it would mean she was under duress. And he'd have been forced to leap from the hotel room window into the branches of a tree below.

Not an option he relished.

He unlocked the door and stepped aside, allowing the woman to enter, feeling the familiar yet contradictory mixture of apprehension and relief that she evoked in him.

When the group had fractured a couple of months earlier, Alex had been faced with a stark choice – stay with Drake and the others, or join with Anya. In the end, it hadn't been a difficult choice.

Anya had saved his life on more than one occasion, just as he had saved hers, and though it would be optimistic to call her a friend, there was no question as to where Alex's loyalties lay. Making contact with Anya hadn't proven difficult. In fact, she had found him. She needed his help one last time.

'I was starting to wonder if you'd make it back,' Alex said, relaxing his grip on the weapon. 'You're late.'

'I ran into trouble,' Anya explained, dumping her pack on the bed. 'What kind of trouble?'

'Nothing I couldn't handle.'

Alex's eyes widened as she shrugged off her jacket. A bloodied dressing was wrapped around her left shoulder.

'Jesus, you're hurt,' he exclaimed, moving forward to help her.

Anya waved him off. 'It's nothing. Just a flesh wound.'

'Didn't Shakespeare have something to say about that?'

Anya gave him a sharp look. One thing he'd come to appreciate about her – if she didn't want a conversation to continue, then it wouldn't. It was that simple.

'Fine,' he conceded unhappily. 'What about Russo? Did you find him?'

Tracking down Russo's home address in Tel Aviv hadn't been easy. Needless to say, men like him were careful to keep such things hidden, but Alex was skilled, motivated and persistent – a potent combination that had eventually yielded results.

'I did.'

'And?'

Anya lowered herself onto the bed, letting out a sigh of fatigue. She had changed since the events in Afghanistan, he realised. She looked older now, weary both in body and spirit, as if some vital spark within her had been dampened.

'He gave me a name,' she explained, peeling away the dressing. 'Vizur.'

Alex frowned. 'Mean anything to you?'

The woman nodded slowly. 'Vizur Qalat was the ISI agent that Cain met with in Pakistan last year.'

'When Drake and the others got captured?'

A dark look passed over her at the mention of Drake's name.

'The same,' she confirmed at length. 'Clearly the two men have a history.'

'Makes sense, I suppose. But why would a Pakistani agent want to betray you?'

The look of cold determination in her eyes provided all the answer he needed. Alex sensed a trip to Pakistan looming.

'We will find out when we find Qalat.'

He had no doubt that she would. However, another worrying thought occurred to him.

'What if Russo tips him off?'

'Russo won't be talking to anyone now.'

Alex felt his throat tighten. He'd expected her to put the screws on Russo, rough him up and interrogate him, but it hadn't really occurred to him what she would do afterward. A man was dead, and he had made it possible.

'Do you have a problem with that, Alex?' she asked him bluntly.

'I didn't think it would come to that.'

His online forays on Russo had included an inspection of the man's personal history. Chanan Russo had a daughter, grandchildren. A family who would mourn his death.

'This is what we do, Alex. This is the world we live in now,' Anya said, her voice quieter yet somehow harder and more compelling as she took a step towards him. 'It is a world that doesn't reward compassion. If you can't live with that, then you should leave.'

The world *we* live in, he thought. He had ceased to be some outsider looking in. Now he was up to his neck in this mess with her, blood on his hands and no way out.

Her gaze was penetrating. 'Are you in or out, Alex?'

There was no getting out of this, he knew. Not until it was over. Alone, he would be hunted down and killed. The only option was to keep moving forward.

'You know I'm in,' he said, giving her the truth. That was all Anya would accept.

She held his gaze a moment longer before nodding. 'Good. Then pack your gear. We leave in twenty minutes.'

Alex blinked, caught off guard. 'We're leaving tonight?'

'It's not safe in Israel now. We can't afford to stay any longer.'

Alex didn't respond. His gaze lingered a moment too long on the laptop, weighing up the message from Frost. A message he had neither replied to, nor mentioned to Anya.

'Is something wrong?'

'Hmm? No, not really.' Then, remembering that Anya was adept at sensing lies, he added, 'You should know, there's talk about you online. The Russians have raised the bounty on you.'

Anya sighed and nodded grimly. 'So I've heard. Pack your gear. I'll be back soon.'

She was just picking up her pack when Alex spoke up again. 'Tell me one thing. Did he deserve it? Russo, I mean.'

Anya was silent for a time, weighing up the question.

'We all deserve it, Alex.'

Saying nothing more, she let herself out.

Chapter 26

Amesbury, UK

Located deep in rural Wiltshire in the south-west of England, the small town of Amesbury was a place of thatched roofs, small fields and country lanes flanked by high unkempt hedgerows. A world away from the frantic bustle – not to mention the pervasive threat of surveillance – of central London. More importantly, the area was dotted with British military installations and garrison towns, which saw a frequent turnover of personnel from all corners of the UK.

This was the kind of area where two new arrivals would attract little attention. In short, it was the perfect place to lay low and regroup.

Scouring local hotels, Drake had found one on the edge of town that still had vacancies. Some quick excuses about a broken-down car had been enough to allay any suspicions about the late hour, and before long he and Jessica were ensconced in a cramped, cheaply furnished room on the top floor.

Drake was by the window, staring out across the darkened rural landscape. He couldn't see it from here, but he knew that somewhere out there in the darkness to the west, amidst the wide grassy expanse of Salisbury Plain, stood the ancient Neolithic monument of Stonehenge.

The nocturnal tranquillity was bisected by a thin ribbon of road in the distance, but otherwise all seemed quiet. There should have been comfort in that, but he found none. The silence felt heavy, the stillness foreboding.

Reaching for the takeaway pizza box beside him, he pulled free a slice that reluctantly parted company from its fellows, and got stuck in.

'Can't believe you're hungry at a time like this,' Jessica remarked disapprovingly.

He wasn't, but he knew he needed to eat. One lesson he'd learned in the military was that you took food and rest whenever you could. You never knew when the chance might come again.

'Needs must,' he reminded her. 'You should eat something too.'

Jessica eyed the greasy conglomeration of meat, bread and cheese, wrinkling her nose in distaste. Instead she held up the miniature of vodka pilfered from the minibar.

'I'll stick with this, thanks,' she said, taking a gulp.

He shrugged. Drinking on an empty stomach wouldn't do her any favours, but he figured she could use something to take the edge off.

'How's the computer coming?'

At Drake's insistence, they had stopped off at a pawn shop on their way out of London. Situated in one of the arches beneath a railway bridge, the place sold everything from jewellery to cell phones to electric guitars. They took payment in cash, probably because most of their gear was stolen, not that Drake was one to judge. After parting with £200, he'd returned to their car with a well-used but functional laptop.

Jessica had been busy running a factory reset just in case the previous owner had left behind anything that could corrupt the memory stick. They'd also physically removed the laptop's wireless card to prevent it sending out any signals. It was unlikely, but ops had been compromised by less.

'Almost ready,' she announced. 'Five minutes.'

She sighed and leaned back against the wall, allowing herself to process everything that had happened.

'None of this feels real,' she said quietly after a time. 'I told myself I knew what I was getting into, that I was prepared for it. I'd spent four years preparing for it. But...'

'It's a different story when it's actually happening to you, right?'

His sister smiled bitterly. 'You always were a smart arse, Ryan.' The smile soon faded however as she looked at him, trying to work him out. 'How did you... get past it? Stop being afraid?'

'I didn't,' Drake admitted. 'I just got good at hiding it.'

Jessica laughed at this. 'Well, I'll try to hide it better next time.'

The laptop pinged to notify them its task was complete.

'Looks like we're ready.'

Drake produced the memory stick and moved over to join her. Inserting it into a spare port, Drake opened the video file, skipped to the point where they'd been obliged to abandon their viewing, and hit Play.

Once more his mother's face appeared on screen.

'—seemed almost like we shared the same mind, like there was nothing we couldn't do if we worked together. I'd never met a man like that before. And… I suppose what happened next was inevitable.'

Berlin – October 3rd, 1990

The atmosphere on the streets of the German capital was one of euphoric celebration, music blaring from countless buildings, fireworks bursting overhead, and ecstatic crowds bearing the national flag. Tens of thousands of people marching through the Tiergarten Zoo and along the great avenue of Unter den Linden, all of them converging on the Reichstag building, the symbol of German government.

And Marcus Cain had a front row seat, standing at the balcony of his hotel suite in the Westin Grand, facing out towards the Brandenburg Gate. The energy on the streets below was infectious, and he couldn't help but feel a swell of excitement and elation, and perhaps a little pride at what he'd accomplished.

An entire country, an entire continent reunited after generations of repression and division. Freedom, democracy and opportunity spreading to millions of people who had known only fear and suspicion.

And as for the once-powerful empire that had kept them behind the Iron Curtain, the Soviet Union was in its death throes – a spent force, bankrupt and exhausted, riven by internal strife and division, teetering on the brink. A giant that had finally been felled.

Because of him. And the woman beside him.

'Here,' Shaw said, handing him a flute of champagne as she glided in beside him. Cain could smell the scent of her perfume, feel the warmth of her body.

'No James tonight?' Cain asked, looking around for her ever-present assistant.

The woman chuckled. 'James has other business now. I wanted to share this moment with you, and you alone.'

He took a sip, relishing the taste, relishing the moment.

'It's beautiful, isn't it?' Shaw whispered.

He looked over at her. She was staring out across a city united in celebration, the fireworks bursting in the night sky, her lips slightly parted, eyes shining in triumph and wonder. She was like a drug, dangerous and intoxicating, and the more time he spent with her, the more he wanted her.

'The end of the old world,' Cain said, reflecting on the Wall that once divided this city, now being joyfully demolished. A whole way of life, the balance of power that had held for half a century, gone in just a few short months.

'And the beginning of the new.' Shaw turned towards him, moving a little closer, her eyes searching his as she gently reached up and touched his chest. A touch that sent electricity through him. 'For us too, Marcus. We're going to do incredible things together, you and I.'

You and I, he repeated to himself. Yes, they would do incredible things together, he realised in that perfect, exhilarating moment with the whole city before them. As the crowds below sang and cheered and waved their flags, he pulled Freya Shaw to him, her body melting into his as he kissed her.

–

Drake and Jessica watched, numb with shock, as their mother went on to describe something that should have been impossible. Something neither of them had ever considered.

'Marcus was different back then,' Freya said, her expression one of sorrow and regret. 'Younger, brighter, always with an eye on the future. It must sound hopelessly clichéd and romantic, but it really felt like something special. Like it was meant to be. I thought he and I were going to take on the world together.'

She stopped to clear her throat, and Drake could see her struggling with what she was about to reveal.

'And for a while, it seemed I was right. We lived and worked together... well, as much as we could, at least. But things began to change once we had a child.'

The word was dropped in so suddenly, so abruptly, that neither Drake nor his sister registered it immediately. It took a second or so for it to sink in, for each of them to process what she'd said.

Their mother had had a child in secret. Marcus Cain's child.

Drake watched in utter silence, not moving, not even breathing as his mother, clearly pained by the memory, leaned back in her chair.

'I'm sorry you had to find out this way, Ryan. I really am. But I tried to keep the truth from you, from Jessica, from everyone. It was the only way to keep her safe. But now...' She sighed. 'You deserve to know. You have a half-sister. Her name is Lauren...'

Reaching out with a trembling hand, Drake hit the pause button to stop the video, stood up and walked over to the room's minibar.

'Ryan…' Jessica began.

Drake didn't respond. Opening the minibar, he popped the lid on a miniature of whisky and downed it in one gulp. The cheap alcohol blazed a heated trail down his throat, lighting a fire in his belly that sent a chill through him. He needed it at that moment, because he knew something about Lauren Cain, the half-sister he'd never even realised he'd had.

Not until it was too late.

'What is it?' Jessica persisted, moving closer. 'Talk to me.'

Downing a second whisky, Drake looked at his sister.

'She's dead,' he said bluntly.

'Lauren?'

He nodded.

A moment of dismay passed over her. The confused emptiness where there should have been wrenching grief. The loss of a sibling she would never get to know.

'How did it happen?'

The only thing he could offer was the truth.

'In Berlin,' he admitted. 'When our team got captured in Pakistan, Anya used Lauren to trade for our lives. But the trade went bad, things went wrong. You remember what I told you about Berlin, don't you?'

'I remember,' she confirmed darkly.

'People died, and Lauren was one of them.' He closed his eyes, hardly able to conceive the cruel twist of fate that had conspired to make this a reality. 'Jesus Christ, it was my fault. She's dead because of me.'

The death of an innocent young woman had weighed heavily on Drake ever since that day, but what he'd just heard had recast the whole thing in a terrible new light. A tragic casualty of war had become a personal loss.

Jessica shook her head. 'No, Ryan. You didn't kill her. This isn't on you.'

'She wouldn't have been there if it wasn't for me.'

'Maybe not, but bringing her there wasn't your choice. That was on Anya, and Cain. They created this whole mess, and they pulled us all into it. Including Lauren.' She glanced away and swallowed. 'Whatever she… whatever Lauren might have been to us, she's gone now. We can't do anything for her.'

Drake sighed. Jessica might have been able to make that emotional break, because she hadn't been there. She hadn't been involved. Lauren was just a name, an abstract identity with no grounding in reality. For Drake, she had been flesh and blood. A person, a life, a future.

He was almost afraid of what he might learn next, but he knew they had to see the message through to the end. Collecting themselves, they sat down to watch the final segment.

'Things began to change after that,' Freya continued. 'Marcus became distant, detached, obsessive about his work. He was determined to rise through the ranks, both at the Agency and within the Circle. It wasn't until later that I began to understand what was driving him. Or rather, who.'

A shadow passed over her then.

'Anya. As hard as he tried, he could never let her go. But she had her own path to follow by then. The Circle had seen her potential, her growing power and influence, and they wanted her as their next rising star.' She allowed herself a bitter, sardonic chuckle. 'They were like children, competing against each other for their parents' favour. Each trying to outdo the other. I tried to turn Marcus around, but… he wouldn't hear me. I imagine he had grander plans in mind. So… I left. Just like that. I ended it. And they continued their little cold war.

'By the end of the decade, Anya had amassed even more influence than Cain himself. He couldn't outdo her, so I suppose he took the only option open to him – he fought dirty. He sabotaged her unit, turned them against each other just as she was preparing to join the inner Circle. He destroyed everything she'd built in a single night. He broke her.'

Drake knew the grim tale well enough, having heard it from Anya herself. Convincing her chief lieutenant that she was planning to take her unit rogue, Cain manipulated a coup against her, resulting in the virtual destruction of Task Force Black.

'That was the breaking point for me,' she went on sadly. 'Something had to be done, not just about Cain, but the Circle themselves. They had changed, I realised. The rot had been slow to set in, and maybe that was why I didn't see it, but now I understood they'd become something very different. They had been created to change history, to build a new world that was better than the one we overthrew.

But when the moment finally came, they failed. They became short-sighted and ruthless, starting wars for money or resources, amassing power for power's sake. I didn't recognise what they were anymore.'

Her expression hardened with grim, unyielding resolve then.

'That's why I'm going to destroy them.'

Chapter 27

Berlin, Germany – October 3rd, 1990

Marcus Cain might have been lost in his greatest triumph, but there was one person in the crowds below who wasn't celebrating that night.

Standing in a doorway on the opposite side of the busy thoroughfare, a hooded jacket hiding her face from view, Anya was silently watching the man she had once loved.

She had come here tonight to seek him out, fully expecting him to grant her an audience. Whatever their differences or difficulties, Cain had never once refused to speak to her, and she'd never doubted that he would see her tonight.

After all, so much of this was happening because of her. She was the one who had risked her life to venture into East Berlin, to threaten the Stasi officer into letting the Alexanderplatz rally go ahead. Just as she was the one who had risked her life time and again in Afghanistan.

She was certain that Cain would embrace her, congratulate her on her accomplishments, thank her for everything she had done and sacrificed. And in some tiny, barely acknowledged part of her heart, she'd hoped that reconciliation might have led to something more.

Time had passed for both of them, and her anger had cooled a little. She'd begun to reassess the choices she'd made over the past few years, whether she'd pushed him away too hastily, dealt with him too harshly. And tonight she'd resolved to reach out to him.

But it wasn't to be. She'd barely entered the hotel lobby before being accosted by a pair of burly security operatives, who had informed her in no uncertain terms that she was not welcome there.

She'd felt it straight away. The disapproving stares, the curious looks, the muttered comments from the other guests as they took in her torn jeans, scuffed shoes and frayed leather jacket that blended in so easily on the streets of Berlin. Now they marked her out as someone different, someone beneath them.

How dare they? She'd thought. She wasn't some piece of trash off the street, some stupid girl to be idly dismissed. She could have taken them both on, armed or not. But even if she'd won, what good would it have done?

They were simply messengers, and the message was clear – she wasn't wanted.

She should have just left, gone back to her temporary apartment and let it go, but she hadn't. She couldn't. Instead she had slunk outside and waited in the shadows of an empty doorway across the street, ignoring the cold and the revelry all around, focussing her attention on the balconies above.

And now she saw why she wasn't wanted tonight. As Cain pulled his female companion close and embraced her, Anya felt her cheeks flush with jealousy. And worse, shame. Of course Cain would take a woman like that, she told herself angrily. Beautiful, sophisticated, intelligent and captivating; the sort that any man would be drawn to.

She felt suddenly angry – not at them, but at herself. Angry at her own foolishness and naiveté, angry at the ridiculous hopes and myopic ambitions she'd nurtured. Next to them in their majestic hotel suite with their grand plans, she was a child. A child playing at adult games, flattering herself that she could be part of their world.

Were they laughing at her, she wondered in a sudden, excruciating moment? Finding amusement in the silly young woman who wanted to play soldiers and spies? Joking about how she'd tried to intrude on their evening?

She could watch no more. Turning away from the heart-breaking sight, Anya strode off down the street as the city celebrated and fireworks blossomed in the skies above, her head down to hide the tears in her eyes.

Jerusalem, Israel

Splashing cold water on her face, Anya straightened up and looked at herself in the bathroom mirror, surveying the face staring back at her.

You're getting old, she thought to herself with a kind of reluctant acceptance. Vanity had never been one of her vices, yet even she recognised the subtle, inexorable changes that were taking place within her. The life she'd lived had been neither short nor easy, with few occasions in which she could recall true happiness, and it was beginning to show.

She was almost at the end of her long road now, her best and brightest years behind her, a dark and uncertain future ahead. And if she was honest with herself, who would really miss her when she was gone?

Anya inhaled deep, gripping the sink tight and tensing her muscles, rallying her strength and resilience, just as she'd done so many times before. She'd been betrayed, written off, used and discarded by almost everyone she'd ever put her faith in. She was a relic of another time, a ghost haunted by old failures and mistakes.

But she wasn't finished yet. She had one last mission to complete, and she wouldn't stop while there was breath in her lungs and blood in her veins.

She heard the patter of something on the sink, and looked down to see a spot of blood smearing the white porcelain. The dressing around her shoulder must have come loose, she realised, surprised by the chill of foreboding it sent through her.

Turning away from the mirror, she removed the bloodied dressing and inspected the wound. It wasn't all that severe, but it had required stitches and would leave a scar for sure. Another to add to the list, she thought with a grim smile.

Changing it for a fresh dressing, she found her cell phone and dialled a number from memory, waiting a few seconds while the encryption software did its work.

'I'm here,' the recipient answered. No greetings, no preamble, no emotion. All business. That was the nature of their relationship.

'What's your situation?' Anya asked.

'I've found him.'

Anya closed her eyes, letting it sink in.

'Is he… what's his status?'

There was a short, questioning pause. 'He's active, and unharmed. I can make contact…'

'No,' Anya said right away. 'Keep him under observation for now.'

'Understood.' Another pause. 'What about you?'

Anya thought for a moment about what she'd learned from Russo tonight, and the next man on her list.

'I have another lead. I'll be following up on it soon.'

Chapter 28

It was dawn, the April sun just rising over the open moorland of Salisbury Plain as Jessica approached her brother. He was standing with his back to her, facing out towards the towering megaliths of the ancient henge, lit by the glow of the new day. Lost in his own thoughts.

They both had much to think about. They had listened to the remainder of their mother's message; her growing suspicion and distrust of the Circle, her fear of Marcus Cain's ruthless ambition, and finally her resolution to bring an end to them both. She had even identified a few others that she'd recruited to her cause, who might be able to help.

This recount of her life had ended with a chillingly pragmatic conclusion.

'If you're watching this video, then it's safe to say my efforts failed. I can only hope it was quick.'

Jessica had felt her brother's tension, the anger and pain eating away inside him as Freya's final words played out.

'I wanted you to know all of this, Ryan. Because you deserved a lot more than you got from me. I've spent most of my life dealing in secrets and lies, but for once I wanted to give you the truth. I know that can't begin to make up for everything I've done, the people I've let down, but maybe it will help make sense of it. And as for you... I can't tell you what to do next. I won't tell you to finish what I started, or let it all go and leave this whole mess behind. All I ask is that you take care of your sister. I can't protect her anymore; only you can do that now. But whatever choice you make, I want you to know that I loved you both, right to the end. And I'm sorry... for all of it.'

Jessica's memory of what had happened afterward was hazy. She remembered crying, drinking some more, and finally surrendering to a restless, troubled sleep.

She'd awoken with the dawn, and Drake had been gone. But she had an instinct about where she would find him.

She moved up beside him, taking in the view. The ancient monument that had stood here for hundreds of generations before they were born, and would still be here long after they and all their cares and worries had crumbled to dust.

'We were here once before,' she said quietly. 'When we were children. Mum and Dad brought us. I couldn't have been more than... five, maybe six years old.'

Drake didn't respond. His expression was glacial, his gaze lingering in the distance, his mind harbouring dark thoughts.

'You took me climbing on the stones,' Jessica carried on. 'I suppose you were allowed to do things like that back then. I was afraid to climb up. I was little, and I wasn't used to things like that. I never had been. But... you gave me your hand, and you told me there was nothing to be scared of. Not while you were around.'

She heard him exhale, his expression soften a little. 'I didn't think you'd remember.'

'I remember,' she assured him, then gave him a rueful smile. 'Just like I remember slipping and scraping my knees coming down. And screaming like a banshee because it hurt so bloody much.'

Drake chuckled faintly at the memory. 'So much for the protective older brother,' he mused. 'If it makes you feel better, I got my arse kicked for that one.'

'Yeah, it kind of does,' she decided, though she soon grew more serious. 'But I knew you did your best, Ryan. Just like Mum did for us.'

Drake shook his head. 'She should have told me. We could have helped each other.'

'She was trying to keep us out of it, just like she always did,' Jessica reminded him. 'Maybe she was right, maybe not. But it was her choice to make.'

'Her choice,' he repeated. 'Now it's mine.'

Jessica could see the look in his eyes now. It was a look she'd seen before. She knew that her brother had already decided on his course.

'I came back here looking for answers, and I got them.' He nodded faintly, as if to himself. 'I know what I have to do. The only thing that still matters.'

'Your life matters, Ryan. It always has.'

Drake smiled sadly. 'This is bigger than me now, bigger than any of us. This is about the future.'

If what their mother had revealed in her last message was true, then the power of the Circle left unchecked would keep growing exponentially, until there was nobody left with the will or the means to oppose them. They would control everything and everyone.

And in the centre of it all would be Drake's nemesis.

'What are you going to do?'

He paused, contemplating the future that could still be his if he walked away. An uneasy peace perhaps, but peace all the same. Contemplating it, then letting it go.

His answer, when it came, was delivered with cold unyielding conviction.

'I'm going to kill Marcus Cain.'

Part Three

Something to Fight For

The only thing necessary for the triumph of evil is for good men to do nothing.

Edmund Burke

Chapter 29

The upper floors of *Waziristan Haveli* commanded impressive views across Abbottabad, though the ever-present threat of surveillance prevented the residents taking advantage of them. Instead, a balcony enclosed by a high privacy wall had been constructed.

Now into late April, the afternoon sun was high enough to peek over this concrete surround, allowing the Master to take his tea in the fresh air and sunlight.

He had spent much of the long winter cocooned in his darkened office, idling away his days replaying old news coverage like some forgotten movie star rewatching their own films.

The Master laid his cup of tea on the little table beside him and eased back into the recliner chair with a sigh, his long thin legs stretched out. The afternoon sun played across a gaunt and pallid face, deeply lined by years of care and worry, the jaw covered by a grey, straggling beard.

'I have missed this.' He spoke with his customary quiet, soft tone. 'To breathe the fresh air, feel the sun on my face.'

He turned to regard Bashir Shirani who sat by his side, patiently attending him. 'During the Soviet invasion we lived in the mountains for months on end. It was so long since I ate a hot meal or slept in a real bed that I began to forget what it was like. We all did. Maybe we stopped *wanting* to remember after a while.' He chuckled to himself. 'Those were great days. We felt strong, invincible, like real men should. We felt we could fight the whole Soviet army ourselves, because God was with us.'

Shirani smiled and nodded indulgently, as was expected. He had heard many stories and legends about this man, most depicting titanic battles against the infidel invaders and feats of unparalleled heroism.

Only in his later years had he begun to learn the more mundane and honest interpretations of events, told by men who had actually been there. Stories of arms deals and financial negotiations – not quite the heroic life of fighting and sacrifice that many imagined. But as Shirani had come to learn, it was the prerogative of old men to embellish past glories.

The Master's dark eyes carried a sad, reflective look. 'Today, I live in comfort and luxury,' he said, gesturing to their heavily fortified surroundings. 'I wear clean clothes, eat good food, sleep in a warm bed. But I would gladly give it all up to be that young man again, living cold and hard in the mountains. To be strong and fearless and free again.'

He fell silent, and Shirani could almost feel his aching sense of longing. He knew he must say something.

'Perhaps one day you will, if God wishes it,' he ventured.

'Perhaps,' the Master agreed.

Though in their own way, they both sensed it wasn't to be.

–

In a small apartment situated on a hillside overlooking the target building, a pair of CIA operatives armed with high-power telephoto lenses were observing the entire compound, making careful and diligent notes of everything that happened there.

They, and men like them, had been on station for several weeks now, allowing the Agency to keep constant tabs on the property. It was dangerous and nerve-wracking work, with the constant fear of discovery vying with the greater danger of missing some vital piece of intel that could change the entire operation.

'Got a vehicle coming in,' operative Cory Linfield announced, hunched over his tripod-mounted camera. He would rather be behind a sniper rifle, but their objective was to gather intel only.

His colleague Rolf Ulland, busy preparing his next report for transmission back to Langley, glanced up from his laptop.

'Make and model?'

'Late model Toyota cruiser, dark blue. Looks like four bodies inside,' Linfield replied, tracking the vehicle as it approached the main gate. 'They're opening up.'

Ulland frowned. That was a sizeable contingent. It could mean nothing, or it could mean a high-value target who travelled with several bodyguards. Abandoning his computer, he moved over and took up the secondary observation position, training his lens on the compound's main parking lot as the Toyota came to a halt.

His finger hovered over the snapshot button as the doors opened and the passengers exited. He didn't recognise the driver or front passenger, though he took shots of them anyway. Both were big and heavyset, likely a protective detail.

Then the rear door swung open and a third man emerged into the afternoon sun. Short in stature, mid-forties, average height, and with a thick beard that reached almost to his chest. His dark hair was receding a little, his deep-set eyes nestled beneath dark, heavy brows.

Both men recognised him immediately.

'Fuck me,' Ulland said, snapping off more shots while the man's face was briefly turned towards them.

'Son of a bitch, that's al-Kuwaiti,' Linfield confirmed. 'I'd bet my life on it.'

Al-Qaeda had largely abandoned cell phones, email and other modern communications tools, instead relying on a network of human couriers to share information. And the most senior of them all, Abu Ahmed al-Kuwaiti, was strolling casually into the target building, flanked by a pair of bodyguards.

'Get Langley on the horn,' Linfield instructed as he flicked through the digital shots he'd managed to snap. 'They're gonna want to hear this.'

Chapter 30

CIA Headquarters, Langley

It wasn't long before the news made its way to Langley, and a special operational planning session was convened, headed up by Dan Franklin, the director of the Agency's highly secretive Special Activities Division. He was responsible for overseeing what had now been officially dubbed Operation Neptune Spear.

Representatives from the NSA and the Pentagon, as well as the director of National Intelligence and the White House chief of staff, were also conferenced in via video link. Some of the most powerful men and women in the country were watching him.

'As you can see from our intel, we now have a confirmed sighting of Abu Ahmed al-Kuwaiti in the target compound,' he summarised, calling up a surveillance photograph on the wall-mounted TV. 'Al-Kuwaiti is believed to be Bin Laden's top man, and his own personal courier. His presence is the strongest indication yet that *this* is the place they're keeping him.'

'But no confirmed eyes on Bin Laden?' the chief of staff asked probingly.

'No, sir,' Franklin admitted. 'The entire compound is fortified with two fundamental objectives in mind – security and privacy. Both of which are highly effective.'

'So you're saying he may not be there at all?'

Franklin knew why he was pushing so hard, because ultimately the president was the one who would have to sign off on this operation. He was seeing the political angle, gauging the potential fallout if the whole enterprise was a bust. It was well known that the president's approval ratings had been on the slide ever since taking office, hampered by a divided congress and struggling economy.

A major victory in the War on Terror could turn his first term around, and dramatically improve his chances of a second. On the other hand, a high-profile failure that got American soldiers killed – and caused a major incident with Pakistan – would be used against him all the way to the next election.

'It's a possibility, sir,' he allowed. 'In situations like this, there are rarely any guarantees. Most of the time we deal in probabilities rather than facts. But everything we've seen so far indicates this is the place. If I had to lay odds on it, I'd bet he's there.'

'What's our operational readiness?' the director of National Intelligence asked. 'If we have to move, how soon can we act?'

For this, Franklin deferred to Chris Kennedy, one of his most senior Shepherd team leaders, and the man he'd tasked with coordinating the assault. A sharp, diligent operative who had served as an Army Ranger before transitioning into the Agency, it was his job to know every step of the operation, from the second the team left their base in Afghanistan, to the moment they stepped off the chopper for debriefing.

'We have a JSOC task force on station just over the border in Afghanistan,' Kennedy confirmed, his manner tense and guarded. 'Fully prepped with stealth air assets.'

Joint Special Operations Command was an umbrella organisation that could draw on special forces personnel from all branches of the military and intelligence communities, including the CIA. Some of the finest operators on the face of the earth had been assembled for this op.

'In terms of readiness, they're currently on active standby. We give the word right now, they can be geared up and airborne in sixty minutes.' Kennedy paused before adding, 'If we bump them up to maximum readiness, that drops to ten minutes.'

'In other words, sir, we're about as ready as we can be,' Franklin said bluntly. 'It's not likely to get much better than this.'

Having al-Kuwaiti and Bin Laden in the same compound at the same time was a golden opportunity that might not come again for weeks, months or possibly ever. Franklin had seen too many targets slip through their grasp while the so-called decision-makers fretted and delayed, hoping for some mythical perfect scenario that would never come.

The White House chief of staff exhaled slowly through his nose. He sensed that Franklin was trying to push the issue, and didn't appreciate being backed into a corner.

'Is that Director Cain's assessment also?' he asked.

'Director Cain gave me full operational authority. I speak for him on this matter.'

'That's a pretty big call to make for a divisional director.'

Franklin said nothing to that.

'All right,' the chief of staff conceded. 'I'll brief the president. You will of course keep us in the loop if anything changes?'

'You'll be the first to hear about it,' Franklin assured him, managing to mask his irritation. The one thing almost guaranteed to fuck up any military operation was political interference.

With the meeting concluded, Franklin returned to his own office on the top floor of the New Headquarters Building, sank into his chair and gratefully loosened his tie. He felt mentally drained after the fraught meeting. With so much at stake, tensions were running high, and many of the key players were quietly compiling lists of people to blame if this thing went south.

Maybe that was why Cain had invested so much operational authority in him, he reflected grimly. Such a thought weighed heavily on him, but in truth it wasn't the only matter he was wrestling with at that moment.

Logging into his terminal, he pulled up an active case file he'd been diligently monitoring. A file detailing the hunt for Ryan Drake.

Nothing had changed since the last simple, terse update.

Last Confirmed Sighting – London (04/26/11)

Franklin was well aware of the failed attempt to apprehend Drake. Hell, an underground explosion in central London followed by a house assault and a high-speed chase through the UK capital wasn't the kind of thing one could sweep under the carpet. Even the news networks had caught wind of it, running stories speculating on everything from a terrorist attack to an organised crime ring.

They were all equally wrong, but it didn't change two stark facts – Drake was alive, and he had chosen to show himself in London. It would be wrong to say he wasn't relieved to know his old friend was still alive, but why reappear now? What was the man after? And why take the risk of venturing into a city like London?

To attempt to learn more would risk drawing attention to himself. Cain had him on a short leash, and wouldn't hesitate to act against him if given any cause to doubt his intentions.

And yet he couldn't let it go. Whatever had passed between them in recent years, he and Drake had been firm friends once. He owed his life to the man, in fact. That wasn't the sort of thing you just chose to forget.

What he needed was someone with more investigative skills than himself, but less history with Cain. Someone who could dig deeper without attracting attention. The question was whether that person would be willing to risk their career, and perhaps their life, to help him.

Unlocking his desk drawer, he fished out the burner phone he kept there and quickly punched in a number, waiting while it rang.

'Kennedy.'

'Chris, it's Dan. I need to speak with you.'

'Sure, boss. I can be in your office in five.'

'I'd rather talk privately.' He thought on it for a moment. 'Meet me at Kryptos.'

The CIA's headquarters was set within an extensive campus of office buildings, guard posts and training facilities, but the original designers had also sought to provide outdoor spaces where employees could relax and exercise. One of the most significant was an open courtyard between the two main office blocks, flanked by tall trees and bushes, and overlooked by the New Headquarters Building cafeteria.

In the north-west corner of this courtyard stood an intriguing and rather bizarre metal sculpture known as Kryptos. It had been commissioned to mark the opening of the New Headquarters Building back in 1990, and took the form of four large copper plates formed into an S-shape, resembling reams of paper emerging from a printer.

Each plate had been engraved with an encrypted message, encouraging aspiring code breakers to attempt to decipher their meaning. Three of them had since been broken, revealing various pieces of enigmatic text, but the fourth remained stubbornly unsolved.

Franklin had always been of the opinion that it couldn't be broken, that it was designed to be meaningless; a little joke by the artist to keep generations of young code breakers scratching their heads. And perhaps a subtle reflection on the realities of their job – not everything was meant to be known, not every mystery could be solved.

Kennedy was waiting for him, sitting on a bench facing the sculpture. He stood up as Franklin approached. 'You wanted to talk. What's up?'

'Walk with me,' Franklin said quietly, handing him a takeaway coffee cup.

It was a pleasant spring day and the courtyard was already busy. Franklin headed away from the hustle and bustle, waiting until they were well out of earshot before speaking.

'If you're worried about the op—' Kennedy began.

'It's not about the op,' Franklin assured him. 'This is something else.'

'I'm listening.'

Franklin stopped, turning to face the younger man. 'It's about Ryan Drake.'

A shadow seemed to pass over the younger man then. Drake was wanted for murder and treason, and there remained a lingering suspicion towards anyone formerly associated with him. He was the reason the Shepherd programme had been shut down for more than a year.

'What about him?'

Franklin took a sip of his coffee, glancing around before speaking. 'He's alive, Chris. He was spotted in London two days ago.'

'The explosion, the armed pursuit?' he asked.

'All Drake.'

Kennedy was silent for a few moments while he took this in. 'Fuck.'

'Pretty much,' Franklin agreed. 'Field teams tried to intercept him, but he got away and vanished.'

'Knowing Ryan, I can't say I'm surprised,' Kennedy mused. 'But why resurface now, when everyone thought he was dead?'

Franklin fixed him with a hard look. 'That's what I'd like to know.'

It didn't take long to guess why Franklin had summoned him. 'You want me to set up a case on him.'

He nodded. 'Under the radar. Nobody can know about this.'

'My entire team got cut loose once already because of that asshole,' Kennedy said, the heat in his voice betraying the old anger and resentment. 'Good people, Dan.'

'You should consider yourself lucky. Cain wants Drake dead, and he'll stop at nothing to make it happen. No matter who gets caught in the crossfire.'

'Why? What's his beef with Ryan?'

That would take a lot more time than they had. 'Long story. The short version is that Cain isn't what you think. He's been involved in a lot of shit over the years, most of it bad. When Ryan got caught up in it, he painted a target on his own head.'

Kennedy took a step closer. 'Dan, are you telling me Ryan's an innocent man?'

As much as he wanted to believe Drake had been unfairly persecuted, he was under no illusions that his former friend had always worked on the right side of the law. He had done many questionable things in his time, that he must still answer for. But he at least deserved a fair hearing.

'That's what I need you to find out,' Franklin instructed him. 'I need to know what Drake was doing in London, and where he's going next. And I need to know fast. If I'm right, we may not have much time.'

'What do you mean by that?'

Franklin glanced back the way they'd come, to the metal sculpture standing in the shade of the big office tower, the stressed-looking analysts and technicians milling around it. Rarely had the Agency been as busy as it was now, with so many global events happening simultaneously.

The wave of revolutions and coups in Africa and the Middle East, the hunt for Bin Laden, the assassination of a high-ranking Mossad agent, the recent attack in London... On the surface it might have been easy to dismiss them as a series of unrelated events, a chance convergence. But not for him.

Where others saw chance, he saw a pattern, an invisible and intangible web binding all of this together. Each one of them, willing or unwilling, was a part of it. And each of them was caught by it. He felt as if the pieces of a jigsaw had been laid out, the pieces moving slowly into place, yet the final image still eluded him.

'A feeling,' he said quietly, his expression distant. 'I can't explain it, I can't prove it... but I feel it. This is bigger than Drake, bigger than all of us. It's been coming for a long time, and when it does, it's going to change everything.' He frowned, struck by the phrase that had leapt unbidden into his mind. 'The end of the old world.'

He blinked, pushing the odd feeling of premonition away, annoyed with himself for voicing such vague notions. But when he looked at the Shepherd team leader standing beside him, he could tell that Kennedy knew it too.

'I'll see what I can do,' he promised.

Chapter 31

The cramped, low-rent apartment in which Keira Frost found herself was the kind of place you ended up out of necessity rather than desire. A one-bedroom affair with a combined kitchen/living room, and grimy windows overlooking a litter-strewn residential block where functioning streetlights were a distant memory.

The trickle of slightly-less-hot air that the worn air conditioner managed to put out was no match for the heat of the Mexican evening. Still, it was a roof over her head. And for all the stifling discomfort, the balmy weather sure beat winter on the streets of Chicago.

Tijuana had been her base of operations for the past couple of months. It was easy to get to, even easier for someone like her to blend in to, and with ongoing gang warfare between rival drug cartels, it was the kind of place where the police didn't get involved.

A pair of high-end laptops were humming away next to each other on her makeshift desk, nestled within a maze of cables, portable hard drives and flickering internet routers. Lines of code streamed across open debug windows as Frost fought a losing battle to pin down her opponent's location. Much as she hated to admit it, the man she'd pitted herself against was more than a match for her, and had so far resisted every effort to break into his system.

Turning her attention to the laptop on her left, she tapped in a series of commands, trying to adjust her strategy. Much to her annoyance, one of her fingers came down on the wrong key, forcing her to start again.

She clenched and flexed her hand a few times, noting the scar in the centre of her palm. A little reminder of the time her hand had been cruelly impaled by a knife. She'd recovered most of her motor function, but it would never be quite what it was. And that realisation made her all the more determined to pay back the man responsible for it.

That would have to wait for now, though. Today she had a more pressing task.

And that task was tracking down Alex Yates, who had chosen to side with Anya when their group disbanded. As adept as she was at disappearing, Alex was her weakness. He was the one who would lead Frost to Anya.

That was the theory, at least. But no matter what she threw at him, he always seemed to be one step ahead.

She was about to turn her attention to the other laptop when suddenly a dialog window appeared on her screen, displaying a simple, terse message.

YOU'RE WASTING YOUR TIME. STOP
TRACKING ME.

Frost practically leapt out of her seat. This was the first time Alex had openly communicated with her. But why now? Either he was willing to talk, or she was close to finding him.

Whatever the reason, she hurriedly tapped out a response.

WE NEED TO TALK. THINGS HAVE CHANGED.

Alex's reply came through seconds later.

NOT FOR ME. STOP TRACKING ME. I WON'T
ASK AGAIN.

Frost's jaw clenched at such a naked threat, but resolved to press on.

RYAN'S BEEN HIT. THEY ALMOST GOT HIM IN
LONDON.

He didn't answer for nearly thirty seconds.

THAT'S HIS PROBLEM, NOT MINE.

'God fucking damn it, Alex. Don't be a dickhead all your life,' she muttered, hammering the keys harder than necessary for her next message.

THIS IS SERIOUS. TELL ANYA WHAT
HAPPENED... PLEASE.

Alex's response wasn't the message of reconciliation she'd been
hoping for. Instead, the dialogue box vanished and all her active
programs abruptly froze.

'What the...'

A second or so later, a stark blue error screen appeared, advising
her that the system had encountered a fatal error and had shut down.

'Fuck!' she snapped, slamming the laptop closed.

Alex's threat had not been an idle one. She had no doubt the
machine was a total write-off. She had backups of her most important
data, of course, but it would take time to restore everything. Time she
didn't have.

'Asshole,' she muttered, heading for the fridge, deciding a few
bottles of Sam Adams might take the edge off her anger.

She was just popping the lid on her first one when there came a
pounding at the door. Instantly alert, Frost opened a kitchen drawer
and pulled out the Beretta 9mm automatic inside. Racking back the
slide to chamber a round, she checked safety, then approached the
door with the weapon tucked behind her back.

With the beer in one hand, she undid the deadbolt and opened the
door enough to get a look at the new arrival. Her face lit up right
away.

'Ryan,' she said, regaining her composure. 'Shit, you took long
enough.'

Drake flashed a grin, though he looked tired and drawn despite his
relief at being reunited with his teammate.

'Been a busy few days,' he explained. 'Mind if we come in?'

Frost frowned. 'We?'

His companion moved into view; a woman Frost vaguely recognised from their one and only meeting several years earlier. It was
Drake's sister, Jessica. The resemblance between them was obvious,
though she looked in worse shape than him, her face marked by cuts
and bruises that were only partially covered by heavy make-up.

'Christ, are you out of your mind?' she asked, unlatching the
security chain to let them in. 'What are you thinking, bringing her
into this?'

She and Drake had agreed to rendezvous here as soon as he could get into the country, but there had been no mention of his sister. Frost had assumed he would find some safe house for her to hole up in until this was over.

'*She* has a name,' Jessica retorted, snatching the beer bottle out of Frost's hand. 'And she's not in the mood for any more bullshit.'

As Jessica took a gulp of the beer, Frost shot Drake an angry look. Had Jessica not been under his protection, he suspected Frost would have laid her out for what she'd just done.

'I can see the family resemblance,' Frost replied testily.

'Save it. I didn't come here to argue.' Drake glanced around the cramped, untidy apartment, unimpressed by what he saw. 'We need to talk. There's a lot to fill you in on.'

Frost took the hint. 'I know a place. But you're buying.'

Fifteen minutes later, they were ensconced at a beachfront bar with a round of drinks in hand, their table facing out onto the sandy expanse of Tijuana Beach. Beyond, the rolling waves of the Pacific stretched all the way to the horizon, aglow with evening sunlight. It was a lively place, with a heady mix of tourists looking for a good time, and locals willing to accommodate them, all thrown together with loud music and cheap drinks.

Frost listened while Drake and his sister poured it all out – the attempted abduction of Jessica, followed by her unexpected rescue, the discovery of their mother's hidden message leading to the Vault in London, and their desperate escape from the authorities. Lastly, Drake explained the contents of his mother's final message.

Frost's expression darkened as the full impact of his words sank in.

'Jesus Christ,' she said at length. 'This whole goddamn mess is tied together. Cain, Anya, the Circle… Your mom was working for them the whole time.'

'Working *against* them, actually,' Jessica corrected her. 'She was planning to bring them down from the inside.'

'How did that work out for her?'

Jessica clenched her jaw, about to let fly a stinging rebuke, but Drake jumped in before she said something they all regretted. 'She joined them because she believed in what they represented. Only later did she realise what they'd become. She was trying to make things right.'

Frost didn't look convinced, but decided not to press the issue. 'So what about you, Ryan? Why are you here?'

Drake turned his head away for a moment, looking out to sea. Taking in the emptiness, the endless horizon, the chance to start a new life.

'I'm here to finish what she started.'

'Bullshit,' she snorted. 'You're out for revenge. I've seen that look before.'

Drake didn't try to dispute her claim, because there was no need. They both knew she was entirely correct.

'Call it what you want. Cain knows I'm alive now, and he won't stop until I'm dead. No matter where I go or what I do, eventually he'll find me. One way or another, this has to end.'

'Ryan, think about what you're saying here,' Frost said, leaning over the table to get eye to eye with him. 'Your mom tried to take on Cain, and she ended up dead. We tried in Pakistan, and we lost...' Her voice caught for a moment before she could go on. 'We lost Cole, almost got killed ourselves. Every single time we've gone up against him, he's won, and we've lost. What makes you think this would play out any different?'

'Because this time we have an advantage.'

Frost's eyes narrowed. 'What do you mean?'

'A man on the inside,' Jessica announced.

Seeing her confusion and surprise, Drake added, 'Freya wasn't the only one working to bring the Circle down. She had allies.'

Frost listened while they told her everything. There was a man, well placed and well trusted within the Circle, with whom Freya had been working to gather intel and evidence. A man who had begun to see the corruption within the organisation, the danger posed by Cain, and who might just be willing to help them now.

'You're sure of this?' she asked dubiously. 'What if this is all some kind of play?'

'She recorded that message in the Vault, alone, in secret. I don't see how she could have been under duress. And if they'd wanted us dead, they could have made it happen easily enough.'

'But do you *trust* her?' Frost pressed him. 'I mean, you said it yourself – her whole damn life was a lie.'

'You didn't know her,' Jessica said with barely concealed irritation.

Frost regarded her coolly. 'Neither did you, apparently.'

The animosity between the two of them was palpable. Drake was quick to interject before it erupted into a full-blown confrontation.

'Look, I won't pretend that Freya never made mistakes. She did, and she paid for them with her life. She died trying to make things right. I believe that, and I believe we have a chance to finish what she started.'

'You willing to bet everything on that?' she said quietly. 'All or nothing?'

He nodded. 'All or nothing.'

They had come down to it at last. The end of the line. The last chance to stop Cain before he became untouchable. No mercy, no hesitation, no quarter given. Only one side was walking away from this alive.

'I'm doing this with or without you, Keira.' He glanced at his sister. '*We're* doing this. But we stand a better chance with your help. I came here to give you a simple choice, one last time. In, or out?'

Frost regarded him for several seconds in tense, anxious silence, watching him as if she could somehow discern their chances of success. But she couldn't. None of them could know how this was going to play out, whether they would prevail against their greatest enemy.

Whether any of them would live through it.

Drake could offer her no reassurance. As he'd said, it came down to a simple choice.

That was when he saw it. The smile. The lopsided, wolfish smile he'd come to know so well. The smile he'd been looking for.

'Course I'm fucking in,' Frost said, raising her bottle and clinking it against his. 'Let's go kill this asshole.'

Chapter 32

The top floor apartment was luxuriously appointed and tastefully decorated, its big floor-to-ceiling windows offering excellent views over the Potomac and the suburban sprawl beyond. And with sunset approaching, the room was flooded with its fiery incandescent glow, the sky ablaze with colour.

But the view was lost on Marcus Cain as he paced the living room, waiting impatiently for his contact to arrive. The waiting was always the worst part.

Pouring himself a glass of whisky from a crystal decanter, he moved over to the windows and looked out. This building was formed around a big semi-circular apartment and office complex, though it was perhaps best known for its infamous name.

Watergate.

From here, he could actually see the office building in which the notorious break-in had taken place two decades earlier, starting the escalating chain of cover-ups and investigations that would ultimately doom the presidency of Richard Nixon.

The door opened behind him and a pair of high heels strode into the room. Cain tensed, bracing himself.

'Well?' he said without turning around. 'What's the decision?'

He heard a faint sigh.

'They voted,' Shaw announced bluntly. 'It's not good news.'

Cain closed his eyes, swallowing down the bitter frustration that welled up inside him.

'Do I get to know why?'

'They feel that further conflict in Afghanistan isn't in our strategic interests. There are other priorities now.'

Other priorities. In other words, Afghanistan had served its purpose to help bring down the Soviet Union. Now it was to be discarded and forgotten.

Cain had lobbied the Circle to intervene there, where simmering tensions between the victorious Mujahideen groups threatened to boil over into civil war.

A war that the hard-line Islamists were likely to win, plunging a once-moderate country into religious oppression, and leaving a whole generation betrayed and abandoned by America, sowing the seeds of future wars.

'You know what this is going to mean,' he said. 'You know we'll be back there one day, fighting the war all over again.'

'Like I said, there are other priorities,' Shaw repeated coldly. He heard her open the decanter, heard the splash of whisky being poured.

Cain turned to face her, his expression dark and hostile. Shaw was still a beautiful woman, still elegant and alluring, but she was different now. The fire and energy that first drew him to her was missing. The connection between them was broken, severed by growing disillusionment and distrust.

'And you? What did you say?'

Shaw lifted the glass to her lips. 'I take my orders just like you, Marcus.'

'Bullshit,' he snapped. 'For once in your life, have the balls to be honest.'

She sighed. 'You're too close to this, you've made it personal. You're not seeing the situation clearly anymore.'

'I'm trying to save lives. I'm trying to stop another war before it happens.' His anger was threatening to break through the walls of self-control now. 'What the fuck have you ever done that didn't benefit yourself?'

'What have I done?' she repeated, laughing to herself. A laugh that was cold and hard and mocking. 'What have I done, Marcus? How about believing in you? That was the biggest mistake I ever made.'

'You brought me into this,' he reminded her. 'After all the promises, all the big speeches about changing the world, you're just like the others. Weak.'

'You still don't get it, do you?' she snapped back. 'You still don't understand.'

She allowed those words to hang in the air, allowed the seconds to stretch out before she delivered her final blow.

'It was Anya they really wanted, not you.'

'Bullshit!'

The woman shook her head slowly, her expression one of pity and disgust. 'You were just a tool, Marcus. That's all you ever were, all you could ever be – a tool to keep her in line. They won't listen to you, because they don't care what you think. They never will.'

Cain didn't speak. He couldn't. He felt like a knife had been driven into his guts. Just like Afghanistan, he was simply an asset to be used and discarded when he'd served his purpose.

'It was all a lie,' he said, his voice hollow. 'All of it.'

'I thought you could become more than that. I saw that potential in you,'
Freya went on. 'But I was wrong. You'll never see the big picture, because you
can't see past her.'

Cain hadn't missed the way she'd spat the word 'her'.

'So that's what this really is,' he said bitterly, sensing the undertone of
jealousy in her harsh words. 'You told them to vote against me. You wanted
to see me take a fall, because your pride and ego couldn't handle being second
best. Yeah, you were right about one thing, Freya. I couldn't see past Anya,
because she was better than you. She was always better.'

Draining the last of her drink, Freya laid the glass down. 'A new handler
will be in touch soon. I don't imagine we'll be working together again.'

She was about to leave when Cain called out to her. 'Answer me one thing.
Was it worth it?'

Freya stopped, keeping her back to him.

'Goodbye, Marcus.'

Washington DC – April 28th, 2011

Marcus Cain shifted slightly in his seat, resisting the urge to reach up
and loosen his tie, a gesture which would be interpreted as a sign of
discomfort and unease by the panel of senators arrayed before him.
Sixteen men, three women. All with their poker faces on.

The Senate Select Committee was here to assess not just his background and accomplishments, but also his personal life, his character and temperament. Their job was to push and prod, look for
weaknesses, to determine if he was fit to lead the nation's premier
intelligence service.

And it was a job they took seriously. Cain had had to answer more
than a few difficult questions designed specifically to trip him up.
There were elements of his life and career that he was not eager to
divulge, and having it all placed under the spotlight wasn't an easy
thing to deal with.

Some, however, were more zealous about this duty than others.

'I'd like to thank you for your cooperation today, Director Cain.
Your answers have been very informative,' said Senator Thomas Barr,
a thin-faced, sharp-tongued Republican from Missouri, as he leafed
through his paperwork. 'I can assure you, we're almost done.'

Cain fought to contain his disdain for the man; his turkey neck that wobbled when he spoke, his unusually large glasses, his thin and nasal voice, his endless questions intended to annoy and provoke.

Cain's recommendation had come from the president, a Democrat, so naturally the Republican contingent were geared up to resist it. Barr had been leading the charge since day one, focussing on the sudden death of the previous CIA director last year, making thinly veiled insinuations that Cain had benefitted greatly from his passing.

'Before we deliver our closing remarks, I'd like to ask a question of a more... personal nature.'

Cain reached for the glass of water beside him. 'Yes, sir?'

'Your daughter... Lauren, wasn't it?'

Cain's grip tightened on the glass. 'That's right.'

'Your daughter Lauren... lost her life during a terrorist attack in Berlin last year. My condolences for your loss, sir.'

'I appreciate your compassion, Senator,' Cain managed to say.

'Quite so. My question, if you'll forgive my directness, is how has this affected you?'

Cain frowned, feigning confusion rather than the open anger he truly felt. The bastard was going after him for losing a child. He could see the barely disguised glee in Barr's expression as he awaited an answer.

'I'm not sure I understand?'

'You lost your own flesh and blood to a terrorist attack. Your job as CIA director is to prevent such attacks, with a clear head and unbiased judgement. Don't you worry those two things may not sit well together?'

Cain could see exactly the trap he had laid. To admit personal grief at the loss of his daughter might call his judgement into question, but to deny any impact whatsoever might paint him as a liar attempting to deceive the panel. Or worse, a sociopath who felt no emotion whatsoever.

At this point, one of Barr's colleagues on the panel cleared his throat. 'While I'm sure Senator Barr's question is well intentioned, I think we ought to be mindful of the standards of professional respect this committee is bound to uphold.'

'I disagree, sir,' Barr countered. 'Personal losses, no matter how tragic, can and do impact on a man's thinking. It's not unreasonable to question whether the loss of a close family member could affect

Director Cain's professional judgement in a crucial moment. A painful question it may be, but it's our responsibility to ask all the same.'

He was looking at the committee chairman now. Although not a voting member, it was his duty to make rulings where protocol was called into question.

'My colleague Senator Barr has raised a valid, if indelicate, question,' he conceded. 'I'll allow it to stand. However, I'd ask that committee members respect the sensitivity of this matter.'

Cain took a sip of water, composing himself before offering his response. Despite the chairman's tacit defence of him, he knew that dodging the question would not be viewed favourably. They were willing to grant him some latitude, but they expected an answer.

'Thank you, Mr Chairman. Out of respect to this committee and the responsibility it's charged with, I'll answer Senator Barr. The loss of my daughter Lauren was one of the most difficult moments of my life,' he said, speaking with complete honesty now. 'When it happened, I felt like I'd lost my hope for the future. I asked myself again and again, why did it happen? What more could I have done? How could I have failed her so badly?

'And I suppose it would have been easy to lose myself in that. But I believe the thing that helps us move past grief and loss is purpose. And for me, that purpose was my work. Now that I've known how it feels to have a loved one torn away from me, it's made me even more determined to spare other innocent people that pain.

'It's not for me to say whether Lauren's death made me better or worse at my job, whether it cleared or clouded my judgement, but I can tell you one thing for sure – I've never been more sure about what I want to do with my life.'

He fixed Barr with a hard, penetrating stare. The man's look of glee and triumph was fading now. 'Does that answer your question, sir?'

Barr cleared his throat, reached up and adjusted his tie. 'It does, Director. Thank you.'

Cain's first action on emerging from the committee chamber was to power up his cell phone. He had been out of the loop for the past several hours and was eager for news. His first point of contact was the man tasked with hunting down Ryan Drake.

'Hawkins.'

'Talk to me,' Cain commanded as he strode across the building's massive central atrium. 'Where are we on Drake?'

'Latest intel suggests he chartered a private flight to Mexico.'

Mexico. An easy entry point into the US.

'What about the London Vault? Tell me you found something useful.'

Hawkins had breached the facility on his own initiative – a decision that was likely to have serious repercussions. Cain would handle that in due course, just as he would handle Hawkins himself, but for now he still needed the man.

'The Vault's mainframe was wiped before we could stop it. Digital forensics are going over it now, but it was pretty thorough. It's unlikely we'll recover anything usable.'

'Give me some *good* news, Jason,' Cain warned him.

'We recovered a laptop from the facility's conference room, and we've been able to reassemble fragments of the last file accessed on it. They think it was some kind of video. All we've got so far are a few still images.'

'Show me.'

A few seconds later, an image file appeared on his cell phone. Straight away Cain opened it up, and felt the breath catch in his throat. The face staring back at him was chillingly familiar. A ghost from his past.

'Freya,' he said under his breath.

'The one and only,' Hawkins confirmed. 'My guess is she left some kind of message for him.'

An edge of concern crept into Cain's mind then. Drake had been a thorn in his side for some time, and although he'd failed to eliminate the man, he'd been able to control him to some extent. But now he had been left a message by Freya. This changed everything.

How much did Drake know? How much had she told him? He had no way of knowing. But Freya had known everything about him. He now had no choice but to prepare for the worst-case scenario: Drake could be coming for him.

'Get to Mexico, Jason,' he instructed. 'Drake knows too much now. Find him and stop him before he gets across the border.'

'I'm on my way there already,' Hawkins confirmed. He paused before adding, 'And the… other problem?'

Cain was in fact facing two separate threats. Not only had Drake slipped through their fingers in London and set his sights on Cain, but in Israel, Anya had reappeared and assassinated a senior Mossad agent.

Cain had learned of the death barely an hour after the body had been discovered, just as he'd learned of the murder of four more men in Jerusalem. Bounty hunters, gunned down during a deadly confrontation in a back alley. It hadn't taken much effort to connect the two events, and surmise that those men had tried and failed to intercept her.

Their deaths meant nothing to him, of course, but the murder of Russo was far more concerning. He was the first link in the chain of events that had taken place eight years earlier. Though Cain was separated from him by several layers, such precautions would do nothing but delay the inevitable.

After vanishing for months, Anya was back, and she was killing her way to the truth. Nothing would stop her.

Two separate adversaries, each following different lines of investigation. But both trails would ultimately lead back to him. The only question was, how best to deal with them?

'If she got to Russo, then she knows what he knows,' Cain reasoned. Anya wouldn't have killed the man until she'd gotten what she needed from him. 'That being the case, we know where she'll be heading next.'

'Qalat,' Hawkins said, making the same connection.

'Get your best people on it,' Cain instructed him. 'If she makes a move against him, they need to be ready. We get one chance at this.'

'It'll be done.'

'We're almost at the finish line now,' the CIA director reminded him. 'No more screw-ups. Are we clear?'

'Crystal,' Hawkins said, an edge in his voice now.

Hanging up, Cain immediately dialled Franklin's number as he headed for the parking garage, where his official car was waiting. Events were moving faster than he'd anticipated. It was time to put the final stage of his plan into action.

'Marcus, we've had some developments in Pakistan,' Franklin began. 'I need to brief you as soon as possible.'

'I'm on my way in,' Cain confirmed. 'Right now, put our assault team on heightened readiness. On my authority.'

'You sure? Only the president can give the order to go.'

Cain smiled at that. The president did what his advisors told him to do, and Cain owned his advisors. He was almost there now. After so many years of planning, the time had almost come.

'He will. Trust me.'

Chapter 33

Tijuana, Mexico

With the sun down, the city had come to life as the local bars, restaurants and nightclubs began to fill up. Bright lights illuminated beachfront dance floors that were already busy, music reverberating from a dozen different directions.

Drake and Frost had their minds on other matters as they made their way to a quieter area of the beach, where the sound of waves crashing against the breakwater was a more welcome backdrop.

With their course of action decided, they had put out a call to their few remaining allies, Jonas Dietrich and Olivia Mitchell, instructing them to rendezvous once Drake and the others had crossed the border.

'How are you holding up, Keira?' Drake asked honestly. He knew Frost wouldn't open up until they were alone.

The young woman snorted in amusement. 'Just peachy. I mean, what's not to like? We're being hunted by every major intelligence agency on earth, not to mention a group of secret assholes that make the Illuminati look like the Girl Scouts. Best of all, we're about to venture into the lion's den with our dicks hanging out. And all of it depends on a guy who might sell us out the moment we make contact.'

'So pretty good, then?'

Frost punched him in the arm hard enough that it wasn't quite playful.

'What about you?'

'Almost as good,' he evaded.

'Don't make me hit you again, you asshole. Level with me.'

Drake sighed, turning more serious. 'They came after Jess,' he said quietly. 'I almost lost her again. I would have done, if it hadn't been for... *her.*'

'Anya?'

He shook his head. 'Doesn't fit. We know she was in Tel Aviv the day before. What are the odds she could have got to the UK just in time to intercept Jess?'

'Can't argue with that, I guess. But if not Anya, then who?'

For that, Drake had no answer. Clearly he was missing something, but he had precious little time to devote to it now. There were too many other things happening.

'Any luck finding her?' he asked instead.

It was Frost's turn to sigh. 'Yes, and no.'

'Meaning?'

'I was getting close to Alex, even made contact with him.'

Drake looked at her incredulously. 'I told you to track him, not start a conversation.'

'It's not that easy, Ryan,' she admitted. 'Alex may be an asshole, but he knows his shit. I couldn't break into his system. This was my last shot.'

'And?'

Were it not for the darkness, he was sure he would have seen her blush. 'He shut me down. Nuked my system remotely. It'll take days to rebuild.'

Drake looked away in disappointment. 'Great.'

'You're missing the point. He wouldn't have done that, except as a last resort. So either he was pissed at me and lost his temper, or...'

'Or he had something else going on,' Drake finished for her.

'Exactly,' Frost agreed. 'If I had to put odds on it, I'd say he and Anya are gearing up for something. Another operation, maybe.'

'Another killing, you mean?'

Whatever Anya had learned from Russo in Tel Aviv, it had led her to the next step in her plan. Where it would end, Drake had no idea. But he sensed more people were going to die before she was finished. And in a moment of stark premonition, he wondered if Anya might be amongst them.

'We have to track her down,' he decided. 'There's got to be a way.'

'Has it occurred to you that she doesn't *want* to be found?' Frost asked.

'We need her,' Drake said bluntly. 'If we're going to make this work, we need everyone we can get.'

'Bullshit. We both know that's not the real reason.'

Drake could feel her looking at him, knew she wouldn't give up unless she got an answer. He had to give her one, and it had to be the truth.

'I did her wrong,' he admitted. 'I took something that I can't give back.'

He looked down, allowing himself to feel some measure of the anger and longing he'd kept carefully locked away since that day in Afghanistan.

'You know, for a while I actually believed we might make it, the two of us,' he mused sadly. 'I could almost imagine a life after this. A real life.'

'Nothing's real if it starts with a lie.'

To his surprise, he felt Frost's hand on his arm. He turned to look at his comrade, his teammate, his friend. One of the few he had left.

It wasn't much, but Drake appreciated the sentiment.

'It's time,' he announced, fishing out the encrypted satellite phone in his pocket. 'Will this hold up?'

'It's the best encryption system on the market,' Frost explained. 'But considering who you're calling, might want to keep it short and sweet.'

'It will be,' Drake assured her as he dialled the contact given to him in his mother's final message. The man who just might hold the key to bringing down Marcus Cain.

Standing on the beach with the moon rising over the sea and the waves breaking against the shore, Drake waited while the phone rang out.

It took all of five seconds for it to happen.

'Yes?'

'My name's Ryan Drake. I think you've been expecting my call.'

Chapter 34

Washington DC – June 10th, 1999

Anya had been to this place many times in her career. Yet even now, the sheer scale of Arlington National Cemetery never ceased to amaze her. Four hundred thousand of America's war dead had been laid to rest here, their graves marked by neat rows of identical white tombstones that stretched off into a gently rolling landscape of grass and scattered woodland. Order and solemn uniformity in death, as there had once been in life.

But her thoughts were less on her surroundings than on the increasingly turbulent and monumental events overtaking her.

Task Force Black, the small, clandestine special forces unit that she'd reluctantly assumed command of nearly ten years earlier, had slowly but surely blossomed into a sprawling and powerful organisation in its own right. Their ranks had swollen with new recruits, their reach had greatly expanded and their capabilities enhanced.

Anya now found herself at the head of a de facto private army, running simultaneous operations in half a dozen countries, with hundreds of people now answering directly to her. And much of it was paid for by the river of money now flowing out of the Circle. Whatever she requested, it was granted without question.

It was as daunting as it was exhilarating. She had entered a world of which she had little experience or understanding: a world of subtlety and negotiation, of power plays and political manoeuvring.

The simple task of coordinating and organising it all took up so much of her time and effort that she was no longer involved in tactical planning and operational execution.

Was this to be her future, she wondered? From a soldier to a spy, and now a bureaucrat? No longer leading her men, but directing them from some office in Washington? That prospect left her with mixed emotions. On the one hand, it meant the chance to set the objectives instead of simply fulfilling them, to be a shaper of policy instead of an instrument. And yet the thought of never being out in the field again, of never leading from the front but expecting others to do it in her place... it was as if she was cheating somehow. Shirking her responsibilities and turning her back on the men who had risked just as much as her.

The sound of approaching footsteps caused her to turn. Her contact had arrived.

'Good morning,' Freya Shaw said, her tone light and airy.

Her eyes were hidden behind dark sunglasses, and while she was still a strikingly attractive and elegant woman, Anya could see the subtle changes wrought by time. The little winkles around the mouth and eyes, the strands of grey in her raven black hair, the hardening of her features. Freya Shaw was growing old.

'A little morbid for a meeting place, don't you think?'

Anya had set the location. She'd been doing it for a while now, in fact.

'Not at all,' she countered. 'It gives me perspective.'

Freya's eyes fastened on the great marble sarcophagus of the Tomb of the Unknown Soldier. The marine honour guard were, as always, silently standing watch in front of it.

'Well, let's hope we don't end up here permanently,' she remarked with a wry smile. 'Walk with me, would you?'

Anya followed as she led the way uphill, Freya moving a little slower than in her younger days.

'Things have been going well for you lately,' the older woman remarked conversationally. 'A string of successful operations, increased funding, more recruitment into your unit. I'm impressed.'

'I do what I can,' Anya replied, a little uncomfortable with the praise. It wasn't something she'd received much of in her life.

'So I've noticed. And as it turns out, I'm not the only one.'

'What do you mean?'

Halting, Shaw removed the sunglasses and looked Anya up and down, as if assessing her for the first time. The two women were about equal in height, one older, more experienced and powerful, the other younger and stronger, with her best days still ahead of her. Shaw seemed to recognise it in that moment.

'Our... mutual friends feel it's time you took the next step.'

Anya's eyes opened wider. 'The Circle?'

A smile flickered on Shaw's lips. 'They've been following your progress these past few years, and they like what they see. They think you're ready to take your place at the top table. And, as it happens, so do I.'

Anya was struck dumb by this news. She knew only a little about the mysterious group that had so aided her career over the past decade, most of which information had come from Shaw herself. So many layers of power and influence one might rise through, without ever knowing where the true decisions were made.

But the Inner Circle, as it was informally known, represented the very top of this vast pyramid. The governing body. The select group of individuals who ran it all.

And they wanted her to join them. Anya – the orphan girl from Lithuania.

'Chances like this only come once, Anya. People could work their entire lives, and never get to where you are,' Freya said. 'Bloody hell, try not to look too miserable about it!'

'I understand, and I… I'm honoured,' Anya said, still struggling to process it. 'I just never expected this. When I imagine the Inner Circle, I think of…'

'Old men?' Shaw prompted helpfully. 'Old men with white hair and expensive suits, meeting in dark board rooms?'

Seeing Anya's rueful expression, she smiled in amusement. 'Well, who can blame you? Just like the president, like congress, the military, the Agency…' She lowered her voice conspiratorially. 'Maybe that's the point, Anya. Maybe we have enough old men in expensive suits. Maybe it's time for something different.'

'But I'm just a…' She stopped herself then, realising the world had moved on since the formative experiences of her own childhood. 'What I mean is, I don't know if I can be like them. Think like them. I am not… cunning, or political, or anything like that.'

'Like I say, that's the point,' Freya explained, regarding her with fond amusement. 'When the Circle was formed, the hammer and sickle was still flying over the Kremlin. But the world has changed, and it's time the Circle changed with it. The men who sit at the top table are the past; they've sat there too long, become too rigid in their thinking. But you… you can be their future. A better future, for them and for us.'

It was only then that it all seemed to come together for her.

'It was you, wasn't it?' Anya asked. 'You made this happen.'

Again that smile, knowing and enigmatic. 'Like I told you all those years ago, Anya. You don't need to be anyone's pawn. Not anymore.'

Anya was struck by the enormity of this moment. For all the battles she'd fought and the challenges she'd overcome, she had never courted power or influence over others. All she had really wanted was to make a difference.

But at last she realised how inextricably linked the two things were, how it was impossible to achieve one without embracing the other.

And how important it was not to abuse either.

'But my men...'

'Your men will be just fine,' Shaw assured her. 'Task Force Black practically runs itself anyway. Your second in command is more than up to the job, if I recall.'

Dominic Munro, the tactically brilliant and driven special forces operative, had risen swiftly through the ranks of Task Force Black, becoming her most senior lieutenant in just a handful of years. And with her recent absence from operational leadership, he was now the de facto commander of the unit. A good man. A strong man. A man that she could rely on.

'Well?' Shaw prompted the younger woman. 'You've just been offered the keys to the kingdom. What's your answer?'

Islamabad, Pakistan – April 29th, 2011

Anya gripped the edge of the sink tightly, her head lowered as she let out a slow, calming breath, before looking up at the mirror. The reflection staring back at her was a far cry from the naïve young woman who had stood at Arlington more than a decade earlier, so caught up in the whirl of opportunities that she failed to notice the ground shifting beneath her feet. She could scarcely have imagined the cruel fate that would overtake her and her entire unit just weeks after that meeting.

She blinked, forcing the memories away. That was the ghost of a future that never came to pass, and the woman at the heart of it was long dead. Now she had more pressing matters to attend to.

Leaving the bathroom, she strode through to the apartment's cramped living space, where Alex was bent over his laptop.

'How close are we?' she asked.

'Almost there,' he replied without looking up. 'Their network protocols are pretty old, but the configuration is kind of weird so it takes a while to get a—'

'I don't need the details,' Anya interrupted. Computer hacking was neither a skill nor an interest she possessed. 'How much longer?'

'Ten, fifteen minutes. Once I'm in, I'll have everything you need. Radio frequencies, deployment patterns, everything.'

'Good.'

Crouching down, Anya grabbed the holdall lying on the floor, hoisted it up onto the table and unzipped it.

'I can delay reinforcements and generally fuck up their response, but I can't do anything about his protective detail,' Alex warned. 'It's you against them. And last time I checked, there's only one of you.'

'I only need one of me,' she replied, removing a disassembled M4A1 assault rifle.

A lightweight submachine gun might have been preferable, but going up against men in body armour, she needed the extra stopping power of the 5.56mm weapon. She'd even procured armour-piercing rounds.

Alex didn't say anything to this. Something was on his mind, she knew. Something more than just the dangerous mission ahead.

'You want to tell me something, Alex,' she stated, pulling back the ejector handle to check the firing assembly. 'Do it now, while we still have time.'

The young computer specialist sighed. 'Frost has been tracking me online.'

Seeing Anya's darkening expression, he held up a hand to forestall any reprimand. 'Relax, she doesn't know where we are.'

'But there is something else,' Anya prompted him.

He nodded. 'She contacted me by encrypted message. Neither of us could see the other, but we could talk.'

Anya's grip tightened on the weapon. 'I told you not to make contact with Drake's group,' she said icily. 'You promised you wouldn't.'

'I know. And you know I'd never tell them anything.' Alex was speaking slowly and quietly, aware of the delicate situation. 'But Frost said that something had changed, that they were all in danger.'

'I know all of this already,' Anya said dismissively.

Alex's eyes opened wider. 'And you didn't tell me?'

'It wasn't for you to know. Drake and the others are no longer your concern.'

'But *you've* been keeping tabs on them.'

Turning away, Anya laid the assault rifle down hard on the table, and reached for the case of ammunition. 'Like I said, it's not for you to know.'

'He hasn't given up on you, you know,' Alex said gently. 'All this time, he's been looking for you. Maybe you shouldn't give up on him?'

Whirling around, Anya grabbed him by his T-shirt and shoved him against the wall, pinning him with her forearm pressed against his neck. A single, sharp blow there would collapse his trachea and kill him within minutes. She had done it enough times to know.

She saw a brief flare of shock and fear at her sudden outburst, but it soon gave way to a growing sadness. And worse, pity.

'You going to kill me, Anya?' he asked, staring into her hard, cold eyes. 'Is this what we are now?'

She'd gone too far, she realised; lost control in a way she never did. When had she become like this? Exhaling, Anya relaxed her grip and pulled away.

'I'm sorry,' she whispered, ashamed. 'You didn't deserve that.'

'They're asking for our help,' Alex implored her. 'Are we really going to ignore them?'

Anya avoided his gaze, turning her attention back to her gear. She couldn't afford distractions like this, especially now. She needed her head in the game.

'We have our own mission now. That's what matters.'

Chapter 35

Sheffield, Texas – April 29th

Situated in southern Texas, about 50 miles north of the Mexican border, and with a population of less than a thousand people, the small town of Sheffield was about as remote a backwater as one could find. The kind of place where the younger residents spent every night dreaming about leaving.

A single main road ran through the dusty conglomeration of sun-bleached wooden houses that had taken root in the midst of the Texas desert. It was serviced by a gas station, a couple of convenience stores and cheap bars, and a single motel used mostly by truck drivers stopping off for the night.

Drake had picked this place as their rendezvous location for two reasons. Firstly, because it was easily 100 miles from the nearest FBI field office, and secondly because the name Sheffield appealed to him. He'd always been amused by the American penchant of naming their towns and cities after existing places.

Either way, it had made for as good a place as any to regroup with the rest of his team after the tense border crossing from Mexico. Normally the loosely enforced southern border was a piece of cake even for untrained civilians to cross, never mind a team of former Shepherd operatives, but there had been a major increase in border patrols over the past few days. The added security had forced them to head further east to a more remote stretch of the frontier, not to mention parting with a healthy wad of cash for a local 'expert' to guide them through winding mountain passes, where a 4x4 was waiting to pick them up on the other side. By the time they made it to the small town of Sheffield that evening, they were all hot, tired and thirsty. One of Sheffield's local bars was a perfect place to remedy all three problems.

Their two teammates, Dietrich and Mitchell, were waiting for them, both nursing beers and looking annoyingly rested and comfortable. Drake had to admit he was relieved to see them again. It had been a couple of months since the group had parted company, and as much as he hated to admit it, he'd missed them.

With greetings exchanged, Drake duly presented his summary of everything that had happened to bring them here, and his intentions now that they were back in the US.

'Ha!' Dietrich snorted once Drake had finished. He tipped his bottle of beer back – his third so far – draining the remnants. 'Good fucking luck, Ryan. You'll need it with a plan like that.'

A burly, grim-faced man who had served in both the West German intelligence service and the CIA, Jonas Dietrich's personality and sense of humour – if it could be called that – very much matched his appearance. In this case, however, his doubts weren't entirely unwarranted.

'Nobody said this would be easy, Jonas,' Drake replied.

'Okay, say for the sake of argument this contact of yours *isn't* full of shit and *doesn't* have you killed the moment you show up, *and* he's somehow able to get you access to Cain. And through some miracle you manage to take the asshole out *without* getting killed yourself, you're still going to be wanted for murder and treason. And the Circle will still be hunting you. Explain to me how this plan improves our position again?'

'Thanks for the vote of confidence, Dietrich,' Jessica said, none too impressed by his cynical attitude. 'I can see you're a real asset to the team.'

'And what exactly have you done for us, *Mädchen*?' he challenged her. 'Because last time we met, *my* team had to save your ass from a prison cell in Iraq.'

'Actually, they weren't *your* team at all, they were Ryan's,' she pointed out politely. 'And last time we met, you were a barely functioning heroin addict.' Seeing his dark expression, she added, 'Things can change, Mr Dietrich. People can change. Perhaps you should remember that.'

For once in his life, Dietrich seemed to have no comeback. Instead he snorted with grim amusement and rose up from the table, towering over her for a moment.

'I need a piss,' he announced.

With the tense atmosphere somewhat eased by his departure, Mitchell offered a more diplomatic view. 'Dietrich might be an asshole, but he does have a point. That's a long chain of Ifs and Buts you're depending on there, Ryan. A lot of ways to get killed.'

A former investigator with the US Army's Criminal Investigation Division, Olivia Mitchell had become embroiled in the conflict with Cain a couple of years ago. The encounter had nearly cost her life, but a daring rescue by Drake's team had freed her from CIA custody. She'd since become a useful ally, with a clear, analytical mind and a calmness under pressure that helped balance out the more fiery members of the team.

'I know the risks,' Drake assured her. 'But everything we've learned so far tells me Freya was on the level. I believe this man can give us what we need: one good shot at Cain. That's all I'm asking.'

'You still have to get away with it,' she reminded him. 'Killing Cain is no good if it costs your life.'

Drake fixed her with a hard look. 'Like I said, I know the risks.'

'That's why we need you,' Jessica chimed in. 'The more of us there are, the better chance we have.'

'We?' Dietrich said, picking up the conversation as he returned to the table. 'Are you coming in with the rest of us?'

'I'm not afraid to risk my life,' she said firmly. 'Even if you are.'

'Easy, Dietrich,' Frost said, before the man could rise to the bait. 'Try not to be an asshole every day of your life.'

Dietrich glowered at his young colleague but said nothing.

'Look, the first step I'll take alone,' Drake said, leaning forward and looking at each of his comrades in turn. 'If the meeting turns out to be a trap, then I take the fall. If he can't help us, we walk away. But if not, then we decide whether or not to go for it.'

His determined expression, however, made it clear his mind was already made up.

'When's the meeting?' Mitchell asked.

'Tomorrow night in DC,' Drake explained. 'I'll be leaving first thing in the morning. All I need to know is who's with me.'

Silence descended on the table. If they wanted to walk away, he wouldn't blame them. Their contact was dubious to say the least, never mind their odds of success, but it was all they had left. Their last chance.

Frost was first to voice her thoughts. 'Shit, Ryan. You know I'm in.'

Mitchell considered it a moment longer before nodding. 'Okay, let's hear what he has to say.'

With two of the party now committed, all eyes turned to Dietrich, who sipped his beer apparently without concern. Only when Frost aimed a kick at him beneath the table did he finally respond.

'Fuck it,' he grunted irritably. 'I'll go just to watch the fireworks.'

Chapter 36

Ojinaga, Mexico

Antonio Gomez brought his truck to a halt in front of his modest single-storey house and killed the engine, sighing in satisfaction at what had proven to be a very profitable day. The wad of dollar bills from his client still bulged in his jeans pocket.

Gomez was no stranger to guiding people through the arid mountains across the US border, using the remote passes and trails in which he'd played as a boy, but usually his clients came from the south. Refugees from Guatemala, Honduras and Nicaragua, or families from Mexico hoping to find a better life. But this group had been gringos; two white women and a man, at least one of whom was American.

It didn't take much imagination to surmise why they wanted to avoid the law. But then, who cared? Gomez certainly didn't. They were out of his hands, his country was safer for it, and he was a good deal richer.

With that thought fresh in his mind, he stepped out into the warm evening air and strode towards his house, lighting up a cigarette. He might head out later, have a few drinks to celebrate. What the hell, maybe find a woman to fuck. It wasn't hard when you had money in your pocket.

Preoccupied as he was with these promising thoughts, he didn't notice anything out of the ordinary as he unlocked his door and stepped inside. But just as it swung closed behind him, he sensed movement coming from his left and instinctively turned towards it.

Too late. Something swung down against him, crashing against the side of his head. There was a flash of white light, and a vague sensation of falling as the world blurred and darkened around him.

When Gomez woke up, he was bound to a chair in the centre of his kitchen, his hands and feet secured with thick loops of duct tape. His mouth had been covered in similar fashion. The electric light overhead hurt his eyes, exacerbating a throbbing headache.

Vaguely he became aware of a splashing noise, then a harsh chemical smell – one as familiar as it was terrifying. The smell of gasoline.

As his assailant casually emptied a jerrycan of petrol over the floor, panic seized him and he began to strain and twist against his bonds. It was a wasted effort.

Hearing his struggles, his attacker turned to look at him. Another gringo, tall and powerfully built, with dark hair and a malicious smile that seemed accentuated by the faint scar running down one side of his face.

'Ah, good. You're awake,' he said. He spoke fluent Spanish, though his accent was American. 'I've been looking forward to talking.'

Gomez let out a muffled scream as the man turned the jerrycan towards him and emptied the contents across his lap. The cold sting of gasoline immediately soaked into his clothes and skin.

Having finished his work, the American set the can aside, moved to the far end of the kitchen and fished a lighter out of his pocket. Gomez's pathetic screaming intensified as he ignited it, smiling with malicious glee.

The bastard was going to burn him alive. He was about to die in agony.

Then, to his surprise, the American reached for a packet of cigarettes on the kitchen counter – his cigarettes, he noticed – and lit one up.

'That's better,' he said, exhaling a cloud of grey tobacco smoke. 'There's nothing like a good smoke at the end of a long day. And it's been a very long day for me. I had to talk to a lot of your fellow guides to find you, Antonio.'

Gomez felt a chill run through him. The man knew his name.

'I'm going to take off your gag now, my friend,' the American informed him. 'I know you won't be dumb enough to scream, because I don't want to have to burn you alive. You know what human flesh smells like when it's burning?'

Gomez stared at him, shaking and sweating in terror.

'Bacon,' the American explained. 'Can you believe that? Every time I go to a goddamn diner and smell bacon cooking, all I can think of is stupid fucks like you screaming.'

Clamping the cigarette between his lips, he moved towards Gomez, grasped the duct tape secured across his mouth and ripped it away. Gomez let out a gasp as it took some facial hair and a layer of skin with it.

'Please,' he gasped, forcing his stinging lips to move. 'I have money. Take it. Take it all.'

'Ah, come on, man,' the American replied, sounding disappointed. 'Do you really think I came all this way, killed half a dozen other guys like you, just to hold you up for a few hundred bucks?'

Gomez said nothing.

'No, my friend. You have something more valuable. Information. See, I know you guided some people across the border earlier today. Gringos. A man and two women.'

Gomez's eyes grew wide with recognition – an expression the American was quick to pick up on.

'Ah, you *do* remember.' Taking another draw, he exhaled another cloud of smoke into Gomez's face. 'Tell me everything you know about them.'

'I... I...' he stammered, trying to get his thoughts in order.

'Antonio, I need you to work with me, buddy,' the American warned. 'Patience is not one of my virtues.'

'There were three of them, just like you said. A man and two women.'

'Did one of the women look like him? Like a sibling?'

'Yes.'

'And the other?'

'She was... short, small. With dark hair.'

A smile spread across the American's face. 'Where were they going?'

'I don't know.'

The smile quickly faded. 'Come on, Antonio. Don't let me down now.'

'I told you, I don't know! I had a man pick them up on the other side. His job was to take them where they wanted to go.'

'What was his name?'

'A truck driver. H-his name is Ruiz.'

The American must have taken Gomez's cell phone while he was unconscious, because he produced it and flicked through the contacts list until he found the right entry.

'Is this his cell number?' he asked, holding the device up.

'Yes. He can tell you where they went.'

Satisfied, the American slipped the phone into his pocket. 'That's good, Antonio. You've been real helpful.'

Drawing a silenced weapon from behind his back, the American brought it to bear in one swift, efficient motion and pulled the trigger, putting a round straight through Gomez's forehead. The man barely even saw it coming.

A short while later, Hawkins exited through the back door and quietly slipped into an alleyway, the gathering gloom of dusk illuminated by the glow of the flames consuming Gomez's house. By the time firefighters arrived from two towns away, there would be little left of the building and its owner but smouldering ash.

Leaving the scene at a brisk walk, Hawkins put through a call on his own phone. 'I need you to trace a cell number.'

Chapter 37

Sheffield, Texas

Dusk had fallen on southern Texas, the first stars already glimmering in the eastern sky as the last light of sun illuminated a few high, trailing clouds far above. It was a quiet, peaceful sort of evening in a sleepy town far from anywhere.

With a long and tiring day behind them, and an even longer day ahead tomorrow, Drake knew he ought to turn in soon. Instead he found himself on a low, rocky hillock not far from their motel, looking out across the sprawling desert.

Tomorrow night at around this time, he would meet with his contact in DC. And despite his reassuring words earlier, he had no way of knowing what might happen. He was risking his life on the word of a dead woman he'd barely known, but desperately wanted to believe in now.

And yet, despite the challenges that lay ahead tomorrow, his thoughts kept drifting back to a different woman. A woman who was out there at this very moment, pursuing a mission of her own. A woman who might hate him for the rest of her life.

Would he see her again, he wondered? Would they encounter each other one more time before this was all over? And what would happen if they did?

He heard the crunch of footsteps approaching.

'Doing your Luke Skywalker thing again?' Jessica asked.

Drake raised an eyebrow. 'Luke Skywalker?'

'You know, the binary sunset, poignant music, soul searching...?' Sensing she was getting nowhere, she shook her head. 'Forget it, never thought I'd be a bigger nerd than my brother.'

Drake smiled as she lowered herself to the ground beside him.

'It *is* beautiful here, though,' she said quietly.

'Pretty different from Wales in springtime, eh?'

'Just a little. Can't say I miss the rain.'

She was quiet for a time, content to share his company in silence and think her own thoughts. But before too long, she decided to voice them.

'Listen, about tomorrow...'

'I have to do it,' he said firmly.

'I know.' She paused. 'I want to go to the meeting with you.'

Drake turned to look at her then. 'Jess...'

'I know I'm not... trained like the others. I'm not a soldier. But this is as much my fight as it is yours. I lost just as much as you did. I need to look him in the eye and ask him why she died.'

'Even if you get those answers, it won't bring her back.'

'Neither will killing Cain,' she reminded him. 'But you're doing it anyway.'

'Because I have to. There's nothing else left. Nothing except you,' Drake said quietly. 'I could never forgive myself if something happened to you.'

'And you think I'd feel any different if I lost you?' she asked. 'You think it's all right to put *your* life at risk, but not mine?'

'Of course not,' he conceded. 'But we do what we have to. We risk what we *have to*. No more than that.' He laid a hand on her arm. 'You'll get your answers, Jess. I promise you that. But this is something I have to do alone.'

His sister glanced away, her hair stirred by the breeze. Reluctantly she nodded.

'Come on,' Drake said, standing up. 'Let's get some rest.'

–

The convoy of three blacked-out SUVs rocketed down the empty desert road, bouncing over hidden bumps and rumbling through potholes, headlights jumping up and down with the movement. Their normally gleaming paintwork was dulled by the dust and sand kicked up by their wheels.

They were closing in on their destination fast. A tiny speck of a town out in the middle of nowhere, 50 miles north of the Mexican border. Well away from Federal law enforcement, and an ideal spot to rest up before moving on.

'Heads up,' the driver called out. 'We're two minutes out.'

Hawkins nodded. 'Gear up. Let's get this done!'

After tracing the cell phone belonging to Gomez's associate Ruiz, Hawkins had dropped in on the man and made sure he told him everything he knew. It was amazing how persuasive a can of gasoline could be, particularly with your girlfriend bound up next to you. Her death had been collateral damage, but Hawkins could live with it.

As the convoy approached the small town up ahead, weapons and body armour were checked, and radios tested. Hawkins savoured the atmosphere of focussed, controlled tension as the moment of deployment drew near. It was like a drug, powerful and intoxicating.

'Thirty seconds,' the driver warned. A couple of hundred yards ahead, the neon lights of a motel advertising vacancies stood at the edge of the main road, flickering garish red and green in the darkness.

They had called ahead to follow up on the tip, and sure enough the hotel clerk had confirmed that three people had checked in that afternoon – a man and two women. Two of the group were British.

'Slow it down,' Hawkins instructed. 'We don't want to tip them off.'

–

Lying atop the sheets in his cheap, uncomfortably warm motel room, Drake stirred and rolled over, awoken from his troubled sleep. His eyes opened slowly, taking in the dimly lit room, the faint glow of streetlights peeking through gaps in the blinds.

For a moment he watched and listened, allowing his senses to tune into his surroundings. All was quiet and still, save for the low rhythmic hum of the air conditioner. Outside, he could hear nothing at all. No cars, no movement. The town slept.

But his intuition told him otherwise. Something wasn't right.

Sitting up, Drake reached beneath the pillow and removed the Browning 9mm he'd stashed there, quietly pulling back the slide half an inch or so. There was just enough light to make out the glint of brass in the chamber.

Thus armed, he slipped out of bed and crept across the room, heading for the window. Even as he drew near, he could feel the hairs on the back of his neck bristling, and gripped the weapon tighter in response.

This was it. All three SUVs pulled into the motel parking lot, killing their lights to avoid disturbing anyone in the rooms facing onto it. Braking sharply, the assault teams piled out, one circling around to the rear of the building to cover possible escape routes, while the other two converged on the accommodation block from two directions, covering each other as they advanced.

'Talk to me, Team Three. Any movement?' Hawkins hissed as he crossed the tarmac lot, approaching rooms three and four, where Drake's group were staying.

'Nothing out back,' the leader of Team Three reported. 'No contacts.'

'Copy that.'

Mounting the covered walkway that provided access to the rooms, Hawkins and his team advanced from one side while the second fireteam came from the other.

Each of the rooms was accessed by a single point of entry, with no connecting doorways between them. One way in, one way out.

Reaching out with his thumb, Hawkins gently switched the fire selector on his MP5 submachine gun to full automatic.

He took a breath, then issued a single command. 'Go.'

The door flew open, the lock blasted apart by a breaching shotgun. Hawkins was moving before the shattered fragments of wood had even hit the ground, forcing his way through the doorway, his laser-sighted weapon sweeping the room before homing in on the bed, where a huddled figure lay beneath the sheets.

Without hesitation, Hawkins brought the submachine gun around and opened fire. The MP5 spat a long burst of silenced rounds, the mattress thudding with the impacts, clumps of foam padding and feathers flying into the air.

But there was no scream of shock and pain, no sudden splash of red from torn flesh. No indication that he'd just ended a life.

Moving forward, Hawkins grasped the edge of the bedsheets and yanked them aside, exposing a small pile of torn and singed pillows, placed there to look just like a body.

'Son of a bitch,' he said, turning away in disgust. 'Nice move, Ryan.'

Unlatching the door, Drake eased it open and stepped outside, sliding the gun down the back of his trousers. He remained motionless for the next few seconds, watching and listening.

Beyond the motel parking lot and a couple of residential houses, the ground sloped upwards to a low, brush-covered hill overlooking the town. The weak glow of nearby streetlights illuminated the road and parking lot, but not much else.

Overhead, tiny flies lazily circled one of the motel's exterior lights. Further off, he heard the distant clicks and chirrups of cicadas and crickets.

He inhaled, seeking any unusual odours, but found only the faint scent of garbage in the dumpsters out back, waiting to be emptied.

Wary of the man hired to pick them up, Drake had made a point of being taken to a different town named Juno about thirty miles away, even booking a couple of rooms in the motel there to maintain the illusion, before hitchhiking to Sheffield. It was unlikely anyone could have tracked them here, but that didn't rule it out.

He couldn't shake the feeling that he was being watched, that somewhere beyond the pools of dirty sodium light, a pair of eyes were following his every move. But to whom did they belong? Friend, or enemy?

He remained there for a good ten minutes, watching and wrestling against his better judgement, questioning whether fatigue and paranoia were playing tricks on his mind.

As time passed and nothing happened, the feeling began to wane. Drake shook his head and reluctantly returned to his room. Sleep, however, remained elusive.

A dark figure stirred from its vantage point on the hill overlooking the motel, rising silently from the ground like a ghost and moving off into the night.

Leaving Drake alone. For now.

Chapter 38

Don's Auto Salvage, situated on the south side of DC, had once been a thriving garage and repair shop. But the financial crisis and subsequent recession had left the owner with mounting debts, forcing him to close his business and sell off his assets.

The building was now little more than an empty shell, damp and rusting, its roof leaking in places. The kind of building that people walked right by without interest. Just another failed business venture in a country filled with them.

All in all, it wasn't much of a base from which to stage the most dangerous mission of their lives, but it was big enough to fit a couple of vehicles inside, and the walled yard out back offered a degree of privacy. And more importantly, the owner was an old friend of Frost's who used to do repair work on her bike. A quick phone call had been enough to convince him to part with the keys.

It was here, in this most inauspicious of settings, that Drake and his small team were now working to create a makeshift comms centre, armoury and motor pool. His meeting was now less than an hour away, and there was much to be done.

'Okay, listen up,' Frost said, finishing up with the tracking device she'd secured inside the lining of his jacket. 'This is a Mode 7 satellite tracker operating on an encrypted frequency, designed to go passive in the event of a security scan.'

She held her laptop up to demonstrate. And sure enough, a pulsing green dot indicated the location of the tracking unit, projected onto a street map of DC.

'Great. What does any of that mean?' Jessica asked.

'It'll stop transmitting if someone tries to search me for bugs,' Drake explained.

'More or less,' Frost agreed. 'The downside is a less powerful signal. You go inside a heavy concrete structure, or underground, I won't be able to track you. Same with your comms unit.'

Opening a small plastic case, she held out a little flesh-coloured earbud that resembled a miniaturised hearing aid. Designed to fit inside the ear canal, it would be virtually invisible to anything short of an invasive search.

'Isn't there anything you can do?' Jessica asked as Drake fitted it.

Frost held up her hands. 'Can't change the laws of physics. You can have small and covert, or big and powerful. Pick one.'

'This'll do fine,' Drake assured her, tapping the comms unit to activate it. 'Radio check. Testing. Testing.'

'Got it,' Frost confirmed, checking the output on her computer.

Just as she said this, an odd rumbling sound echoed up from deep beneath them, the vibrations shivering through the old building's structure. A half-finished cup of coffee on the workbench rattled slightly, tiny ripples appearing on its surface.

'What's that?' Jessica asked, glancing around for the source of the disturbance. As far as she knew, Virginia wasn't prone to earthquakes.

'Subway train,' Frost explained as the vibrations and noise faded away. 'One of the main Metro lines runs right beneath this place.'

With Drake's tracking and communications set up, Dietrich stepped forward with a compact semi-automatic handgun.

'Here,' he said, holding it out. '9mm Glock 26. Small but effective. It won't penetrate body armour, but it's the best concealed carry weapon we've got.'

Drake regarded it, then shook his head. 'No weapons.'

The veteran operative frowned. 'Tired of being alive, Ryan?'

'That was our agreement. No weapons.'

'You really think he'll honour it?' Mitchell chimed in dubiously. 'I'd rather have it and not need it.'

Drake looked at them both. 'If he wants me dead, then he'll make it happen. One Glock isn't going to change that.'

Neither of them could think of an answer to that. Sensing their wavering confidence in the meeting, Drake carried on.

'Have a little faith. He wouldn't go through all this just to kill me.'

With the matter decided, if not entirely resolved, Drake snatched up the jacket Frost had prepared and threw it on, turning towards the used car they'd brought inside. They'd bought it from a dealership in one of the less affluent areas of town, paying cash in exchange for minimal paperwork, and had already swapped out the license plates.

The only question now was where the meeting would take place. Drake had been told only the city and the date. The rest would be given when it was required. He knew the drill, and the reasoning behind it, but it didn't make him feel much better.

'Ryan.'

Jessica had approached, wishing to speak in private. She looked tense and uneasy, and he didn't blame her. He just hoped she didn't want to revisit last night's debate.

'You know I have to do this alone, Jess.'

'I know,' she conceded. 'I just… want you to be careful.'

He laid his hands on her shoulders and looked his sister square in the eye. 'I'm going to find him, I'm going to get the answers we need, and I'm coming back in one piece. Okay?'

Swallowing, she nodded. 'Okay.'

On Frost's workbench nearby, Drake's encrypted cell phone buzzed with an incoming message. Hurrying over, he picked it up and read it. As expected, it was from his contact, giving the first waypoint in his journey.

'We're on,' he announced. 'Let's get it done.'

Chapter 39

CIA Headquarters, Langley

'Talk to me, Chris,' Franklin said as soon as he and Kennedy were alone, making their way across the central square of the Agency's main campus. The look on Kennedy's face told him the man had news for him, and he wasn't to be disappointed.

'Some serious shit went down in London,' he began. 'The building they assaulted was put on complete lockdown after the attack, total news blackout. We did some digging into the place, and it looks like it was owned by a front company. No records of any business dealings or activity in all the years they were operating.'

'Okay, but a front for what?'

'We've heard of a place like this once before, during an op in Ukraine. Highly secured but totally invisible. A black hole of intel that everyone can see but nobody knows about, like it doesn't even exist.' He paused, before adding, 'I think Ryan was in a Vault.'

Franklin halted abruptly. Vaults were reserved for the highest of high-level operatives; major global players with the cash and the connections to qualify for access. The idea that Ryan Drake would have gained entry to such a place was outlandish at best. The further notion that Cain might have sanctioned a raid against such a protected space was even more so.

'How could Ryan have found a place like that?'

Kennedy threw up his hands. 'That, I can't tell you. But whatever he found in there must have been pretty fucking important, because Cain mobilised just about every resource in London to stop him.' Glancing around, he added, 'I spoke to a buddy of mine seconded to British intelligence. He says the op was led by an American with top-level clearance, the authority to requisition anything he needed.'

'Who, exactly?'

'Man by the name of Hawkins.'

Franklin felt his heart rate rise further. Jason Hawkins, Cain's own personal attack dog. The man responsible for a string of murders, assassinations and unsanctioned operations all across the globe.

'You know him, then?' Kennedy remarked, reading his expression.

'Yeah,' Franklin replied quietly. 'Yeah, I know him.'

The Shepherd team leader studied him a moment longer before carrying on. 'Well, you should know that Hawkins bailed out of there not long afterwards.'

'Where did he go?'

'Back here, to the US. He was on a dark flight laid on by the Agency, so there was no record of his transfer, but we did some digging and tracked it to Laughlin Air Force Base in Texas.'

'Laughlin?' Franklin said, scanning his knowledge of military bases in that area. 'That's right on the Mexican border.'

'It is.'

'Son of a bitch,' Franklin gasped.

'I know. Join the dots on this one, and...'

'They're trying to stop Ryan coming into the country,' Franklin finished for him. 'He must be trying to cross over the border from Mexico.'

'Yeah, but what does he want?'

'Cain,' Franklin decided, the disjointed pieces of the puzzle suddenly coming together. 'He's coming to DC. He's coming after Marcus Cain.'

Silence descended between them as the implications of this settled on each man.

'Look, I know you only brought me in to do some digging, but we're talking about a credible threat on the CIA director's life,' he pointed out. 'God knows, I got no love for Cain. The man may be dirty, he may be all kinds of things, and he ought to answer for that. But this isn't the way to do it.'

'Who else knows about this?' Franklin asked, his mind racing.

Kennedy hesitated, struck by the man's change in demeanour. 'Just my team.'

'And you trust them?'

'With my life,' the team leader promised. 'They're solid.'

'Good. Keep it that way.'

Kennedy was silent for the next few seconds, clearly unhappy with his instructions. 'Dan, if something happens, if it comes out that we knew about this and did nothing...'

'I know the situation,' Franklin shot back. 'And so does Cain. That's why he's got his people all over it.'

'So what do we do?'

Franklin was quiet, trying to decide which was the lesser of two evils.

'We wait,' he said at length. 'Stay on it. Keep looking for Ryan, and call me as soon as you have something.'

Chapter 40

The Washington National Cathedral was a massive neo-Gothic structure situated far to the north-west of central DC. Its towering facades,
flying buttresses, soaring windows and grand columned interior had
all been constructed to mirror the great religious edifices of medieval
Europe. And yet the building itself was barely a century old. A valiant
but unnecessary attempt at historical splendour by a young country
lacking an identity of its own.

The place, however, had seen a lot of use in the past hundred years, a
favoured site for state funerals and other important memorials. Ronald
Reagan's funeral had been conducted there just a few years earlier.

The cathedral was open to visitors throughout most of the week,
but now, in the early evening, most of the tourists had trickled out.

That suited Drake just fine as he advanced down the central nave,
passing row after row of empty pews. He kept to the right, using the
pillars as cover and sticking to the general shadows as much as possible.
He was acutely aware of how exposed he was in this place, how easily
this could turn out to be an ambush, leaving him with few avenues of
escape.

There were no guarantees in what he was doing. He could only
hope that his mother's contact proved to be genuine.

Approaching the far end of the massive vaulted room, Drake paused
for a moment, listening and looking around, allowing himself to tune
into his new environment. He heard some hushed words between a
couple of elderly sightseers over by the main altar, their conversation
magnified by the room's acoustics, but otherwise all was quiet. The air
was cool and dry, and smelled of dusty stone.

No sign of any threats.

Satisfied that nothing appeared out of the ordinary, Drake turned
left at the transept, where a set of stone steps led down to the cathedral's
crypt. The passage was blocked by a red rope with a brass plaque that
read, *Closed for Renovation Work – No Unauthorised Entry.*

Drake slipped past this minor barrier and descended into the depths.

–

Jonas Dietrich sat parked on the street opposite the cathedral, the afternoon sun glinting off the towering stonework. Having tailed Drake across town, he'd finally parked up and watched as his companion ventured alone through the cathedral's huge carved entranceway. Alone and unarmed, and meeting with a man of unknown intentions – in his view, Drake was either extremely brave or extremely foolish.

Then again, the two things weren't mutually exclusive.

Reaching up, he hit his radio transmitter to report in. 'He's inside.'

'Copy that,' Frost's tinny voice buzzed in his ear. 'Any sign of activity?'

'Sure, but I thought I'd sit back and watch.'

Theoretically Dietrich was there as backup, with an MP7 machine pistol stowed in the car's glovebox, though none of them were under any illusions that he'd be able to save the day if things turned sour. The best he could hope for was to cover the entrance and report on what he saw.

'Very funny. Sit tight, call out if you see anything.'

'Roger that.'

Shifting position, Dietrich resumed his tense vigil.

–

Drake descended the steps slowly and carefully, his senses straining to detect anything out of the ordinary. The primal instinct that once kept our distant ancestors alive in a harsh world is still remarkably adept at discerning potential threats. The problem is that centuries of safety and comfort have dulled our conscious minds to its subtle warnings. One of the skills an operative like Drake learned was to heed this primitive but effective warning system. In this case, however, there was nothing to concern him yet.

Soon enough, the stairway bottomed out into a large chamber deep in the bowels of the building. Despite their sinister connotations, the crypts of most cathedrals are in fact quite unremarkable places, often serving a plainly utilitarian function. In the case of the Washington

Cathedral, however, the crypt actually contained an extensive series of chambers and no fewer than three underground chapels, allowing people to worship or reflect in relative privacy, away from the larger crowds upstairs.

Creeping forward, Drake advanced deeper into the crypt, following the signs for the Chapel of St Joseph of Arimathea. He was neither a religious scholar, nor familiar with the cathedral layout, but he did know that this particular chapel was located at the base of the cathedral's massive central tower, making it the heart of the entire complex.

As he emerged into the vaulted underground chamber, lit by soft lights placed around the perimeter to create an atmosphere of quiet reverence and reflection, it was easy to tell from the huge, squat supporting columns that this place was structurally critical. Thousands of tonnes of stonework rested on those four pillars.

He stopped, held his breath and waited.

It took all of five seconds to realise he wasn't alone down here. In the cool, dry, sterile air, he caught the faint scent of aftershave. And more than that, he could sense he was being watched.

'You asked to meet,' he announced, his voice echoing around the chapel. 'Here I am.'

'Here you are,' a voice repeated.

Drake watched as a figure emerged from the shadows on the far side of the room. A figure that quickly resolved itself into the shape of a man; slender and well dressed, his greying hair neatly combed.

'Hello, Ryan,' Richard Starke said. 'It's good to meet you, at last.'

–

'Goddamn it,' Frost said under her breath.

The atmosphere inside the disused garage was tense and fraught as the team waited for news on Drake, none of them quite sure what to do with themselves.

Jessica was by her side in moments. 'What is it?'

'Lost his signal,' the young woman replied, checking the tracking software. 'No comms, no GPS.' She shook her head. 'Ryan's off the grid.'

'We knew this might happen,' Mitchell reasoned, though she was no less anxious for her friend's safety. 'His contact chose that location specifically. I guess he didn't want anyone snooping on them.'

Frost clenched her jaw unhappily. 'I don't like it. Shit doesn't feel right.'

'We could go in,' Dietrich suggested over the radio. 'Recover Ryan and his contact, and bring them back for interrogation. Then we'll have all the time we need to question him.'

'Really?' Mitchell asked. 'You think a guy like that would let himself be abducted?'

Dietrich was silent for a second or so. 'He wouldn't have a choice in the matter.'

Frost was torn, struggling to decide between her concern for Drake and the obvious dangers of blowing the entire operation with a hasty assault.

'Give him a chance,' Jessica said, much to her surprise. 'Ryan knows what he's doing.'

Frost glanced up at her. 'That's what I'm afraid of.'

–

Drake watched as the director of the NSA moved out into the centre of the chamber, his hands at his sides, eyes on the only other man in the room.

Unlike the director of the CIA, who often found himself at the centre of various controversies and investigations, Starke had spent much less time in the public eye. Drake had never been in the same room as him, and couldn't recall much news coverage on the man.

What little he did know had come courtesy of his short official biography. As was mandatory for the NSA, Starke was from a military background, graduating top of his class at West Point in 1973 and going on to serve nearly two decades in the US Army. Eventually he'd transitioned over to the National Security Agency, where he rose quickly through the ranks. Unusually quickly, from what Drake understood.

Because of the complex machinations of government positions like this, Starke was also the de facto head of the Central Security Service, US Cyber Command, and technically held the rank of a four-star general, though he had long since swapped his dress uniform for a conservative, unremarkable civilian suit.

A career military man who walked and dressed like a civilian. One of the most powerful men in America, who looked as unassuming as a low-level office manager.

'I'm unarmed, and I came alone,' Starke said in a calm, composed voice. 'Just as we agreed.' He halted and looked Drake up and down. 'I assume you reciprocated?'

'If I wanted you dead, you would be.'

'I don't doubt it.'

The older man's lined features betrayed a trace of a smile. 'You know, I was beginning to wonder if you'd ever make contact. After all this time, I figured her message must have been lost.'

'I've been busy.'

'So I've noticed. Caused quite a stir over the past few years. There are a lot of people who want to see you dead.'

'I get that a lot,' Drake assured him. 'But here I am.'

'Here you are,' Starke agreed. 'So now that we've established what we're *not* here to do, let's talk about why we *are* here. What do you want from me, Ryan Drake?'

'You worked with my mother,' Drake stated. 'Freya Shaw.'

Starke nodded. 'You look a little like her, you know. I didn't really appreciate the resemblance until now.'

Drake ignored that. 'The two of you were part of the Circle.'

'If that's how you'd choose to describe it,' Starke observed coolly. 'What exactly did she tell you?'

'Enough.'

'Oh, I doubt that,' Starke promised him.

'Then why don't you help me out?' Drake suggested. 'What were the two of you doing together? What was she trying to achieve?'

Smiling faintly, Starke moved over to one of the pews that encircled the room and eased himself into it with a sigh. 'That's… a long story.'

'I'm used to long stories, mate.'

The NSA director cocked a greying brow. 'Fair enough.'

Leaning back in the pew, he regarded Drake for a moment or two before he began.

'You're quite right, of course,' he admitted. 'Your mother and I served in what you refer to as the Circle for almost as long as you've been alive. Long enough to see the changes that took place.'

Drake's eyes narrowed. 'What sort of changes?'

'The organisation was formed with two major objectives. Firstly, to facilitate the collapse of the USSR and bring about the end of the Cold War, using any means necessary. And secondly, to establish a new world order favourable to American interests for the foreseeable future.'

'So what went wrong?'

'Wrong?' Starke gave a resigned shrug. 'They won. That's what went wrong.'

'I don't understand.'

'The Circle's entire purpose was to win not just the Cold War, but the peace that followed,' Starke explained. 'Without an enemy to overcome, the organisation began to stagnate and drift. Their goals shifted from using power as means to end division and conflict, to using division and conflict as a means to accrue more power. They sowed the seeds of proxy wars and revolutions all over the world, to take advantage of the chaos and instability that followed. The rise of the internet gave them the ability to control global communications and reshape public opinion. And as their power and influence grew, so did their ambition and hubris. I imagine you're familiar with the old maxim of power corrupting?'

'I've heard of it,' Drake replied, thinking of the man poised to become head of the biggest intelligence agency in the world.

'The Circle weren't immune to that either. I saw it, and so did your mother. We knew we couldn't simply resign and walk away, so... we resolved to do something about it.'

Drake moved forward, approaching the NSA director. 'What did she do?'

'Your mother believed the Circle could be steered back on the correct path by altering their leadership. She felt they needed a fresh perspective. Someone... less influenced by the past. In this case, a young operative recruited into the Agency.'

Drake's heart began to beat faster. 'Anya.'

'Correct,' he confirmed. 'Anya was quite unlike the rest of the Circle. A soldier, a spy, a person with courage, intelligence and a natural flair for leadership. But more importantly, a sense of conviction and morality. She was your mother's biggest hope, and she convinced me to help her. Together we saw to it that Anya grew quickly in power and influence, to the point where the Circle began to take notice. They agreed to meet with her, intending to bring her into the fold.'

'So what happened?' Drake asked, though he sensed he knew the answer.

'Marcus Cain happened,' Starke said grimly. 'He knew that if Anya was inducted into the Inner Circle, he never would be. So he turned her own unit against her, convinced its leader that she was planning to betray them.'

Drake knew this part of the story well enough, having heard it from Anya herself. Munro, her most trusted lieutenant, had attempted a coup against her. In the resulting bloodbath, Task Force Black practically tore itself apart.

'The Circle's faith in Anya was broken after that. And your mother,' Starke added. 'She knew neither of them would reach such a position of influence again.'

'So what did she do?'

Starke spread his hands. 'What *could* she do? She accepted it. Meanwhile, with Anya neutralised, Cain became the favourite. Your mother knew that if he joined the Inner Circle, there would be no limit to his power. She knew she had to stop him. He knew it too, so he recruited *you* into the Agency as a precaution.'

Drake closed his eyes as the truth dawned on him. 'Leverage.'

'Precisely. If Freya made a move against him, he would take revenge on you. And so the balance was maintained, for a while at least.'

Drake hadn't known. He hadn't suspected the real reason his mother had never tried to reach out to him, never attempted to make contact. She'd been prevented from doing so by Cain himself.

'By 2007, Cain was a rising star in both the Circle and the Agency. But he also had a lot of loose ends to tie up: men whose services he'd used to rise to power; men who could compromise him. He needed someone with the right skills to take them out, who couldn't possibly implicate him if they were discovered. In other words, he needed Anya. She was still alive in a Russian prison, so he broke her out, knowing she would kill the men he needed killed in search of answers. And who better to break her out than you?'

Drake was obliged to sit down on the pew beside him at that point. His head was whirling as the complex machinations of the past few years were at last laid bare, outlined in curt, efficient fashion as if Starke were a history teacher recounting some long-forgotten battle. The sheer scope and complexity of Cain's plans was simply staggering.

'But with Anya free and you now working against Cain, your mother sensed an opportunity. A chance to join forces with Anya and take Cain down together. At least, that's what she planned.'

Starke was silent once she'd finished outlining her plan, staring pensively into the flames flickering in the fireplace beside him. She had travelled all the way to his private residence to present her plan, arriving late at night.

Thoughtful and meticulous as always, she could sense Starke's potent mind churning through everything she had told him, considering the risks and the rewards, the variables and the possibilities.

Freya didn't rush him. Starke was a man who spoke when he was ready, who waited until he'd thoroughly arrived at a conclusion before voicing his thoughts.

'Are you sure this is what you want?' he finally asked.

'I am.'

She knew it was possible to reach out to Anya through their old communication channels. Whether or not the former Agency operative would agree to the meeting was uncertain, but she had to try.

'Anya put her faith in you once before, and it didn't work out well,' Starke warned her. 'She won't have forgotten that.'

Freya sighed and nodded, the sting of Cain's betrayal still cutting deep after nearly a decade. 'That's what I'm counting on. She's angry, she's dangerous and she wants revenge. Maybe we can use that.'

'Suppose she takes out that revenge on you. What then?'

Freya took a drink of the Scotch he'd poured for her. The potent drink brought little comfort, but it helped take the edge off her restless thoughts.

'Then I die,' she conceded, her eyes turning towards the fire.

She sighed, thinking of the long series of tumultuous events that had led up to this decision. The triumphs and the failures, the alliances and the betrayals. And all of it amounting to one thing – nothing.

'I'm sixty years old, Richard. I'm an old woman,' she reflected. 'This may be my last chance to make a difference.'

Starke turned towards her, struck by the finality in her tone. 'You helped reshape the world, Freya. Nobody can take that away from you.'

'And I flattered myself that I'd made it a better place,' she remarked sharply. 'I didn't… we didn't. It was sheer arrogance to presume something like that. The world would have been better off without me, without the Circle, without the mess we've created.'

'Do you really think it can be undone now, after all this time?'

'I don't know,' she admitted. 'But I think the world deserves a chance to find out.'

Starke sighed and nodded, recognising that she wouldn't be swayed from her course. 'Let's just hope it's ready when the time comes.'

Freya drained the last of her Scotch. 'There's one thing I need you to do for me.'

'Name it.'

'In case… something goes wrong, I left a message for my son, Ryan. I told him to find you. If that time ever comes… do what you can to help him. Please.'

'Of course.' Starke laid a comforting hand on her shoulder. 'I won't let you down.'

–

'I warned her against it, but she was adamant,' Starke said, shaking his head sadly. 'Freya wasn't the kind of woman to change her mind.'

Of that, Drake had little doubt. As he was discovering, Freya Shaw had proven to be an extraordinary woman, not just in her accomplishments, but in her strength of character and resolve. Willing to risk everything, to sacrifice anything for what she believed in.

'I think she saw it as a chance at redemption. Your mother had carried the guilt of what happened to Anya for years, never forgave herself for it. She believed that taking down Cain together would help make things right. That was her hope.' He looked down at his hands, clasped in his lap. 'But it never happened.'

North Wales, UK – May 1st, 2009

Yanking her arm free, Freya whirled around to face her adversary, eyes gleaming with defiance. She wouldn't give them the satisfaction of putting a bullet through the back of her head.

'You look me in the eye, you coward,' she said, staring right at them. 'Look me in the eye when you pull the trigger.'

If she'd expected her words to strike a chord, to engender some kind of reaction, she was to be disappointed. A second came and went. A second broken only by the sigh of the evening breeze, and distant hoot of an owl, and the hammering of Freya's heart.

She saw the barrel of a weapon raised, saw the long snout of a silencer gleaming in the thin sliver of moonlight.

Freya let out a breath. 'Of all the people to do this—'

A 9mm slug passing through her chest silenced that sentence for her. She let out a strangled gasp, as if in surprise, then fell backward and collapsed to the ground, her body skidding down the rocky slope until it came to rest in the pool of stagnant water.

—

Starke let out a breath, his gaze unfocussed as he replayed an old memory. 'Your mother was willing to risk everything to stop Cain. And in the end, it cost her everything.'

'You think he had her killed,' Drake prompted him.

'It's the only logical conclusion.'

Drake leaned forward, staring him hard in the eye. 'You're sure it was Cain?'

Starke turned to regard him. 'The balance of power had changed. Freya had become a threat to him, and Marcus only knows one way to handle threats like that. Just like Carpenter, just like Surovsky, just like everyone who stands against him.' He nodded. 'Yes, I'm sure it was him.'

Drake leaned back against the pew, his mind racing along with his heart. He'd long suspected Cain's involvement in his mother's death, but knowing the circumstances that had led to it was another matter altogether. The more he learned about his mother, the more he realised how wrong he'd been about her.

'You knew this, and you let him get away with it,' Drake said, his shock and turmoil crystallising into the most inevitable emotion of all – anger. 'You stood back and did nothing.'

Starke considered that carefully for a second or two, not as a man fearing for his life and wondering what plea or intimation might save him, but as someone genuinely reflecting on their own actions and motivations.

'Yes,' he conceded. 'I did.'

'Why?'

'Because I didn't want to end up like her,' Starke said, a harder edge in his voice now. 'Marcus Cain is an enemy unlike any other. Every time you make a move, he's three steps ahead of you. Every plan you come up with, he has a contingency for it. He's been playing this game almost as long as you've been alive, he knows every trick, anticipates every strategy. That's why he's still standing when everyone else around him has fallen. What can you expect to do against a man like that?'

Drake's gaze didn't waver for a second. Everything Starke had said was perfectly true, as he knew from bitter experience. Marcus Cain was a man of immense cunning and intelligence, commanding virtually unlimited resources and unparalleled power, with no weakness or compassion left to hold him back.

All of that was true, but none of it mattered to Drake any longer.

'I'm going to kill the bastard. And you're going to help me.'

Chapter 41

An hour later, Drake returned to the disused garage with Dietrich in tow, giving the team a hasty summary of what had taken place at the cathedral – everything he'd learned from Starke, and the plan he'd put forward.

Needless to say, the revelations about their mother hit Jessica particularly hard. Drake could see his sister struggling with her emotions as he relayed her final conversation with Starke. He would speak with her more later, but for now there were more urgent matters to discuss.

'He's willing to help us,' he concluded. 'He recognises the threat Cain poses now, not just to us but to everyone if he joins the Inner Circle. The only way to stop him is to take him out.'

'Well that's great, but what can he actually do?' Frost asked. 'No offence, but he didn't do jack shit for your mom.'

'That was different. He underestimated Cain's reach, and he trusted Freya to cover her own back.' Drake sighed unhappily. 'He was wrong on both counts. He won't make that mistake again.'

'Which brings us back to the original question,' Mitchell pointed out. 'What can Starke do for us?'

'He's the director of the NSA, and a senior member of the Circle. He can give us intel on Cain's movements and communications that nobody else has access to. And he can make contact with the man himself. That gives us what we need – a target window.'

The most fundamental aspect of any assassination was knowing where and when your target was going to be vulnerable. Security and physical defences could be overcome, but finding that precious window of opportunity was crucial.

For this reason, presidents, heads of state and even high-profile celebrities employed misdirection as their principle defence. Avoiding routine and regularity, they never travelled the same route twice, often using multiple vehicles with fake passengers to confuse pursuits and confound ambushes.

Marcus Cain was no different. The man was well aware of the enemies he'd amassed, and made use of every defensive measure in the arsenal. His home was like a fortress, impossible to assault without heavy casualties. He rarely ventured beyond the highly secure environment at Langley, and when he did, he was never without an armed escort. The only window of opportunity was when he was on the move. Now, with Starke's help, they might just have it.

'But even if we can listen in on him, how do we get to him?' Jessica asked. 'He must have security.'

'We can't get within a mile of Langley,' Frost agreed. 'Even if we could, we'd never make it out.'

'We don't need to. There's one place we know Cain has to be soon,' Drake said, bringing up a news article on his cell phone and holding it up. 'Here.'

The title of the article read: *A New Era – CIA director expected to be confirmed soon.*

'Son of a bitch,' Frost muttered as the implications sank in.

'The Select Committee is going to vote to confirm him anytime now,' Drake explained. 'Cain has to be there for the confirmation hearing.'

'He'll be vulnerable,' Dietrich realised.

Their timing was indeed fortuitous, arriving in DC mere days before he was expected to be sworn in. Marcus Cain's rise to power might, if they were lucky, also prove to be his undoing.

'The confirmation ceremony is done in the Capitol Building,' Drake went on. 'We can't hope to get past the security there, but Cain has to get to and from that location, probably by motorcade. If we can track him, that's our best chance to make the hit.'

'Jesus,' Mitchell said, rapidly considering the implications of his plan. 'Taking out an Agency motorcade in the middle of DC...'

'I know,' Drake said, grimly acknowledging the potential for collateral damage. Not just amongst Cain's protective detail, but also any DC civilians who might get caught in the crossfire. 'This could get messy.'

'Is that who we are now?' Frost asked bluntly.

'Nobody's saying this will be easy—'

'You're talking about starting a war in the middle of Washington,' the young woman protested. 'That's not "*difficult*". That's insane.'

'It's our best shot at ending this. Maybe our only one.'

'Not if you get killed in the process, and take half the city with you,' Jessica chimed in. 'This isn't supposed to be a bloodbath, Ryan.'

Drake let his breath out slowly, considering this. A protracted firefight on the streets of Washington would almost certainly result in heavy casualties, not to mention drawing in law enforcement and military units from all over the city. But there was no alternative that he could think of.

'You said yourself, we can't get within a mile of Langley,' he retorted. 'And there's no way past the Capitol Building's security. So both locations are a no-go.'

As the seat of the US Congress, the Capitol was one of the most secure buildings in the world, particularly during a confirmation hearing, when many high-ranking executives were likely to be in attendance.

Frost too was well aware of this fact, and had no comeback for him.

'That leaves us with an ambush en route. It's the only way this can work.'

It was an inelegant plan at best, but the only one that offered a chance of success. Drake had been on his share of ops that had begun under less than ideal circumstances, and pulled through all the same.

'But—'

'I hear what you're saying,' Drake cut in impatiently. 'We can't treat this op like downtown Baghdad, so the blood and guts routine is out. We need a way of doing this quick, smart and clean, and it starts with figuring out Cain's movements. I need to know what he's doing, where he's going and who he's talking to. Get me some options for surveillance, then we can use Starke to make it happen.'

Frost opened her mouth to protest, then thought better of it. 'Fine,' she conceded.

As the young woman set to work, Drake turned his attention to the others. 'Mitchell, Dietrich, we need to be prepared for different assault plans. Where are we on weapons and equipment?'

An op like this would require specialist weaponry and equipment – the kind you couldn't purchase from a local hunting store. But one of the advantages of their line of work was having a network of contacts in the weapons trade, with access to gear stolen or 'misplaced' from military arms depots.

'I've got some guys in Baltimore who can set us up,' Dietrich confirmed. He paused, adding, 'Won't be cheap, though. They charge a lot of money not to ask questions.'

Drake shook his head. Money was of little concern at this point. 'Do you trust them?'

The German gave a thin smile. 'As much as you trust Starke.'

'Very funny,' Drake hit back. 'We need the full package. Assault, breaching and sniping work.'

Glancing past the big imposing operative, Drake spotted Jessica over by the perimeter of the room, her arms folded and her shoulders hunched over. Drake could guess what was on her mind.

'Get in touch with them,' he instructed. 'I'll draw you up a list soon.'

Dietrich nodded. 'I'm on it.'

Moving past him, Drake approached his sister tentatively. He knew all too well how difficult it was to hear how their mother had died and, more importantly, who was responsible.

'I'm sorry you had to hear that, Jess,' he said quietly.

'Don't be,' she replied, keeping her back to him. 'I came here for answers, knowing I wouldn't like them. I got what I wanted.'

'She tried to make things right.' Drake sighed, reflecting on all the things he'd once believed about Freya Shaw. 'I was wrong about her. All those years, it was so easy to blame her... hate her even. All that time wasted. I wish I could take it back.'

The woman he'd once viewed as distant, selfish and dismissive, then as a ruthless, power-hungry operative working for a shadowy clandestine organisation, had finally been revealed. He saw her now as a good woman forced to make difficult choices and painful compromises, giving up parts of herself in pursuit of a higher goal, only to be thwarted time and again.

His sister didn't respond for a time, and he began to wonder if she might be holding back tears. But when she did finally speak, her voice wasn't strained or wavering. It was cold, and hard and resolute.

'Promise me something, Ryan.'

Drake took a step closer. 'What?'

She turned to face him, her eyes locking with his. 'Promise me you'll be the one to kill him. Not Frost, not Dietrich, but you. Promise me you'll look him in the eye when he dies.'

At any other time, Drake might have been taken aback by the change in her, but not now. She'd been through too much, lost too much, suffered too much. He understood her sentiment, her desire for retribution, because it burned just as fierce and cold inside him.

'I promise.'

Swallowing, Jessica nodded. 'Thank you.'

'Ryan!' Frost called out from the other side of the room. 'I've got something you should see.'

Drake looked at her, then back at his sister. He was reluctant to leave her alone.

'Go on,' Jessica urged him. 'I'll be fine.'

Drake strode over to join the technical specialist at her makeshift work terminal. 'What have you got?'

'I may have a lead on Anya,' Frost replied. Seeing his change in expression, she added, 'Don't get too excited. It's not a precise address or anything.'

Drake frowned. 'So what *do* you know?'

'I told you that Alex nuked my computer when I tried to make contact. Little shit sent a virus that wiped my entire hard drive.'

'Okay, so he fucked you over,' Drake conceded. 'What about it?'

'You only pull a move like that as a last resort.' She paused for a moment, searching for a suitable metaphor for her computer-illiterate comrade. 'It's like... a boxer throwing a big haymaker. He doesn't do it often because it'll leave him wide open if it doesn't connect.'

'But it did connect,' Drake reminded her. 'He wiped your computer.'

Frost shook her head. 'That was never much of a problem. The only thing it really cost me was time, and he knew it. He was trying to delay me. He knew I'd back up everything online, just like he knew I'd be able to reconstitute the drive and find his virus.'

'And?'

'It's a nasty piece of work, but at the end of the day it's just computer code. Once you pick it apart, you can learn a lot about it. Such as where the activation command came from. He was using a VPN to mask his IP address, but—'

'Skip to the interesting part,' he advised. 'Where is he?'

'Pakistan.'

Drake cocked an eyebrow. 'Pakistan?'

'I don't know what he's up to, but I'd bet my ass he isn't there alone.'

Drake rubbed his jaw, deep in thought. 'Can you communicate with him again?'

'I don't think so,' she admitted. 'He wiped everything I used to track him before. He won't make the same mistakes again.'

She gestured to the makeshift terminal she'd established.

'I can keep trying, but I can't do that and plan our op against Cain. So… which do you want me to focus on?'

Drake was silent for a few seconds. Much as he wanted to re-establish contact with Anya, the pragmatic part of his mind knew she would resurface only when she was ready. In any case, they had a more important task at hand. Finding her had to take a back seat to their mission against Cain.

'Leave it,' he decided. 'Put everything you have on Cain.'

He'd made the only decision he could under the circumstances, yet he remained troubled and preoccupied with more new questions that had sprung up. What was she looking for in Pakistan? And what would she do when she found it?

Chapter 42

Islamabad, Pakistan

Reclining in the back seat of his luxury SUV as it slowly advanced through evening traffic, Vizur Qalat was in an upbeat mood. He had good reason to be. His recent ascent to the top position within the ISI, Pakistan's premier intelligence agency, had allowed him to usher in a series of sweeping changes that had greatly bolstered his position.

Old enemies and political rivals were either eliminated or quietly ushered into meaningless figurehead roles, while long-time allies and younger, more easily influenced personnel were phased in to replace them.

In barely six months, Qalat had reshaped the most influential organisation in the country, consolidating power around himself. He had spent most of his long career preparing for this, operating on the periphery of major events, biding his time and waiting for the right moment to make his move.

That moment had come in the summer of the previous year, during a tense but ultimately fruitful meeting with Marcus Cain, the interim head of the CIA. Each man had come away from that meeting with something he'd long sought, or at least believing he had.

Qalat smiled faintly at the memory. Powerful and ruthless he might have been, but Marcus Cain still had much to learn. He would come to understand that in due course, as they all did.

The traffic up ahead had slowed to a crawl. Curious, Qalat leaned forward to peer between the two muscular bodyguards seated up front. Pakistan could be a dangerous country, and a man in his position couldn't afford to put himself at risk.

'What's the hold-up?' he asked, his mood soured by the delay. It had been a long day; he was tired and hungry, and entirely unwilling to be waylaid.

'Looks like a breakdown up ahead, sir,' the driver replied. 'Engine trouble, maybe.'

A rusted old panel van had shuddered to a halt in the middle of the road, the rear end sagging noticeably on old suspension. Busy oncoming traffic meant it was impossible to go around the obstruction.

Qalat made a dismissive gesture. 'Get them out of the way. Push them off the road if you have to.'

Nodding, the driver leaned on his horn, sounding an angry blast to the van's owner. Doubtless he hoped to avoid the indignity of getting out and helping push the dilapidated vehicle aside himself.

As if in response to this, the van's rear doors suddenly swung open. Qalat's first assumption was that the van's passengers were preparing to push the machine off the road, but a sudden flash from inside the darkened cargo area caused him to jump in surprise.

It was followed an instant later by a thunderous bang that reverberated through the SUV's frame, and the crunch of disintegrating machinery. With a terrible surge of alarm, he realised that someone was shooting at them, targeting the car's engine bay.

It was an ambush!

'Get us out of here!' he screamed as a second violent impact shook the SUV.

The driver threw the gear stick into reverse and stomped on the accelerator, but his effort yielded nothing. The car's power plant had been reduced to a mess of broken cylinders and ruptured fuel lines by a pair of heavy calibre armour-piercing rounds.

'Unit One, we're hit!' the driver yelled into his radio. 'Shots fired at the corner of—'

His voice was silenced abruptly by an explosion of glass from the supposedly bulletproof windshield, followed by a kind of wet popping sound as his head was blasted apart. Qalat instinctively shrank away from the gruesome sight, his face and expensive suit sprayed with blood and fragments of bone.

'Get down! Down!' the second bodyguard called out, taking cover just as a figure emerged from the van's cargo bay.

Qalat could only stare in disbelief through the broken, blood-splattered windshield. Their adversary was encased head to toe in a suit of heavy, cumbersome ballistic armour that reminded him obscenely of a knight from some medieval battlefield. Even his head and face were obscured behind an armoured mask and helmet. An assault rifle hung from one shoulder, the weapon's frame bulked out by an extended drum magazine.

Behind him, Qalat could see the long barrel of an anti-armour sniper rifle mounted in the van's rear bay, probably a big .50 calibre unit designed to punch through armoured military vehicles like Humvees and APCs.

'Get our backup in here now,' he demanded, his shock and surprise giving way to colder, clearer thinking. As brutal as this ambush might have been, they had anticipated such attacks.

'Unit Two, we're pinned down!' his bodyguard spoke urgently into his comms unit. 'Target is in the open. Take him out!'

A second vehicle had been trailing them a short distance behind, ready to lend assistance. Qalat heard the sound of doors slamming, and twisted in his seat as a pair of agents advanced past his window, one armed with a sidearm, the other clutching a P90 submachine gun.

Both men opened fire in unison, spraying their target with a deadly hail of mixed calibre gunfire. All around them, panicked civilians screamed and shrank away in terror, while nearby motorists abandoned their vehicles and fled for their lives.

The would-be assassin staggered backwards under the impacts, his ballistic armour rippling with each hit. But instead of crumpling to the ground in a pool of blood as he should have done, he instead swung the M4A1 assault rifle around on the agents and opened up with a long, sustained burst.

Spent shell casings clattered to the ground all around him as he cut down his enemies like a scythe through standing grass. Their light Kevlar vests offered almost no protection from the unrelenting hail of fire.

Qalat jumped back as one man slumped against the window, his fading eyes filled with pain and fear, before sliding out of sight, leaving a long smear of blood on the glass.

'Where are our reinforcements?' Qalat demanded as the masked figure ejected the spent drum magazine and reached for a fresh one. 'We need them here now!'

'Mayday, mayday.' His sole remaining bodyguard had switched his comms unit to an open frequency, appealing for help from anyone in the vicinity. 'We are under attack. Officers down, requesting backup.'

His look of growing panic made it clear he was getting nowhere.

'Can't get a signal out. They're jamming all frequencies.'

Qalat clenched his jaw, considering his limited options as their enemy slapped a fresh magazine into place and raised their weapon.

'This car is armoured. He can't get in. We sit tight and—'

His voice was drowned out by the staccato hammering of gunfire against the window, the glass cracking and buckling under the relentless assault. Somehow the window held, but not by much.

Lowering the assault rifle, the attacker paused to consider this problem. Then, reaching into his webbing, he withdrew a small metallic object and held it up in plain sight. Qalat was familiar enough with military hardware to recognise a white phosphorous grenade when he saw one. Armoured or not, no vehicle was going to protect them from the lethal incendiary.

Then, to his surprise, the masked gunman held something else up against the window. Something less dangerous but, as it turned out, far more effective.

A piece of paper with two simple sentences written in Punjabi.

All I want is Qalat. Give him to me, and you get to live.

To emphasise his point, he waved the grenade slowly back and forth, taunting them. The bodyguard's gaze slowly turned towards the passenger in the rear seat, splattered with the blood of his fallen comrade.

'You stand your ground,' Qalat ordered, sensing his wavering loyalty. 'If he doesn't kill you, then I will. And your whole family.'

A potent threat under normal circumstances, Qalat's words lacked their usual authority. It took the bodyguard all of three seconds to make his decision.

Drawing his sidearm, he held it up by the trigger guard, then unlocked the door with shaking hands and stepped out. The masked assailant kept him covered as he dropped his weapon and backed away with arms raised, finally breaking into a run and fleeing.

With his last vestige of protection running like a frightened child, Qalat could only watch in simmering anger as the assault rifle poked in through the door, trained on him.

'Out!' a voice commanded.

The voice that spoke was strong and authoritative, but also distinctly female. His entire protective detail had been dismantled in under a minute by a woman.

'Now!' she repeated. 'Hands where I can see them.'

Qalat reluctantly opened his door and stepped out, keeping his hands raised.

'You won't get away with this, my friend,' he said calmly as she yanked his hands behind his back. 'My people will come for me. They will repay this attack tenfold.'

'You and I will talk soon enough, Vizur,' she replied, securing his wrists with cable ties and leading him towards the waiting van.

He was shoved roughly inside, landing hard on the dirty floor of the cargo deck. Clambering in beside him, his abductor swung the rear doors shut then hammered a gloved fist against the driver's cab.

'We're in! Go!'

In seconds, the engine roared back into life and they were moving, leaving behind a scene of utter devastation.

Chapter 43

Washington DC

'All right, listen in,' Drake said, beckoning his team over to the makeshift planning table he'd set up, which was already strewn with design blueprints and maps of central DC – everything from street layouts to satellite images, subway maps and even sewage and utility tunnels.

Frost's computer skills had unearthed a treasure trove of information on their proposed Area of Operation, much of which was freely available online as a matter of public record. This intel had allowed Drake to put together the outline of an attack plan, including potential ambush points and escape routes. It was still sketchy, but it was the best they had.

'We know that Cain's confirmation hearing will take place in the Senate chamber on Capitol Hill,' he began, indicating the Senate building on the map spread out before him. 'We also know he's likely to use the underground parking area beneath the South Capitol Park, so there's no way to get to him once he's in there.'

'So we hit him before he gets there,' Mitchell reasoned.

'Exactly. We know he'll be travelling by armoured motorcade, so our best shot is to lay down an ambush en route. The objective will be to intercept his motorcade, neutralise his security detail and take him out before they can call in reinforcements. Preferably with minimal civilian casualties.'

Dietrich folded his arms. 'That's a tall order, Ryan.'

Drake nodded, acknowledging his reservations. 'To do this, we have three main problems to overcome. One, we need to know where and when to hit him.'

'I've got you covered,' Frost said.

The last time Drake had found himself standing at the Thomas Jefferson Memorial late at night, it had been on New Year's Eve two years earlier. The night he'd discovered that Anya was still alive, after believing her killed in Moscow.

The place was exactly the same as it had been back then, save that the cherry trees encircling the rotunda were now in full spring blossom. He was lingering in the shadows of one of the building's arched entryways, the cold steel of a concealed sidearm pressed into the small of his back. Beside him, Frost was similarly armed.

Hearing the click of shoes on the flagstones surrounding the memorial, Drake swapped a glance with his younger companion. She nodded, ready to follow his lead. Ascending the steps into the rotunda, the new arrival advanced into the big open space and halted, scanning the darkness around them.

'I'm here,' Starke announced with mild impatience. 'And I don't have much time.'

Drake emerged silently from the shadows, with Frost right behind him.

'You're late,' he announced.

Starke turned casually to face him. 'And you're good. I didn't hear a thing.' Turning his attention to Drake's companion, Starke inclined his head in greeting. 'You must be Keira Frost, if I'm not mistaken?'

'What's it to you?'

'A matter of professional interest. I make a point of knowing the people I work with, and I know a good deal about you, Ms Frost. A teenage runaway, living homeless on the streets for almost a year, a string of criminal convictions...'

'We're not here to swap tragic life stories,' she said tersely.

Sensing he'd made his point, Starke turned his attention back to Drake. 'So, what do you need from me?'

'Access to Cain's communications,' Drake explained.

Reaching into her pocket, Frost fished out a cell phone and held it out. To the untrained eye it looked like a standard, commercially available smartphone.

'There's a custom tracking program built into this unit,' she explained. 'It'll automatically lock onto and clone the SIM details of any other phone nearby. With this, I can make a copy of Cain's private cell. I can read any incoming or outgoing communications, and track his movements just like with any other cell phone.'

Starke raised an eyebrow. 'Very impressive. What's the catch?'

'The catch is you have to be close to him for it to work.'

'For how long?' he asked.

'Sixty seconds at least, maybe more.'

Starke eyed the device dubiously, mulling over what he'd been told. 'Say I do this,' the NSA director asked. 'What then?'

'Let us handle the rest.'

The less Starke knew about their plans, the better.

'Last chance to back out,' Drake prompted him, sensing the doubts creeping in. 'Whether we go or not depends on what happens in the next ten seconds. Are you in or out?'

'If it's discovered that I was complicit in this...'

'Then you go down, just like us,' Drake finished for him. 'Either we're all in this together, or none of us are.'

This was the crucial moment. If Starke backed out now, Drake would need to find two things – a whole new way of approaching his plan, and a place to hide Starke's body where it would never be discovered.

The NSA director stared at him long and hard, as if trying to see the future that lay ahead with this man. Then, reconciling himself to the risks and uncertainties, he reached out and took the cell phone from Frost.

Drake let out a barely perceptible breath and relaxed his grip on the weapon.

Before either man could say anything more, Frost handed Starke a concealed radio earpiece set inside a clear plastic case. 'You'll be needing this. It's encrypted, and pre-tuned to our frequency. Don't power it up until you're ready to make your move. The battery only lasts a couple of hours.'

'I'm familiar with the routine,' he replied, slipping both items into his coat pocket.

'Cain's confirmation could come at any time. I assume you'll know before they make it public?' Drake said.

The NSA director gave a wry smile. 'It's my business to know things.'

'That'll be your chance. Contact us when you're ready.'

'I will.' Glancing back the way he'd come, he nodded to himself. 'I'm out of time here. For all our sakes, I hope you know what you're doing, Ryan.'

He wasn't the only one, Drake thought.

'You do your part. Let us do ours.'

Saying nothing more, Starke turned and strode out of the building.

Chapter 44

Alaska – September 27th, 2001

The morning sun rose on the ancient primeval forest, the boles of towering spruce and birch trees casting long shadows across the rich, loamy ground, still damp from overnight rain. Bees and small insects circled in the hazy green light, while golden leaves drifted down from the canopy above.

The seasons were turning, the brief, vibrant flourish of summer slowly fading.

At the base of a shallow valley, a small Sitka black-tailed deer lowered its head to drink from a stream. A buck, his antlers small and unimpressive compared to the elaborate displays found on other species. He too was changing with the turning of the seasons, shedding his reddish-brown summer coat in favour of a thicker dull grey covering that would see him through the bitter Alaskan winter.

A faint breeze sighed through the trees, carrying with it an unfamiliar scent. He paused, stretching up his long neck, his dark and sombre eyes scanning the woodland around him for predators. His nostrils flared as he breathed in, seeking the source of the elusive smell.

He didn't see the arrow coming. He was aware only of a sudden movement behind a stand of bushes in the distance. The deadly missile arced through the air and struck him in the neck. Instinct took over and he tried to flee in panic, only to stumble and fall in a heap of flailing limbs.

His killer was moving before he'd even hit the ground, sprinting across the valley floor towards him, boots churning the muddy ground, leaping nimbly across exposed roots. There was a scrape of metal on metal as a knife was drawn.

Skidding to a halt beside the stricken animal, Anya grasped the antlers and yanked the head back, exposing the vulnerable throat.

'I thank you for your sacrifice, brother,' she whispered in her native language, before severing the arteries in its neck.

An hour later, Anya returned to her log cabin overlooking a fork in the river below, with her hunting bow in hand and the deer carcass slung over her shoulders. Though belonging to a smaller species than most, the buck was still heavy and bulky, fattened for winter, and hauling it over a couple of miles of rugged terrain had been no easy task. Really it should have been a two-man job, but there was no man to assist her. It was just her out here. Alone.

That was exactly how she wanted it.

She had spent more than a year in this place, purchasing a dilapidated old cabin the previous summer and resolving to fix it up. Though she considered herself only a mediocre carpenter, she had set about her task with steady determination, working late into the long summer days. By the time winter rolled around, she'd made the dwelling more or less habitable.

In truth, the simple, strenuous work was exactly what she'd needed. It had been easy to lose herself in it, to slowly forget the disastrous events of the year before, when she'd been forced to fight and kill her own men. Her unit was effectively destroyed, her power wiped out, her plans in ruins.

And now she was done. Done with the Agency, the Circle, the life she'd once had. Done with people. Out here in the primeval wilderness that reminded her so much of her childhood home, where her only concerns were the practicalities of survival, she had found a measure of peace. Maybe she would live out her days here, growing old in contented isolation.

She detected the distinctive thump of rotor blades off in the distance and instinctively stopped, turning her head slowly until she picked out the source. A small dark shape had appeared on the horizon, emerging from behind one of the towering peaks that dominated the region. A chopper.

Maybe it was nothing to do with her, she told herself. There were gold mining operations off to the west, which often used choppers to ferry in personnel or equipment. Maybe that was all it was.

Her heart sank as the chopper swung towards her, following the course of the river valley. As it drew closer, she saw the distinctive drab grey paint job. Military.

In response, Anya drew an arrow from the quiver over her shoulder as the Bell Huey circled overhead, the thump of the rotors and the shriek of the engines deafening.

Finding a suitable landing spot at the far end of the open meadow, the pilot eased the Huey lower until the skids touched down. As the engines fell silent and the big blades slowly spun down, the side door slid open and a lone man leapt out.

Anya's throat tightened as Marcus Cain approached. He moved slowly, warily, his eyes on the notched bow. He looked older, she thought. His face drawn and lined, strands of grey showing at his temples.

'You're not an easy woman to find,' he remarked.

'Go home, Marcus,' she warned him. 'There's nothing for you here.'

He halted a few feet away, looking her up and down. Perhaps thinking the same thing about her as she'd thought about him. 'I need your help, Anya. We need your help.'

'No.' Anya shook her head. 'No more help, no more missions. I'm finished with the Agency, and with you.'

'Things have changed—'

'Goodbye, Marcus,' she said, turning on her heel and striding away. She had nothing more to say to him. No more anger or pain. She just wanted to be left alone.

'There's been an attack.'

Anya halted, struck not so much by his words, but by the gravity of them. This wasn't something normal, the kind of predictable tragedy that people like Cain had long since become numb to. This was something more.

'In New York, two weeks ago,' he went on. 'The World Trade Centre, the Pentagon... Thousands are dead, tens of thousands injured. It was the worst terrorist attack in history.'

Anya was no stranger to loss and death, but the scale of this was far beyond anything she'd experienced. And she'd been completely ignorant of it. Out here, cut off from the world, she might have lived out the rest of her life, never knowing.

But now she did know.

'Why are you telling me this?' she whispered.

Cain sighed. The pained, weary sigh of a man forced to confront his own failings. 'The attack was staged by al-Qaeda.'

Anya closed her eyes, her mind immediately grasping the shattering implications. Al-Qaeda, the terrorist organisation born from disaffected Mujahideen fighters embittered by the perceived betrayal by America. Operating under the protection of the Taliban, who had seized power after the long, brutal civil war in Afghanistan.

Just like they'd predicted.

'I warned you this would happen, Marcus,' she said, her voice cold and dangerous. 'I begged you not to abandon Afghanistan, and you ignored me.'

'I did what I could—'

'We had a chance to help them!' she shouted, rounding on him. She'd been wrong earlier – she did have anger for Marcus Cain. She had a great deal of it, and it had all come rushing to the surface in this moment.

The lies, the excuses, the hubris… all of it had made this happen.

'Afghanistan tore itself apart in civil war, terrorists and fanatics took over, and we stood by and did nothing. Nothing! You used them to fight your dirty war, just like you used me, and then you threw them away when it was over. Their blood is on your hands.'

'Goddamn it, three thousand people are dead!' he exploded, grabbing her by the jacket and pulling her close. 'And who knows how many more are going to die before this is all over.'

'You mean…'

'We're going to war in Afghanistan,' he said bluntly. 'Congress is screaming for it. The Pentagon's already drawing up invasion plans.'

'And you want me to run off and join them, just like before,' Anya said, laughing bitterly. 'Sorry Marcus, but I'm not that young, or that idealistic, anymore.'

'We're calling up every asset we have left,' he explained. 'You fought in Afghanistan for years. You know the land, you know the people—'

'And now you want me to go back there and kill them.'

Whatever their affiliation now, the prospect of fighting and killing the same men she'd once fought alongside was abhorrent to her.

'I want you to save lives,' he countered. 'The invasion will be a bloodbath, for them and for us. People like you are our only chance to prevent it.'

'What more do you want from me, Marcus? Haven't you taken enough already?' Backing away, Anya spread her arms to encompass the wilderness around them. 'This is all I have now. I'm not a soldier anymore. I… can't be that person again.'

She saw a brief flicker of something in him then. Compassion, regret, she couldn't say. But it was soon gone, replaced by something colder and more pragmatic.

'Task Force Black are going in,' he said firmly. 'I'm offering you command of the unit, if you want it. We both know you can lead them better than anyone else.'

Anya could feel it now. The invisible tendrils of her past, reaching out for her, grasping, tearing her away from the new life she'd tried to build. The killer she'd tried to leave behind, stirring out from the dark recesses of her psyche.

'Just like the old days,' she said, her voice bitterly mocking.

*'I'm asking you to go in one last time.' His voice was quieter now, softer.
'Help us end this thing. Help us make this right. After that...' He glanced
around at the forests, the river, the mountains. 'You can rest.'*

*Anya turned away, taking in the same view, thinking of the life she had
here. The life she was about to give up. She closed her eyes to hide the tears
that threatened.*

Islamabad, Pakistan – April 30th, 2011

'You're wasting your time,' Qalat's voice echoed around the empty
warehouse, deceptively calm and composed given his situation. 'My
people are on their way as we speak. If you have any sense, you will
run and pray they never catch up with you.'

Anya wasn't listening to him. Not yet at least.

Secluded in a small, disused storage area, she winced in pain as she
stripped off the bulky ballistic armour that had kept her alive during
the ambush, unlatching straps and dropping the chunks of reinforced
steel plate and Kevlar on the ground, revealing the all-too-frail human
body beneath.

The armour might have protected her from fatal injuries, but all
that kinetic energy still had to go somewhere. The multiple high
velocity impacts had inflicted a series of painful welts and deep bruises
across her torso, arms and legs. She felt like she'd been held down and
pummelled relentlessly by fists and boots.

'Jesus Christ,' Alex gasped at the doorway. 'How much more of this
can you take?'

'I'll be fine,' Anya replied, her voice strained. 'We knew this would
happen.'

The ambush plan had been neither elegant nor sophisticated. Anya
had opted for a brute force approach that she never would have
contemplated before, eager to get her hands on her target. Perhaps
too eager, she reflected, holding in a gasp as she stretched her bruised
muscles.

'Keep watch on Qalat. I need to finish up here.'

'He's handcuffed to a chair,' Alex reminded her. 'He's not going
anywhere. Anyway, I scrambled the ISI's alert system, sent them on a
dozen wild goose chases all across the city. They won't be finding us
any time—'

'Just go, Alex,' she said sharply. 'I'll join you soon.'

Alex backed away, knowing better than to debate the matter.

As soon as he was gone, Anya's facade of strength and composure slipped away, and she wilted visibly as pain and fatigue clawed at her. Head low, she clutched at the wall for support, breathing slow and deep as she fought to maintain control.

Not now, she told herself. Not now.

Reaching into her pocket, she popped the lid on a jar of painkillers and dry-swallowed several. Then, digging deep, she slowly and defiantly straightened up.

When she emerged onto the warehouse floor a minute or two later, she walked tall and confident, her bruises hidden beneath fresh clothes, her face an impassive mask as she approached the prisoner.

Qalat glanced at her with mild interest, but this professional curiosity quickly gave way to something else. Recognition. Even though Anya was certain they'd never met.

'I must admit, I'm surprised,' the ISI director began, quickly masking his lapse. 'Most people in our line of work are not so... feminine. Tell me, what—'

Drawing her sidearm, Anya took aim at his left leg and pulled the trigger. The dull thud of the suppresser was followed by a startled cry of pain from the bound man as blood began to leak from the torn skin of his thigh. It was superficial injury at worst, but a painful reminder of who was in charge here.

'Stop whimpering. It's a flesh wound,' Anya explained, adjusting her aim so that the weapon was trained on his groin. 'The next one will be more... permanent.'

She had run plenty of interrogations before, and knew how important it was to establish dominance right away. There were few better ways than the prospect of a .45 calibre round in the genitals.

'What do you want?' Qalat demanded.

'I want information.' Picking up a battered old wooden chair lying near the wall, she took a seat in front of him. 'Before we begin, know that I'm very good at spotting liars. No matter how good you think you are, I will know. And every time you lie to me, I will put another round in you.' She gestured to the silenced M1911 in her lap. 'I have seven more bullets in this magazine, Vizur. You really don't want me to use them.'

Qalat said nothing. She sensed her point had been made.

'Now, tell me how you know me.'

His eyes narrowed, but the man remained silent.

'Don't test me, Vizur,' she warned. 'You recognised my face when I walked in. How do you know me?'

Qalat sighed, raising his eyes towards the ceiling before he finally spoke.

'I've known you for a long time, Maras,' he admitted. 'Marcus Cain's little protégé, his pet project. The beautiful young woman who caught his eye.' He looked her up and down. 'Not quite so young now, of course, but I can see why his head was turned.'

Anya's jaw tightened. 'Go on.'

'When you were captured by the Soviets in 1988, Marcus was all set to rescue you, no matter the cost to himself. But you had a little secret of your own, didn't you?'

Anya could feel her heart beating faster as he spoke.

'You were a KGB agent, sent to infiltrate the CIA. And you did an exceptionally good job – getting your case officer to fall in love with you, no less.' He smirked. 'After all, who would ever suspect a woman?'

'Clearly you did,' she prompted him. This man knew things about her that even the Agency still hadn't discovered.

Qalat nodded. 'You had made a lot of enemies for yourself by then. The Soviet handlers you betrayed, the American military who never fully trusted you, the factions in the CIA who wanted to see you fail…'

Anya didn't need to be reminded of that. She remembered all too well.

'But Marcus believed in you. Right up until I showed him your KGB file. The look on his face was… tragic.' He sighed, feigning sympathy. 'No rescue for you.'

Leaning forward, Anya jammed the muzzle of her silencer into the flesh wound at his thigh, eliciting a growl of pain and a fresh surge of blood. Nearby, Alex looked away uncomfortably.

'It was you,' she snarled. 'You convinced him to call off the rescue.'

'I did,' he said, gritting his teeth.

'Why?'

'We thought you had betrayed the Agency, gone back to your Soviet handlers. We assumed the whole thing was a trap to lure in the rest of the unit.'

Anya released her grip, leaning back in her chair as her mind raced. Cain hadn't abandoned her willingly. He had been forced into it, in the mistaken belief that she'd betrayed him. The traumatic, life-changing event that had driven a permanent wedge between them had started in a way she hadn't understood.

What else did she not know or understand about the man?

'You and I both live in a world of lies,' Qalat went on. 'It's the life we chose. But somehow... it never makes it any easier when we're the ones being lied to.'

Enough, Anya told herself. Whatever had driven Cain's decision to abandon her in Afghanistan all those years ago, it didn't change who he was now. And it certainly didn't change her mission here.

'If you know me as well as you claim, you know I was captured by the Russians a second time,' she said, refocussing her mind on the interrogation. 'Eight years ago, they found me again.'

'I know this,' Qalat confirmed grimly.

'Then you also know of an Israeli agent named Russo,' she explained. 'He told me that Pakistani operatives coerced him into selling me out. Operatives answering to you, Vizur.'

Qalat had once again fallen silent. She could tell he was thinking fast, weighing up how much she knew and what he might say in response.

'It was Cain who handed you that mission, wasn't it?' she pressed him. 'He wanted plausible deniability. He used you and your men to locate me, so he could sell me out to the Russians. Tell me the truth, and I'll let you live.'

She expected him to break in light of such damning evidence, expected him to confirm that everything she'd said, to vindicate her anger and justify her betrayal. But instead, to her utter dismay, the man shook his head and chuckled softly to himself.

'You still don't understand, do you?' he said, still chuckling to himself. 'This is bigger than Marcus Cain, bigger than you or I. We are simply pawns in a much grander game.'

Clenching her jaw in anger, Anya pressed the silenced automatic against his other leg and pulled the trigger. Qalat's chuckling, mocking amusement was suddenly replaced by screams of pain as he slumped forward, straining against his bonds.

'Enough!' Anya shouted, grasping his hair and yanking his head back just as she'd done with that deer ten years earlier, forcing him to look at her. 'This is no game! Give me answers, or I will torture you until you beg me for death, Vizur.'

'Anya—' Alex began, his voice edged with alarm.

'Stay out of this, Alex!' she warned him. 'Tell me why I was betrayed!'

'I told you… we live in a world of lies,' Qalat said between ragged breaths. 'Even Marcus.'

'Anya!' Alex repeated, more urgently now.

'What is it?' she demanded, furious at the interruption.

His attention was focussed on the laptop computer beside him. 'The motion sensor's been tripped. Someone's outside.' He looked up at her then, his face tight with fear. 'They've found us!'

Chapter 45

Washington DC

'Once we're tied into Cain's comms, we'll know where and when he's going to make his move,' Drake went on, 'and where to make ours.'

'It's just over ten miles from Langley to the Capitol Building,' Mitchell said. 'About twenty minutes in normal traffic.'

Drake nodded. 'That means twenty minutes of vulnerability.'

'Yeah, but look at the map, Ryan. There are a hundred different routes he could take,' the former CID officer pointed out. 'We can't set up an ambush like this on the fly. Even if we know when he's moving, we also need to know *where*.'

'Mitchell's right,' Dietrich agreed. 'We need to prepare our ground in advance for this to work.'

That much was certainly true, Drake conceded. Taking out an armed Agency motorcade with the resources available would require every advantage they could muster. The attack, when it came, would have to be hard, fast and highly coordinated.

'Holy shit, Dietrich. You're actually agreeing with me?' Mitchell quipped.

'Don't get used to it.'

'We can't get to Cain, so we make Cain come to us.' Drake pointed to the map, where the city was bisected by the meandering curve of the Potomac river. 'No matter which route he takes, he still has to cross the Potomac.'

Jessica's eyes lit up. 'The bridges.'

He nodded. 'There are three possible crossing points – the Key Bridge in the north, the Thomas Jefferson Bridge in the centre, and the Fourteenth Street bridges off to the south.'

'What about this one?' Jessica asked, pointing to one crossing that lay between them. The Arlington Memorial bridge.

Frost shook her head. 'Unlikely. The main highway from Langley runs right underneath it,' she explained, pointing to the road the motorcade was most likely to take. 'He'd have to double back on himself to cross there.'

'That leaves us with three likely candidates,' Drake concluded.

'Not bad, Ryan,' Dietrich agreed. 'No buildings nearby, not many civilians on the sidewalks. All we'd have to worry about is passing traffic.'

'It narrows down our options, but we still can't be in three places at once,' Mitchell reminded them. 'How do we make him go where we want?'

Drake looked up at his German comrade. 'That's where you come in, Jonas.'

Fort Totten Waste Disposal Site

'Fucking place stinks,' Dietrich muttered as he strode across the vehicle storage depot, passing lines of bulky dump trucks, loaders and tracked excavators. All of them silent and motionless in the early morning gloom, waiting for the first shift of the day to arrive.

'It's a landfill, Jonas. What do you expect?' Mitchell replied, though she had to admit the stench of rotting garbage hanging in the air was not a pleasant one.

Dietrich ignored the quip. 'Ever wonder why we get landed with the shitty jobs?'

'Because Ryan doesn't like you.'

'The feeling's mutual,' he snorted, slowing as he approached one garbage truck in particular, taking note of the license plate in the sickly orange glow of nearby security lights. 'This is the one.'

Mitchell nodded. 'Get on it. I'll keep watch.'

Clambering up to the cab, Dietrich tried the door on the off-chance it might have been left unlocked. Stranger things have happened, but not in this case. Instead, Dietrich retrieved his lock picking gear and set to work.

As he attacked the lock, Mitchell touched her comms unit. 'Keira, sitrep?'

On the other side of town, the young technical specialist sat hunched over her computer. Having easily hacked the depot's surveillance system and routed the feeds to her terminal, she now had a decent view of her two comrades.

'Smile, you're on candid camera.'

Mitchell smirked. 'How's my hair look?'

'Great. Local security feeds are running on a loop, so they can't see you on CCTV. Might want to make this quick, though.'

'Copy that.' She glanced up at Dietrich as he fumbled with the lock. 'I'd like to say we've got our best man on it, but…'

'I heard that,' Dietrich muttered. Moments later, the door lock clicked as the lock disengaged. 'You were saying?'

She smiled innocently. 'Never doubted you for a second.'

Dietrich disappeared from view as he set about stripping the ignition system to hotwire it. Hollywood makes it look easy; in reality, itis much more technical, and more time consuming.

'Hate to interrupt you two lovebirds,' Frost said, her tone urgent, 'but you've got incoming.'

'Hey, you guys over there!' a voice called out from further down the line of vehicles. 'What you doin'? First shift doesn't start for another hour.'

'Fuck,' Mitchell said under her breath, pasting on a fake smile as she turned to face the man striding over. He was in his mid-fifties, his close-cropped hair bristling like a scrubbing brush, his stout frame straining against his night watchman's uniform.

'That's why we're here,' she began, her tone confident and relaxed, almost to the point of boredom. She'd long since learned that if you look and act like you're supposed to be there, most people will assume that you are. 'Got a problem with one of your trucks. We're here to take it in for an overhaul.'

The night watchman frowned. 'What kind of problem?'

Mitchell made a show of inspecting the folder she was carrying, containing some hastily forged work sheets. 'Says here you've got noises and vibrations coming from the front wheels. Probably a worn bearing. Pain in the ass to strip out, that's why they sent us here early to pick it up.'

'Keep him talking,' Dietrich's voice buzzed in her ear. 'I'm almost done.'

Approaching, the night watchman looked her up and down. She and Dietrich were dressed in the blue overalls and hard hats of vehicle mechanics.

'That's weird. Usually they leave an entry in the vehicle logbook,' he mused, an air of suspicion creeping in now.

Mitchell shrugged dismissively. 'Hey, I don't run things at this end. They tell us to come pick up a truck; here we are.' She paused. 'Whatever. Call it in if you want.'

Hesitating, the man reached for his walkie talkie and put in a call to the security hut. 'Hey Mike, you got a copy?'

'Go.'

'Yeah, I got a maintenance crew in here to pick up one of our dump trucks. You got anything on the job sheet for today?'

'Wait one…' A few seconds passed. 'Nah, nothing on the log.'

Mitchell felt her heartbeat surge, and thought of the weapon tucked into her work belt behind her back. She could fight her way out of this if need be, but the prospect of killing an innocent man was not an appealing one.

'What about the computer log?' the watchman asked.

'They've seen your face. If this goes to shit, you know what must be done,' Dietrich's monotone voice warned her. He was out of sight for now, but she took his meaning well enough. If she didn't drop the night watchman, he wouldn't hesitate to do it for her.

'Erm, yeah I got it here,' the second security man confirmed. 'One of the garbage trucks is down with bearing problems. A crew's scheduled to come pick it up before first shift. Guess they forgot to fill in the paperwork.'

Mitchell relaxed instantly. Frost had managed to insert a fake log entry. The ruse would likely be discovered before too long, but it wouldn't matter. They had what they needed now.

She gave the watchman a world-weary shrug. 'Red tape, am I right?'

He grinned. 'You know it. Need any help getting this thing out?'

In response, Dietrich sat up straight in the driver's cab and rolled down the window. 'No, we're good to go here,' he said, putting on a fake American accent.

The watchman seemed momentarily perplexed, but Dietrich fired up the engine before he could question it further.

'Have a good one!' Mitchell called out over the rumble of the engine, clambering up into the passenger seat.

Driving away hesitantly as he tried to get a feel for the clutch and transmission, Dietrich glanced at his partner in crime. 'You're a hell of a bullshitter, Mitchell.'

The woman flashed a grin. 'I learned from the best.'

Chapter 46

'Once you have the truck, your objective will be to cause as much chaos as possible and block off the southern approaches, leaving Cain with only one option.'

Drake circled the Key Bridge, better known as the Francis Scott Memorial Bridge, the northernmost of the possible crossing points.

'Once we've funnelled Cain's motorcade into the kill zone, our final objective is to spring the trap,' he went on. 'This is where things get interesting.'

'That's one word for it,' Frost remarked.

Giving her a brief glance, Drake carried on. 'The standard official motorcade for an agency director is three vehicles – one on point, one follow-up car behind, and the main limousine in the centre. That means about a dozen armed agents in total.'

The CIA director wasn't quite on the same level as POTUS, who travelled with a veritable army of Secret Service agents, police, White House officials, emergency doctors and dozens of other personnel to protect every aspect of his wellbeing. Nonetheless, it was an important government position, with an appropriately comprehensive security package.

Springing the trap would be one thing. Making sure Cain was caught in it would be quite another.

'Lot of guns,' Mitchell mused.

'The guns we can take care of. It's the limousine that's the problem.'

With that, Drake spread a photograph on the table before them. It was a picture of an imposing executive limousine, snapped en route to some official function.

'Say hello to the CIA director's official vehicle,' Drake began. 'Bulletproof glass, run-flat tyres, fully armoured with Kevlar and ceramic plate. This is going to be a tough nut to crack.'

'So what do you suggest?' Jessica asked.

'A hammer,' Dietrich replied. Striding over to the panel van parked in the centre of the disused garage, he slid open the side door and hoisted out a large reinforced plastic carry case. After setting it down on the table with a heavy thump, he unlatched the catches holding it closed, glanced at the others like a magician about to perform his trick, and flipped the lid open.

'Jesus Christ, Dietrich. Do you think you could have found something bigger?' Frost asked, running her eyes over the heavy-calibre sniper rifle set within the case's foam packing. It was far larger and bulkier than anything she'd handled before.

Dietrich flashed a sardonic smile. 'I suppose most things look big to you, little one.' Hefting the weapon carefully, he lifted it out of its protective case for inspection. 'This is an AS-50 anti-materiel rifle with integrated scope and collapsible bipod. Accurate up to fifteen hundred metres.'

The AS-50 was a British weapon released by Accuracy International just a few years earlier, designed to take out armoured personnel carriers, low flying aircraft and other lightly protected vehicles. The concept was based on the anti-tank rifles of the first and second world wars, though the design was distinctly cutting edge, making use of an array of composite materials and recoil-absorbing mechanisms to create a weapon that was both powerful and usable without injuring the operator.

He held it out to Drake, who accepted the heavy weapon and raised it up to his shoulder, testing the weight and balance. Even without ammunition the rifle weighed a good 30 pounds. Firing it while standing upright would be impossible; this was a weapon that needed to be emplaced in a prepared position.

'Good,' he decided, lowering the gun.

'Damn right it's good,' his colleague snorted. 'Had to call in a lot of favours to get that.'

'Will it be enough, though?' Mitchell asked.

Dietrich flashed a wolf-like grin. 'It will with these,' he said, opening an ammunition box and holding up one of the AS-50's formidable-looking cartridges. 'Raufoss Mk 211 .50 calibre rounds. Armour-piercing tungsten tip with a high explosive incendiary core. It's got as much penetrating power as a 20mm round, but only half the size. Theoretically you could shoot down a Hind chopper with one of these.'

Raufoss rounds were particularly nasty projectiles, able to punch through plate armour before detonating a high explosive incendiary element, killing or severely injuring anyone trapped inside a target vehicle.

'It'll be enough,' Drake decided, laying the weapon down.

The plan was simple. After disabling Cain's limousine, he would pepper the stationary vehicle with Raufoss rounds, turning the interior into a killing zone. If direct fire or shrapnel didn't kill Cain, the incendiary element would ignite the car's interior and burn him alive. If he bailed out, Drake would be standing by to drop him.

The other two vehicles in the motorcade would, at that point, be irrelevant. Cain and everyone else in the limo would be dead before they could do anything to assist. Such collateral damage would, Drake knew, weigh heavily on his conscience for a long time to come, but it was the only plan that offered a decent prospect of success.

'Where will you be?' Mitchell asked. 'Where will you take the shot?'

Drake turned his eyes to the map once more.

'Here,' he decided, circling a building on the northern side of the bridge. A well-known landmark amongst university students in the area, the 150-foot-high clock tower provided a perfect field of fire across the bridge below. 'Georgetown University.'

A silence descended on the group then as each of them stared at the innocuous-looking building marked on the map. That was where it would happen. That was where Marcus Cain would die.

Chapter 47

Islamabad, Pakistan

Instantly Anya's mind snapped back into the moment, her anger and desire for vengeance replaced by quick, calculating decision-making. Rushing over to Alex's laptop, she surveyed the images from the wireless surveillance cameras installed outside.

Sure enough, a pair of vans had pulled up and at least a dozen armed operatives were converging on the warehouse, kitted out in full body armour and clutching submachine guns. Somehow the Pakistani intelligence service had found them, despite Alex's best efforts.

'Wipe everything. Now,' she instructed, hurrying to retrieve the assault rifle she'd left beside the van. 'Get to the emergency exit as soon as it's done!'

Qalat, seeing the urgency of her situation, smiled despite the pain. 'Time to fly, little bird,' he taunted. 'I told you they would find me.'

Snatching up the assault rifle, Anya turned towards the prisoner. Clearly there was more to learn from him, but she couldn't do it here. Qalat would have to come with them.

She'd just taken a step towards him when the sudden tinkle of broken glass caught her attention. She looked up in time to see a couple of small metal objects fly in through the ventilation windows high above.

Instinctively she turned away and squeezed her eyes shut just as a pair of thunderous bangs shook the building. The assault team wouldn't risk using fragmentation grenades with a friendly in here, forcing them to employ stun grenades instead.

Her ears were ringing when she opened her eyes and glanced towards the main doors. They were heavy steel units, mounted on rollers and secured with a heavy padlocked chain from the inside. A formidable barrier.

But the sudden roar of a vehicle engine told her they had found their own solution. A second later, the doors crashed open, peeling inwards and collapsing as one of the vans burst through, venting steam from behind the crumpled front grille.

Even before it had come to a halt, the side door slid open and black-clad assault operatives began to pile out, with more surging in through the breached doors.

Turning away, Anya leapt for cover behind her own parked vehicle just as one of the attackers raised his weapon and snapped off a burst.

'Contact!'

The warehouse echoed with the rattle of automatic fire as a stream of 9mm rounds zipped past, screaming off the concrete floor just metres away. Anya backed up against the van as more gunfire peppered the sides and rear, bursting the tyres and punching holes in the thin metal skin.

Rolling over and flattening herself against the ground, she peered beneath the van, spotting a pair of booted feet advancing towards her. Hefting the M4 into position, she let loose a prolonged burst of fire. The weapon kicked and bucked against her shoulder, spent shell casings rattling against the underside of the vehicle to land smoking on the ground beside her. Zipping along beneath the van, the 5.56mm projectiles tore into the feet and shins of the unfortunate operative, shattering bones and blowing flesh apart.

She saw him stumble and fall, heard his agonised scream, then rolled aside to avoid an answering hail of gunfire. A couple of rounds even ricocheted off the ground and the underside of the van to howl past her, missing by less than a foot.

Nearby, Riley smiled as she let loose another volley, relishing the satisfying kick of the MP5 against her shoulder. She had been dispatched here to this hot, stinking country on the far side of the world with one mission – to find and kill Anya.

Now her goal was within sight.

'Move up,' she commanded. 'Take her out.'

They had her pinned down, Anya knew. It would only be a matter of seconds before they outflanked her, or flushed her out with grenades. Either way, she'd be cut down by automatic gunfire.

Reaching for her comms unit, she hit the transmit key. 'Alex, come in.'

'Anya! Where are—'

'I'm pinned down!' she interrupted. 'I need cover. Fire in the hole!'

'Are you sure?'

Another round ricocheted off the paintwork beside her, tiny flecks of semi-molten metal spalling off and peppering the side of her face.

'Fire in the hole!' she repeated. 'Now!'

Nearby, the three operatives on point were closing in on the now-ruined van, weapons up and ready. At a signal from Riley, one man peeled off left while the other moved right, outflanking their target. Dangerous and well trained she might have been, but she was alone and cut off. They had the advantage of numbers and firepower, and Riley was determined to make use of both.

Gripping the MP5 submachine gun tight, she spoke into her comms unit.

'In position?'

'Roger.'

'Standing by.'

Both men were standing by with stun grenades. Either Anya would be forced to break cover, in which case Riley would drop her, or they'd rush her while she was blinded and deafened. Either way, she wasn't getting out of this.

She took a breath, readying herself, before giving the word.

'Go!'

But just as she issued her command, her voice was drowned out by a high-pitched, shrieking whine from somewhere up above. Glancing up in alarm, Riley was just in time to see a bright red projectile screaming towards her, trailing smoke and sparks.

'RPG!' she cried out, throwing herself aside.

The strange missile hissed over her head before detonating with a flash and a shower of sparks. It was followed almost immediately by another, and another. Within seconds, the warehouse was alive with pyrotechnics surging down from both sides, flashing and shrieking and bursting apart around the assault team in a loud, blinding, disorienting display.

'Fuck!' Riley shouted in anger, ignoring the barrage now that she understood its origins. 'It's just goddamn fireworks. Move in now!'

The improvised explosive devices raining projectiles down on them might have been loud and alarming, but they posed little threat to a fully armoured assault team. Leaping to their feet, the operatives surged through the drifting sparks and brightly coloured smoke towards their target, weapons up and ready.

Anya, however, had used the brief distraction to abandon her position, and was now sprinting towards the metal stairwell at the far side of the warehouse, ducking and doing her best to avoid the flying projectiles. The armoured assault team might have been able to shrug it off, but she had no such protection.

She also knew the surprise and disorientation wouldn't last long. She had mere seconds to rendezvous with Alex and make her escape. She could only hope the young man was smart enough to pull out.

No sooner had this thought crossed her mind than a figure emerged from the smoke right in front of her, coalescing into solid reality before her eyes. She saw him just as he saw her, and raised his submachine gun to fire.

Her first instinct was pull away, but in one of those split-second decisions that often mean the difference between life and death, Anya instead rushed forward, angling slightly to the right, then shifting her weight, allowing herself to fall back. Her momentum carried her on so that she skidded along the ground past him.

She saw him adjust his aim, saw him twist the weapon downward and heard the rattling crack as it spat out a burst that chewed into the ground behind her, but it was too late.

As she skidded past, she angled the M4 towards him and returned fire. Unable to aim with any degree of accuracy, she simply held the trigger down and emptied the entire magazine into him. Many of her rounds missed altogether, others flattened themselves against his armour or ricocheted away, but enough found their mark to knock him off balance.

Sliding to a halt, Anya discarded the empty, smoking weapon and leapt to her feet. Ignoring the pain in her bruised body, she drew the M1911 automatic and kicked the stricken operative to the ground before he could fire again. Jamming the barrel beneath his chin, she fired a single round upward. There was a dull crunch and a metallic whang as the .45 calibre projectile tore up through his skull before impacting the inside of his helmet.

He was down, but others would be here soon enough, alerted by the sound of gunfire. She had to get out—

Her thoughts were cut short when something struck her hard across the back of the head, jerking her forward. White light exploded across her eyes as she went down, the pistol falling from her grip.

Anya landed in a heap beside the man she'd just killed, stars dancing across her vision and pain blazing from the back of her head. She'd been hit. How bad, she couldn't say. But she was alive. She had to get up.

Struggling to rise, she saw the bleary shape of the dead trooper's submachine gun just a few feet away, and groggily stretched out her hand for it. A sudden kick to the ribs put an end to such a meagre effort, knocking her over onto her back.

'Not this time, you little bitch,' a voice said, muffled by a face mask.

Looking up, Anya could see the man who had struck her with the butt of his weapon. The man who loomed huge and menacing, silhouetted against the flash and smoke of the fireworks as he raised his gun to fire.

A shot rang out, followed by another, and another. Anya flinched with each sharp crack, not understanding how she was still alive.

The operative in front of her jerked and staggered under the impacts, before a final round blasted straight through his face mask. He toppled backward, triggering a wild uncontrolled burst in his death throes that tore into the ceiling overhead, before collapsing in a twitching heap.

A moment later, a second figure leapt into view. A young man, his face etched with fear and concern, a smoking automatic clutched in his hand.

'Anya, are you okay?' Alex asked, his voice shaking. 'Can you walk?'

She stared back at him, dazed, struggling to understand. 'Alex…?'

'Get up!' he hissed. 'We have to go now!'

Hooking a hand beneath her arm, Alex managed to haul the injured woman to her feet and half-dragged her towards the metal stairwell. The blood pounded in her ears and her vision swam, yet she retained enough awareness to realise the urgency of the situation, and somehow found the strength to put one foot in front of the other, stumbling and lurching up the stairs.

'Hurry!' Alex urged her, coughing as he inhaled the thick cordite smoke all around.

The barrage was sputtering out now as the last of the pyrotechnics were expended, leaving a thick, choking cloud of acrid smoke hanging over the warehouse, but they both knew it wouldn't last long.

Anya managed to reach the top of the stairs, leading to a catwalk that ran just beneath the roof, and together they staggered along to the far corner, where a ladder led up to a rooftop access hatch.

Leaving his injured friend, Alex ascended the ladder, unlocked the hatch cover and heaved it open. Smoke poured through the gap, providing glimpses of a dark sky beyond.

'Come on!' the young man hissed. 'Let's go.'

The world was spinning around Anya, but through some great exertion of will she clutched at the metal rungs, hauling herself up one at a time.

Her vision was growing blurry again, the pain and disorientation assailing her. She felt like lead weights had been anchored to her body; every rung was like climbing a mountain, but still she forced herself upward.

Almost there.

Then she slipped, her hand missing the final rung above. She felt herself tumble backwards, already bracing herself for the bruising impact with the grate below. She knew even as she fell that she wouldn't have the strength to make the climb again.

Suddenly she felt something close around her wrist, felt herself jerked to a stop, and looked up to see Alex in the open hatch above her. His arm was shaking, his face contorted with the effort of holding her, but his grip was unfailing.

And with some titanic effort born out of desperation and sheer stubborn refusal to give in, he hauled her upward until she managed to grasp the edge of the hatch. Hooking her feet into the rungs below, Anya was at last able to lend her own meagre strength to his efforts, and with an exhausted gasp, she heaved herself out of the opening.

Drained by the exertion, they collapsed together on the rooftop.

–

Down below, Vizur Qalat crouched in a corner of the smoke-filled space. The sudden and unexpected barrage had bought him the time he needed to free himself, tipping his chair over so that it broke on impact.

Thus able to move, he'd limped away from the desperate gun battle and taken refuge at the rear of the building, where he waited for the assault team to take care of Maras and her accomplice. Now he sat slumped against the wall, silent and wary, teeth gritted against the pain of the gunshot wounds. True to her word, she'd made sure to administer flesh wounds only, though it scarcely lessened his animosity towards her.

He fervently hoped the team was able to capture her alive. He wanted to repay today's little interrogation session personally. Not to mention the security operative who had abandoned his post and fled to save his own sorry life. Qalat would ensure he made good on his threat to kill the man and his family for such cowardice.

The sound of footsteps approaching drew his attention back to more immediate matters, and he looked up as a pair of men in full assault gear approached him with their weapons up and ready.

'You took long enough,' he snapped in Pashto, his authority as director quickly reasserting itself. 'Get me a medic.'

Neither man responded, nor did they lower their weapons.

'Are you deaf?' Qalat demanded. 'Can't you see I've been shot?'

Reaching up slowly, one of the operatives pressed the transmit button on his comms unit. 'Alpha team. Principal is secure, requesting orders.'

Qalat blanched. The operative had spoken English, and it was a woman. This assault team was American.

'Copy that,' a voice replied. 'What's the status on the target?'

'They were expecting us. We've got men down.'

'I don't care about casualties. I want her dead.'

'Marcus Cain sent you, didn't he?' Qalat said, his heart beating fast and urgent now. 'He knew Maras was coming for me. You tell him I can help find her. I know what she's looking for.'

'You hearing this?' Riley asked, keeping her radio link open so that Hawkins could listen in.

The few seconds of silence that followed seemed to stretch out into hours.

'I've heard enough from him,' Hawkins decided. 'Kill him, and find Anya.'

'Wait!' Qalat pleaded as the woman trained her weapon on him. For the first time in his long career of careful planning and manoeuvring, of calculated risks and negotiation, of betraying and sacrificing others to further his own interests, at last he knew true fear.

'Cain needs me. There are things he doesn't know. We... we have a deal!'

'*Had* a deal, asshole,' Riley said calmly before putting three rounds through his chest. As the dead man slumped to the floor, his blood painting the wall behind, Riley turned to her second in command. 'Spread out. Find her!'

–

For the next few seconds, neither Anya nor Alex could say a word as they lay gasping for air, hearts pounding, muscles aching. They were each exhausted and hurting, but they weren't out of danger yet.

Rolling over, Alex grasped the hatch cover and swung it closed. Lacking anything to bolt it with, he hastily unbuckled his belt and looped it through the internal bolts, tightening the leather strap as far as it would go.

'That won't hold them long,' he warned, turning towards his companion. 'We have to move.'

Rousing herself, Anya gestured to the far end of the rooftop.

'The line,' she mumbled. 'Get it ready.'

'You be right behind me,' Alex said as he hurried away.

Their warehouse sat amid a heavily industrialised area, one of nearly a dozen identical units arrayed in rows along a main access road, with a stretch of brush-covered dead ground behind. Between each warehouse stood a gap of at least thirty feet – too far for any human to jump.

Fortunately, they had a different escape route in mind. Anticipating a possible attack, Anya had run a length of cable down from the roof of their warehouse and across the open ground behind, securing it to a support post for the chain link fence that encircled the site. The line had deliberately been left slack, even buried in places to avoid drawing attention.

Rushing over to the edge of the roof where this line had been coiled around the perimeter rail, Alex spotted the stack of cinderblocks attached to the end, grasped them and heaved them over the edge. The heavy counterweight plummeted away into the darkness below, drawing the cable with it until the line snapped taut, the old rail straining visibly.

'It's ready!' he called out. 'Hurry!'

Struggling to her feet, Anya limped over to him. Alex meanwhile snatched up the simple pair of leather straps that would serve as an improvised descent harness, wrapping one end around his wrist.

'Go,' she instructed him. 'I'll follow behind.'

Alex glanced uncertainly at the line stretching off into the darkness, then back at Anya. 'Maybe you should go first.'

A loud thump caused them both to turn as the hatch cover jump upward an inch or so before Alex's improvised binding held it back.

'No time to argue,' Anya decided. 'Go now, Alex!'

Swearing under his breath, Alex looped his descent harness over the cable and gripped it tight, testing the weight. A whole lot of things could go wrong in the next few seconds. The cable could snap, the harness could give way, or he could lose his grip and fall. Not to mention the prospect of getting shot while hanging suspended and helpless.

'Fuck it,' he muttered, pushing himself away from the edge.

The line jerked and flexed under his weight, swinging him from side to side and threatening to tear the harness right out of his grip, but he clung doggedly on as he began to slide down the cable, rapidly picking up speed. The wind whipped past his face and the ground rushed beneath him as the rooftop, and Anya, receded into the distance.

Alex tensed up, bracing himself as the perimeter fence hurtled towards him, bringing up his feet to cushion the impact as he slammed into the barrier.

Behind him, Anya watched as the young man disappeared into the darkness, the metal rail threatening to buckle under his weight.

The rattle of automatic fire drew her attention back to the access hatch, where a burst of gunfire had punched through the metal sheeting, tearing apart Alex's belt. As the hatch cover swung open from inside, Anya knew she was out of time. There was no choice but to risk it.

Looping the descender around the still-jerking cable, she gripped the leather straps tight, closed her eyes and threw herself off the roof.

The sickening moment of plunging vertigo was halted by a violent snap as the cable took her weight, very nearly tearing the straps from her grasp. She was weakened and disoriented after the fight, and quite possibly nursing a concussion. In short, she was in no condition to attempt a fast rope descent like this, but there was no alternative. She either went for it, or she died.

Another burst of gunfire crackled somewhere behind, but Anya paid it little attention. Every ounce of willpower and strength was now focussed on maintaining her grip as the ground soared by below, every second carrying her further from the rooftop and the armed men sent to kill her.

She could feel her grip weakening, the strap beginning to slide through her fingers. Desperately she tried to hold on, but her body was reluctant to obey her commands, and little by little she could feel herself losing her hold.

Up ahead, she saw the perimeter fence rushing towards her, with Alex crouched down beside it, and gritted her teeth as she fought to keep hold for a few more seconds.

It was no good. The strap slipped through her hand and disappeared. She fell, plunging through the air, waiting for the crushing impact as the ground rushed up to smash her like a giant fist.

But to her surprise, she tumbled to the ground a mere moment later, pitching forward and instinctively rolling to absorb the impact and bleed away some of her forward momentum.

'Anya! Are you okay?' Alex asked, hurrying over to her.

Picking herself up with difficulty, Anya gingerly moved her limbs. Pain radiated from a dozen bruises and cuts where sharp stones had gashed her skin, but she couldn't feel anything broken at least. What she hadn't realised was that her weight on the line had caused the weakened railing to buckle outward, adding enough slack to lower the height of the cable and save her from serious injury.

It had been a lucky escape indeed.

'I'm all right,' she confirmed, not entirely sure how true that was.

Alerted by distant shouts on the rooftop, Alex pointed towards a gap in the dilapidated fence. 'We can't stay here. Come on!'

As they slipped through the ragged gap in the chain links and into the darkness beyond, Anya spoke up. 'I have to warn Ryan.'

'Ryan?' Alex exclaimed. 'I thought you wanted nothing to do with him?'

'Things have changed,' the woman replied. 'Everything has changed.'

Part Four

Something to Kill For

He who seeks revenge should remember to dig two graves.

Chinese Proverb

Chapter 48

At just after one p.m., Marcus Cain's desk phone bleeped with an incoming call. Steeling himself, he lifted the receiver. 'Director Cain.'

The crisp, efficient voice of a female operator greeted him. 'Please hold for the president, sir.'

The line went silent again. He heard a few distant clicks and buzzes as the lines were synched up and the encryption software at both ends did its thing. Then a second or two later, Cain was connected with the president of the United States.

'Marcus, good to speak with you again,' POTUS began, speaking in the smooth, measured cadence he'd become so well known for. 'How have you been?'

'I've been just fine, Mr President,' he lied. 'Thank you for asking.'

'Well, I've got a feeling your day's about to get a whole lot better,' POTUS said, clearly pleased with news he was about to give. 'The vote just came in from the Senate Select Committee. It's my honour to inform you that they've approved your appointment as permanent director of the CIA. Congratulations, Director Cain.'

Cain closed his eyes and exhaled, allowing it to sink in. Allowing himself just a moment to appreciate the accomplishment.

'The honour is mine, Mr President.'

'Look, I know you've worked long and hard for this. And I know you've given a great deal in service of your country. I'm confident you'll make an excellent director, and I have a feeling we'll be needing men like you in the years ahead.'

'Thank you, sir. I won't let you down.'

'Good man,' POTUS said, and Cain had the impression he genuinely meant it. 'Now, I believe the DNI will be in touch shortly to invite you for the confirmation ceremony later today. It's a formality of course, but we have to go through the whole nine yards. If you don't mind heading over to this side of the Potomac one more time, that is?'

Cain managed to force a laugh. 'Of course, sir.'

'Good. My people will arrange the swearing-in ceremony at Langley once you've finished at the Senate. We'll try to keep press involvement to a minimum, given everything else that's going on right now. And maybe then we can get down to some real work, huh?'

Cain smiled at the thought. Yes, there was indeed a lot of work to do.

'Thank you, Mr President.'

—

Barely twenty minutes after Cain's momentous call with the White House, Drake's cell phone started buzzing. Bracing himself, he hit the Receive Call icon.

'Yeah?'

'It's me,' Starke announced. 'Cain's office just took a call from the White House. It's happening today.'

Standing in the midst of their makeshift base, Drake raised his free hand and snapped his fingers to get everyone's attention. All work and conversation ceased as the others looked expectantly towards him.

'When?'

'The confirmation ceremony is at six p.m.'

Drake looked at his watch. Barely two hours to have everything in place. It would be tight, but they could do it.

'You know what you have to do?'

'I do,' Starke confirmed.

'Good. Activate your comms unit and get to Langley. We'll talk you through it.'

'I'm on my way there now,' the NSA director confirmed. He paused before adding, 'This is it, Ryan. Don't let me down.'

'I won't.'

Closing down the call, he looked around at his companions. The small group of friends, of family, who had followed him all this way, who had risked their lives for him more times than he could count. The people he was asking to help him one last time.

They were watching him now. Waiting. Ready.

'We're on,' he stated. 'Get ready.'

Chapter 49

Golyanovo District, Moscow – March 10th, 2003

Marcus Cain inhaled, tasting the frigid night air as he stood in the shadow of a half-built concrete wall, waiting for his contact to arrive. The construction site in which he was standing had been started when the hammer and sickle still flew over the Kremlin: a grand housing scheme for the good workers of the city that had never come to fruition.

With the fall of the Soviet Union, construction had halted in the early 1990s and never restarted. Ghostly frames of half-finished buildings stood everywhere, most covered with graffiti, their concrete supports crumbling away to expose the steel reinforcing rods beneath. Everything of value had long since vanished, leaving just the bare bones standing as silent reminders of what might have been.

Not for the first time, he caught himself reflecting on his own involvement in that. Were it not for the actions of himself and others, might the hammer and sickle still be flying? Might Europe still be divided, and the Cold War still be raging?

He shook his head, banishing the notion. He wasn't here to reminisce about past wars, but to avert future ones.

He reached beneath his coat to feel the solid shape of the Glock pistol he'd brought with him. When someone arranged to meet with you in waste ground on the outskirts of Moscow in the middle of the night, the chances of a violent confrontation were high. Especially if that man was Viktor Surovsky.

Cain had done his research on the man. A career KGB agent, he had served as an intelligence officer in Afghanistan in the 1980s, conducting a brutal and highly effective campaign against the Mujahideen. He'd gone quiet after the dissolution of the USSR, falling off the Agency's radar, only to re-emerge during the recent conflict in Chechnya where, by all accounts, he'd continued the ruthlessly efficient tactics learned in Afghanistan.

A hard, dangerous man who had lived a hard, dangerous life.

'A cold night, my friend.'

Cain whirled around to see a figure standing in the shadows of a gutted apartment block. It took most of his self-control not to reach for the pistol on instinct.

The figure moved, resolving itself into the shape of an elderly man in a black overcoat and an ushanka, the traditional fur hat ubiquitous in Russia. Even in the poor light, Cain could make out the sallow, gaunt face of Viktor Surovsky.

'In my country, we are well used to the cold,' the Russian went on.

His English was excellent, with only a mild accent. Smiling, he reached into his coat pocket, and again Cain resisted the temptation to grab for the pistol.

An anxious moment later, Surovsky produced a small hip flask, undid the stopper and took a generous swig. Satisfied, he held it out to Cain, who shook his head.

'I didn't come all this way to share a drink.'

The Russian snorted with amusement. 'Indeed not. You're here because you want information from me. Information that could prove extremely valuable to you.'

Cain's look was dubious. 'That depends on what you want in return.'

'We will talk about what I want in a moment. First, let's talk about what you want, Marcus Cain,' he said. 'The United States is preparing to invade Iraq. The war could start within days.'

None of this was a secret, of course. The build-up of military forces in the Gulf had been well documented by the world's news media.

'We both know this invasion will be a costly mistake,' Surovsky went on, speaking with absolute confidence. 'Believe me, we Russians know the cost of ill-conceived invasions.'

There was a glimmer in his eyes as he said this. An old fire of anger and hatred kindled briefly into life by the humiliating defeat in Afghanistan. Another event that Cain had played a part in orchestrating.

'You are here, Mr Cain, because you're looking for a way to stop this war before it happens. A way to save hundreds of thousands of lives.' The man smiled, though it was as cold as the night around them. 'What if I told you I could give it to you?'

Now they were getting down to it. 'What are you offering?'

'I am offering you the president of Iraq.'

Cain's eyes lit up. Saddam Hussein was the rock on which the Iraqi regime was built. Without him, the government would collapse within days, allowing more moderate successors to take over. Removing the need for armed invasion.

'How, exactly?' he asked warily.

'One of the members of his inner circle is willing to trade his location in exchange for money and a guarantee of freedom. Once you know this, a simple drone strike would be all it takes to eliminate him. You could go down in history as the man who stopped a war and saved thousands of lives, Mr Cain. Is that not a legacy to be proud of?'

It was indeed. America had already been drawn into one costly and fruitless foreign war in Afghanistan. They had been fighting for two years already, with no end in sight. The last thing they needed was to start another.

'That's what you're offering,' he said. 'What do you want in return?'

The FSB agent took another drink from his flask, relishing both the drink and the moment that was about to come. 'What do I want?'

–

Cain was making his last-minute preparations before departing Langley when his desk intercom buzzed. It was his personal secretary in the outer office.

'Yeah, Martha?'

'Sir, I have NSA Director Starke here to see you.'

Cain frowned. In all the time they'd worked together, Starke had never sought him out at Langley. Their meetings had been conducted in secrecy, far from prying eyes. Why come here today?

He glanced at his watch. His executive motorcade was already on standby downstairs, ready to ferry him to the Senate. He could ill afford a lengthy delay.

Still, curiosity compelled him to accept.

'All right. Show him in.'

Moments later, the door opened and Richard Starke strode into the office. Unusually, he was wearing his official naval uniform rather than the drab grey suits he traditionally favoured. He was even walking straighter and taller, carrying himself with the confidence and bearing of the military man he'd once been.

'Richard, this is… unexpected,' Cain began, putting extra emphasis on that word as he rose from his desk. 'Not often we have the NSA director here at Langley.'

Cain's secretary discreetly closed the door behind him. Given the gravity of events that were discussed in this office, the room was soundproofed and free of recording devices. They could talk freely.

'Well, it's not every day we get a new CIA director,' Starke replied. 'I hear congratulations are in order, Marcus?'

–

On the other side of the Potomac, Keira Frost sat hunched in the back of her panel van, doing her best to ignore the steady drumming of rain against the roof.

They had pulled into a layby along the tree-lined Clara Barton Parkway just over the river, barely 1000 metres from Cain's office. It was as close as they could get legally.

'I'm ready to begin my sweep,' she said, speaking calmly and efficiently into her headset. 'You need to get close to him, Starke.'

'How long is this gonna take?' Mitchell called from the driver's seat up front, keeping a wary eye on passing vehicles.

'There are too many variables at play,' Frost replied briefly, the tension and pressure of the moment obvious. 'But we get one shot, and that's it.'

–

'You hear a lot, Richard,' Cain acknowledged.

A flicker of a smile brightened the man's normally stoic features. 'Wouldn't be a very good NSA director if I didn't.'

He moved forward, approaching Cain's desk so that the two men faced each other across the shining expanse of teak.

'Officially, of course, it's tradition for other agency directors to welcome new appointments into their roles. I imagine we'll be working together closely in the years ahead.'

–

The modified cell phone, scanning for other devices to copy, finally found what it was looking for and transmitted a result that pinged on Frost's laptop a fraction of a second later.

'Yo! I got something,' she exclaimed, leaning forward to study the data on screen. Her elation soon turned to a frown of confusion. 'Wait, what the fuck?'

Mitchell twisted around in her seat. 'What's wrong?'

'There's two cell phones in range,' the tech specialist replied. 'Either there's someone else in the room we don't know about—'

'Or Cain's got a hidden burner,' Mitchell finished for her. 'Can you clone them both?'

Clearly the burner was likely to yield the most useful intel. The problem was that they didn't know which was which, and there might not be time to clone both.

'Yeah, but it'll take time. Isolating the first one now.' As the cloning process began and the on-screen progress bar slowly began to fill up, Frost unmuted her headset to speak with Starke. 'It's working, Starke. Keep him talking, and for Christ's sake *don't let him leave.*'

–

Cain raised an eyebrow, regarding his NSA counterpart with curiosity. 'And unofficially?'

Starke eased himself into the chair opposite, regarding Cain across the desk. 'We've known each other a long time, Marcus.'

That was an interesting statement, Cain thought. For all the times they'd met and exchanged information over the years, they had never talked of personal matters. Cain knew the true personality of the man seated opposite no better than a stranger on the street.

'And I've always played it straight with you,' Starke went on, looking oddly uncomfortable now, as if he was struggling to find the right words. 'Given your new... appointment, I'd like to think you'll keep that in mind. When the time comes.'

–

Frost's eyes were glued to the progress bar on screen as it crept agonisingly slowly towards completion. The tension in the van was palpable as the early evening rain continued to patter off the metal roof.

'First cell is at fifty per cent,' she said, flexing and tensing her fingers anxiously. There was nothing she could do to hurry the process. All she could do was watch. 'Keep him talking, Starke.'

–

Leaning back in his chair, Cain surveyed his counterpart. In official terms at least, they were equals: heads of their respective organisations, commanding considerable authority and influence. But in the true race to the top, Cain was about to pull dramatically ahead of his rival. A fact that was doubtless weighing heavily on his mind now.

'Come on, Richard. You don't really think I'm that petty, do you?'

Starke shifted a little in his seat. A minor change in posture, but a significant show of discomfort all the same. He wasn't a man accustomed to being put on the spot like this.

'The measure of a man is how he treats the people he *doesn't* have to be kind to,' Starke said, paraphrasing the well-known proverb.

–

'Come on, come on,' Frost whispered, desperately willing the computer to work faster. The time between incremental movements looked to be growing longer, the seconds stretching out into hours.

'How long?' Mitchell demanded. She was just as edgy as her younger companion, but completely ignorant of how their efforts were progressing.

'We're at seventy-eight per cent on the first cell. Stay with him, Starke,' she commanded the NSA director.

–

It was Cain's turn to offer a faint, knowing smile. 'You know, the last we spoke, you offered me a few words of advice. It seems only fair that I return the favour now.'

Starke sat watching him in silence.

'Do you want to know your problem?' Leaning forward, Cain rested his hands on the desk and looked him in the eye. 'You think small, Richard. You view the world in such narrow terms, obsessing over the little details but missing the big picture. Maybe if you saw things as I do, we'd be in different positions right now.'

He saw something flare behind Starke's eyes then as the man sat stock still on the other side of his desk. Anger, resentment, jealousy... perhaps all of those things. He couldn't quite say, but it was there all the same.

However, he never got the chance to respond. No sooner had Cain spoken than his intercom buzzed.

'Sir, your motorcade is waiting downstairs,' Cain's secretary advised. The tone of her voice warned him that time was growing short.

'I'm sorry, Richard, but duty calls,' he said, rising from his chair and flashing a charming smile. 'Wouldn't want to miss this one. You understand, right?'

'Of course.' Starke stood up stiffly. 'We all have our jobs to do, and I wouldn't want to keep you from yours.' Rounding the desk, he stepped close and held out a hand.

Cain took it, noting the strength behind Starke's grip.

'Enjoy today, Marcus,' he said quietly. 'You deserve it.'

That look was there again, and Cain briefly wondered at the intent behind it. Had he mistaken jealousy and envy for something colder and more menacing?

Then he released his grip and the look vanished.

Cain was out of time. He had to leave now.

'Thanks for coming over, Director Starke,' he said, turning away and opening his office door so that his secretary could hear them once more. 'Looking forward to working with you. Oh, and see yourself out, will you?'

–

'Fuck, he bailed on us,' Mitchell hissed. Twisting around in her seat, she looked at Frost, who was still staring intently at her computer screen. 'Tell me you got it.'

'Only had time to clone one cell,' she replied, though her expression betrayed her familiar lopsided grin. 'But we've got the son of a bitch. Give me a couple of minutes to reconstitute it here, and we're ready to rock.'

Excitement and anticipation surged through her. They had him!

'Keira, remind me to buy you a drink when this is all over,' Mitchell said, switching channels to speak with Drake.

'Make mine a tequila,' Frost called back.

'Ryan, come in. Over.'

'Go.'

'Cain bailed on the meeting. He's got two phones, we only had time to clone one.'

'Copy that. What's his status?'

'He's preparing to leave Langley. His motorcade's standing by.' She looked around at Frost again, sensing the anticipation, the tension rising by the moment. 'It's your call. What do you want to do?'

Drake was silent for a few seconds, weighing up everything that was at stake, everything they stood to lose. Everything they'd given to get this far.

'We're going for it,' he said firmly. 'Get everyone into position. This is it.'

Chapter 50

A light rain was falling as Cain strode outside towards the waiting vehicle, typical of springtime in Virginia. He made no attempt to shield himself from the inclement weather, however. Instead he paused, closed his eyes and raised his face up to the sky, feeling the droplets of water on his skin.

This was the day, he knew. The day that would change everything.

'Sir?' the protective agent waiting by the car said uncertainly. 'Everything okay?'

Opening his eyes, Cain gave a faint smile. 'Sure. Everything's just fine.'

Slipping into the vehicle, he dug his phone out and dialled an internal Agency number, waiting a few seconds before it was answered.

'Franklin.'

'Dan, it's Marcus,' he began. 'What's the status of Neptune Spear?'

'We're green across the board,' Franklin confirmed, an edge of anticipation in his voice now. 'The assault force is on ten-minute standby, just like you ordered. Say the word, and we're ready to move.'

'The word is given, Dan. Contact Vice Admiral McRaven at JSOC and tell him he has authorisation to proceed immediately,' Cain instructed. 'Alert all members of the National Security Council, and get the Situation Room prepped. They're not going to want to miss this.'

'What about you?' Franklin asked. 'Shouldn't you be here for this?'

'I've got business to take care of. You're head of Special Activities Division. I want you to lead the session.'

Cain heard his subordinate let out a breath as the magnitude of what was about to happen settled on him. 'I understand.'

'Let's make history,' Cain said as the car pulled away from the main building.

Jalalabad, Afghanistan

It took less than five minutes for Franklin to put a call through to Vice Admiral William McRaven, the head of Joint Special Operations Command, and the man charged with overseeing Operation Neptune Spear on the ground.

From there, the deployment instructions were issued to the task force itself, stationed at a Forward Operating Base in the mountains of south-eastern Afghanistan. Night had already fallen there, the rugged peaks showing black against a starlit sky.

'All right, hustle up! We have final authorisation, we go tonight,' the SEAL team leader shouted as his men hurried back and forth inside the hangar that had been their home for the past several days, snatching up weapons and equipment. 'This is it, gentlemen!'

Behind him, pilots strapped themselves into the cockpits of their transport choppers, quickly running through pre-flight checks, while high overhead, unmanned drones were repositioned, vectored in towards the target area. The entire might of the US special forces machine now mobilising behind their objective.

Washington DC

'He's on the move!' Frost called out, studying her screen. 'Heading south-east towards central DC. Right on the money.'

'You copying this, Ryan?' Mitchell asked.

'Roger that,' Drake replied. He was breathing a little heavier as he hurried to get both himself and his heavy load into position. 'What's his ETA on the bridge?'

'About ten minutes.'

'Understood. Dietrich, are you ready?'

'Say the word,' the German operative grunted.

'Do it.'

–

The Theodore Roosevelt Bridge crosses the Potomac just north of the huge white marble columns of the Lincoln Memorial. One of the main arteries leading into the heart of the capital, its eastern side terminates in a complex series of junctions and off-ramps as the main highway splits in different directions, including Constitution Avenue, which runs along the northern side of the National Mall all the way to Capitol Hill.

Now heavy with evening traffic as weary commuters made their way home, few took notice of the garbage truck heading in the opposite direction. Most were trying to get *out* of central DC rather than back in, so one of the city's municipal vehicles was of little interest.

However, rather than slowing down as it approached the eastern end of the bridge, where the roadway curves sharply right, the lumbering truck sped up, surging past the slower-moving cars in the right lanes. Horn blasts sounded in its wake from angry motorists forced to move aside, but still it continued onward, the driver seemingly oblivious.

At the last moment he swung the wheel hard right, causing the rear tyres to skid and lose purchase on the slick tarmac. Fishtailing out of control, the truck clipped the concrete lane divider and spun violently left, threatening to tip over as its own momentum worked against it.

With the crunch of buckling metal and shattered concrete, the truck shuddered to a halt, smoke and steam rising from the crumpled engine bay, oil leaking from the broken transmission. At a stroke, the entire eastbound side of the bridge had become blocked by the wreck.

–

In the motorcade heading south-west along the banks of the Potomac, lead protective agent Sarah Watts frowned as the report of the crash came through her comms unit.

'Unit Two, be advised. RTA on the Roosevelt Bridge eastbound, traffic's already building up on the western approach.'

Watts frowned. 'Copy that, Dispatch. What's the sitrep?'

'Looks like a garbage truck hit the central reservation at the east end. Local PD are on it, but right now its FUBAR,' the dispatch officer replied. 'Recommend you take an alternate route.'

Watts felt a momentary sense of unease. One that she couldn't quite articulate, but which stirred memories of a similar incident several years earlier. Road accidents were as common in DC as any other major city, but what were the chances of such a crash happening at this very moment, right on their intended route?

'Understood, Dispatch,' she confirmed. 'Switching to Alternate One now.'

Switching radio frequencies so that each driver in the motorcade could hear her, she issued her instructions. 'All teams, be advised. We have an RTA on the Roosevelt Bridge. Switch to Alternate One now. Repeat, switch to Alternate One now.' She paused before adding, 'And look sharp. Call out anything that doesn't look right.'

'What's on your mind, Watts?' the driver asked as she clicked off her transmitter. It wasn't often she felt the need to remind her people of their jobs.

Watts was reluctant to voice her fears, born from the irrational belief that speaking of them would somehow make them more real and therefore more likely. And yet she couldn't quite shake the sense of déjà vu, that something was coming for them. Just like several years earlier, when a routine prisoner transfer had turned into an absolute clusterfuck, ending with a CIA operative pointing a gun in her face.

That too had begun with a truck crash.

'Just a feeling,' she replied, scanning the highway ahead. 'I hope I'm wrong.'

–

Overlooking the placid, muddy waters of the Potomac, the Georgetown Car Barn was a large, red-bricked structure dating back well over a century. Starting out as a streetcar manufacturing plant, it had fulfilled various roles during its long history before finally falling into disuse.

After years of neglect, it had eventually been leased by Georgetown University, who converted it to house their School of Arts and Sciences – a popular place for graduate students to continue their advanced studies. At this time of day, however, the academic work was winding down and most students were packing up for the day.

Amongst this general hustle and bustle, few took notice of the man in a drab grey maintenance uniform carrying a heavy tool bag as he made his way along the building's central corridor. The campus and its facilities were old, and such maintenance personnel were a common sight.

His head was down, his face hidden by a baseball cap, his height and build unremarkable. Nobody questioned him as he ascended the stairwell, and nobody took notice when he produced a little handheld device, using it to pick the locked access door leading up to the clock tower. In a matter of seconds, he'd disappeared inside and eased the door closed behind him.

Alone in the narrow stairwell, Drake removed the hat, hoisted the heavy bag over his shoulder and started his climb. His heart was beating hard and urgent as he ascended, the bag and its bulky contents bumping and jolting against his back.

His radio earpiece crackled. 'It's done. The bridge is blocked,' Dietrich reported.

'Copy that. What's your status?'

'Had to get out of there fast before local PD showed up,' he explained, panting. 'But it's out of action for sure. I can see tailbacks all the way to the western end.'

'Good man,' Drake said, satisfied. 'Keira, what's the ETA?'

'Just a few minutes. Better hurry.'

'I'm on it.'

Reaching the top of the stairwell, he tried the door. Just like the one at the bottom, it too was locked, but a couple of attempts with the lockpick gun was enough to 'ping' the tumbler system, forcing them to align as if a key had been inserted.

Gripping the handle, he stopped. 'I'm at the door. Kill the rooftop cameras.'

'Roger that,' the tech specialist replied. 'Looping external cam footage… now. You're clear.'

Drake didn't hesitate for a second. He trusted Frost's technical expertise with his life. Opening the door, he emerged onto a covered walkway that ran along the rooftop, with arched gables set at intervals facing out onto the street below. These unusual architectural features were likely a holdover from the building's original function, retained for cosmetic value only.

However, they provided a perfect vantage point over the bridge below, now shrouded in low-lying cloud. The rain was coming down harder now, dripping from guttering, running in tiny rivers down the tiled roof and sluicing down drainage pipes from the clocktower above. The air was warm and humid, typical of the time of year.

Staying low, Drake hurried over to the nearest gable and set his burden down, glad to be rid of the heavy weight. Unzipping the bag, he carefully removed the components of the dismantled sniper rifle and set to work.

First he inserted the barrel and breech assembly into the stock and trigger mechanism, exerting downward pressure until it locked into place, then working the action a few times to check the feed system was functioning properly.

'Target's approaching the bridge,' Frost warned. The tension was almost palpable now. 'Two minutes out.'

Drake didn't respond; he just carried on working with the same quick, calculated efficiency. The high-powered telescopic sight was next, sliding easily onto the top-mounted rail. Last out was the large, heavy magazine, loaded with five rounds of high-explosive, armour-piercing incendiary .50 calibre ammunition. Each projectile powerful enough to bring down a low-flying chopper.

Five rounds. Five chances to kill Marcus Cain.

Drake paused then, contemplating everything that needed to happen in the next two minutes. The magnitude of what he was about to do. Another man might have been keyed up and anxious, filled with nerves, even shaking at the thought of what he was undertaking, but not Drake. Not now. He'd been through too much to let those kinds of emotions interfere.

His only sense was one of calm, controlled and absolute resolve. All fear and doubt had fallen away, leaving nothing but the mission. His companions had risked their lives to make this happen, to give him this one perfect chance, but the final step was for him to take.

Pushing the magazine home until the retainer pin locked it firmly into place, he reached forward and extended the bipod legs mounted on the underside. With the weapon now loaded and assembled, Drake set it down on the rim of the window and took up position behind it, sighting the bridge below.

'I'm in position,' he reported, his voice icy calm. 'Standing by.'

Chapter 51

Afghanistan

The assault force of about two dozen operatives, loaded aboard a pair of stealth-modified Black Hawk choppers, lifted off from their staging area just before midnight local time. They were accompanied by two Chinook heavy transport helicopters, with a number of ground attack aircraft flying in support.

The Chinooks would fly only part of the way to the target, peeling away and landing in open desert where they would remain on standby as a rapid-response force. When it came to the assault itself, the Black Hawks would be on their own.

As soon as they were airborne, the Black Hawks descended to less than a hundred feet and accelerated up to maximum cruising speed, flying nap-of-the-earth through the winding mountain valleys all the way. With no recognition lights and only a sliver of moonlight overhead, the pilots were forced to rely on night vision equipment and advanced avionics to avoid a fatal collision.

In the crew compartments of both choppers, the mood was tense and anxious as SEAL operatives went through weapon and equipment checks, readying themselves for what was about to happen. They had trained and prepared for this mission for months, had done everything they could to anticipate every scenario, but they were all veterans of previous operations. They knew how easily things could go wrong.

'Time on target, sixty minutes!' the team leader called out. 'Sixty minutes!'

CIA Headquarters, Langley

Seated in the conference room on the top floor of the New Head-quarters Building, Dan Franklin clenched his fists as he stared at the

TV screen opposite, showing the position of the strike force as they approached their target with, it seemed to him, glacial slowness.

He could imagine the mood onboard those choppers. The tension, the anticipation, the adrenaline high. He'd been through it himself, had experienced the fear and the elation of combat, but this was different. The importance of this mission went far above anything he'd taken part in.

This mission could change the course of history.

'National Security Council is convening right now,' Kennedy reported, checking his laptop. 'The president and his staff are in the Situation Room at the White House. They should be online any minute.'

'Copy that,' Franklin replied, acutely aware that some of the most powerful men in the world were about to get on the line. And he was the one who would have to answer to them.

'Where the hell is Cain?' Kennedy asked, vexed by the director's absence. 'He should be here overseeing this.'

'Keep your mind on the job,' Franklin ordered. 'This is bigger than Cain now. Bigger than any of us.'

Kennedy glanced up at him, but wisely remained silent.

–

As his car made its way towards central DC in heavy traffic, rain pattering around them, Marcus Cain took out his phone and put through a call to his subordinate.

'Franklin,' came the terse response.

'What's the situation, Dan?'

'Strike force is en route to target. ETA, sixty minutes. We're about to go online with the president and the NSC,' Franklin reported. 'You sure you don't want to be here for this?'

How he wished he could be. He wanted to be there in that Situation Room with the rest of them, watching events unfold via satellite link, watching history being made. Sharing in the elation and celebrations, just like he'd done twenty years earlier when the Cold War came to an end. When the future had seemed like some great highway of infinite possibilities stretching out before him.

But he knew he couldn't. For his plan to succeed, for all of this to be worth it, things had to play out the way he'd intended.

'I've got other business to take care of first.'

'I don't understand.'

'I know, Dan. I know.'

He glanced out the window, surveying the muddy expanse of the Potomac as they approached the bridge. Not long now.

'But when this is all over, you will.'

—

'Heads up,' Frost said over the radio. 'Target's on the western approach now.'

Angling the heavy sniper rifle upward, Drake reached up and adjusted the telescopic zoom, focussing on the far side of the bridge. And sure enough, there was the three-vehicle motorcade, moving steadily in time with the traffic. Cain was in there. Heading straight at him, straight into the kill zone.

'Got them in sight,' he confirmed. 'Range, five hundred metres.'

'Copy that. Cell phone tracking is locked.'

Grasping the side-mounted charging handle, Drake racked it back, hearing the crisp click as the first round was drawn into the breach. The convoy was already well within the rifle's 1500 metre effective range, but he wouldn't open fire yet. He needed to be sure.

Ignoring the black SUVs up front and trailing behind, he focussed on the limousine at the centre of the convoy; the windows were darkened, masking the interior from view. Large, bulky and heavy, it moved with the ponderous speed of its powerful V8 engine weighed down by layers of armour and bulletproof glass.

That was where he would concentrate his fire. His first shot would go straight through the radiator, blasting apart the engine block and disabling the limo. After that, he would unleash everything through the windshield, killing the driver before the high explosive rounds detonated inside. The sealed environment would magnify the effects of the deadly projectiles. If Cain wasn't killed by direct fire or flying shrapnel, the incendiary effects would immolate him regardless.

A spare magazine sat beside him, ready to be loaded and used if the opening salvo wasn't enough to finish the job. Drake had practised and rehearsed the magazine changeover to the point he could perform it blindfolded.

'Four hundred metres. I have good line of sight.'

Once the limo had been reduced to a smoking ruin and he was satisfied that every living thing inside it was dead, then would come the final phase of his plan – evacuation. This phase would have to be conducted with the greatest of haste, because his position was certain to be betrayed by the noise of the AS-50. Even if it were possible to fit a suppressor to such a massive weapon, it would do no good – the blast of the .50 calibre rounds would be impossible to mask.

'Three hundred metres.'

They were well within firing range now, and perfectly aligned for a kill shot. Rarely were snipers afforded such an ideal target.

For barely a second, Drake thought of all the people he'd lost because of the man in that limo. Good people who had died because of him. So many others whose lives had been destroyed. He felt as if each of them was with him in that moment – shadowy spectres hovering over him, waiting for him to act.

'It's all on you now, Ryan,' Frost said, her tone hushed and breathless now that the moment had come. 'Take the shot.'

Lining up his sights on the limo's front grille, Drake exhaled slowly, allowing the tension to leave his body as his finger tightened on the trigger. No more questions, no more doubts, no more hesitation.

Just him and his target.

'Firing.'

Then abruptly he stopped, alerted by a change around him. A minor shift in the flow of air, the barely audible thud of a boot on the wet rooftop, the faint scent of another human body close by.

Someone who had been expecting him.

'Don't move,' a voice commanded. 'Take your finger off the trigger.'

Chapter 52

The agonising seconds stretched out as everyone in the van held their breath, waiting for the shooting to start. Waiting for confirmation that their target had been destroyed.

But there was nothing. No distant crack of gunfire. No explosion as the limo's gas tank ignited. No radio transmission from Drake to report the completion of his grim task.

Just the drumming of rain on the steel roof.

'Ryan, he's in range now. I repeat, target is in your sights,' Frost spoke into her radio. Her voice was carefully measured, but the others could see her hand shaking. 'It's now or never. What are you waiting for?'

There was no response except the faint hiss of static over the radio net.

'Something's wrong,' Jessica said. She knew her brother wouldn't hesitate at a moment like this. 'Pull up the cameras on that rooftop.'

Switching screens, Frost accessed the security feeds from Drake's sniping position, which were still feeding looped footage into the building's system, and brought up the camera covering Drake's position.

The moment the footage appeared on the screen, Jessica let out a gasp of horror.

'Oh, God.'

–

'Take your finger off the trigger and put the weapon down.'

The voice that spoke to him was female, American, slightly muffled by a mask or fabric covering the mouth. Whoever she was, she had the drop on him.

The convoy was getting close now. Barely 200 metres away, moving steadily amidst the busy traffic on the bridge. Cain's limo was in his sights, perfectly lined up, but it wouldn't be for much longer.

He had just seconds to make his choice.

'You going to kill me for this?' he asked. 'For him?'

He heard the click of a weapon being cocked, smelled the faint odour of gun oil. It could only be inches from his head.

'Don't make me show you.'

Drake closed his eyes, letting out a faint sigh as he took his finger off the rifle's trigger. A sigh of disappointment at what he was about to do.

It happened fast. Sweeping his arm around, Drake violently smacked the weapon aside, hearing the distinctive clang of metal as it clattered to the ground nearby. He didn't care where it landed right now; what mattered was that it was out of the fight.

Now he needed to deal with its owner.

Rounding on his opponent, he lashed out with a strike to the throat, knowing that a hard blow there would collapse her larynx and drop her like a stone. She saw it coming and twisted aside, deflecting the blow with her forearm. Drake noticed the sudden shift in posture, knew a retaliatory attack was coming, and instinctively threw up his arms to parry it.

He and his adversary were different but equally matched; one larger and stronger, the other faster and more agile. For a few seconds, they traded blows, ducking and blocking and looking for an opening, a moment of vulnerability.

Drake had no stomach for a prolonged fight; not with the mission hanging by a thread. He had to end this quickly.

As his opponent tried to grab for his arm, hoping to twist it and force him off balance, Drake countered with a kick to the leg that buckled her knee. An open strike to the centre of the chest sent her reeling.

But far from being out of the fight, she used her momentum, rolling backward and springing into a crouch. At the same moment she drew a knife from her belt, gathering herself to leap at her opponent again.

But her momentary lapse had bought Drake the time he needed to snatch up her fallen weapon and turn it on her.

'Enough, Ryan!' the woman snapped. 'I'm not your enemy!'

Dropping the knife, she reached up and tore her mask off, revealing her face for the first time. It was a face that Drake had never expected to see for the rest of his life, and he let out an involuntary gasp of disbelief.

'Sam?'

–

'Unit Two, what's your status?' Watts asked as the convoy rumbled over the wet tarmac, approaching the eastern end of the bridge, wipers fighting against the rain.

'Two here. All good. No contacts.'

'That feeling still kicking in?' the driver asked with a hint of good-natured mockery. Intuitions and 'bad feelings' weren't unknown in their line of work, but they rarely came to anything.

Her eyes swept the buildings lining the eastern shores of the Potomac up ahead, silhouetted against the sombre grey sky. Hotels, offices and residential blocks were everywhere, but for some reason she felt her eye drawn towards the dominant red brick structure of the Georgetown Car Barn. Especially the big square clocktower that loomed over the entire complex, providing a perfect view across the bridge approach.

If she were planning an ambush, that's where she would be right now.

'Maybe,' she said, trying to shake her unease. 'I guess it was nothing.'

–

'That's right, Ryan,' she said, picking herself up stiffly. 'It's Sam.'

Drake's mind was reeling as he tried to make sense of what he was seeing. Samantha McKnight, once a trusted member of his own team. The woman he'd once even imagined starting a new life with.

The traitor who had been acting as a spy for Marcus Cain since the very beginning, who had compromised their mission in Pakistan, betraying them all. People were dead because of her actions.

Rushing forward, Drake clamped a hand around her throat, virtually lifting her off the ground as he pressed the weapon against her chest.

'Tell me why I shouldn't kill you right now,' he snarled. Whatever shock and confusion he might have felt at McKnight's sudden appearance had vanished, replaced by years of pent-up pain and fury at her betrayal.

'Ryan, the target's almost on top of you,' Frost's voice buzzed urgently in his earpiece. 'Twenty seconds, you're going to lose him!'

'I'm here to stop you,' McKnight said, her voice rasping as his grip tightened. 'You're making a mistake.'

'My biggest mistake was trusting you,' he spat. 'You sold us out, you piece of shit!'

'Ryan, what's going on there?' Frost pleaded over the radio.

'I didn't sell you out!' McKnight protested, grasping at his wrists, trying to pull his hand away from her throat. 'I want Cain dead as much as you, but it won't happen this way!'

'Bullshit!' His grip tightened further, the tendons in his arms standing out hard and sharp. 'You'll say anything to save your own life.'

Then, just like that, she stopped. McKnight stopped fighting, stopped resisting. Instead she went limp, making no attempt to protect herself.

'Then kill me,' she said, her voice little more than a hoarse whisper now. 'End it, Ryan. Because that's what it'll take to stop me. If you fire on that convoy, this is all for nothing.'

The two warring sides of Drake's psyche rose to a crescendo within him. One side was utterly focussed on ending Marcus Cain's life, and the other was struck by the impassioned plea from the woman standing before him. Would she really go through all this for a man like Cain? Or was he wrong? Was there something about this he didn't understand?

McKnight made no further attempt to sway him. She just stood there, waiting for him to make his choice. Ready to accept it either way.

In the end, her silence was what decided him.

Drake lowered the weapon and released his grip just as the convoy passed below, moving beyond his line of sight. His chance to take out Marcus Cain had just come and gone. Everything he'd risked and sacrificed, he'd just given up for the woman standing in front of him. All he could do was hope he hadn't just made the biggest mistake of his life.

'Thank you,' McKnight rasped, rubbing her throat.

Raising the weapon once more, he took aim over her shoulder and pulled the trigger. However, instead of the thump of a suppressed gunshot, he heard only a crisp metallic click as the hammer struck an empty chamber.

Drake let out a breath. The gun had never been loaded. It had been a bluff. She couldn't have killed him, just as he couldn't have killed her.

The woman sighed. 'I'm sorry. I had to know whether you would trust me.'

'What the hell are you doing here, Sam? What the fuck is going on?'

He might have relented on killing her, for now at least, but that didn't mean her betrayal was forgotten or forgiven. What she said in the next minute would determine whether she lived to see the one after.

'I'm trying to protect you.'

'Protect me?' he sneered. 'Like you protected me in Pakistan?'

'What happened in Pakistan wasn't me. I wish I had time to explain it all, but I'm telling the truth.' She looked away, seething with frustration at all the things she wanted to say but couldn't. 'As for now, who do you think saved your sister when they came for her?'

Drake's mind suddenly flashed back to the conversation with his sister a week earlier, as she recovered from her near abduction at the hands of Cain's people.

They told me they were going to take me away forever. Torture me, kill me...' Her voice grew strained, 'That's when she showed up.'

'She?'

'I never saw her face. But she was waiting for them. She took out their convoy, got me to safety. She's the only reason I'm not dead or captured.'

'That was you,' Drake said quietly, his mind racing as a big piece of the puzzle suddenly fell into place. 'The woman in the mask.'

McKnight nodded solemnly.

'Why?'

'I was ordered to protect your sister,' she explained.

Drake looked at her sharply. 'Ordered by who?'

Chapter 53

Two months earlier

She was dead.

A ghost; just a vague memory of a life that had ended the previous year. And not with any sense of finality and closure – it had simply stopped, her very existence erased like the markings on a chalk board.

Remembered by few, mourned by none. Least of all the small group of men and women she had once considered friends. To them she was worse than a ghost. She was a pariah, a traitor whose deception had undone everything they'd worked and sacrificed for. An outcast whose name was spoken only with disgust.

She had accepted this fact as one must accept all uncomfortable realities one can't change. She didn't deserve pity or grief, much less forgiveness. Not from them or anyone else. On balance, she didn't recall much in her former life that she could feel proud of.

And sitting alone in a darkened prison cell with nothing but her thoughts for company, she'd certainly had time to ponder it.

Her captor had more than lived up to his word, promising a lifetime to relive her decisions and mistakes, and realise the cost of betraying him. He'd devoted all the time and resources needed to keep her alive, though she could hardly be called 'well'.

She was watched constantly in her miserable isolation, her food intake carefully monitored, her behaviour scrutinised for possible suicide attempts. She had learned this the hard way when she'd tried to end her life after several days of quiet, logical deliberation, internal debate and grim planning, only for three guards to storm in and forcibly restrain her. She'd spent a week strapped to a bed for that little infraction.

Unable to live and incapable of dying on her own terms, she had spent her existence trapped in some shadowy in-between as the days and weeks slowly blended into months, and finally all concept of time seemed to disintegrate. The world carried on without her as she brooded alone in the dark.

She let out a sharp gasp as the truck hit another pothole, jarring her back against the bare metal sidewall and eliciting a stab of pain deep inside. Her body was still recovering from the exhausting ordeal it had so recently endured – an ordeal that had forced her reluctant transfer to a proper medical facility that could deal with her – yet there was little chance to rest and recuperate.

As soon as her guards could force a discharge order, she was off, bundled into the back of an armoured car for the journey back to the black site where she'd been held ever since that terrible day in Pakistan.

'Vacation's almost over,' one of her guards taunted. 'Soon you'll be back, home sweet home. Feels good, doesn't it?'

The second man sniggered in amusement.

Ignoring his mockery, she glanced towards the rear doors, where she fancied she saw a sliver of daylight through a gap in the hatch. Not much, just a faint glow of natural light against the metal. She could tell it was hot outside. She could feel the heat radiating through the truck's metal skin, leaving the interior stifling.

She imagined a hot sun outside and felt a sudden, crushing pang of longing. She would have liked to see sunlight one more time before she was returned to her cell, just to remember what it was like.

Just once.

'Eyes front.'

She didn't move, didn't acknowledge the command.

A sharp elbow to the ribs was enough to remind her who was in charge, and she turned to glare at the guard beside her. He was overweight, perspiring visibly in the hot air. She could taste the stink of his sweat.

'I said eyes front, convict,' he repeated, spitting out each word. 'You got a goddamn problem with that?'

Her hands slowly curled into fists as she stared back at him in silent hatred, wishing with all her heart that the cuffs and chains holding her back would slip away. Just a few seconds would be enough. Enough to strike upward, palm open, catching the base of his nose, driving it upward into his skull. Enough to shut the fat prick up forever.

It would be worth any beating she had to take. Worth anything they might do to her. After all, what did she have to lose now?

She saw him reach for the taser holstered at his waist, saw him thumb back the retaining strap holding it in place, and readied herself for the pain that was coming.

But it didn't come. Something else did.

A violent, thunderous boom resounded outside, sending a shiver through the chassis around them. Debris ricocheted off the truck's armoured exterior.

'What the fuck?' her guard yelled, looking around in fright.

She was pitched sideways as their driver threw the wheel over, trying wildly to evade whatever obstacle lay in their path, but another loud thud accompanied by the crash of a reinforced windshield giving way told her his efforts had been in vain.

'Oh shit! We've been hit!' the other guard screamed as their truck slewed sideways, the road disappeared beneath them and they rolled over.

The next few seconds were filled with terrifying, painful chaos as the truck pitched over and tumbled down an embankment, its reinforced chassis all that kept it from buckling entirely. The three human passengers were hurled against the walls and floor and roof with bruising force as their world turned upside down.

When at last the stricken vehicle rolled to a halt, she was lying on what had once been the wall. Heart pounding against her chest, body bruised and aching, she opened her eyes, looked around and moved her limbs experimentally. Nothing seemed to be broken.

The truck's engine had stopped, but the dim internal lights were still flickering uncertainly. Something was dripping down her cheek. She thought it might be blood, but the acrid smell told her otherwise. It was gas from the punctured fuel tank.

Her survival instinct kicked in. She was alive, the truck was crippled and at risk of burning up. Anything beyond that was irrelevant. What mattered was what she did right now. She had to get clear before it ignited, perhaps make a break for it.

Wild, unfettered, irrational hope rushed through her like a raging torrent.

She heard a low, pitiful groan beside her, saw a fleshy face smeared with blood and contorted in pain, and lashed out viciously with both shackled feet, knocking the guard unconscious. She wished she had more time to appreciate the visceral satisfaction of that, but survival was the priority now. Scrambling over to him, she felt around his belt kit for his set of keys.

The other guard was lying sprawled near the rear doors, his head bent at an unnatural angle. A broken neck, instantly fatal. Maybe he'd been a good man. Maybe he had a wife who loved him, children who would mourn his passing.

Maybe. But she certainly wouldn't.

Her search was interrupted by a sudden thump against the doors. She froze, straining to listen, hearing movement outside. Footsteps moving quickly through undergrowth. Another thump.

She returned to the guard's belt kit, unlatching his set of keys and getting to work on her restraints. Another noise outside as the handcuffs clicked, and fell away. She attacked her leg irons with eager, frantic haste.

She heard a faint click as the lock was disabled, and yanked the metal links off her ankles. But no sooner had she freed herself than the interior reverberated with what sounded like the boom of a shotgun discharge. An explosive breaching device, planted on the doors. She flattened herself against the floor as the lower door collapsed outward and harsh, blinding sunlight streamed in.

Eyes watering in the stinging cordite smoke, she watched as the other door was hauled open, revealing a lone figure silhouetted against the searing light outside. A figure clutching a weapon. She tensed up, wondering if this was it. Wondering if this was how she would finally die.

Maybe it wasn't so bad, given the alternative. As far as the world was concerned, she'd been dead for a long time anyway.

'Go on, then,' she spat, straightening up, staring defiantly at her executor. Ready to take what was coming. 'Do it! I'm not afraid of you.'

'Good,' a hauntingly familiar voice replied. 'Because I need your help, Samantha.'

Samantha McKnight gasped in disbelief, unable to comprehend how the person standing there could possibly have found her. Or why they would risk their life to free her.

'Well?' Anya prompted. 'Are you coming?'

–

'Anya saved my life, when everyone else had given up on me,' McKnight said, her tone one of distant sadness.

'Why you?'

She looked at him then, her expression one of grief and longing. 'Redemption.'

Drake couldn't begin to understand Anya's reasoning. They had given up on McKnight for a reason – she had betrayed the team, cost them their chance at bringing down Cain. If she expected redemption from him, she was looking in the wrong place.

'She never gave up on you,' McKnight went on. 'No matter what happened, she wanted me to keep you safe. I've been shadowing you ever since London.'

Suddenly Drake was reminded of that night just after crossing the border, when he'd stood outside the motel and stared off into the darkness. That feeling of being watched. It hadn't just been some erroneous intuition, then. It had been real. McKnight had been tailing them, unseen and unheard.

'I don't expect you to forgive me, but—'

'Never mind that,' he cut in. Their past would have to wait. There were bigger issues at play now. 'Why did you interfere tonight? Why are you protecting Cain?'

'I'm not. I want that son of a bitch dead as much as you.' McKnight pointed down to the bridge below. 'But that wasn't Marcus Cain. It was a trap.'

Drake shook his head vehemently. 'Bullshit. We tracked his cell phone.'

It wasn't possible, he told himself. They had covered every eventuality tonight. The confirmation ceremony, the contact with Starke, the motorcade route, the cell phone hack. Everything told them Cain was here.

'His cell phone, but not him,' she countered. 'Don't you understand, Ryan? The motorcade was a lie, just like everything else. He knew you were coming to kill him, when you'd make your move, and he was ready. Just like he always is.'

Drake's mind was racing as he replayed the events that had led him here. The attempted abduction of his sister, the raid on the Vault, the near miss as they crossed the Mexican border. Cain had tracked his movements across the world, guessed his intentions, and set the perfect trap to draw him in.

And he'd fallen for it.

'How do you know all this?'

'Because I've tried to play Cain's game myself,' she said, and he caught the flash of pain and anger. 'It's a game you don't win.'

Her expression told its own story, but it was one that would have to wait for now. 'Anya sent you to watch over me. Which means she couldn't,' he reasoned. 'So where is she?'

McKnight glanced away, torn about what to do.

Tossing aside her empty weapon, he drew the Smith & Wesson automatic hidden inside his jacket and turned it on her. Her gun might have been unloaded, but his wasn't.

'You might be telling the truth about Cain, or you might not,' he reluctantly conceded. 'But don't think for one second I'll hesitate to put you down if you hold back now.'

McKnight tensed as he thumbed back the hammer.
'Where is Anya?'

Chapter 54

Golyanovo District, Moscow – March 10th, 2003

Standing in the midst of that lonely, abandoned construction site, with a chill night wind sighing through crumbling concrete and only an old enemy for company, Marcus Cain waited for Viktor Surovsky to state his demands.

'Let me tell you what I know. I know that you had an American-trained special forces team operating illegally against Soviet forces in Afghanistan fifteen years ago, and that many of my countrymen died as a result.'

'Mr Surovsky, even if I—'

The Russian waved a bony hand dismissively. 'Do not waste your breath. I care nothing for them. Young men die – there will always be more of them.'

Cain fell silent, struck by the man's callous disregard for human life. Even amongst the hardened echelons of the Agency, the deaths of one's own servicemen were still mourned.

'But what I do care about is the team itself. Specifically the woman who served with them,' Surovsky went on. 'A woman answering to the codename Maras.'

The chill that ran through him had nothing to do with the cold. This man knew all about Task Force Black, formed to wage a guerrilla war against Soviet forces in Afghanistan. The group that had helped win the war, ultimately hastening the downfall of the USSR.

But more importantly, Surovsky knew about Anya.

'Your reaction tells me I'm not wrong,' the old man remarked shrewdly. 'I know she and her team are still active. They have been a thorn in my side for a long time. One that I wish to see removed.'

'Suppose you're right,' Cain said. 'Why now?'

Surovsky took another drink from his flask, shuddering a little as the liquid settled on a troubled stomach. An ulcer perhaps, or some other complaint common in men of his generation. Hard men, who lived harder.

'I have plans for my career in the FSB,' he explained cryptically. 'Plans that will soon make me more... visible.'

Cain took his meaning well enough. Viktor Surovsky, who had dropped off the map since the end of the Cold War, was planning a major power play.

'But a man does not rise to that level by leaving loose ends untied. And Maras is a loose end I have been meaning to tie off for some time now.'

At last Cain understood why Surovsky wanted her so badly. Anya had been an asset of the KGB once, back in the dark days of the Cold War. Sent to the West to infiltrate the CIA, only to turn her back on her former masters. Even worse, she had gone on to wage a brutal and very effective war against them.

Anya had been the KGB's biggest failure, and doubtless there were plenty of men in Moscow who still wanted her dead. One of whom was standing before him.

Surovsky straightened up, having said his piece. 'That is my price, Mr Cain. Give me Maras, and I will give you Hussein. It is a good trade, I think.'

Even Cain, a man for whom very little was surprising, had to take several seconds to compose himself. Task Force Black was still one of his best deep strike assets, particularly now, with the War on Terror in full swing. And aside from their military value, they were real people who had served him faithfully for decades.

More importantly, how could he possibly sacrifice Anya? How could he betray her, giving her up to this brutal, vengeful man? Her death at his hands would be neither quick nor painless.

'You ask a lot of me.'

'And I offer a lot in return,' Surovsky reminded him. 'Think on it – the man who helped take down the dictator of Iraq, prevented a war, saved thousands of lives. You would be a hero in your country, and heroes get rewarded.' He shrugged. 'In a position of greater power, you could do even greater good. Isn't that what it always comes down to in the end – the greater good?'

Cain looked away for a moment, utterly torn. Anya and the others had carried out countless missions for him, done everything that was asked of them and demanded little in return. Could he really abandon them to this Russian bent on revenge? Could he live with himself afterward?

But balanced against the lives of a dozen operatives were the thousands, perhaps hundreds of thousands, that would die in the coming war. Not just American soldiers, but Iraqi civilians. Women and children, whose only crime was being born in the wrong place.

Could such cold and pragmatic arithmetic really condone what he was being asked to do? As far as justifications went, it was pretty poor, but for Marcus Cain, standing in that cold wasteland that night, perhaps it was enough.

Washington DC – May 1st, 2011

'Welcome to *Meridian*, Mr Cain,' the receptionist said, smiling in greeting as Cain ascended the stairs into the building's plush main foyer. 'It's a pleasure to have you with us.'

Cain had to commend his contact's sense of nostalgia. The name on the door might have changed, the artwork and furniture might have been updated to reflect changing fashions, but this was still the same place he'd stepped into twenty years earlier.

It had been called *L'infini* back then, and the woman who had once summoned him was long dead, but here he was. Preparing for another meeting.

'It's good to be here,' he replied, striding confidently across the marble floor.

The hesitation and self-consciousness that had gnawed at him back then was gone now. He was no longer an uncertain young man taking his first steps into a new world. Now he was something very different.

His journey here from Langley in a plain, anonymous car without escort or protection had passed without incident, just as he'd known it would. Drake's attention would be focussed on the official motorcade making its way towards Capitol Hill, allowing Cain to go about his real business tonight.

'I presume my associate knows I'm here?'

The woman nodded. 'He does, sir.' She indicated the arched doorway leading into the club's main room. 'If you'll follow me, he's waiting for you.'

'Lead the way.'

Cain followed as the young woman conducted him through to the expansive, high-ceilinged dining area, which was about half full. The steady hum of conversation accompanied by the clink of glasses and cutlery echoed off the marble pillars and the grand vaulted roof overhead.

Unlike last time, when his arrival had gone largely unnoticed, he sensed eyes on him now, conversation faltering a little as he passed each table. He wasn't just some anonymous DC worker this time. He was a man of standing and power, well known both in Washington and elsewhere. A man whose arrival was always remarked upon.

In turn, Cain's eyes swept the room, seeking out his contact, wondering which table would be his. The leader, the peak of the vast pyramid that Cain had slowly but surely climbed over twenty years.

Turning right, the young woman led him to a table in the centre of the room. A table at which a lone diner sat waiting for him, glass of wine in hand and a half-eaten meal before him. A man whose appearance here almost caused Cain to laugh out loud, struck by the absurd irony of this moment.

'Mr Cain to meet with you, sir,' the woman said, excusing herself.

Dabbing his mouth with a napkin, the man rose to his feet and smiled in greeting, amused by the look of astonishment on Cain's face.

'Marcus, good to see you again. It's been a long time.'

Pakistani Airspace

Hanging onto his restraining harness as the Black Hawk yawed hard to port, following the tortuous contours of the mountain valley, the SEAL team leader could do little more than trust to the skill and competence of the two pilots as they wrestled with the heavily laden aircraft.

The Chinooks and close assault aircraft had parted company with them about ten minutes earlier, peeling away to land and remain on standby. They were on their own now.

Outside the dimly lit interior, he could see only darkness. They could be ten feet off the ground or ten thousand for all he knew. The other Black Hawk could be right in front of them, or a thousand yards behind. What he did know was that they were pushing the chopper's twin turbo-fan engines to the limits of their performance. Speed and concealment were everything now as they strove to reach their target before they were detected.

The Pakistanis didn't know a thing about this mission, and might attempt to shoot them down if they were discovered. Stealthy or not, a pair of Black Hawks laden with troops and equipment would be easy prey for a surface to air missile.

These grim thoughts were interrupted as his headset crackled into life.

'Viper One, Actual. This is Eagle. What's your status?'

'This is Viper One Actual. We're ten minutes out. All elements are green. Good to go. Repeat, good to go.'

'Copy that, Viper One.'

Ten minutes, the team leader thought to himself. Ten minutes until they made history.

Washington DC

For a few seconds, Cain said and did nothing. He just stared at the man standing opposite, taking in every detail of his appearance. A man he hadn't seen in almost two decades.

He had certainly changed a good deal since their last meeting. The thinning brown hair was mostly gone now, leaving just a few close-cropped, silvery strands around the sides. The skin around his face was sagging noticeably, the cheeks hollow, the forehead lined and creased, the eyes framed by a pair of expensive glasses. He was also considerably less trim around the midsection now.

And yet he was unmistakably the same man who had conducted him to his first meeting in this club in the summer of 1989. James; Freya's loyal assistant and bodyguard. The man willing to follow her every order without question. This man was the head of the Circle. The summit of the pyramid. The most powerful and dangerous man on the face of the earth.

The realisation was as fascinating as it was incongruous.

'What's the matter?' James asked, smirking. 'You look like you've seen a ghost.'

Clearing his throat and recovering his poise, Cain replied, 'In a manner of speaking. You're...'

'Not what you were expecting?'

The man's smile broadened. He was looking at Cain as he had twenty years ago, not far from this very spot, when he'd pulled a gun on him and stood there, waiting for the command to fire. Watching Cain sweat.

'That's rather the point though, isn't it? To be the one thing, the one man, that no one expects,' he went on. 'My role demands that I perform many duties, Marcus. Some are pleasant and rewarding; others... less so. But I have to admit, meetings like this are my favourite. Each of your predecessors reacted a little differently at this point. I've seen shock, denial, amusement, even anger. Each reaction told me a little more about that person.'

'My predecessors?'

'You don't think you're the first person to stand in this spot, do you? Or that you'll be the last?' Leaving that thought to hang in the air, he gestured to the second chair at their table. 'I imagine you have a lot of questions. Please, take a seat. Make yourself comfortable.'

As he eased himself into a chair, Cain watched as the man casually resumed his meal, slicing off a piece of steak and popping it in his mouth.

'This is a big day for you, Marcus,' he remarked. 'Promotion to director of the CIA.'

'I have you to thank for that, it seems.'

James nodded acknowledgement. 'I may have had a hand in it. You came well recommended, of course. But that's not why I picked you.'

'Then why?'

He smiled. 'Because I like you. I liked you from the first day we met.'

Cain was beginning to understand why this man had chosen to reveal himself under a different guise all those years ago. 'It was a test, wasn't it? Twenty years ago, pretending to be Freya's "assistant": you were testing me.'

Reaching for the bottle of red wine in the centre of the table, James poured Cain a glass. 'I've always believed the measure of a man is how he treats those he *doesn't* have to be kind to. And I wanted to get the measure of you, Marcus. I wanted to know what kind of man you really were.'

He spread his hands out to encompass their surroundings.

'And now, here you are. At the top table, as it were.'

Reaching for his glass of wine, he rose slowly to his feet. All talk in the dining room ceased, all eyes turning towards James as their fellow diners waited, hushed and expectant. Each of them had sat where Cain was now, each had proven themselves through long years of dedicated service, careful manoeuvring and flawless strategizing. Each of them belonged to the Inner Circle, bound by their shared web of secrecy and deniability.

James held up his glass in a toast. 'To your success, Marcus. Congratulations.'

With little choice but to respond, Cain took up his glass, raised it in acknowledgement and drank. And as he did, the room erupted in applause.

Just for a moment, he allowed himself to appreciate the gravity of this night.

He had made it. After twenty years of striving and sacrifice, he had reached the summit of the seemingly insurmountable mountain, found both the beginning and the end of the Circle.

—

Ignoring the rain sluicing down around her, Anya crept to the edge of the rooftop and looked out across the street at her target. It wasn't much to look at from the outside. Though elegantly designed and tastefully appointed like many of the embassies and diplomatic institutes in this part of town, there was nothing obviously imposing or ostentatious about it.

That didn't surprise her in the slightest. The people who made use of that place didn't announce their power and influence to the world. It was what lay beyond that innocuous facade that mattered. It was why she was here tonight.

Reaching up, she hit her radio transmitter.

'I'm in position,' she said quietly. 'Did you get what you need?'

'Working on it,' Alex replied, sounding tense and harassed as he strove to complete his task. 'How did you know he'd be here?'

'I've been here before,' Anya replied. A long time ago, she too had stood where Cain was now. 'Can you patch us through to his cell phone?'

Given the right circumstances, it was possible to hack virtually any cell phone and set it to passively transmit anything in range, effectively turning it into a makeshift listening device. The NSA and various other intelligence services had been using the technology for years now to spy on their own citizens.

Aside from considerable technical expertise, all that was required to make it possible was the phone's SIM number. Anya had obtained that very thing just minutes ago, planting a scanning device near the entrance to *Meridian* and waiting until Cain approached the doorway. She just hoped he'd been in range long enough for Alex to get what he needed.

'I'm working on it,' Alex confirmed. 'Stand by.'

'Understood.' Clicking off her radio, she whispered, 'Hurry, Alex.'

–

Taking his seat once more, James set his glass down on the table and resumed his meal, slicing off another piece of meat. His razor-sharp steak knife slid through it like butter.

'Now, let's get down to business,' he said briskly. 'You have questions, starting with the same one that every other person who's sat in your place has asked. We might as well get it out of the way.'

He was right, of course. Cain did indeed have questions. And as he'd correctly surmised, they all began with the most fundamental of all.

Leaning forward, he looked his host in the eye and spoke. 'Why?'

James met his searching gaze and smiled.

'As I said, just like the others,' he mused thoughtfully. 'The same human need to ascribe reason and motivation to everything that happens around us. It's the reason our ancestors established religion and superstition to rationalise disease and natural disasters, until we outgrew them and replaced them with science and logic. All of it to answer that most fundamental question – why.'

Cain didn't say a thing. He just waited for James to go on.

'You want to know why the Circle exists. I can tell you, but some answers can be more difficult to accept than others. That's why our candidates are so carefully chosen and tested, to make sure they're ready and prepared for it. Are *you* ready, Marcus?'

Never had he been more so. 'I am.'

'Good,' James nodded. He paused briefly before going on. 'Fundamentally, the answer is as simple as the question – chaos.'

Cain frowned, perplexed by his answer. 'I don't understand.'

'Nor should you. Not without first understanding how I arrived at the answer.'

–

'We're in!' Alex called out over the radio net. 'Patching you in now.'

Perched on her rooftop observation point, Anya waited while he set up the link. The audio signal was muffled and of low quality, probably because the phone was in Cain's jacket, but the conversation was audible all the same.

Anya was now listening in as if she were right there beside him.

She tensed as she felt her cell phone vibrating in her pocket, but made no attempt to answer it. It was McKnight, but whatever she had to report, it would have to wait.

Right now, all her attention was focussed on events playing out in that building opposite. That was all that mattered now.

–

'God fucking damn it!' Drake snapped, hammering his fist against the steering wheel as his call failed to connect once again. 'She's ignoring the call.'

He and McKnight were speeding across town, dodging and swerving to avoid the congested traffic. Drake had brought her with him, partly to guide him to Anya, and partly because he didn't trust her enough to leave her behind.

He had no idea who Samantha McKnight really was, why she'd done the things she'd done or what she wanted, and right now there was no time to sort it out. That would have to come later, assuming any of them made it through the night.

'She won't answer,' McKnight confirmed as he floored it through an intersection, running a red light. 'Not when she's this close.'

Drake didn't respond to that. He gripped the wheel tight, his eyes on the road ahead as he fought with the busy traffic.

'She knows what she's doing, Ryan,' McKnight ventured. 'She doesn't need you or anyone else—'

'Shut up!' Drake shouted, in no mood for advice. 'The only reason you're still breathing is because you might be useful. That can change very fast.'

With McKnight wise enough to hold her tongue, Drake fired up his comms unit. 'Keira, come in.'

'Ryan, where the fuck have you been?' Frost demanded. 'What's going on?'

'Long story. McKnight's with me—'

'Samantha McKnight?' Frost put in, her shock and dismay obvious. 'What the—'

'What part of "long story" don't you understand?' Drake interrupted. 'Listen, the motorcade was a fake. It was all fake. Cain knew we were coming. He's not going to Capitol Hill tonight.'

'So where is he?' Frost asked, struggling to get to grips with the barrage of new information.

'Thirteenth Street, North-West.' She listened as he reeled off the exact address. 'We're on our way there now. I need everything you can get me on that building.'

'I'm on it,' she said, already setting to work. 'But what are you expecting to find?'

Drake glanced over at his passenger. The woman who, until a few minutes ago, he'd been ready to kill.

'The Circle.'

Chapter 55

James settled back in his chair, hand on his wine glass as he began his tale.

'The Circle was formed in the dying days of the Cold War, by myself and a few other like-minded individuals who understood the storm that was coming. It was begun with the most noble of intentions – to create order from the coming chaos. A new world order, where prosperity and freedom would reign supreme.' He cocked a greying eyebrow. 'Peace in our time, you might say.'

Cain nodded. None of this was news to him so far. It was this very same ideal that had so captivated him all those years ago: to leave the world a better place than the one he'd found.

'With the combined efforts of people like yourself and… many others, we were ultimately able to realise our goal. The Cold War was ended, the Soviet Union toppled and the world freed from the threat of nuclear war. It should have been a time for celebration. Unfortunately, our greatest success ultimately proved to be our biggest mistake. Or should I say, our most formative lesson.'

'How so?' Cain asked.

'The end of half a century of global conflict ushered in a new way of thinking. A relaxation, a complacency. Without an enemy to strive against, our country began to lose its way. Little by little, our military withered under years of cutbacks, and our government and intelligence agencies followed suit. Our culture became soft and self-absorbed, consumed by materialism and small-minded thinking. Progress and development stagnated. Whereas before we built space rockets, now we created…' Reaching into his pocket, he held up a sleek black smartphone. 'These.'

His disgust was evident as he tossed the phone into the table.

'America's global power and influence declined throughout the 1990s. Old enemies were replaced by new ones that we had neither the will nor the interest to deal with. Our greatest victory was slowly defeating us.'

Cain's mind was racing as the man's words sank in. The end of the Cold War, the collapse of the Soviet Union, the liberation of half a continent from totalitarianism and repression... All of it was a failure in this man's eyes.

'The question of course was what to do. Our efforts to end war and conflict had failed to reap the rewards we expected. If anything, we were regressing. Eventually it became clear that our failure to find a solution was based on a false understanding of the problem.

'Peace and order weren't the answers I'd hoped for – in fact, they were fundamental elements of the problem. Prolonged peace leads to stagnation and corruption, which in turn leads to societal decay and, ultimately, total collapse. It's been the same story with almost every empire and kingdom in human history, yet no one ever fully grasped the implications. Instead we strive for the same flawed ideals again and again, each time expecting a different result, but instead meeting the same inevitable outcome – failure.'

He glanced at his wine glass, swirling it slowly and watching the scarlet liquid sway back and forth.

'That's when I realised the true solution required a... different philosophy.'

–

Roaring out of the winding valley that had shielded the two Black Hawks from the outside world, the choppers skimmed low across the arid landscape of dusty scrubland and small irrigated fields, each passing second bringing them closer to their final destination.

'Five minutes to target!' the team leader called out, scanning the SEAL operatives lining the cramped compartment. Even in the dull red glow of emergency lights he could make out their tense, eager expressions.

'Final weapon and equipment checks!'

Craning his neck to see out the cockpit window up front, he could just make out the distant glow of lights from a small town directly ahead. Somewhere in amongst that suburban sprawl lay their target building, and the man they'd travelled halfway around the world to kill.

And in just a few minutes, they would be going in.

–

In the midst of that plush, extravagant dining hall in central DC, Marcus Cain listened as his companion brought his narrative to a close.

'If peace and prosperity were the problem, then it was logical to conclude that the opposite conditions were required for society to thrive. Which brings me back to the answer I first gave you – chaos,' James explained patiently. 'Human beings thrive on war and conflict. It's what's driven the most significant advances in our history. Aircraft, computers, space travel, nuclear power, advanced medicine... all of it created to satisfy a fundamental need. The need to prevail against an enemy. That's when the true solution came to me. We'd pursued war and conflict as a means to an end. But we were wrong. War wasn't a means, it *was* the end. A world of endless war and conflict, driving greater and greater advances, maintaining the strength and resolve of the population, and the governments they elected. Maintaining the balance of true power. Not order *from* chaos, but order *within* chaos.'

He smiled, taking another sip of wine.

'But even chaos requires a degree of control. Escalating conflicts left unchecked might eventually spill over into global catastrophe. Disease, famine and revolution allowed to spread too far and wide could undermine the entire system. What the world needs is balance, and that's where we come in. That's the true purpose of the Circle, Marcus – to balance the chaos of the world. To give humanity what it needs but would never admit to.'

Cain sat back in his chair, stunned into silence by everything he'd heard. He was no stranger to hard truths and unpleasant facts, but to hear the fate of humanity laid out in such cold, practical, analytical terms was something altogether different.

The true purpose of the Circle at last laid bare. Not to save humanity from war and create a better world, but to preserve it through endless conflict and destruction. And for twenty years, he had been a part of it.

As he sat there, his hands resting on the table, his eyes briefly flicked to his watch, making a mental note of the time. Almost there.

–

In the conference room at Langley, Franklin watched as the two Black Hawks swept in over the target compound, one taking up position over the main yard while the other hovered over the further end of the open space used as a garden. The images were being beamed live from a Reaper drone orbiting the target.

'Viper One in position. Deploying now.'

'Copy that, Viper One. You are go.'

But just as ropes were hurled out and the assault teams prepared to deploy, the first Black Hawk began to sway and pitch alarmingly, struggling to maintain position. As it swung out of control, the tail rotor clipped one of the high walls.

'Shit,' Franklin said under his breath as the chopper pitched over and ploughed into the ground, crashing against the compound's outer wall. 'Eagle, what's the status on Viper One?'

'We're okay,' a clearly shaken team leader reported. 'Viper One is good to go.'

Within seconds, bright green shapes began emerging from the crashed chopper, moving fast and orderly despite the chaos of their rough landing, and joining forces with the team deploying from the second Black Hawk.

Light spilled out from nearby buildings as residents were startled awake, but the SEAL team paid them no heed as they swept in against the target. A secondary unit peeled off to breach a smaller structure on the south side of the yard, while teams from the other chopper quickly and efficiently scaled the inner defensive walls, but the main force advanced on the central three-storey residence.

'Team One and Two in position.'

'Copy that. Breach! Breach!'

Franklin could do nothing but wait now as the team disappeared inside, moving beyond sight of the drone. Whatever happened in the next couple of minutes, he could do nothing to influence it.

–

'It's interesting to observe your reaction, Marcus,' James observed, noting Cain's gaze as it moved to his wristwatch. He didn't appear remotely surprised or curious. Rather, he looked like he'd just caught out a magician in the middle of his trick. 'Waiting for something?'

'I...'

'The mission tonight will be a failure, of course,' James went on.

Cain leaned forward. 'Excuse me?'

'Operation Neptune Spear,' James explained patiently. 'The target location your teams are raiding at this very moment is a fake. Bin Laden is quite some distance away, safe and accounted for.'

Cain could feel his heart pounding. 'You know where he is?'

'Of course we know. We've known for the better part of a decade.'

'Why did you...'

'Why did we protect him?' James finished for him. He leaned forward, folding his hands on the table. 'Didn't it ever occur to you that he was worth more to us alive than dead? His military value is negligible at this point of course, but his symbolic value is beyond measure. He's an enemy to hate, but never truly defeat. A target to strive for, but never quite reach. Just like war and chaos, the hunt for him is more useful than his actual death would be.'

The cold, pragmatic logic of the Circle at work again. They were willing to protect the most wanted terrorist in the world in order to stoke fear and hatred, sowing conflict and chaos wherever it suited them.

'It took some work on our part to convince you that you'd found the right place, of course,' the leader of the Circle went on. 'Feeding false information to your contact Qalat in Pakistan, getting all the right people to fall into line. And of course, making sure the illusion was maintained until the crucial moment.'

–

As the prisoners below were secured, the rest of the assault team advanced up the central stairway, heading for the upper floor. Their hearts were pounding as they ascended the steps. They were close. The man they'd been hunting for so long was just yards away from them.

The faint thump of footsteps on the landing above caused them to freeze for a moment, waiting and listening, their weapons trained upward at the closed door at the top of the stairs.

And then, slowly, the door edged open to reveal a tall, lanky figure clad in a loose-fitting nightshirt, a greying beard trailing down to his chest, his thinning hair in disarray. He peered out into the stairwell, and for a heartbeat his gaze fastened on the SEAL team below.

It happened so fast that those involved would struggle to recount exactly how it played out. The lead SEAL team member raised his assault rifle, took aim just as the target retreated into the room, and uttered a single word.

'Contact.'

—

Cain sat in rigid silence, watching the man opposite. James' earlier relaxed joviality had departed now, giving way to something colder and more clinical as he delivered his instructions.

'There will be blowback from this, of course. Blame and recriminations, but most of it will be deflected away from you. Your subordinate Franklin will take most of the heat, and probably be forced to stand down. But we already have someone more... reliable in mind to replace him.'

It had all been a lie. Just like everything else, it had been one giant game of deception. The realisation was written plain on Cain's face.

'One thing you still need to learn, Marcus, is that every man has his place. Every man needs to recognise his limits. You may have earned a seat at this table, but you don't control what happens here. You never will. I trust we understand each other?'

—

Franklin could do nothing now but wait, hunched over the conference table, staring at the night vision aerial image of the compound half a world away.

He didn't speak, didn't move a muscle. There was no point in pressing the mission commander or the team leaders for an update. They would report back when they had something to report.

Glancing momentarily at Kennedy, he saw the man's eyes were closed, his fists clenched as he whispered, 'Come on, come on.'

The seconds stretched on without an acknowledgement. And with each moment that passed, more doubts began to creep into his mind. Were they wrong? Had this all been a mistake? Was their intel flawed?

Had Cain led them astray?

Then just like that, a crackly, distorted voice came over the radio net.

'For God and country – Geronimo, Geronimo, Geronimo.'

–

The world around Bashir Shirani felt like the aftermath of a tornado. Everywhere he heard the sounds of women and children crying, men yelling orders and defiant outbursts, the stench of burned plastic, wood and cordite, the destruction wrought upon the dwelling that had been his home for the past several months.

All of it shattered by the American assault team that had swept through the place, killing and destroying everything in their path. Nothing could stand against force like that. Nothing.

'Up!' the operative behind him said, grabbing his cuffed hands and hauling him to his feet. He saw other prisoners, members of the Master's household, likewise restrained, some hurling abuse and impotent threats at their captors. Most fell silent when thick felt bags were placed over their heads, and a moment later his world went dark as he too was hooded.

He could do no more here. He would be taken away for processing.

–

Cain could feel his phone vibrating in his pocket, though he made no attempt to answer it. He knew what it meant, and smiled faintly as he regarded the man seated opposite.

'Yes, James. We understand each other.'

Unknown to the leader of the Circle, a trio of figures had slipped into the room behind him, moving swiftly and silently into position. Just like him, they had had to manoeuvre carefully to reach this point, overcoming many defences and security measures, killing many people who stood in their way. But they were here now, and they were ready.

'But there's something I want you to know before we go on.' He paused, savouring the moment. Relishing what was about to happen. 'My team are exactly where they need to be.'

Just for an instant, Cain saw a flicker of doubt. This man who had spent his life planning for everything, foreseeing every possibility, countering every strategy, sensed that something wasn't right. He sensed a flaw in his position.

A flaw that was suddenly revealed by the thump of suppressed automatic gunfire. Seated at a table nearby, a man and woman cried out in shock as a stream of projectiles tore into them. Tumbling backwards, the man pulled the tablecloth with him, upending glasses, plates and cutlery that crashed to the floor.

More panicked shouts and screams erupted across the dining area as the shooting continued and the occupants were mercilessly cut down.

Instinctively James turned towards the source of the commotion, tearing his attention away from Cain. It was the opportunity he'd been looking for. Cain had brought no weapon with him, but he didn't need one.

Seizing up the steak knife that James had left unattended on his plate, he seized it up, drew back his arm and plunged it into the man's hand with every ounce of strength he could summon. The sharpened blade carved its way through skin, muscle and bone before embedding itself deep in the table surface.

The man's face crumpled, twisting in agony, and he opened his mouth to scream. He never got the chance. Before he could utter a sound, the operative who had approached from behind looped a length of rope around his neck and pulled it violently taut, jerking his head back and cutting off his scream before it began.

Jason Hawkins was no stranger to this method of killing, and had always found it oddly satisfying to literally crush the life out of a man. He smiled as he tightened his grip, confident that the feeble old man couldn't possibly escape, but held back enough to keep him alive. His master had given explicit instructions that this wasn't to end until he said so.

Oblivious now to the chaos and death all around him, Cain stood up from his chair and slowly approached the terrified man, one bloody hand still pinned to the table while the other pawed uselessly at the rope.

Cain's eyes were alight with sheer, absolute hatred as he leaned in closer. Hatred that had been carefully suppressed and controlled for twenty years.

'Right now, you're probably asking yourself that most fundamental question of all – why?' he said, mockingly repeating the man's earlier words. 'I think now, at the end, you deserve a little truth. The truth is, I knew exactly what the Circle was, long before I came here tonight. I've known for a very long time. Just like I knew you were protecting Bin Laden, feeding me false information, leading us to the wrong place. And I let you believe it. That's why he's dead now, just like you're about to be. That's why the Circle ends today.'

The smell of burned cordite was thick in the air as the assault team swept through the room, dispatching anyone who had survived the initial onslaught. The entirety of the Inner Circle, everyone responsible for commanding the whole corrupt organisation, was either dead or dying.

They had exposed themselves today, believing nothing could touch them. Believing they could trust him. That was their biggest, and last, mistake.

'Do you have any idea how long I've waited for this moment?' Cain asked, his voice shaking a little as he spoke. 'How many times I've thought about killing you?'

This was the culmination of Cain's plans. This was everything he had worked towards for twenty long years. And at last, he had what he wanted.

James' other hand pulled and wrenched at the knife pinning it to the table, tearing the flesh even further and bringing fresh jolts of agony.

'All this time, you thought you controlled me. You thought you knew me. And little by little, year by year, you began to trust me. And this is where it brought you. Everything you worked to build, every person you betrayed, everything you achieved… it was all for nothing. I wanted you to know this, James. I wanted to look you in the eye at the end.'

Straining, grunting and gasping desperately for breath that wouldn't come, James looked up at the man looming over him. The man he'd always believed he could control and manipulate. The man who was about to kill him.

And at last, as the darkness closed around him, he knew true fear.

'This is your reward,' Cain informed him, relishing his moment of triumph. 'This is peace in our time.'

Giving Hawkins a nod, he watched as the big, powerful operative increased his grip, muscles and tendons straining with the exertion. James' eyes bulged in agony and horror, his face turning purple, spittle flying from his mouth, his arm flailing uselessly as the pain and terror and desperation reached a final, unbearable peak.

And then, at last, he went still as death found him.

Bashir Shirani blinked as the bag was whipped off his head, a pair of bright flashlights shining into his eyes. He was in a small outbuilding at the far side of the compound. Outside, he could hear the high-pitched whine of helicopter engines spinning up, accompanied by urgent shouts from the assault team as they fell back.

Their mission accomplished, they were preparing to pull out before Pakistani military and police units arrived. All that remained was to deal with one loose end.

'Name?' one of the troopers barked at him, his voice wary and tense. Tonight had been the biggest night of their lives, and the last thing they wanted was for something to go wrong just as the mission was winding down.

'Salah ad-Din,' he replied without hesitation.

There was a moment of silence as the armed men around him considered his answer. Then at a nod from the team leader, one of them drew a knife and brought it down on him.

Shirani felt the plasticuffs at his wrists fall away, and brought his hands around in front, rubbing the raw skin. All things considered, it was a small price to pay for what he'd accomplished tonight.

Bin Laden was dead, as were most of al-Qaeda's senior leadership.

'Thank you,' he said quietly, rising to his feet.

'No. Thank *you*,' the team leader said, shaking his hand. The Nomex combat glove was coarse and rough against Shirani's palm, but he didn't care. 'America owes you a debt. And... Director Cain sends his thanks.'

Shirani nodded, some of the pressure of the past few months undercover finally starting to come through. He had been Marcus Cain's hand-picked operative, entrusted with the most important and secretive mission imaginable, and he had completed his task.

He knew there would be a lengthy debriefing, and an even longer spell needed to readjust to normal life – he'd almost forgotten what 'normal' meant – but for now, he simply felt exhausted.

The team leader seemed to sense it too, and smiled encouragingly at him.

'Let's get the hell out of here, shall we?'

Chapter 56

Washington DC

Marcus Cain felt as if he were in a dream as he strolled out of the smoke-filled restaurant, leaving the assault team behind to begin the clean-up operation. A good number of people were going to have to 'disappear' after tonight, but that no longer mattered to him.

His work was done, his task complete. He was witnessing the beginning of a new age. An age free from the insidious influence of the Circle. The new world he'd hoped to create twenty years ago had at last come to fruition.

His cell phone was ringing again, and this time he answered. 'Cain.'

'We got him,' Franklin informed him, his simple statement belaying the gravity of the situation. 'It's done.'

Cain sighed, closed his eyes and nodded. After so long, so many setbacks and challenges, he could hardly accept that it was all over.

'Well done, Dan,' he said, genuinely meaning it. 'I knew you wouldn't let me down.'

Franklin didn't say anything to that, but his momentary silence told Cain the sentiment was acknowledged. 'The White House is going apeshit. They want to put out a statement as soon as possible. The president wants to congratulate you personally. Where are you now?'

Cain glanced back into the dining area, where broken plates, glasses and dead bodies lay strewn across the floor, tables upended and chairs toppled. The Inner Circle, the most powerful and untouchable men and women in the world, lay dead, their blood pooling on the expensive imported marble tiles.

'Just finishing up here.' The heaviness in his voice told Franklin that more information was unlikely to be forthcoming. 'Listen, once the dust settles, the Agency's going to be needing a new deputy director. I can't think of anyone better than you.'

Silence greeted him once more, though it wasn't grudging, uncomfortable silence. This time it was shocked, stunned muteness.

'Marcus, are you... sure about that?' Franklin asked, regaining his voice.

'I already raised your name with the president. He agrees you'd be an ideal choice.' He sighed. 'You're a good man. Better than me, I think. The Agency's going to need men like you.'

'No conditions?'

'No conditions.'

'I don't know what to say...'

'Say yes,' Cain advised. 'Make this easy.'

Franklin exhaled slowly. 'Okay. When you get back to Langley, we'll talk.'

Footsteps on the marble floor behind drew Cain's attention back to the present, and he turned as Hawkins approached, his expression one of satisfaction and contentment. Death was his business, but it was more than just an occupation for Jason Hawkins. He enjoyed it, thrived on it.

'We're all done here,' he reported.

'That's good,' Cain replied absently.

The veteran operative cocked an eyebrow. 'Thought you'd be popping the champagne right around now.'

'The Circle might be gone, but the work's just beginning,' Cain reminded him gravely. It would take a long time to undo everything they'd wrought. He gestured back into the wrecked dining area. 'How long to make all this disappear?'

'Two, three hours, tops. We've got a clean-up crew on it already,' he confirmed. 'By the time we're done, nobody will even know we were here.'

'Good work, Jason. I want you to head to the rally point near Capitol Hill. Prepare the field teams for my arrival.'

Hawkins frowned at the change of plan. 'Shouldn't we finish up here first?'

Cain shook his head. 'Drake never made a move on the motorcade. That means he's still out there. I want you on standby in case he tries something.'

'Fair enough.' He was about to turn away but halted, a smile forming. 'Lighten up, Marcus. We won. Enjoy it.'

Saying nothing, Cain turned away and strode out through the main entrance. Once he was certain he was away from the building and out of earshot, he fished out his phone once more and dialled a new number.

It was answered within moments. His call was expected.

'He's on his way. Have your team ready.'

'They're already there,' a distorted voice responded. 'I hope for your sake there are no surprises.'

'None,' Cain promised. 'He's all yours.'

An effective tool he might have been, but Jason Hawkins had outlived his usefulness tonight. A man like that had no place in the new world he'd brought about. And if his death helped to make amends for the Vault attack in London, then so much the better. It had been easy enough to convince them Hawkins had exceeded his authority and launched the attack without permission, because it wasn't a lie.

They were welcome to him.

His short call concluded, Cain slipped his phone back into his pocket and took a deep breath. The rain had eased off at last, the air cool and fresh as the warmth of the day bled away. Traffic rumbled by on the main drag, pedestrians strode past on the sidewalk, and a chopper thumped its way through the darkness somewhere overhead.

The world continued as it had before, unaware that a seismic shift had just taken place. Most people would never learn of the events in that restaurant, and that was fine with him. That was the life he'd chosen.

He started walking, heading down the street and away from the vehicle that was waiting for him. 'Sir!' his protective agent called after him. 'Sir, where are you going? We have a car standing by.'

Cain glanced at his watch. He was expected at Capitol Hill for his confirmation ceremony shortly, and to delay much longer would arouse suspicion. But he had time. After everything he'd done, he figured he could keep them waiting a few minutes.

'I need ten minutes, son,' Cain replied. 'Alone.'

The young man didn't look happy. Cain's safety was his responsibility, and it went against protocol to leave him unprotected. 'Sir, my orders are—'

'You take your orders from me,' Cain reminded him sharply. Softening his tone a little, he added, 'Anyway, this won't take long.'

Hesitating, the operative looked towards Cain's destination, guessing his intentions. Given everything that had happened tonight, it seemed understandable that a man would seek out such a place.

Reluctantly he nodded his assent.

Cain strode off down the street, his hands in his pockets and his coat turned up against the light drizzle. He could scarcely remember the last time he'd walked alone, unguarded, unwatched. Free.

The years of care and worry and pain seemed to fall from him with each step. It's over, he told himself again, still struggling to come to terms with it. It had been worth it. It had all been worth it.

Cain's eyes rose skyward as he drew near his destination, taking in the lofty bell tower and soaring columns of the National City Christian Church. One of the big neoclassical religious edifices erected throughout the city, this one overlooked the famous Thomas Circle, named after the famous Union general George Henry Thomas, whose mounted statue rested on a massive stone plinth in the centre.

Ignoring the sounds of traffic surging around the huge road conglomeration, Cain ascended the stone steps up to the church's main entrance, mounting them slowly, as if each were a significant undertaking.

The doors were closed but unlocked, allowing worshippers to enter. Pushing the heavy barrier open, Cain stepped inside and gratefully allowed it to swing closed, shutting out the world. Cool, reflective silence closed in around him like a blanket. He breathed deep, taking a moment to appreciate the peace.

Making his way up the central aisle, he approached the altar near the massive pipe organ, where rows of candles burned gently in the cool, subdued gloom.

Reaching into his pocket, he carefully produced a small photograph that he'd kept with him every day for almost a year now. A picture that was just starting to fade and fray at the edges. His daughter, Lauren, killed the previous year in Berlin.

Another casualty of war. Another sacrifice.

Cain paused with the picture in his hand, allowing himself to reflect on everything he had done to get here, every person he'd manipulated and betrayed, every sacrifice he'd made, every sin he'd committed.

He couldn't rightly say if he was deserving of redemption and forgiveness. He couldn't even say whether James had been right after all, whether humanity was doomed without the Circle to maintain the balance of conflict and chaos. Perhaps it was futile to strive for something better.

All he knew was that he'd done his part.

And perhaps that was enough.

Placing the picture gently against one of the candles, he reached for a taper and used it to light the wick, saying a silent prayer for the young woman he'd lost. The flame was just sputtering to life when he became aware of footsteps approaching, soft and muted.

Coming for him.

'I had a feeling you'd be here,' he said quietly, blowing out the taper. 'I knew you'd find me sooner or later.'

'You know why I've come.'

'I do.' Cain turned slowly to face the new arrival. 'It's good to see you, Anya.'

Chapter 57

Behind the wheel of a black unmarked Agency service vehicle, Hawkins was en route to the rendezvous point in an underground parking lot just north of the Capitol Building. From there, he was to take command and coordinate the various field teams who would oversee Cain's journey back to Langley.

The Circle might have been eliminated, but both Drake and Anya were still out there somewhere. Killing them as well would be the crowning achievement in what had, so far at least, proven to be an extremely satisfying day.

He glanced up, taking in the sight of the huge white building with its grand columns and towering central dome about a mile distant. An impressive building, he conceded. Shame about the assholes who worked there.

His attention was drawn back to the vehicle when his cell phone started buzzing. It was an unknown number.

Frowning, Hawkins hit Receive. 'Who is this?'

'Listen carefully, Mr Hawkins,' the caller instructed. 'If you want to live through the next hour, you'll do exactly what I say.'

–

For the next few seconds, neither Cain nor Anya made a move. They stood their ground in silence, each taking the measure of the other, each subconsciously comparing the person before them with the one they'd thought they'd known.

She's older, Cain found himself thinking. There were lines around her mouth and eyes that hadn't been there the last time they'd met. Her blonde hair was wet from the earlier downpour. She looked tired, and in pain. A woman for whom life had been particularly harsh and unkind.

And yet here she was. Hurt but undaunted. Scarred and embittered, but resolute.

She had carved a trail of blood and death from one side of the world to another, each step bringing her closer to this moment.

'Twenty years,' the woman began, her voice calm, hushed. No anger, no hatred. Just a quiet resolve to learn the truth. 'Everything you did for twenty years: every lie and secret and betrayal. It was all for tonight, wasn't it?'

He had lied many times in his life, but not tonight. 'Yes.'

Anya tilted her head slightly, trying to fathom the mind of the man in front of her. The phenomenal reserves of patience and mental fortitude needed to maintain the ruse for so long, to prove himself time and again. To win over their trust until at last, the time came to strike them down.

'Was it worth it?' she asked. 'Was it worth it to stand here now?'

Cain's eyes strayed to the photograph placed carefully against the candle, the image aglow with the flickering light. His only daughter, taken from him just like so many others. Some of them had been good, others bad. Some deserved death, others a chance at life. All of them weighed heavily on him, and would do for the rest of his days.

But the woman standing before him now endured more, sacrificed more, lost more than almost any other. If only she understood the decisions he'd been forced to make, the impossible choices that had been thrust upon him, the cruel twists of fate, circumstances and mistakes that had conspired to drive them apart.

'Do you remember what you told me once?' he asked, revisiting an old memory from two decades ago. 'You said they'd use us until there was nothing left. They would take everything from us, destroy everything we were.'

Anya's haunted expression told him she remembered it all too well.

'You were right about them, Anya,' he whispered. 'Even back then, you knew what they were. You're the reason I turned against them, made it my life's work to destroy them. And tonight, I made them pay for that. I took back everything they stole from us.'

'No,' she retorted, a flicker of cold anger showing behind those steely blue eyes for the first time. 'I can't get back what I lost. My family, my freedom… my future. I gave you my life, Marcus.'

Her voice wavered as she struggled to keep control. She looked lost and vulnerable in that moment, desperate for understanding.

'I did everything that was asked of me. Why wasn't it enough?'

'I wish I knew,' Cain admitted.

Anya swallowed hard, and he saw tears glistening in her eyes.

'I have to know one thing... before the end,' she managed to say. 'Why did you sell me out to the Russians? Why did you betray me?'

They had come at last to the final moment. Anya's brutal and relentless quest for answers had carried her all across the world. She had evaded every trap set for her, had killed men both powerful and dangerous, had pieced together every clue, until at last she'd ended up here.

Yet the final answer still eluded her. *Anya*, he thought as he looked at her then, seeing a shadow of the bright, vibrant young woman she'd once been. *There was a time when I would have died for you. You were the bravest and most incredible woman I ever knew, and I loved you. But still you don't understand.*

Without hesitation, Marcus Cain gave his answer.

'I didn't betray you, Anya.'

Golyanovo District, Moscow – March 10th, 2003

'No,' Cain said.

Even in the half-shadows of the dark, abandoned construction site, Cain saw the older man's face fall.

'What did you say?'

'I said no, Viktor,' Cain repeated, *his heart pounding as the words came out. But the moment they did, he felt a surge of something he hadn't felt in a long time. The sure and certain knowledge that for once in his life, he was doing the right thing.* 'I won't sell her out. Not to you, not to anyone. That's a line I won't cross.'

'You would sacrifice thousands of lives, to save just one?' Surovsky asked, *incredulous at the thought.* 'No woman is worth that much.'

'She is to me,' Cain retorted. *No matter their differences, no matter how distant they'd become, Anya had never once betrayed him. She had never sold him out. How could he do any different?*

'Do you have any idea what I am offering?'

'I know exactly what you're offering, and I know I'd never be able to live with it,' Cain said truthfully. 'If I betray the people who risk their lives for me, I'm no better than you, Viktor.'

At this, the old man snorted with grim amusement. 'I imagined you to be many things, Mr Cain. A hopeless idealist is not one of them.'

'I'm happy to disappoint you.' He turned to leave, then halted. 'Oh, one more thing. In case you find yourself in a position of power someday, know this – I won't forget our conversation tonight.'

With that, he turned his back on the man and departed, leaving Viktor Surovsky alone in the darkness.

–

'I refused,' Cain finished, bringing his short recount to an end. 'The chance to kill Hussein, stop the war before it began... I gave it up. For you, Anya. I couldn't betray you.'

Anya stood in stunned silence, eyes wide, mind racing, trying to understand what she'd heard. Trying to comprehend how it could match up with everything she'd discovered. Then slowly she turned to look at him, her expression hardening.

'You're lying.'

'It's the truth. Only the truth.'

'Enough!' she yelled, her voice echoing across the huge, empty church. In a flash she had drawn her sidearm and trained it on him. 'I was captured, handed over to the Russians like a piece of meat. Carpenter, Surovsky, Qalat... every link in the chain led back to you.'

She stepped closer, the gun trembling slightly.

'Every single one of them told me the same story – that I was betrayed by my own people. How else do you explain that?'

Cain sighed; he'd known this moment had been coming. And he knew what he had to tell her. He did indeed have an explanation, however difficult it might be for her to hear. All he could do was present the truth.

'Because I wasn't the only one there that night.'

–

Viktor Surovsky was just turning to leave, still marvelling at Cain's arrogance and stupidity, when suddenly another figure appeared in front of him, emerging from the shadows like a ghost.

Surovsky drew back, reaching for the weapon inside his coat. Perhaps Cain had not been as forthcoming as he'd claimed, bringing some hidden assassin to the meeting with him, ready to strike him down.

'Wait,' a woman's voice urged in Russian. 'I'm not your enemy.'

The FSB agent stopped, surprised and intrigued.

'Really?' Surovsky asked warily. 'Then tell me, what are you? A lost tourist?'

'Not quite.'

The mysterious interloper stepped forward, allowing the pale moonlight to play across her face. Even in the poor light, Surovsky made out long dark hair and an elegant, attractive countenance. No longer young perhaps, but strikingly beautiful all the same.

'Think of me as an… intermediary,' she explained. 'Someone who can provide what you're looking for… if you give me what I want.'

Surovsky's eyes narrowed. 'Clearly Mr Cain doesn't know about this.'

'Marcus Cain is weak and sentimental. His judgement on this matter is clouded,' the woman said disparagingly. 'Mine is not.'

'Perhaps so.' Surovsky conceded. 'But how do I know you can deliver Maras?'

In the wan moonlight, he saw her smile faintly. 'Because I know a great deal about her. I helped train her, in fact. I know where she's going and why. And because I helped broker the meeting she's rushing to attend.'

'And you would betray this woman?' he asked, dubious. 'Someone you trained?'

'To stop a war? Absolutely. Some things are bigger than personal loyalty. Cain never understood that, but I do.'

Reaching into his coat, Surovsky produced his hip flask once more and took a gulp, grimacing as his stomach knotted in protest. An ulcer, flaring up again. He held out the flask to her, and this time she took it and swallowed a generous measure.

'What should I call you?' he asked.

'You can call me Freya.'

Chapter 58

Pulling into a vacant space in the underground parking lot, Hawkins killed the engine and stepped out of his SUV, glancing along the rows of parked vehicles in search of the field team that was supposed to meet him.

'Come out, come out, wherever you are,' he said under his breath.

As if in response, a pair of headlights flicked on at the far end of the underground space, accompanied by the rumble of an engine firing into life. A panel van, judging by the general dimensions.

Hawkins stood his ground as the van approached, squinting a little in the glare of the headlights. Coming to a halt just a few yards away, the driver left the engine running as he opened the door and stepped out, accompanied by two more men from the sliding door on the side.

'I don't recognise you guys,' Hawkins remarked as the trio approached, each wearing hard, serious expressions. 'You new?'

The driver, evidently the leader, spoke a single, terse command. 'You're coming with us.'

Hawkins' eyes narrowed. 'Am I?'

At a nod from the leader, all three men drew down on him. Hawkins didn't make a move. Cain had sold him out, he knew then. Discarding him now that he'd served his purpose. Giving him up to people who wanted him dead.

'That wasn't a request.'

Hawkins glanced from one man to the next, taking note of the weapons in their hands, the look of cold, ruthless determination on their faces. Each of these men was a professional killer – of that much he was certain – and was no stranger to moments like this. He had been on the other side of this particular situation many times.

'Three of you, huh?' Hawkins taunted them. 'Thought they would have sent more.'

'Get on your knees and put your hands behind your head.'

Hawkins considered it, then shook his head. 'I don't think so.'

A trio of silenced gunshots rang out, coming in such close succession that they seemed to blend into one. All three men jerked convulsively as the projectiles impacted, then fell to the ground like marionettes with their strings severed.

Hawkins watched without emotion as his would-be abductors lay twitching at his feet, their blood pooling on the concrete.

'Clear!' a young woman called out.

Glancing up from the dead bodies, Hawkins smiled as Riley rose up from behind one of the parked cars and approached him, flanked by two other members of Hawkins' team. All three were holding silenced M4 assault rifles with telescopic sights.

'Good shooting,' Hawkins commended her.

Riley's face darkened with anger as she regarded the dead bodies. 'Cain fucked us,' she spat. 'What the hell are we going to do now?'

'We're on our own. Once this is over, we're officially freelance.'

He was done taking orders, done risking his life for causes he didn't care about, done answering to fools who would sell him out at a moment's notice. When this was all over, he was taking his unit and packing up. A group like his would have their pick of ops anywhere in the world.

Riley's smile was eager and predatory. 'About goddamn time.'

'But first we've got some business to finish,' Hawkins said, turning away.

'What kind of business?' Riley asked.

He smiled, anticipating the payback he was owed. 'Marcus Cain.'

–

'She must have followed me there that night,' Cain explained. 'She cut a deal with Surovsky by herself. By the time I figured out what had happened, they had you.'

Cain fell silent then, watching the play of emotions across Anya's face. She looked as if her world was collapsing around her. Everything she had believed, the ruthless and single-minded search for answers that had sustained her for the past four years, gone in an instant.

'If you are lying to me...'

'Look at me, Anya,' Cain implored her. 'I'm done lying. Everything I've told you is the truth. No more, no less.'

The look in Anya's eyes confirmed she believed him.

'Freya was the one who betrayed me.'

'She did what I couldn't,' he grimly acknowledged. 'For the… "greater good".'

'But it was all for nothing,' Anya whispered. 'Freya's deal changed nothing. The war happened anyway.'

Once more, Cain found himself reflecting on James' haunting sentiments on the value of war, and the hunt for Osama Bin Laden.

Didn't it ever occur to you that he was more useful to us alive than dead?

'Don't you get it? The war was always going to happen. The Circle made sure of that.'

Turning away, Anya looked at the row of candles arrayed in front of her, most of them unlit. Then, in a sudden fit of anger, she swept her arm across them, scattering them across the floor.

'It was a lie,' she said, her voice nearly breaking as she leaned on the empty stand for support. 'Another lie. All this time, I have been chasing a ghost.'

Cain hesitated, caught by the once-familiar urge to reach out to her. This woman who had once been such an integral part of his life, who he would have given anything for, and who had ultimately cost him so much.

'I know. But it's over now,' he said quietly. 'It's over, Anya.'

'No. Not yet,' another voice announced.

Both Cain and Anya looked toward the arched doorway on the far side of the altar as a man emerged from the shadows, his weapon trained on Cain, his eyes alight with vengeance.

'Ryan,' Anya gasped. 'What are you doing here? How did you find us?'

'Because he had help.'

A second figure emerged from behind a pillar, taking up position alongside Drake. A woman that Cain had never expected to see again.

'Remember me?' McKnight spat as she took a step towards him. 'You said I'd have a long time to think about my mistakes, and you were right, Marcus. Just like I've had a long time to imagine this moment.'

'Wait!' Anya implored them, stepping between Cain and his two would-be assassins. 'You are making a mistake.'

'Stand aside, Anya,' Drake warned, his voice icy cold as he approached his nemesis. 'This has to happen now.'

'No, it doesn't,' she countered. 'You don't know what you're doing.'

She didn't fully understand how Drake and McKnight had forged this unlikely alliance, but it didn't matter now. They were here, and they had come for one thing only.

'I know this man took everything from me,' Drake hit back. 'He's not walking out of here alive. Stand aside.'

With no other option, Anya turned her weapon on Drake. 'I can't let you do it.'

'Are you going to kill me, Anya?' Drake challenged her. 'For *him*?'

'You don't understand—'

'This man destroyed our lives, took everything we had,' McKnight countered. 'Why in God's name are you defending him?'

'Because I was wrong, Samantha,' Anya admitted. 'About everything. He didn't betray me to the Russians. He was working all this time to bring down the Circle.'

'He had my father executed,' McKnight said through clenched teeth, tears stinging her eyes. 'I heard him die.'

'No, you heard a gunshot over the phone,' Cain interrupted.

The woman froze, struck numb by his words. 'What did you say?'

'Your father is alive, Samantha,' he stated. 'I'm not a monster, despite what you might think. Killing an innocent man wasn't necessary. I needed you to believe he was dead.'

'You're lying!' she cried, refusing to let herself believe it.

'Am I?' he asked. 'Or is it easier to pull the trigger, and tell yourself I deserved it?'

'You locked me up, told me I'd never see daylight again. Told me my life was over.'

'You were a risk. I needed you out of the way until this was all over.' He glanced at Anya. 'If you'd stayed where you were, you would have been released.'

McKnight's eyes were wide with shock, the weapon trembling in her hands as Cain took a step towards her.

'You have every right to hate me. I used you, put you in an impossible position, forced you to work against the people you valued most. I know you didn't want to do it. I know you're a good person.'

Another step closer.

'You could kill me, take revenge for everything I did.' He sighed. 'And spend the rest of your life running from it. But it doesn't have to end that way. You can still have a life of your own, Samantha,' he said gently. 'A future. A family...'

'No more, Cain,' Drake snapped.

'Let him speak, Ryan,' McKnight countered, clearly swayed by his words.

'For Christ's sake, can't you see what he's doing? He's telling you exactly what you want to hear.' He shook his head. 'No more. This ends here.'

Cain turned slowly to regard him.

'Ryan Drake,' he said, facing his adversary down. Looking at him not as an enemy to be overcome, but as a survivor like himself. A man worthy of respect. 'Out of all the people I've dealt with, I don't think I've ever met one as persistent as you.'

'You have to answer for what you've done.'

'We all do,' Cain fired back. 'Tell me, how many men have you killed to be here tonight, Ryan? How many deaths do *you* have to answer for?'

Drake hesitated, momentarily daunted by his question. Because he sensed the truth in it. He had killed men – and women – in his long battle against Marcus Cain. Many had deserved it, others hadn't. But they had died anyway.

Because of him.

'I did what I had to do to survive,' he said quietly. 'I didn't want it.'

'And Lauren?' Cain challenged him. 'Did you want that?'

A muscle tightened in his jaw as he thought of the sibling he would never know, lying dead on a sidewalk in Berlin. 'Lauren... your daughter... was an accident. We didn't kill her.'

'But you *were* responsible. She would never have been there if not for you.'

'Don't, Cain!' he retorted, gripping the weapon tight. He refused to play this game. Not now. 'We never asked for any of this. You backed us into a corner, took everything we had, left us with no choice. This all began with you, and it'll end with you. Tonight.'

Cain straightened up a little then, raising his chin as he faced Drake down without fear. 'Then do it,' he said simply. 'If you're as righteous as you believe, then pull the trigger. Tell yourself you did the right thing, punished the evil man, made the world a better place.'

'First *you* tell me something. Tell me why you killed Freya.'

He had held himself in check until this moment, but now they'd come down to it. Now he was going to get the answers he'd come for, and then he was going to kill the man.

'What do you mean?'

'Enough!' Drake shouted, struggling to hold his emotions in check. 'Enough lies. For once in your life, tell the truth. Tell me why you had her killed.'

'Ryan...' Anya began.

'Stay out of this!' he snapped, turning his attention back to his most hated enemy. 'It's just us now, Marcus. We're all that's left. Don't you want to be honest, just once, before I kill you?'

Cain shook his head slowly. 'You still don't understand, do you? You've got the wrong man.'

'You're lying.'

'What have I got left to lie for?' Cain asked frankly.

'You want to stay alive.'

Cain spread his hands. 'My work's done. What happens now doesn't matter.'

Drake had stepped right up to him, the barrel of his weapon pressed against Cain's forehead. One pull of the trigger, and it was over.

'Then this won't matter to you.'

'Stop, Ryan,' Anya interrupted. 'He's telling the truth.'

Drake looked at her. 'How do you know?'

He watched as she swallowed, her throat tightening, then closed her eyes as if seeking some inner reserve of strength and willpower. Then, opening them, she raised her chin and gave Drake his answer.

'Because I'm the one who killed her.'

Chapter 59

Yanking her arm free, Freya whirled around to face her adversary, eyes gleaming with defiance. She wouldn't give them the satisfaction of putting a bullet through the back of her head.

'You look me in the eye, you coward,' she said, staring right at them. 'Look me in the eye when you pull the trigger.'

If she'd expected her words to strike a chord, to engender some kind of reaction, she was to be disappointed. A second came and went. A second broken only by the sigh of the evening breeze, and distant hoot of an owl, and the hammering of Freya's heart.

She saw the barrel of a weapon raised, saw the long snout of a silencer gleaming in the thin sliver of moonlight.

Freya let out a breath. 'Of all the people to do this—'

A 9mm slug passing through her chest silenced that sentence before she had a chance to complete it. She let out a strangled gasp, as if in surprise, then fell backward and collapsed to the ground, her body skidding down the rocky slope until it came to rest in a pool of stagnant water.

Her killer lingered a moment longer, waiting to be sure the gunshot had done its work. Waiting to confirm her target really was dead.

'You shouldn't have come looking for me,' Anya said, looking down on the dead woman with a hint of regret.

Her work done, she turned away and started her walk back to the waiting van.

–

Drake let out a strangled breath. Cold, invisible fingers were clamping around his throat, slowly squeezing the life out of him. What Anya had just said made no sense. Every atom of his being instinctively rebelled against it.

'No. No, that's not possible.'

Anya said nothing, but the look of utter desolation on her face told its own story.

'Anya, tell me this isn't true,' he implored her. 'Tell me you're wrong.'

The woman for whom he'd risked and sacrificed so much was looking back at him, her expression a mixture of grief and desperate longing for understanding.

'I'm so sorry, Ryan,' she whispered. 'But I won't lie. I killed Freya.'

Drake closed his eyes, feeling like a knife had just been driven into his chest. All this time he'd been tracking his mother's killer, looking for the one responsible, and she'd been right in front of him all along.

He could feel his heart rate rising, could feel the blood pounding in his ears as the awful, incomprehensible truth sank in.

'Why?' he asked, barely able to get the word out. 'Why did you do it?'

'I did not know who she was.'

Drake glanced at the weapon in his hands. It was starting. The red darkness gathering in his mind. The monster he'd thought long banished, rising up once again.

'Why did you kill her?' he repeated.

He watched the muscles in her throat tighten as she took a tentative step towards him. 'Freya… your mother wasn't who you think she was,' Anya said, keeping her voice carefully measured and controlled now. 'I can explain everything, I just need time.'

Drake could feel his body tensing up involuntarily, his heart pounding, preparing itself for what was coming. Anya saw it too. Sensing his intentions, she backed off a pace.

Drake took another step towards her, only to feel a forceful hand on his arm, pulling him back. He turned to see McKnight holding him back.

'Don't do this, Ryan,' she urged. 'Please.'

Drake lowered his head, allowing himself just a moment to contemplate her plea, to imagine how this might play out if he let it go. Maybe there was an explanation. Maybe Anya did have a reason for what she'd done.

An instant later, the thought vanished and everything became clear. Yanking his arm free, he lashed out at McKnight, catching her with an elbow strike to the face that sent her crashing backwards off the edge of the raised altar and onto the stone floor below.

Switching his attention to Anya, he saw the woman raise her weapon, ready to gun him down just as she'd put down his mother before him. Moving with fluid, terrifying speed, he caught her wrist and yanked it upward. The suppressed weapon thumped as she squeezed the trigger, a stray round sailing harmlessly over his shoulder.

In response he brought his own automatic to bear, ignoring the second shot that thumped past him, the exhaust gasses from the suppressor stinging his eyes. Anya was fast; fast enough to duck before he could pull the trigger.

But Drake wasn't aiming for her head. Instead he swept the gun around, the butt striking the suppressor on Anya's own weapon like a hammer blow. Metal clashed against metal and the gun was torn from her grip, clattering to the ground a few yards away.

Unarmed now, Anya lashed out with her naked fists, trying to take him down hand to hand. She had faced Drake before and prevailed against him, her superior training and experience giving her the edge she needed. She knew his capabilities and his limitations, and how to exploit both.

But this was a different man from the one she'd fought before. A man seasoned by unforgiving experience, hardened by brutal adversity, driven by rage and fury.

A man who blocked and deflected her increasingly desperate attacks, driving her backward, wearing her down. And for the first time, a doubt crept into her mind. Catching her outstretched arm, Drake yanked it upward and drove a knee into her stomach with every ounce of force he could summon, knocking the breath out of her. Coughing and gasping, Anya went down on one knee, struggling to rise.

Never before had she faced an opponent like this.

Face tight with pain, Anya looked up as Drake loomed over her, a dark and menacing figure that seemed to have grown in stature before her eyes. She saw the glint of a weapon in the overhead lights as he turned it on her, saw his expression twisted with anger and fury, his eyes burning with vengeance.

'Stop!' a powerful voice yelled.

Drake's head snapped around to see Marcus Cain standing a few yards away. He was holding Anya's weapon.

'Anya isn't your enemy, Ryan,' Cain said. 'Put the gun down.'

In another life, Drake might have laughed at the absurd irony of their situation. Him, ready to kill the woman who had been his ally for the past four years. Cain, ready to kill him to defend his nemesis.

'Why don't you both put them down,' McKnight said, leaping back up onto the altar. She was bleeding from a cut above the eye where Drake had struck her, but the injury hadn't slowed her down. Her eyes were still bright and focussed, now filled with cold anger.

'I told you to stay out of this,' Drake said, jaw clenched, weapon still trained on Anya.

'Killing each other isn't going to bring her back.'

'You were ready to kill Cain tonight.'

'I was wrong,' she acknowledged reluctantly. 'Just like you.'

'She killed my mother.'

Anya rose slowly to her feet, hands curled into fists as she faced her former ally. Drake was right there before her, his weapon trained on her head.

'Put it down, Drake!' Cain warned.

'Stay back. This is between us,' Anya said calmly. She made no attempt to stop Drake now. She just stood there, meeting his gaze evenly and without fear. 'I once told you never to point a gun at me unless you were ready to pull the trigger. Are you ready to do it now?'

'Why, Anya?' he asked, anger and betrayal vying with a desperate need for understanding. 'Why you?'

'She gave me no choice. I wish it hadn't come to that, but it did.' She paused just for a moment, settling some silent debate in her mind. 'And if I had to do it again, I would.'

Drake let out a breath, struck not just by the cold pragmatism of her statement, but by the utter conviction in her voice. She was holding nothing back, making no attempt to argue her case or justify herself.

Challenging him to pull the trigger.

But looking her in the eye now, could he do it? Could he kill Anya? Did she deserve it for what she'd taken from him?

Before he could contemplate this further, the stand-off was interrupted by a voice that blared suddenly throughout the vast empty church, booming and powerful, somehow coming from multiple sources all at once.

'Well done, Ryan,' the voice announced, evidently pleased. 'Not quite how I imagined tonight playing out, but it's good enough.'

All four of them glanced around, seeking the source of the voice but finding nothing. It took them a moment to realise it was being projected through the building's wireless speaker system. Designed to carry a preacher's sermons throughout the vast church, it had been hijacked by a decidedly less pious orator tonight.

'Where's it coming from?' McKnight whispered.

'I don't know.'

'Don't waste your time,' the voice advised. 'I can see you, and hear you.'

Glancing upward, Drake spotted a security camera covering the altar. One of several positioned around the church to safeguard it against theft and vandalism. Whoever was speaking to them must have hacked into this security system.

'Do you really think I'd be foolish enough to come there in person?'

Drake knew that voice. Even over the booming speaker system, he recognised it from their previous meetings. And he was not the only one.

'Starke,' Cain gasped.

'Hello, Marcus,' Richard Starke's voice rolled out. 'Still leaving those loose ends untied, huh? I warned you about that.'

'You made this happen?' the CIA director asked, gesturing to the others. 'You brought them here tonight?'

'No, *you* made it happen. I'm just here to clean up your mess,' he explained. 'Speaking of which, it's time to finish this, Ryan.'

'Finish it?'

'The man who destroyed your life, and the woman who took your mother's. They're right in front of you. All you have to do is pull the trigger, and this is all over.'

'It's already over. Cain destroyed the Circle, just like you wanted.'

'What makes you think I wanted the Circle destroyed?'

'You son of a bitch,' Drake snarled, finally seeing the full extent of Starke's lies and manipulation. 'We trusted you!'

'So did your mother. A Drake family weakness, it seems.'

Drake hadn't missed his implied meaning. 'What are you saying?'

'Enough,' Starke said, his voice booming far louder than any of them could hope to match. 'It's time to finish what you started.'

'Killing me won't bring the Circle back,' Cain reminded him. 'They're gone. It's over.'

'Far from it. You might have taken out the leaders, but everything they created is still intact. All that's needed is for someone to carry on their work.'

It didn't take much imagination to guess who Starke had in mind. He might have failed to protect them from Cain, but he was ready and willing to seize the opportunity and fill the power vacuum that had opened.

'The same offer applies to you, Miss McKnight. Kill them both, and your record will be expunged. You'll get your life back, and all of this will be a distant memory.'

Drake glanced at McKnight, sensing the doubts that were slowly blossoming in her mind, the long-abandoned possibilities awakening once more. She was tempted.

'What's the matter, Ryan?' Starke pressed him. 'Are these people really worth dying for? Would they hesitate in your position?'

Drake backed away from Anya, his eyes flicking between her and Cain. One of them had been his ally, the other his enemy. Now he didn't know what either represented.

But the question remained – would they pull the trigger, in his place?

'Tough decision, Ryan? Maybe you need a little… incentive,' Starke suggested. 'Look up.'

A pair of large-screen televisions had been mounted high on the walls on both sides of the main altar, probably to display hymn verses and other references during ceremonies. Now, however, when they flickered into life, they displayed something very different.

Drake felt the world start to close in around him, narrowing to a single tunnel between himself and the TV. It was displaying camera footage, low quality but clearly distinguishable. He recognised the location and the people in it right away, because he had been with them barely an hour ago.

It was the rest of his team, back at the disused garage. They were clustered around Frost and her computer terminal.

'I think you understand my point now. Finish your mission, and you and your team get to walk away. Refuse, and… well, take a guess.'

Tearing his eyes away from the screen, he looked at Cain and Anya. Two people who had cost him a great deal already, and who might cost him even more depending on what he did in the next few seconds.

Were they really worth it? Were they worth sacrificing everything he had left?

'Take me,' Cain commanded. 'Take me and let the others go.'

'Very noble of you, but I'm not in the business of leaving loose ends untied.'

Drake could almost feel the man's firm resolve to protect Anya, even at the cost of his own life.

'You already lost a loved one because of this, Ryan,' Starke reminded him gravely. 'Are you willing to lose another?'

'Ryan,' McKnight said, her voice hushed. 'He'll kill us no matter what we do.'

'Time to choose,' Starke commanded him. 'Your mission, or your friends.'

Last of all, his gaze came to rest on Anya. The woman at the centre of all of this. The person who had saved, and very nearly ended, his life on more than one occasion. Who had taken and given so much.

She was watching him now, waiting for him to make his decision.

'Remember what I told you once?' she said quietly. 'You're a good man, Ryan. No matter what happens, remember that.'

'No more talk,' Starke's booming voice commanded, everywhere and nowhere all at once. 'Kill them now.'

Drake's finger tightened on the trigger, inching fractionally towards the crucial point. Whatever justifications they might have for their actions, both Cain and Anya had committed terrible acts in their lives. They had each murdered, betrayed and lied in order to survive.

But so had he.

Was he really any better than them? Was he more deserving of life? Was it even his place to make such a choice?

'No,' Drake said at last, lowering his weapon. 'I won't do it, Starke. We both know you'll kill us all, no matter what I do. I'd rather die with a clear conscience.'

He heard the NSA director sigh wearily over the speaker system.

'You know, for a moment I actually thought you might have the balls to do it,' Starke said mockingly. 'But you're right about one thing. You *are* going to die.'

As if on cue, the big doors at the far end of the church crashed open, allowing at least half a dozen figures to rush in through the breach. Drake's head snapped around, taking in the tactical operatives, the heavy body armour, the silenced assault rifles swinging towards him and the others. And in the midst of the assault team, a man he recognised.

Hawkins smiled as he raised his rifle, taking aim. Not at Drake, but at Anya, standing alone and unarmed in the midst of the altar. She would be the first to die.

Drake saw it too.

'Get down!' he shouted, knowing he was too far away to intervene.

It happened so fast, so easy, it almost didn't seem fair. Sighting her centre mass, Hawkins took first pressure on the trigger, exhaled and relaxed his muscles, then unleashed a short, deadly accurate burst that zipped through the air and struck its target.

Except that target wasn't Anya. Just as the assault rifle kicked back into his shoulder, another body moved in between them.

Marcus Cain stumbled backwards as the rounds slammed into his torso, pulling Anya down with him. They landed together on the stone floor of the altar, Cain still shielding her with his dying body, his blood staining the ground around them.

At the same moment, Drake turned his weapon on Hawkins and opened fire just as the man was bringing his weapon around to sight his next target. Out of the corner of his eye he saw Drake take aim, knew the man had the drop on him, and tried to leap behind cover as Drake pulled the trigger. White hot pain seared through him as the round tore into his neck and he went down, his blood painting the pew behind.

In the midst of the unfolding firefight, Cain and Anya lay together behind the altar, holding each other close, everything around them forgotten. For a moment, their eyes met and everything else seemed to fade away. Cain watched as Anya's shock and disbelief give way to growing realisation at what he'd done.

He saw a faint reflection of the young woman who'd once looked at him with love and longing, who had once been willing to die for him, and who now realised he'd done the same for her.

'Anya!' Drake yelled, gripping her arm and trying to pull her away. 'We have to go! Now!'

Nearby, McKnight had leapt down from the altar, trading fire with a trio of assault operatives who were advancing along the edge of the vast room, using the pews and pillars for cover. The room echoed with the thump of suppressed gunfire.

'Hurry, Ryan! Get her up!'

Coughing weakly, Cain nodded. 'Go,' he urged her. 'Get out of here.'

There was so much still to say, so much they might still have done together. And none of it would come to pass now. This was where their story ended, and she knew it.

'I'm sorry,' Anya whispered.

'Come on!' Drake implored her, physically hauling her away.

Cain was oblivious to the desperate battle unfolding around him, the thump of automatic weapons and the frantic shouts. His laboured breathing was growing shallow, his damaged heart slowing as the final moments of his life played out.

His head lolled to the side, taking in the shelves of unlit candles neatly laid out nearby. And in the midst of them, a single one burning brightly, illuminating the photograph he'd carefully placed below it. His daughter, Lauren.

He would see her soon, he thought as the flame of his life flickered out and the darkness closed in around him.

Chapter 60

'Where the hell is he? Talk to me, Frost,' Jessica demanded, pacing back and forth across the dusty, litter-strewn floor of the garage, impatient for news on Drake.

'If I knew what the fuck was happening, don't you think I'd tell you?' Frost hit back.

So far their night had swung wildly from triumph to disaster and back again, leaving them completely in the dark about what was happening. The last they'd heard from Drake, he and McKnight were en route to the church where Anya was planning to confront Cain.

How and why he'd decided to join forces with their traitorous former team member – or even how she'd found him in the first place – was a complete mystery. There simply hadn't been time to question him.

'We should go there ourselves,' Frost decided. 'He may need backup.'

'What about the plan?' Mitchell countered.

'The plan's fucked,' she stated bluntly. 'We're on our own now.'

Mitchell sighed but nodded agreement. 'Fine. What about Dietrich?'

Thinking on it for barely a second, Frost switched comms frequencies. 'Dietrich, come in. Relocate to National City Christian Church ASAP. Ryan's off comms and needs urgent backup. Over.'

There was no answer.

Frost repeated her summons. 'Dietrich, acknowledge this transmission. Over.'

Once again she was met by dead air. Both men had simply disappeared.

–

Anya was in a daze as Drake hauled her away from the altar, barely even conscious of the firefight raging around them. Glancing left, she watched with a strange sense of detachment as the wooden frame of the pulpit shattered under a stray burst of gunfire. On her right, more rounds ricocheted off a stone pillar, busting apart in a spectacular shower of sparks and broken masonry.

And all the while, Drake pulled her onward, with McKnight covering their retreat.

'Changing mags!' McKnight shouted, ejecting the spent clip from her smoking weapon.

Hearing the crash of another door being blown open nearby, Anya looked up as two more men advanced into the room straight ahead, trying to cut them off.

'Contact front!' Drake called out.

Both he and McKnight emptied their weapons into the two operatives, aiming for the head instead of wasting ammunition on their formidable armour. One stumbled backward while the other was spun sideways, triggering a long burst on full automatic that stitched a path across the stonework in front of them.

'Go!' Drake cried, pushing past their fallen bodies and into the corridor beyond.

In that instant, the world snapped back into place for Anya. Reaching down, she snatched up one of the dead men's weapons – a Heckler & Koch G36 assault rifle – and dropped to one knee to present a smaller target.

Sighting the nearest operative as he broke cover, she squeezed off a short, deadly accurate burst that slammed into his upper chest and face. She saw a burst of red, heard a muffled scream as he went down.

'Fall back!' McKnight yelled.

'Go! I'll cover you.'

In response, McKnight grabbed her arm, forcing her to look round. 'You can't win this one, Anya. We have to go. Now!'

Those words seemed to cut through the fog of rage and vengeance that had enveloped her. She could make a stand here, probably take a few of them with her, but in the end they would get her. Her death would serve no purpose at all.

Glancing down at the dead man by her feet, she undid a pouch on his webbing and yanked out the fragmentation grenade within. A few seconds later, she'd yanked the pin free and placed the device beneath the body.

Firing off another wild burst through the open doorway, she retreated deeper into the building with McKnight right behind her.

–

Nearby, Jason Hawkins pulled his hand away from his neck. The Nomex combat glove was slick with his own blood. Drake's hastily aimed shot had grazed him, just missing an artery, but it was bleeding profusely all the same.

'You okay, sir?' one of his operatives asked, eyeing the gory wound.

'It's nothing. Move up!' Hawkins snarled. 'Run those bastards down.'

As his team closed in on the doorway, Hawkins rose to his feet and ascended the steps of the altar, glancing up at the cross overhead before turning his gaze downward to the man lying dead on the floor.

Marcus Cain, the director of the CIA. One of the most powerful men in the country. The man who, less than an hour ago, had tried to have him executed. An eye for an eye, as his father always used to say.

Reaching up, he pressed his radio transmitter. 'It's done. Cain's dead.'

'Good,' Starke replied, speaking directly over the secure comms system. 'And the others?'

'We're on it.'

'I suggest you finish this quickly. Local police have been alerted. I can stall them, but not for long.'

Nearby, his team advanced into the doorway, encountering two of their comrades lying sprawled on the stone floor. One reached down to check for signs of life while his comrades covered him.

What he didn't notice was the grenade lodged beneath the dead man's shoulder. Not until he heard the faint ping of the spring-loaded fly-off handle detaching, and saw the metal sphere roll into view.

'Grenade!'

The roar of the detonation sent a cloud of smoke and stone fragments out into the main altar room, the vibrations trembling up through the building's structure to send shivers of dust down from high above.

Hawkins was obliged to turn away to avoid flying debris. But as the echo of the blast died away, he let out a slow, carefully controlled breath.

'Get in there,' he instructed, seething with rage. 'Find them.'

–

The main body of the church was flanked by a pair of five-storey buildings. Constructed of the same grey stonework as the church itself, they were devoted to less spiritual and more practical matters; mostly administrative duties, project planning and general workspace for the church's sizeable staff. Tonight, however, the place was deserted, the lights turned off, the desks and meeting rooms unmanned.

Weapon in hand, Drake advanced quickly up a flight of stone steps and along the short corridor connecting the church building to the office block, heading for the north end of the building where a stairwell led down to an emergency fire exit. The same way he and McKnight had made entry.

He had no idea what they were going to do once this was over, how he could begin to process everything he'd learned about both Anya and his mother, but that would have to wait.

Don't think about it now, he commanded himself. *Just keep moving.*

Reaching up, he powered up his comms unit and spoke urgently into the microphone. 'Keira, Keira, come in. You need to get out of there now. Repeat, you've been compromised. Get the fuck out.'

Frost didn't respond. Neither did anyone else, for that matter. All he could hear was the faint hiss of static in his ear. Was it the heavy stone structure around him, or something else? Was he already too late?

Catching footsteps behind, he glanced over his shoulder as his two companions sprinted to catch up with him.

'They're coming,' Anya reported, avoiding Drake's gaze. 'We barred the door at the other end, but it won't hold them long.'

'We're almost out,' Drake replied as they pushed through into a large, open plan office area, banks of desks and smaller meeting rooms set at intervals. Everything had been powered down for the night, the lights turned off and the computers shut down. The only illumination was from the glow of street-lamps outside, hazily filtered through the drawn curtains.

'We have to warn the others,' McKnight said.

'Comms are down,' he replied, trying again in growing desperation. 'Keira! Anyone, come in!'

Nothing.

'Fuck!' he snapped. One or both sides of the transmission were being jammed by Starke. The head of the NSA. The man who was tapped into everything.

'They can't hear you,' a woman's voice taunted him. 'You're too late.'

Drake's reaction was born from pure instinct. Twisting aside, he threw himself behind a bank of desks just as a storm of automatic gunfire erupted in front of him, the muzzle flashes bursting across the dimly lit office space like lightning. Glass shattered as rounds blasted apart computer monitors and tore through thin wooden desk partitions, showering him with debris.

Anya and McKnight likewise took cover on the opposite side of the aisle. Angling her weapon over the top of the desk, Anya snapped off a long burst, spent shell casings clattering to the ground around her. It was loud but futile, buying them mere seconds. The answering hail of gunfire was both accurate and sustained, forcing her to flatten herself against the floor.

Quickly assessing the situation, Drake reached his conclusion about the same time as his companions. 'Get out of here, both of you,' he hissed. 'I'll draw their fire.'

Anya shook her head. 'We have to do this together.'

They both flinched as more rounds chewed up the floor between them, some ricocheting wildly into the wall behind.

'No time to argue. Just go!' Drake snapped, readying himself.

Anya stared back at the man who was about to risk his life for her, wishing there was something she could say to him. Some way of making this right.

'I'm sorry, Ryan,' she whispered.

Drake met her gaze, and for a moment she wondered if he might harbour similar sentiments. 'Find a way to warn the others,' he ordered her. 'Don't let this be for nothing.'

Swallowing, Anya nodded.

At the far end of the room, Riley smiled as she gleefully emptied the remains of her P90 submachine gun's magazine in Drake's direction, revelling in the wanton destruction. The short, compact weapon jolted against her shoulder with satisfying power, the smell of cordite smoke thick in the air around her.

Death and destruction had always held a certain fascination and excitement for her, one that was almost arousing in its intensity. But tonight the anticipation was heightened by the knowledge of who she was about to kill. Drake and Anya trapped together. No way out, except through her.

Removing the spent magazine, she reached for a new one and deftly inserted it into the gun's housing. At the same time, her earpiece was buzzing with a new transmission from Hawkins. 'Team Two, sitrep.'

'We've got them in sight,' Riley reported, speaking quietly as she scanned the shadowy banks of desks. 'They'll be dead soon.'

'Negative. Keep them pinned down and wait for support.'

She understood what he had in mind, using Riley and her team to hold Drake up while Hawkins and the others hit them from behind. Caught between the hammer and the anvil, they'd have nothing to do except die.

But there was an edge of something in his voice now. Was it tension, or impatience?

'No time,' she decided. 'We have to finish them *now*.'

She could do it, she knew; the elation and energy of the moment radiated from the very core of her being. She didn't need Hawkins, or anyone else. She would be the one to take down Drake and Anya – their last remaining enemies. And then, finally, they would be free.

Hawkins started to respond, but she reached up and switched off her comms unit. Out of contact now, she glanced at the two operatives flanking her.

'Move up. Flush them out.'

Both men nodded, then began to advance.

'This is it, Drake!' she called as she racked back the weapon's charging handle. 'Don't make it too easy on us. I want this one to be worth it.'

Pressing himself against the floor, Drake crawled to the end of the bank of desks and eased his head out just long enough to take in the scene. Two operatives advancing towards him, both armed with submachine guns, both equipped with night vision scopes. Men who could see through the darkness as if it was bright as day. Riley meanwhile held back, waiting for him to break cover.

Three against one. Bad odds.

That was when he caught sight of something mounted on the wall nearby. A large red cylinder, gleaming dully in the hazy orange glow of streetlights. A fire extinguisher.

'Get ready,' he whispered to Anya and McKnight.

Taking a breath, Drake leaned out, took aim and opened fire. The first round struck the cylinder a glancing blow, ricocheting off without penetrating. However, the second landed true, punching straight through the steel casing. An instant later, the high pressure extinguisher ruptured explosively, ejecting a cloud of white carbon dioxide that enveloped the far end of the office.

'Go!' Drake shouted, leaping up.

Anya and McKnight scrambled to their feet. Unable to make it to the fire escape, they instead rushed at the windows facing out onto the street below. Raising the assault rifle, Anya emptied the remainder of her ammunition into the window, which shattered and collapsed under the onslaught.

She could feel rounds zipping past her as their enemies, sensing their intent, fired blindly into the gaseous haze. There was no way to anticipate or avoid them. All she could do was run and hope luck was on her side.

Closing her eyes, she gathered herself up and leapt through the gap, plunging onto the street about fifteen feet below. Buildings and roads flashed past her before the concrete sidewalk rose up and hit her hard, knocking the breath out of her lungs. Broken glass sliced through clothes and skin, and she felt the familiar hot flash of pain jolting through her already injured body.

McKnight landed beside her a second later, curling into a ball to lessen the impact and rolling to a stop a few feet away. She was wet, bedraggled and bleeding from several lacerations, but she was alive.

'Get up, Samantha. Move!' Anya hissed, pulling her up and moving in close to the base of the building, out of sight of the windows above.

They were injured, but they were clear.

'Hurry, Ryan,' she whispered.

–

Staying low, Drake rushed forward, ignoring the panicked gunfire that sliced through the air just above his head. The laser sights that had

348

helped his opponents aim and fire were now working against them, the beams plainly visible in the swirling CO2 haze.

Taking aim at the nearest one, Drake squeezed off a trio of shots, hearing the distinctive wet crunch as one blew through a human skull. But the muzzle flash of his weapon had given away his position. He rolled into cover to avoid the answering volley that blasted apart the nearest desk.

Riley immediately understood what he was doing, and how to stop him. Turning towards the emergency fire suppression alarm mounted on the wall beside her, she slammed the butt of her weapon against the protective glass panel, reached in and yanked on the lever. Straight away, red lights blazed on and the overhead sprinklers sputtered into action, unleashing a downpour on the office below.

As the gas began to clear under this watery onslaught, Drake knew he had only seconds to act. Leaping out from behind cover, he launched himself at the second operative and smacked the P90 aside before he could bring it to bear. With his enemy temporarily exposed, Drake jammed the barrel of his gun into the man's armpit, twisting it around the fabric of his Kevlar vest and pulled the trigger. The gunshot was muffled by fabric and flesh pressed against the barrel, but the thumping recoil told him the weapon had discharged.

The man jerked convulsively, tried to let out a cry of shock and pain, only to cough up a mouthful of blood. A second shot was enough to deal a fatal blow. It was the last of Drake's ammunition. The weapon was dry.

Holding the man upright, Drake swung this human shield towards Riley just as she opened up, spraying the dead man with automatic fire. Drake could feel the sickening thumps as rounds slammed into his makeshift shield, the Kevlar vest absorbing most of them.

The instant the firing stopped, Drake released his hold, allowing the dead man to flop to the ground, then charged at his remaining enemy. With his gun empty, he drew back his arm and hurled the useless weapon at her, forcing her to throw up the P90 to deflect it. Both guns rang out as the automatic clashed against the P90's polymer coating.

It was a desperate gesture, but it had bought him the time he needed to close the range. Realising she had no time to reload, Riley dropped the cumbersome gun and reached for the knife at her waist, slashing wildly just as he leapt at her. Instinctively Drake tried to twist aside mid-leap, raising his arm to defend himself.

Hot pain flashed up his forearm as the blade bit into his flesh. Caught off balance by his attempt to evade the deadly blade, he slammed into the wall, his shoulder taking the brunt of the impact.

Riley was on him in an instant, trying to seize the momentum and finish him. The blade swept down against him, gleaming in the crimson light, only to tear a ragged gash across the drywall as Drake ducked aside.

–

Outside, Anya and McKnight were retreating down the street away from the towering church building. Already they could hear police sirens closing in, mingling with the blare of fire alarms inside the church. In a minute or two, the whole area would be locked down.

'We can't leave him behind,' McKnight said.

'He made his choice,' Anya replied, fishing out her cell phone and dialling.

'Anya, what the—' Alex began as soon as he'd picked up.

'Don't talk, just listen,' she cut in. 'I need your help right now.'

–

The two adversaries circled each other warily, each looking for an opening as water poured down around them and fire alarms blared.

Riley, however, held the upper hand. She was armed, she was fast, and she knew how to take full advantage of both. Drake was tiring, and already injured. She smiled as she shifted her grip on the blade, feinting and gauging his reactions, muscles tensing as she prepared to strike.

Guns had their place, but there was nothing quite so primal, so visceral, so exciting as a knife. Seeing the agony flare in your enemy's eyes as the blade slid into their flesh.

'I've been waiting for this, Drake,' she said, her eager eyes shining like coals in the red light. 'Just you and me now.'

She came in fast, slashing and thrusting, forcing him backward, keeping him on the defensive. The only good piece of advice Drake had ever had about getting into a knife fight was simple and blunt – bring a gun.

That wasn't an option now. Riley was a vicious fighter, fast and nimble, moving with the easy grace of a gymnast. Sooner or later the blade would find its mark.

He had to disarm her. As she came in again, thrusting the blade at his throat, he shifted his weight suddenly, sidestepping so that the knife sailed past him. Catching her arm, he yanked it down hard, dropping to one knee and exerting all his strength to heave her over his shoulder. Turning over in the air, the young woman crashed onto the desk in front of him, scattering files and other office equipment across the floor.

That was his chance. She was exposed and vulnerable, but she wouldn't be for long. Leaping to his feet, he came in with an elbow strike, but the agile operative saw it coming and rolled aside. Pain jolted up his arm as his elbow slammed against the desk. Before he could recover, Riley's knee swept around and caught Drake squarely on the side of his head.

Pain and white light exploded inside his skull. As Drake staggered sideways, injured and disoriented, Riley leapt down from the desk, her boots splashing in the pooling water.

'The great Ryan Drake,' she said contemptuously, breathing hard with a mixture of exertion and excitement. 'Fucking pathetic. I'm doing the world a favour by ending you.'

Sensing victory, she crept towards her stricken adversary like a predator stalking its prey. He was no threat to her now.

This was it. This was the moment she'd been waiting for.

'It's a shame you won't get to see your friends when we kill them,' Riley said, reversing her grip on the knife. 'You'll just have to imagine it.'

Drawing back her arm, she leapt at him.

But Drake wasn't as injured or helpless as he'd appeared. As she swung for an over-handed strike, he threw up his hands, managing to catch her wrist just as the knife was coming down against him. He saw a brief flash of surprise at his sudden reaction, but her expression quickly changed as a new idea took hold.

Drake knew exactly what she was going to do. He was counting on it.

Releasing her grip on the knife, she allowed the weapon to fall from her grasp as if she'd discarded it. But even as it was falling, her other hand leapt out to catch it and plunge it upward into his stomach.

But her chance never came.

In a flash, Drake caught the blade before it made it into her grip. Riley's eyes opened wide, shock and sudden fear showing for the first time as steel flashed in the glowing red lights. She let out a gasp of pain and disbelief as the knife sank into her chest.

For a second or so they remained like that, frozen in time, water falling in slow motion around them. In a final act of defiance, Riley grasped at his neck, trying to pull him close with her fading strength, her eyes locked with his.

There was neither remorse nor compassion in her opponent's gaze.

As Drake yanked the knife free, her legs gave way and she went down, slumping against the side of a desk. She was still staring up at him, her eyes glazed, blood seeping from the corner of her mouth as she tried to speak, unable to comprehend how she'd lost.

Drake didn't spare her a glance as he snatched up his fallen weapon, ejected the spent magazine and calmly slapped a fresh one into place. She was no threat to him now. With his way now clear, he turned away and vanished, leaving the young woman to die alone.

Chapter 61

In the disused car garage, tensions were rising rapidly as the seconds ticked by with no contact from the rest of their team.

'Scan the police frequencies,' Mitchell said. 'See if there's been a report of gunfire.'

'On it.'

Basic police scanners could be bought even from civilian electronics stores. Frost's set-up, however, was considerably more sophisticated, allowing her to crack many of the encrypted frequencies that were out of reach for the average citizen. If there had been an incident of some kind, she would be able to find out in a matter of seconds.

'What the fuck?' she said, her expression darkening as she tilted her head, listening carefully.

'What is it?' Jessica implored her. 'Is he dead?'

'No, the airwaves are,' the young woman replied. 'No transmissions, no comms, nothing.' She spun around to face the others, her face falling. The conclusion was as obvious as it was chilling. 'We're being jammed.'

'But how could they be jamming us if they don't know...' Jessica trailed off momentarily as the implications sank in, '...where we are?'

Frost's computer pinged and a message appeared on screen. A message just like the ones she'd used to communicate with Alex. Twisting around, she scanned the text on screen, her heart surging with fear.

YOU'RE COMPROMISED. GET OUT NOW!

–

Shoving the silenced automatic inside his soaking jacket to hide it from view, Drake hurried north along the main road, trying to put as much distance as possible between himself and the church. Already he could hear police sirens as local law enforcement rushed to the scene.

Other people nearby were reacting too, many spilling out of a nearby bus station to see what was happening. More than a few smartphones were being pointed towards the church. Drake lowered his head, trying not to be seen.

It was a wasted effort. Not only was he the only person moving away from what was clearly a major incident, but he was soaked to the skin, bruised and bleeding from numerous injuries. He could feel warm blood dripping down his forearm, soaking into his jacket.

'Oh shit, man. What happened to you?' asked a young black man, probably a college student judging by the looks of him.

'What's with this guy?' he heard another man ask. 'Hey, you! You involved in this? What you hiding, man?'

Drake knew this was going downhill fast. For obvious reasons, Americans were particularly sensitive about possible terrorist attacks, and they knew something had happened tonight.

Seeking to put distance between himself and the increasingly hostile crowd, he turned right to cross the road, hoping to find a quieter side street to disappear into. He needed to stop and sort himself out, find a way to warn his friends and rendezvous with Anya and McKnight, but not while he was exposed.

The shouts were growing more numerous as the mood turned against him. Glancing over his shoulder, he saw a couple of the younger, bigger men pursuing him. He couldn't allow them to swarm him. Reaching into his jacket, he closed his hand around the weapon.

The screeching of brakes drew his attention back to the road, and he watched as an old-model Chevy sedan skidded to a halt barely ten yards away, headlights blinding him.

Drake drew his gun without hesitation and turned it on the driver, assuming the car was an unmarked police unit or even an Agency service vehicle.

'Stop fucking around and get in, Ryan,' a gruff voice demanded impatiently.

Drake's eyes opened wide. 'Dietrich?'

'Who else? Now move!'

Hesitating no longer, Drake leapt in and slammed the door shut. Barely was he in his seat before Dietrich stepped on the gas, swinging the car into a U-turn before accelerating away. Leaving the growing mob behind.

'How did you find me?' Drake asked, pulling up his jacket sleeve to expose the deep, snaking gash across his forearm.

'Police scanner,' Dietrich explained. 'You've caused quite the shitstorm, Ryan. What happened back there?'

'Cain's dead. The Circle's gone.'

For once, Dietrich's stoic, dispassionate mask slipped. 'You mean it's over? Finished?'

'No. They're going after Jessica and the others. We have to warn them.'

'They're off comms,' the German explained. 'Haven't been able to raise them.'

'Fuck,' Drake said under his breath. 'Then we have to get there ourselves!'

–

The sprinklers were sputtering out when Hawkins and the assault team swept into the devastated office, two operatives moving over to the shattered window to cover the street below while the others fanned out to secure the room.

In a matter of seconds, Hawkins had taken in the two dead team members lying sprawled on the ground, their blood staining the pooling water. Then at last his gaze settled on the young woman slumped against a desk at the edge of the room. Her head was down, her blonde hair hanging in limp tangles around her face.

'Window clear!' one of the team called out.

'Exit clear!'

Hawkins ignored them as he walked slowly towards the fallen woman and knelt down in front of her. Laying down his weapon, he reached out and cupped her chin, raising her head up to face him. Eyes that had once sparkled with eager excitement and absolute devotion now stared lifelessly back at him.

Hawkins tilted his head, as if puzzled by what he was seeing, as if it hadn't quite registered. She was gone. Brushing the damp hair back from her face, he gently closed the unseeing eyes.

'Goddamn you, Riley,' he whispered. 'I told you to wait for me.'

'Sir!' one of his team was calling to him. 'Sir, we have to go!'

Hawkins bowed his head in silent grief, ignoring the increasingly urgent warnings from his subordinate.

'Sir, the police are on their way! If they find us here—'

Drawing his sidearm, Hawkins turned the gun on his teammate, took aim right between the eyes and pulled the trigger.

The others froze in shock and disbelief, staring at the man who now lay twitching on the ground, his blood and brains staining the floor around him.

'Anyone else?' Hawkins asked, rising slowly to his feet. A powerful, terrifying figure that seemed to grow larger than his mere physical presence. A man whose face was now a mask of barely contained rage.

Not one of them was brave enough to speak up.

Nodding, Hawkins looked at the nearest man. 'Order our strike team to move in now. Kill everyone except Drake. I want him alive.'

–

'Shit!' Frost gasped, turning to the others. 'We're blown.'

Mitchell, realising the urgency of the situation, didn't stop to question it for an instant. Turning away, she reached for the makeshift weapon bench and snatched up an MP5 submachine gun.

Frost, meanwhile, triggered a fast-delete program on her terminal, wiping all trace of what they'd been doing here.

'Jessica, get to the rear office and wait for me there,' she said, her voice low, urgent, frightened. 'Hurry.'

No sooner had she spoken than the lights flickered out. Barely a second later the building reverberated with a sudden, violent explosion from outside. All three women dropped to the floor as the doors were blown off their hinges by carefully placed breaching charges.

'Get down! Cover your ears!' Frost shouted as a trio of stun grenades were hurled in through the gaping hole.

Squeezing her eyes shut, Jessica clapped her hands over her ears just as the grenades detonated, the concussive waves rippling through her body and hammering painfully against her skull.

'Move in! Go!' a voice called out.

Opening her eyes, she watched as Mitchell upended the steel table she'd been crouched beside just as several figures emerged from the swirling smoke and dust.

'Contact! Contact!'

The shooting started then, Mitchell angling the MP5 over the edge of the table and spraying a burst at the lead operative, who staggered backwards under the impacts. Reacting to the threat, the others spread out and returned fire, the flashes from their muzzles illuminating the gloom like lightning. Bullets tore into walls and computer monitors all around.

For a second or so, Jessica froze like an animal caught in the headlights, terrified and mesmerised. For all the dangers she'd encountered, this was the first time she'd witnessed a true gun battle. It was enough to leave her awestruck.

'Jessica, move!' Frost yelled, skidding to a stop beside her and gripping her arm painfully. 'Fall back!'

That was enough to snap her back to reality. She understood Frost's command, but it made no sense to her.

'Fall back to what? There's nothing back there.'

'Just go! I'll be with you soon!' Rising to her knees, Frost took aim and snapped off several shots from her automatic. 'Go now!'

Knowing better than to argue, Jessica leapt up and sprinted towards the small collection of storage rooms and offices at the rear of the building, flinching as several rounds punched through the drywall mere feet away.

As Drake's sister retreated, Frost turned towards Mitchell, who had ducked behind cover long enough to insert a fresh clip into her weapon. Another burst rang out from the other side of the room, tearing holes through the metal table.

'We have to fall back!'

'Go! I'll cover you.'

Rising up, Mitchell brought the weapon up to her shoulder, sighted her next target and pulled the trigger. But just as she did so, another burst tore through the air, one of them punching through her improvised cover and burying itself in her leg.

Letting out a cry of pain, Mitchell went down, scrambling to pull herself behind the table as more fire peppered it. Blood was already pumping from the torn flesh, likely a severed artery.

'Oh Christ,' Frost gasped. 'Hang in there, I'm coming!'

She tried to rise up, but their enemies already had her position covered and a renewed volley forced her back.

'No!' Mitchell called out, holding up a bloodied hand. She was trembling as her body started to go into shock, her face pale and tight with pain. But as her eyes met Frost's, her expression was resolute. Already she'd recognised her hopeless situation, and knew there was only one thing left to do.

'You get out of here,' she commanded. 'I'll give you cover, buy you some time.'

'Fuck that!' Frost shouted. 'You're coming with me.'

Mitchell glanced down at her injured leg and shook her head. She wouldn't make it twenty yards in this condition, and she knew it.

Frost knew it too, as hard as it was. Swallowing, tears stinging her eyes, she uttered her last words to the woman who had become not just a teammate, but a friend.

'I'm sorry.'

Nodding, Mitchell readied the weapon and rallied her flagging strength. 'Go!' she shouted, forcing herself up on her good leg and opening fire.

To have hesitated even for a second would have rendered Mitchell's sacrifice useless. Leaping up, Frost retreated deeper into the building, following the same path Jessica had taken. She didn't allow herself to look back.

Behind her, Mitchell emptied the last of her magazine at the nearest operative. Most of the 9mm slugs flattened against his Kevlar armour, but at least one tore into his left arm, taking him out of the fight.

Her resistance was loud and defiant, but short-lived. As the bolt flew back to expose the empty breech, she sank down behind cover, dropping the smoking, empty gun. The hot surge of adrenaline that had carried her this far was fading. A cold numbness was rising up from her legs, a creeping fatigue clawing at her as her lifeblood seeped away.

She was dying. She should have felt afraid at that realisation, and yet an odd sensation of calm and equanimity had come over her. She had done what she could, fought to the last, but she could go no further.

She supposed that, on balance, she'd been living on borrowed time ever since that mission in Istanbul a couple of years ago. Drake and his friends had risked their lives to save hers. It seemed fitting that she was able to return the favour.

She smiled faintly as a pair of operatives rounded the table, calling out a warning that they'd found one of their targets, and allowed her eyes to close as they raised their weapons.

Drake and Dietrich were speeding towards the scene, all thoughts of maintaining a low profile forgotten now as they raced to reach their friends before it was too late. Maybe it already was, Drake couldn't help thinking. Maybe they were wasting their time, trying to win a battle that had already been lost.

'Drive faster, mate,' he said urgently, wrapping a strip of torn shirt around the gash on his arm. The pain was of little concern, but he needed to get the bleeding under control.

'This is as fast as it goes,' Dietrich warned as they powered through an intersection, jumping a red light and narrowly avoiding a collision with cross-traffic. He glanced at Drake. 'Ryan, what do you think the two of us can do against a full assault team?'

Picking up his sidearm, Drake pulled back the slide to check a round was chambered, then checked the suppressor was securely attached.

'Whatever we can.'

–

Jessica had taken refuge in one of the back rooms that had once contained spare parts and work tools, clutching her automatic in a tight, clammy grip. Her breathing was coming in short, shallow gasps, her heartbeat thundering in her ears, blood rushing through her veins.

Here, so close to death, her body was now painfully, urgently alive.

Hearing footsteps outside, she raised the weapon and flicked the safety off, only for Frost to launch herself through the doorway, closely followed by a volley of gunfire that ricocheted off the walls behind.

'Hold your fire!' she warned.

Jessica lowered the weapon, glad beyond words to see her comrade. However, the other member of their team was nowhere to be seen. 'Where's Mitchell?'

Frost shook her head solemnly, her expression saying it all.

'Oh, Christ...'

'Mourn her later,' Frost commanded. 'Right now, all that matters is getting out of here.'

'How? They've got the place surrounded.'

There were no convenient emergency exits, windows or fire escapes here. The garage was one sealed unit, with cinderblock walls at the sides and rear. The main doors were the only way in or out.

'There's another way,' Frost said, though she didn't look happy about it. 'Get down on the ground, open your mouth and cover your ears.'

'What—'

'Just do it!' Frost snapped.

Outside, a trio of assault operatives advanced down the short corridor, weapons up and ready, laser sights piercing the air that was now heavy with smoke.

'One tango down,' the team leader spoke into his radio. 'Moving up.'

'There's no way out. We've got them cornered.'

They could hear noises coming from the last room on the left. Signalling by hand, the team moved up, one of them reaching into his webbing for another stun grenade. There was no talk now. They'd done this enough times to know how it would play out.

Closing in, the team leader raised his hand and silently counted down.

Three, two, one…

–

The concussive rumble of the blast was so loud that Drake and Dietrich heard it from two blocks away. As Dietrich brought the car to a sudden stop, Drake leapt out to take in the scene up ahead. Car alarms, triggered by the blast, filled the night air with their shrill electronic blare, and nearby pedestrians were shouting and glancing around in fright.

But Drake knew what it meant. He saw the distant plume of smoke rising from the garage. The sight of it was like a hammer blow.

'Frost, come in,' he said, speaking low and quiet into his comms unit.

There was no response.

'Mitchell, do you copy?'

Static hissed in his ear.

Drake swallowed hard, his heart pounding, the pain of his injuries forgotten now.

'Ryan, we can't stay here,' Dietrich warned him, taking in the same grim sight.

'Jess, can you hear me?' Drake closed his eyes, silently praying to anyone who might be inclined to listen. 'Please.'

Again the faint pop and hiss of an empty frequency was the only response.

'Ryan...'

'Wait!' Drake called out. He'd heard something on the comms net; faint, distorted, almost swallowed up by hissing static, but real. Straining to listen, he repeated his hail. 'If anyone can hear me, acknowledge.'

'Ryan... you... copy?' a female voice asked.

Drake's heart leapt. The voice was too garbled to discern the identity, but at least one of the team was alive.

'I've got you. What's your situation?' he asked, forcing calm into his voice.

–

Beneath their feet, Jessica was hurrying along the edge of the underground metro line, struggling to keep pace with Frost in the near-darkness.

'We're on the metro line beneath you,' she explained, her voice echoing in the tunnel. 'We had to blow our way through to escape.'

A series of small but powerful shaped charges planted on the floor of the garage had been enough to blow through the concrete shell and collapse it into the tunnel below, allowing the two fugitives to clamber down. It had been an emergency escape route devised by Frost before the mission even began; a last-ditch option in the event they were cornered.

Her ears were still ringing from the blast, her body bruised from the desperate leap down into the tunnel, her skin and clothes coated with a heavy layer of dust. But she was alive.

For now at least.

'Do *not* go back there!' Frost added, pausing for a second to catch her breath. 'There's nothing you can do now.'

Drake paused, perhaps catching her heavy tone. 'Sitrep?'

Jessica heard her pained sigh. 'Mitchell didn't make it.'

'I see.' He said nothing more on the matter. That was a conversation for later. 'Where… you now?'

'The Green Line, by the looks of it,' Frost said. 'We're heading south. Meet us at Anacostia station.'

'Say again?'

'Anacostia station!' she repeated.

'Negative… breaking up…'

'Goddamn it!' she snarled in frustration. 'Fucking subway tunnels!'

They would have to make their own way out and try to re-establish contact once they were free of interference. Turning away, Frost was about to resume her journey when Jessica suddenly gripped her arm.

'Wait,' she whispered. 'Listen.'

Frost held still, straining to listen. Slowly she turned to look back the way they'd come, though in the near-darkness it was impossible to make out much. In the absence of visuals, her other senses had become heightened.

There! The faint scuffle of a boot on the concrete floor of the tunnel, the clink of a weapon shifting position.

Saying nothing, she gently tugged on Jessica's arm, pulling the woman down into a crouch beside her. No sooner had they done so than the twin flashes of muzzle flares lit up the tunnel about fifty yards back, red-hot projectiles zipping through the darkness.

Their pursuers had caught up with them.

'Stay down!' Frost hissed.

Raising her weapon, Jessica took rough aim at the nearest flash and pulled the trigger, surprised by how hard the weapon kicked back against her wrist. The sharp crack of the gunshot echoed off the tunnel walls to pound her ears again. She smelled the sharp tang of burned cordite, the acrid smoke stinging her eyes, but she ignored it as she pulled the trigger again.

Beside her, Frost had added her firepower to the desperate battle. Though better trained and certainly more accurate, she was just as impaired by the lack of visibility. That certainly didn't stop her trying though. In a matter of seconds she had burned through an entire clip, firing almost blind.

Ejecting it, she slapped a fresh one into place with the speed and precision of the trained operative she was. Rising to her feet, she advanced towards their enemies.

'We can't win this!' Jessica warned her, realising this was more than simple covering fire. Frost *wanted* this fight. She wanted to vent her rage on the men who had killed Mitchell.

'Go! I'll cover you!'

'Keira, listen to me!' Jessica shouted, grabbing her arm and pulling her close. 'If we don't make it out, Mitchell died for nothing. We have to go! Now!'

That harsh recrimination seemed to cut through the fog of her anger. Reluctantly abandoning the fight, Frost turned and followed as Jessica retreated down the tunnel, the sound of their rapid breathing mingling with the rattle of gunfire and the occasional whine as bullets ricocheted off the walls. Up ahead, the tunnel began to brighten as they approached an underground station.

The two women ran with everything they had, pushing their weary bodies to their limits, but their pursuers were both faster and better armed, and the increasing visibility made them easier targets – three factors which inevitably turned the tide against them.

A dull, heavy thump accompanied by a startled cry of pain from behind told Jessica that her companion had taken a hit, and she spun around to see Frost fall.

'Keira!' she called out, rushing to her aid.

Frost was clutching her shoulder, groaning in pain as she tried to pick herself up. Skidding to a stop beside her, Jessica turned her weapon back down the tunnel, sighted a vague shape moving in the shadows and fired off several rounds in his direction.

She didn't know how many were left, but she didn't imagine it was much. Frost too had almost exhausted her ammunition.

'Get out of here,' Frost said through gritted teeth. 'Go, goddamn it!'

Jessica shook her head. 'I lost one friend today. I'm not losing another.'

'We're friends now, huh?' Frost snorted with bleak humour, remembering the contentious start to their relationship.

However, the delay had given their pursuers time to catch up, and a renewed burst of gunfire forced them to flatten themselves against the cold concrete of the tunnel floor. They were pinned down, unable to retreat, unable to hold their ground.

'We've got them!' a voice called out. 'Move up!'

Jessica looked at the young woman beside her, injured and hurting, but defiant to the end. Was this where they would both die, she wondered? In a stinking subway tunnel?

She jumped as a new burst of gunfire rang out – not in front of them, but from behind. Thinking their enemies must have cut them off, she tensed up, bracing herself for the inevitable torrent of pain as the bullets tore into them.

But no such thing happened. Instead she heard a muffled cry from further down the tunnel, accompanied by the heavy thud of a body hitting the ground. Twisting around, Jessica froze at the sight of a woman striding past her, an assault rifle up at her shoulder, her face lit by the flash of each gunshot. Spent shell casings, still red hot, pattered to the ground around them.

Pausing only for a moment, she glanced down at the two fugitives. 'Get up now.'

Jessica knew that voice, even if the face had been hidden last time they'd met. It was the same woman who had rescued her back in the UK. How had she found them again?

Just as these thoughts were flashing through her mind, Jessica felt a sudden gust of air coming from further down the tunnel. Immediately she recognised the phenomenon from her experience on the London Underground, and knew what it meant.

'Hurry!' the woman commanded, snapping off more shots, keeping their enemies pinned down.

Heaving Frost to her feet, Jessica turned and ran just as the tunnel behind them began to grow brighter, suddenly resolving into a pair of headlights, blindingly intense. A subway train, coming right at them.

Their opponents saw it too, turning towards the light and noise, but too late. The sudden screech of brakes was accompanied by a pair of screams as they took the full force of the speeding train, killing them instantly.

'Fuck!' Frost shouted, realising they weren't going to make it. 'Against the wall, now!'

Abandoning their retreat, all three women leapt over the tracks and flattened themselves against the sloping wall as a DC Metro train rocketed past mere feet away, a blur of bright yellow light and blue sparks from the conducting rail. Wind howled past them, mingling with the screeching brakes into a deafening cacophony. The subway train continued on for another fifty yards or so before coming to a shuddering halt.

For a couple of seconds, not one of them moved a muscle. They remained pressed against the tunnel wall, breathing hard, hardly believing they were still alive.

It was their saviour who first managed to rouse herself. 'Hurry! Let's go!'

Advancing past the stationary train and ignoring the warning shouts from the driver, the three women covered the remaining hundred yards or so to the big station up ahead. Abandoning the assault rifle, McKnight leapt up onto the platform and reached down to pull the others up. It was late at night by now, and there had been few people in the station to begin with. The crackle of gunfire from the tunnels had been enough to force the few remaining commuters to evacuate.

Both Jessica and Frost were approaching the limits of their endurance as they sprinted across the main concourse, up the escalators and through the ticket barriers.

'Help!' Jessica called out to the security guard on duty, feigning panic. 'Someone's shooting down there!'

The man was already on his radio, calling it in.

McKnight led them out through the main entrance and into the fresh night air beyond, rain still pattering down. Darting between traffic, she hurried across the busy main drag fronting the station and kept going, not stopping until both her companions were on the point of collapse.

'In here,' she said, indicating a narrow side alley used for garbage collection. Taking a deep breath, she looked back out onto the street to confirm they hadn't been pursued. 'We're clear for now, but—'

She froze, eyeing the weapon now pointed at her.

'Don't fucking move, McKnight,' Frost hissed. Injured and exhausted she might have been, but she was still perfectly capable of using a gun. And by the looks of things, she was eager to do so now.

'Keira, what are you doing?' Jessica demanded. 'She just saved our lives.'

'This bitch is the reason Cole is dead,' the young woman spat. 'She betrayed us, spied on us for Cain. None of this would be happening if not for her.'

McKnight shook her head. 'It's not what you think.'

'Shut up!' Frost moved closer, pressing the gun into her chest. 'You fucking people, you're all as bad as each other. You deserve this.'

McKnight raised her chin, staring her down. 'Then do it,' she said quietly. 'If you think I deserve it, pull the trigger, Keira. I'm not afraid to die.'

'Stop this!' Jessica said, pushing herself between them, shaking with anger. 'Whatever she did before, she saved our lives today. Are you going to kill her for that?'

Gritting her teeth, Frost looked for a second as if she was prepared to fire anyway. But then, letting out a breath, she stepped back, leaning against the wall for support. Her complexion was pale, her face tight with pain, her eyes heavy with grief.

'You live with it,' she said, glaring at McKnight. 'You live with what you did, and you leave. Because if I ever see you again, I *will* pull the trigger.'

Swallowing, McKnight opened her mouth to reply, then thought better of it. Resigning herself to the inevitable, she turned and walked away, leaving them behind.

Chapter 62

'SEAL teams are withdrawing to primary staging area,' Kennedy reported, watching the real-time drone feed as the last Black Hawk chopper lifted off from the Abbottabad compound, taking with them a handful of prisoners for interrogation, a mountain of documents, cell phones, hard drives and other intel that would keep the Agency's analysts busy for months, as well as the body of one Osama bin Mohammed bin Awad bin Laden.

Once his physical remains had been formally identified and DNA tested, confirming beyond all doubt that it was him, he would be handed over to the US Navy for burial at sea.

The compound itself and the low-value prisoners would be left for the Pakistanis to secure. Doubtless there would be fallout from the unsanctioned raid, and the unspoken implication that they'd been sheltering him, but those were concerns for tomorrow.

The president was preparing to make an official announcement, but already it had begun to leak out onto the internet. Crowds were forming outside the White House and other major buildings throughout the capital as the news spread, the entire country rousing itself in anticipation.

'Goddamn,' Kennedy said, shaking his head slowly. 'I can't believe it's over.'

This was what it felt like not just to witness history, but to change it. The world would be a different place tomorrow, in part because of them.

'I know,' Franklin said quietly. He'd expected to be in a jubilant mood right now, but he couldn't quite muster that emotion. Instead he simply felt drained, the tension and drama of tonight taking its toll on him.

So lost was he in these thoughts that he scarcely noticed his cell phone buzzing on the table in front of him. Blinking, Franklin returned to himself, picked up his phone and took the call, expecting yet another White House official, Pentagon representative, member of the National Security Council, or any of the dozen other agencies that had been calling all evening.

'Franklin.'

His weary expression quickly changed as the news came through. 'Excuse me, can you say that again?'

Kennedy watched as the man paled visibly, his mouth opening in shock as he listened in disbelieving silence.

'How... how did it happen?'

Kennedy sat in tense, anxious hush as he waited for the call to end. For a sickening moment he wondered if, somehow, they'd gotten it wrong; hit the wrong compound, killed the wrong man. Perhaps everything they'd worked towards was about to be snatched away.

Ending the call, Franklin rose slowly from his chair, shaken to his core. Kennedy had never seen his boss like this before.

'What is it?' he asked, dreading the answer. 'What happened?'

'It's Cain,' Franklin replied, his voice leaden. 'Director Cain's been assassinated.'

–

As the news of Bin Laden's death finally broke, and crowds around Washington and elsewhere gathered in jubilant celebration, Drake and the others sat alone on a tree-covered hilltop in Rock Creek Park, several miles north of the city.

Four people from vastly different countries and backgrounds, once united behind a common purpose, now left exhausted and broken. After the tumultuous events of the night, everything they had discovered, overcome and lost, they simply had nothing left.

'She knew she wasn't going to make it out,' Frost said, her expression pensive as she stared out across the city, thinking about the friend they'd left behind. 'She gave her life for us.'

'She was a good woman,' Dietrich agreed, for once abandoning his usual gruff, cold demeanour. 'She didn't deserve this.'

'None of us did,' Frost replied.

Jessica, who had been sitting beside her brother, looked up at him. 'Anya was the one who killed our mother.'

She saw the muscles in Drake's throat tighten. 'Yes.'

All this time, it had been so easy to blame Cain for everything – the corrupt, evil, ruthless man, the ultimate enemy to be defeated. Now she was beginning to realise the truth was far more complex than they ever could have imagined.

He nodded, acknowledging the cold, unforgiving reality that now stared them in the face. Freya Shaw hadn't been the ruthlessly ambitious power broker they'd first assumed, but neither had she been the virtuous hero they'd come to believe in over the past couple of weeks, unfairly persecuted and betrayed by her contemporaries.

The truth, as they were now realising, had been more complicated and less clear-cut than that. Just as it always was.

'Fucking lies,' Frost said bitterly. 'All of it. Lies and betrayals and bullshit. They're all as bad as each other, they all got what they fucking deserved. Cain, the Circle, Anya… even your mom.'

Drake felt his sister tense up, felt her start to move, but held her back with a sharp look, knowing Frost needed to get this out.

'They spin their fucking webs and screw each other over, and where does it get them? What's the point?' She shook her head in exasperation. 'People like us get caught in the crossfire. People like Mitchell, Cole, Keegan…'

Her voice wavered a little as she said each name. All of them had been good people who deserved to live. All of them were dead.

'But it's over now,' Jessica said. 'Cain's dead. The Circle's gone. What's left?'

Drake knew the answer to that just as well as his teammates.

'Starke,' he said, sighing as he closed his eyes, realising how badly they'd all been played. Richard Starke, the master manipulator. The man who had successfully played and betrayed everyone who had ever crossed his path, slowly taking down his rivals and enemies, until at last there was no one left to stand against him.

No one except the four exhausted, desperate people sitting on that hilltop.

'He'll rebuild the Circle,' Drake went on, already picturing Starke's unfettered rise to power. 'He knows how they operated, knows everyone's secrets. He's plugged into everything. He'll take over everything they once controlled. And he won't stop until every one of us is dead.'

Silence descended on the small group as each of them played out the same terrifying scenario. One man, assuming all the power and influence once wielded by the Circle, with no one left to check his authority or question his decisions. A man who would never give up until the last remnants of his former enemies, the final people who knew his dark secrets, were eliminated.

'Then we have to take him down,' Jessica reasoned.

'Yeah? With what?' Frost asked. 'We staked everything on tonight, and we lost. What more is there?'

For that, none of them had an answer.

–

'All right, everyone. Listen up,' Franklin began, taking in the sea of faces watching him expectantly. Many of them still held looks of shock and dismay, others confusion, some even grief. All of them were waiting for him to speak.

With the news of Cain's death now circulating the Agency, Franklin had gathered the most senior divisional leaders and department heads into a secure conference room at Langley for an emergency briefing. Others who couldn't be here physically were listening in on a secure line.

'As you all know by now, we recently received word that Director Cain… Marcus Cain, our colleague and our friend, was murdered earlier this evening in an incident in central DC. We're still getting information, so right now it's impossible to say what exactly happened and who's responsible.'

He saw a few people bow their heads. Whatever Franklin's private thoughts on the man, Cain had dedicated a lifetime of service to the Agency. Many of the people in this room had worked with him for years, even decades.

'I know many of you will be feeling grief and anger, and you'll want to mourn him in your own way,' he carried on. 'Unfortunately, we'll have to hold our thoughts of Director Cain until we can get through the present situation.'

There were a few nods from around the table.

'In order to continue to function until the current crisis is resolved, we need a clear chain of command. So, with that in mind, effective immediately I'm assuming the role of acting director. All divisional leaders now report directly to me. We'll be liaising closely with the FBI and other intelligence agencies, so I need situation reports from each of you within the hour. If you have subordinates that aren't already here, bring them in, because we're sure to need them.'

His eyes swept the room.

'Questions?'

There were none.

'Good. Then let's get to work.'

As the senior executives filed out, Franklin glanced up as a single man entered like a warship cleaving through stormy waters. He was dressed in full naval uniform.

'Director Starke,' Franklin began, surprised by the arrival of the NSA director. 'I wasn't told you were coming.'

'I know,' Starke acknowledged. 'I was hoping to speak with you in private.'

Kennedy, who had been acting as Franklin's de facto chief of staff since the news of Cain's death broke, glanced at his boss curiously. Franklin gave him a nod, knowing this was no idle request.

Packing up his gear, he left the room, closing the door behind him.

'With all due respect, sir, I hope you understand that my time is limited tonight,' Franklin began. The prospect of some inter-agency turf war was not something he was prepared to entertain.

'I do,' Starke agreed, pacing the room. 'So I'll get straight to the point. I know who killed Marcus Cain tonight.'

Franklin stared at him. 'How would you know that, sir?'

'Marcus Cain was involved in a highly classified covert operation to infiltrate and destroy rogue elements within the US intelligence community. Not just the CIA, but the military, the NSA, even branches of the government.'

'What?' Franklin gasped, thunderstruck.

'The operation was so sensitive that only Director Cain, myself and a few others were fully aware of its scope and intent. Even you weren't briefed on it,' he added, looking up at Franklin regretfully. 'I'm sorry we kept you in the dark, son. But we had to take every possible precaution.'

Franklin glanced away, his mind in turmoil. Was it true? Had Marcus Cain been pursuing something even bigger than the events of this evening?

'And while the operation was successful, there were… other factors at play.'

'What factors?'

The NSA director sighed, preparing to deliver bad news. 'A former CIA operative named Ryan Drake, and another known by the code-name Maras.'

Franklin felt his blood run cold. Surely what he was suggesting couldn't be true?

'Unknown to us, they were both part of this rogue cabal, and they had managed to make their way to Washington DC tonight. They laid an ambush on Director Cain, and...' He hesitated, taking a moment to compose himself. 'By the time our teams intervened, it was too late.'

He shook his head.

'It was my fault, son,' he said, filled with self-recrimination. 'I should have seen this coming.'

Franklin rested his hands on the table, feeling like he needed the support. 'I need you to be absolutely clear on this one, sir. You're saying Ryan Drake and Maras assassinated Marcus Cain?'

Starke looked him in the eye hard. 'Yes.'

Dan Franklin felt like he'd been punched in the stomach. Was it possible he'd been so utterly wrong about both Cain and Ryan? Was his former friend really part of some cabal operating within the Agency? Had Anya somehow pulled him into it?

'Needless to say, none of what I've told you can leave this room,' Starke went on. 'If the truth gets out, it'll destroy the US intelligence community for decades. We have to find both suspects and bring them in at all costs.'

Franklin understood his meaning well enough: dead or alive.

'I have a lead, but I'm going to need your help.' Starke was coming closer now, staring him down. 'I'm sorry to dump all of this on your lap, Dan, but you're the only man in this situation that I can trust. Can I count on your support?'

Franklin's heart was pounding, his mind racing as he tried to sort it all out. He had felt no great love for Marcus Cain, but the man had nonetheless pulled off one of the biggest victories in the War on Terror. And if he truly was involved in something far deeper and more sinister, then his death might just have been a terrible loss for all of them.

And the revelation that Anya might have been behind it simply confirmed his worst fears about her. At the very least, the two of them needed to answer for their actions.

'You can,' he confirmed. 'Whatever you need, it's yours.'

Chapter 63

Alex was waiting at the pre-arranged rendezvous point, the tiny fishing community of Rose Haven on the shores of Chesapeake Bay. With nothing more to be done in DC, he had packed up his gear and withdrawn here to wait for his contact.

He stood overlooking the town's marina, watching the yachts and fishing boats bobbing gently on the swell. Not far away, he heard the sound of raucous celebration in a tavern overlooking the wharf, accompanied by horn blasts from passing cars.

Barely thirty minutes ago the president had appeared live on TV to announce the death of Osama Bin Laden. The world's most wanted terrorist was dead, and America was celebrating.

But Alex didn't much feel like celebrating tonight.

He looked up as a car pulled into the parking lot, and a lonely figure emerged. Alex could tell by the look on Anya's face just how badly things had played out tonight.

'Did they make it out?' he asked, desperate to know if his warning had made it through.

'Samantha just reported in. Frost and Drake escaped with her.'

Alex could feel a knot of fear in his stomach. 'And Mitchell?'

Anya shook her head solemnly.

Letting out a breath, Alex turned away to hide his grief-stricken look. Olivia Mitchell had saved his life once, very nearly losing her own in the process. And now she was gone. Another casualty in this endless war.

'What the hell happened tonight, Anya?' he managed to ask.

'I don't know,' she confessed. 'How could I have been so wrong?'

'About Cain?'

'About everything. Cain, Freya, the Circle... even Starke. They used me and lied to me, and I walked into it every time.' The woman rested her hands on the metal railing at the edge of the marina, lowered her head and gripped it tight. 'All that time wasted. My own life was the biggest lie of all.'

Alex sighed. He had more bad news to deliver, but was reluctant to burden her with more concerns. Not now, when she had been through so much already.

'You have something to tell me,' Anya prompted him, as if she could read his thoughts. 'Don't be afraid, Alex.'

'You sure you want to hear it?'

'Holding it back won't change it. I would rather know.'

He moved up beside her. 'They're pinning Cain's death on you. The Agency, the FBI... they're coming after you with everything they have.'

'I expected as much,' the woman said grimly. 'Starke knows I'm a threat. He will mobilise every available resource to find me.'

'That's not all,' Alex went on. 'The Israelis have picked up on it, too. They've tied it to Russo's murder. Not to mention the Pakistanis and the Russians...'

Her list of enemies was growing by the day. Anya might well have carved a path of blood and death halfway across the world in her search for answers, but there were always repercussions.

Anya flashed a thin, brittle smile. 'It seems the whole world wants me dead.'

There was a weary kind of resignation in her voice, as if she'd always known it would come to this. As if she'd accepted the price she would pay before her mission even began.

'I could stall them,' Alex offered weakly. 'Create false leads, direct them away, but...'

He couldn't bring himself to say it. They both knew Alex's efforts would only delay the inevitable. Even someone like Anya, who could appear and disappear like a ghost, couldn't hope to escape all the world's major intelligence agencies. Sooner or later they would find her.

She was looking out across the waters of the bay now, her hair lifted by the breeze as she took it all in, contemplating the tumultuous past that had brought her here, and the future that lay ahead. Considering her position and coming to one unavoidable conclusion.

'It's all right,' Anya said gently. 'You've done enough. I can ask no more of you, Alex.'

'What are you saying?'

'You did everything I asked of you. There is nothing more to be done.' She turned to look at him. 'I release you from our agreement.'

'But you need me,' Alex argued, refusing to accept it. 'There's still—'

Anya held up a hand. 'It's all right, Alex,' she said, her voice calm and understanding. She knew why he was protesting, why he was fighting against it, but she also knew it would do no good. 'You have done your part. The rest is up to me now.'

She was saying goodbye, he realised. She had come here to bid him farewell. She was set on her course now. And seeing the sad, resolute look on her face, Alex knew he'd never see Anya again.

He glanced away, unable to meet her eye. It was then that he felt her hand laid on his.

'You know, you are probably the closest thing to a friend I have left, Alex,' she admitted. 'You are a good man. And for what it's worth, I'm glad to have known you.'

Alex couldn't help himself. Though they had rarely shown much affection towards one another, he did so now. Reaching out, he pulled her close and hugged her. He couldn't begin to explain how deeply she had changed him, how grateful he was to her, but perhaps it didn't matter now. Perhaps she understood.

'Live your life,' she said, letting go of him. 'Live it well. Don't waste it like I did.'

His throat was tight, his voice strained when he spoke. 'Where will you go now?'

Anya swallowed and looked out to sea again, her thoughts turned inward, her mind reflecting on a different time. A different life.

'Home.'

Part Five

Something to Die For

We are not now that strength which in old days
Moved earth and heaven; that which we are, we are,
One equal temper of heroic hearts,
Made weak by time and fate, but strong in will
To strive, to seek, to find, and not to yield.

Alfred Tennyson

Chapter 64

Havana, Cuba – May 3rd, 2011

Situated on the northern coast of Cuba, the city of Havana was one of the most vibrantly unique settlements anywhere on earth. Even half a century of communist rule, poverty and economic strangulation had failed to dampen the character and culture of the place.

And given that it was a non-extradition country barely a hundred miles from the southern tip of Florida, with a diverse population and a heavy reliance on tourism, it had seemed like a good location for Drake and his team to rest and regroup while they planned their next move.

Not that there were many options left. Cain and the Circle might be gone now, but a new and equally ruthless enemy had arisen to replace them. Richard Starke was moving swiftly to turn the full weight of the world's intelligence services against them, leaving them with few places to hide and even fewer ways of striking back.

The man was untouchable, unreachable, unbeatable.

As for Anya, she had vanished two days ago. Even now, Drake remained deeply conflicted about her. So much had changed in just one night, so many truths he'd clung to had been exposed as lies, he wondered if he would ever feel sure of anything again.

These thoughts weighed heavily on Drake as he made his way back to the group's low-rent apartment in one of Havana's less affluent districts that night, making use of the network of small, narrow roads and side streets.

Scooters and mopeds zipped past trailing dirty grey exhaust smoke. Occasionally a car would rattle by, some ancient machine older than Drake, painstakingly repaired and maintained. Trade embargoes meant that few modern cars made it onto the market, forcing locals to resort to ever more creative ways of keeping old vehicles running.

He couldn't say exactly when he realised he was being followed. Perhaps some intuition told him someone had been watching him a little longer than necessary. Perhaps he'd heard the sound of the same shoes on the cobbled street too many times.

But whatever it was, Drake's mind quickly switched gears, abandoning his gloomy introspection and flipping into survival mode. He gave little outward sign of this, walking with the same unhurried pace as before, but his eyes now darted back and forth, taking in every detail of his environment, looking for options and threats.

The road split in three up ahead, with a big apartment block jutting out into the intersection like the prow of a ship. One branch of the road veered right, climbing steeply uphill, while the other two went left, sloping gently downward towards the city's harbour area.

Drake took the right fork, ducking into a side alley the moment he was out of sight. Drawing his concealed Browning automatic, he waited, silent and unmoving, for his pursuer to come for him.

Sure enough, a few seconds later he heard shoes on the sidewalk, coming up fast. Waiting until they were passing by the entrance to the alley, Drake leapt out, clamped a hand over his target's mouth and pulled him into the waiting shadows.

'Wait!' a panicked voice cried as Drake pressed the automatic into his neck. 'It's me, Ryan!'

Drake drew back a little, surprised by his unlikely pursuer. 'Alex?'

Yanking the man forward into the light, he stared at the young computer hacker recruited by Anya. Drake hadn't seen the man since their mission in Afghanistan, and in truth, had never expected to lay eyes on him again.

'This how you greet all your friends?' Alex asked, recovering some of his composure.

'What the fuck are you doing here?' Drake retorted. 'How did you find me?'

Alex shook his head. 'I didn't, I found Frost. She's not all that hard to track. I've been wandering all over the fucking city looking for you. It was sheer bloody luck I spotted you tonight.'

'That's how you found us, not why,' Drake reminded him.

Straightening his already crumpled shirt, Alex glanced around at their less-than-auspicious surroundings. The smell of rotting garbage hung heavy in the air.

'I came to talk to you,' he explained. 'Is there... somewhere else we can go?'

Ten minutes later, the two men had found a table at an outdoor bar – one of many in Old Havana – facing out onto a small courtyard ringed by palm trees. A weathered stone fountain stood in the centre of the square, just about managing to put out a trickle of water.

The place was busy, the air filled with the strains of live music, laughter and excited chatter in half a dozen languages. But Drake's focus was less on the nightlife than on the young man seated opposite.

'We're here. Talk,' Drake instructed him.

Alex took a gulp of his tequila, marshalling his thoughts. 'After we left Afghanistan a few months ago, Anya reached out to me with a job offer; finding intel on people, hacking security systems, that sort of thing. The short version is that I was with her right up until a few days ago in Washington. She met up with me after... what happened that night.'

'Go on,' Drake pressed.

Alex looked up from his drink, his expression bereft. 'She did it to say goodbye, Ryan. She said there was nothing more I could do.'

'Any idea where she went?'

'Yeah.' Alex took another drink. 'She said she was going home.'

Drake's mind rushed back to a night several years earlier, when Anya had finally opened up to him, sharing some of the details of her early life; one of which was that she'd grown up in the Baltic state of Lithuania.

'So why come to me with this?'

Alex swallowed, his voice grave. 'Because I think she's going there to die.'

Drake wasn't a man who could be easily rattled, but the finality, the depth of feeling in Alex's voice was enough to send a chill of foreboding through him.

'Anya's a survivor. She always has been,' he countered. 'She doesn't need my help or anyone else's. Maybe she never did.'

Alex shook his head. 'You weren't there. You didn't see the look in her eyes. She looked... beaten. Like she'd given up.'

Drake said nothing to that. Anya possessed a near-indomitable spirit that had carried her through every challenge, hardship and adversity life could throw at her. And until now, he had firmly believed she would never surrender, no matter how dire her circumstances.

Until now.

'I want to help her, but I can't do this alone. I wouldn't know how to find her. And even if I did, I can't protect her from what's coming. But *you* can,' Alex went on. 'Look, I know you've had your... differences.'

'That what you'd call it?' Drake remarked scathingly. 'She killed my mother, Alex. Three of my teammates are dead. Three people I'd have given my life for. That's more than just a fucking "difference".'

Suddenly Alex slammed his fist down so hard on the table that it knocked over his glass, causing some of the nearby patrons to look their way in alarm, wondering if a fight was about to break out. Even Drake took notice.

'Take it easy, son,' he warned.

'She never gave up on you,' the young man said, forcing himself to calm. 'Even after everything that happened, she couldn't bring herself to let you go.' Leaning over the table, he looked at Drake imploringly. 'Please, Ryan... don't let it end this way.'

Drake leaned back in his chair, saying nothing.

Chapter 65

Frankfurt, Germany

Anya was almost at the end of her long journey now. A journey that had taken her from Israel to Pakistan to America, and finally back to the land of her birth. The place where she would make her last stand.

But there was one thing still to do. One last person she had to find. Not for revenge this time, not for information or assistance, but for something more personal.

She found him on his customary route home, knowing that he often took a minor detour through *Grüneburgpark* to relax after a busy day, sometimes buying chocolate from one of the small cafes in the area.

She could feel her heart beating faster as he approached at a leisurely pace. Anya kept to the shade of some trees and bushes that overhung the public footpath, blending into the natural cover as she'd been trained to do. He was just passing her when she at last found the courage to speak up.

'Yasin,' she said softly, emerging from her hiding place.

The young man froze, startled by the voice. Even more startled by the owner. But he didn't turn around. Instead she heard a faint exhalation, saw his shoulders drop a little, his head lower.

'You found me,' he said. His voice was deeper now, she realised. A young man's voice; not the boy she'd once known.

'Yes.'

'What do you want?'

'I...' Anya swallowed, searching for the right words. 'I hoped we could talk.'

At last he turned to face her, taking in her appearance for the first time in nearly a year. Anya did the same, marvelling at the change that had come over him in so short a time. When she'd first met him, Yasin had been a street thief, living homeless in the slums of Pakistan's largest city. Barely twelve years old, skinny, malnourished and unwashed, he'd broken into their makeshift base of operations and tried to steal valuable equipment, forcing Anya to subdue him.

However, he'd eventually proven to be an invaluable ally, saving her life when the team's mission had gone horribly wrong. She'd taken him with her to Europe, where he had again demonstrated remarkable loyalty and resourcefulness.

But hers was no life for a young boy, no matter how brave and cunning, and after successfully rescuing Drake and his team, she had forced Yasin to surrender himself to the German authorities, knowing they would give him the care and protection she couldn't.

That had been almost a year ago.

Things had changed since then, she realised now. The skinny, underdeveloped frame had filled out. His once shaggy, unwashed hair was now neatly cut, his face assuming the more definite, masculine lines of maturity. She thought she even saw sparse hair along his jawline. The boy she'd known was becoming a man.

And she had missed it all. She felt an odd sensation of loss at that.

'Fine,' he conceded gruffly. 'Let's talk.'

A few minutes later, they were walking together through the pleasant parkland in uncomfortable silence, oblivious to the children playing and the families walking nearby. Anya could almost feel the resentment radiating from the youth at her side.

'You look well,' she began awkwardly. When he didn't respond, she added, 'Your new family. They... take care of you?'

'What do you care?'

That hurt more than she'd expected. 'I care, Yasin.'

'Is that why you left me, just like everyone else?' Yasin shot back, bristling with hostility. 'Threw me away when you had no more use for me?'

Turning to face him, Anya gripped him firmly by the shoulder and looked him in the eye. He was almost as tall as her now, and she knew he would soon surpass her.

'You know why I left you.' There was a harder edge in her voice now. She had tried to be patient with him, but now she needed him to understand. 'Where I was going... it was no place for you.'

'I would have come anyway,' he countered stoutly, but this time she could hear the hurt in his voice. The pain of being abandoned.

Anya sighed. 'I know. And if you had, you would have gotten hurt or killed. I couldn't live with myself if that happened. And if not, eventually you would have ended up just like me.' She shook her head. 'That is no life worth living, believe me. You deserved better than that. You deserved a future. That is something I can't give you.'

He seemed to catch the deeper meaning behind her words. Anya saw the anger start to give way to something else – fear and dawning comprehension.

'Why did you come here today? Why now, after all this time?'

Anya glanced away, taking in their pleasant, peaceful surroundings. The people out walking without a care in the world. She had never known such a life. She never would.

'Things haven't worked out as I hoped,' she admitted. 'I have to go away now, and… I don't know if I can come back. But I wanted to see you first.'

'To say goodbye?'

'To say thank you,' she amended, turning to look at the young man again. 'For helping me see what's really important.'

She saw his throat tighten as her meaning sank in, saw him struggling with his emotions. It was a good few seconds before he trusted himself to speak.

'My foster family, they… they are good people,' he managed to say. 'Fair. Trusting. They have been kind to me.'

That was enough for Anya. She pulled Yasin close and hugged him tight in a final embrace, squeezing her eyes shut to hide her tears.

Chapter 66

CIA Headquarters, Langley

Resting his elbows on his desk, Dan Franklin lowered his head and rubbed his eyes, which were dry and red from fatigue. He hadn't gone home in the past two days, had barely slept, and had certainly had no time to devote his mind to anything except the work.

The hunt for Cain's killers was still in full swing, now including not just the CIA and FBI, but foreign intelligence services as well. The Pakistanis, responding to the assassination of their own intelligence director just a few days prior, not to mention the unsanctioned raid on Bin Laden's compound in their territory, were up in arms about it.

The Israelis, too, were on the hunt for the killer of one of their high-ranking intelligence officers, and were convinced that Anya was responsible. Even the Russians now saw it as an excuse to take revenge for the murder of Viktor Surovsky three years ago, and were already making noises about possible retaliation.

Everyone was clamouring for answers, but Franklin had none to give them. Both Drake and Anya had, for now at least, disappeared. And the constant demands of the job were taking their toll on him.

He looked up at the sound of knocking on his door.

'Come,' he called, rallying what patience and stamina he had left.

When the door opened, however, it wasn't some divisional leader come to report in, or a government representative demanding something he couldn't give.

'Dan, you got a minute?' Kennedy asked.

'Can it wait?'

'Not really.'

Sighing, Franklin gestured to the chair opposite. Closing the door behind him, Kennedy approached and sat down. And, typical of the straight-talking Shepherd operative, he wasted no time.

'I don't like this.'

'What's to like?' Franklin countered. 'Cain's dead, the intelligence world's losing its collective mind, and the people behind it have vanished into the wind.'

'That's just it,' Kennedy went on. 'Who's really responsible for this?'

'I haven't slept in thirty hours, Chris. If you've got something to say, just say it.'

Kennedy leaned forward. 'Look, I've been trying to pull security footage of Cain's murder. Churches are like every public building – they've got surveillance systems. But every camera was turned off, every database wiped.'

'So they covered their tracks,' Franklin acknowledged. 'Both of them are professional operatives. They know what they're doing.'

'Which means we've got nothing except Starke's word that they're the real killers.' He clenched his jaw, clearly not relishing what he was about to say. 'It doesn't sit well with me. Cain dies with no evidence about what happened, and within the hour Starke's right here, pressed and dressed, telling us exactly how it went down. Like he was ready for it.'

'You're suggesting Richard Starke had Cain murdered, and blamed it on the others?' Franklin asked him. 'Why the hell would he do that? He doesn't stand to gain anything from the man's death.'

'I don't know. But I'm telling you there's something more going on here. Starke knows more than he's telling us,' the man pressed. 'And if they find Drake and take him down before he has a chance to tell his side, then we'll never know.'

Franklin looked at him. 'What exactly do you want from me?'

'If we get a lead, send my team after him. Give us a chance to bring him in alive, instead of handing him over to Starke.'

'You mean go behind his back?'

The Shepherd team leader shrugged. 'Call it what you want. But I'd rather give the man a chance. He deserves that much, at least.'

Havana, Cuba

'No fucking way,' Frost said, shaking her head. 'Forget it, I won't do it.'

Returning to the apartment with Alex Yates in tow, Drake had related everything the young man had told him about his final meeting, concluding by announcing his decision to travel to Lithuania and intercept Anya.

'I can't make you do anything,' Drake acknowledged. 'I came to tell you what *I'm* going to do. Whether you come with me is up to you.'

'And if you *do* find her?' Jessica asked. 'What then? What is she to you now – a friend, or an enemy?'

'I wish I knew,' Drake admitted. 'I won't know for sure until I see her.'

'Goddamn it, haven't you had enough? Both of you?' she asked, looking accusingly at each man. 'Haven't we lost enough already?'

'She needs our help,' Alex stated.

'Fuck off, Alex,' Dietrich growled. 'We needed *her* help in DC, and guess what? She wasn't there for us. Why should we be there for her now?'

'Anya warned you about the ambush at the garage,' Alex said, then turned his attention to Jessica, who was standing by with her arms folded. 'She's also the one who sent Samantha to rescue you in the UK, and get you out of that subway tunnel. Neither of you would be alive if it wasn't for—'

'Spare me the Monday morning quarterback routine,' Frost snapped. 'You're not one of us, Alex. You don't know jack shit about McKnight or what she did, and you sure as hell don't know what happened at that garage. Maybe if your little warning hadn't been a day late and a dollar short, Mitchell would still be alive.'

That was enough for Alex. Hurling his chair aside, he leapt to his feet and would likely have swung for her if Drake hadn't intervened, forcibly holding him back.

'Fucking say that again!' Alex shouted, his face colouring with rage as he tried to break free. Even Frost seemed taken aback by his outburst. 'Say it, I dare you!'

Mitchell had saved his life in Istanbul years earlier. He had, in fact, known her before any of the others had even met her. None of them had felt her death as keenly as he.

'That's enough, both of you!' Drake commanded, jabbing a finger at Frost. Turning his attention to Alex, he leaned in close, his voice low and faintly threatening. 'Take a breath and back off. We're not doing this here, yeah?'

Exhaling, Alex reluctantly nodded and turned away to compose himself. Leaving the young man to cool off, Drake turned to face the others.

'Whether we like it or not, Anya's the only ally we have left. We need her,' he reminded them. 'I'm going, alone if I have to. Like I said, I can't make anyone else do this.'

'When are you leaving?' Dietrich asked.

'As soon as I can get transport arranged.' Drake sighed and looked at each of them in turn. 'Think it through, but don't take long. If Alex is right, we don't have much time.'

Chapter 67

Lithuania

It had been thirty-four years since Anya had set foot in this place – fully two-thirds of her life. She couldn't rightly say why she had avoided it for so long. Certainly there had been plenty of opportunities to come back over the years, especially once the Cold War ended and the country regained its independence. And yet she had never once returned.

Perhaps she hadn't wanted to be reminded of the life she'd left behind. A simple, innocent, contented life, full of promise and potential and dreams of the future that might be. The kind that might someday have yielded a family, children, a home of her own.

A life she was destined never to have.

So much time had passed, so many tumultuous events had drastically reshaped her future, that this land and the carefree childhood tied to it had long since faded into a half-forgotten past that she thought of simply as Before.

Before the agonising loss of her parents. Before the KGB and the CIA and their endless struggle for supremacy. Before the Circle and their webs of deceit. Before Cain and his betrayals. Before she started on her path to the person she was now.

So deeply had Anya buried this place that she'd actually struggled to find her way here today, taking wrong turns down unfamiliar roads she'd once known intimately, walking in a daze through forested glades that stirred only the shadow of memories, the vague sense that they had once been familiar.

But in the early hours of morning, with the sun just creeping over the horizon, she'd made it, finally arriving at the entrance to the winding, unpaved road, long since overgrown and unused. That was when she felt it. The rush of familiarity, of memories long forgotten, of a life once lived.

She was lost in a haze of wistful emotion as she silently compared her present surroundings to the place she used to know. She remembered driving this way in her father's car, the bump and jolt as the suspension rattled over potholes, the faint smell of petrol and oil and old leather.

To her right, the ground sloped gently downhill towards a lake a couple of hundred yards away. She could still see the rocky outcrop where she used to jump in as a child, emerging from the cold water laughing and gasping for breath.

To her left was the high ground that dominated the area, the slopes heavily wooded but the hilltop itself bereft of cover. That was where she'd sit on the grass, read books and stare out across the wild, empty landscape, daydreaming of the far-off places and adventures that awaited her.

The pine and spruce trees that grew there were bigger now, their soaring branches reaching high into the morning sky. Or maybe the rest of the landscape felt smaller somehow, closer together.

Straight ahead, maybe fifty yards further on, stood the building that she'd once called home.

There wasn't much left now. Decades of neglect had seen the roof sag noticeably, many of the tiles missing. The windows and doors were gone, looters having long since carried off anything of value. It was a shell now, slowly rotting and decaying away.

But it had once been something very different. Just like her.

Anya turned off the remains of the road and into the long grass beyond, now surging with new spring growth. Discarding her heavy pack, she lowered herself to her knees, allowing the green stalks to sway gently around her in the breeze. There was something deeply calming in it, watching the wind shimmer and flow through the sea of grass.

A moment of peace in a lifetime of war.

Reaching out, she allowed her hands to brush the blades of grass, feeling the movement, the life within. It had rained during the night. The grass was still damp, leaving her fingertips coated with moisture.

As she had done so many times before, Anya gently wiped her hands across her face, the cool water refreshing and reinvigorating her, clearing her thoughts and focussing her mind. Closing her eyes, she inhaled, tasting the scent of wildflowers coming into bloom, damp earth and moss and wet leaves. The living world around her, which had survived and thrived long before she had walked the earth, and would continue long after she'd ceased to be.

It occurred to her then that the only times in her life when she'd felt truly comfortable had been in places like this, far away from cities and noise and people. Places that reminded her of Before.

The sun was coming up now, peeking over the distant mountains off to the east, rising into a perfect blue sky. She could feel its warming rays on her face, driving off the early morning chill. The dawn of a new day, perhaps her last.

Anya smiled faintly as she opened her eyes, knowing she was ready for it. Perhaps it was fitting that it ended here, where it had begun so long ago.

With that thought lingering in her mind, she reached for the cell phone in her pocket.

–

Drake was preparing to leave the apartment in Havana, on his way to meet with the man who could arrange transport for them, when he felt his cell phone buzzing in his pocket. He frowned, instantly on guard. The only people in the world who knew this number were in the room with him.

The others sensed it too, and waited expectantly as he took the call. 'Yeah?'

'Ryan,' Anya said, her voice soft, quiet, tinged with sadness.

Drake closed his eyes, doing his best to compose himself. He hadn't realised how much he'd missed the sound of her voice until this moment, hadn't allowed himself to admit it. But here she was, speaking with him now.

Realising the opportunity that had just presented itself, Drake looked over at Frost and snapped his fingers. Straight away she set to work, running a trace on the call.

'Keep her talking,' she mouthed.

Turning away, Drake moved towards the balcony overlooking the Havana waterfront.

'Anya. Where are you?'

'It doesn't matter now.'

'Yes, it does,' Drake promised her. 'We can help you.'

'No, Ryan. No more.' There was an air of finality in her voice when she said this. A sad acceptance of something she'd always known. 'I don't want you to come for me. That's not why I called.'

Opening the door, Drake stepped out onto the balcony. 'So what do you want?'

'To say that… I'm sorry. For everything. I took something you can never get back. And I wish…' She sighed, searching for the right words. 'I wish things had not been this way. I wish we had met in a different life.'

Drake swallowed and nodded, feeling like a weight had lifted from him. The weight of guilt and remorse he'd carried since learning the truth of his own past.

'I'm tired, Ryan,' Anya said, her voice betraying just how much of a toll this life had taken. 'Tired of running, tired of fighting… tired of losing. I just want it to be over. And I think that soon, it will be.'

Taking his eyes off the moonlit bay stretching before him, Drake turned his gaze upward, taking in the great dark sweep of the night sky.

'Don't do it,' he said suddenly, putting forth everything in a last-ditch plea. 'Whatever you're planning, whatever you've got in mind, don't do it. *Please.*'

'Why not?'

'Because…' Drake let out a breath, holding nothing back now. 'Because I don't want you to die. Not now, not for this. Don't let it end this way.'

The woman was silent. And as the seconds stretched out, Drake began to wonder if his words had struck a chord. For a moment, he allowed himself to hope she would change her mind.

'Do you remember what I told you once?' she finally said. 'I would rather die for something, than live for nothing. Some things *are* worth dying for.'

Drake gripped the rusted balcony railing tight as the woman spoke. She wouldn't be swayed. Her mind was made up, her fate decided.

'I know what I have to do now, and… I'm not afraid. Not anymore.'

'Anya…'

'Goodbye, Ryan. Live a good life.'

As the line went dead, Drake released his white-knuckle grip on the railing and swept back into the apartment.

'Tell me you found her.'

Frost, glancing up from her laptop, nodded confirmation. 'I've got her.'

NSA Headquarters, Fort Meade, Maryland

Deep within the huge, monolithic black building that was the NSA headquarters, Richard Starke stood with his arms folded, waiting expectantly while technicians worked to decrypt the phone call they'd intercepted. They were backed up by networks of supercomputers running the most sophisticated codebreaking software humanity had ever produced. This one building contained more computing power than NASA, the FBI and the CIA combined, and all of it was under his command.

'Well?' he prompted as the senior analyst scanned the results.

'We've got her,' the young man confirmed. 'GPS tracking is locked in. The call originated in Lithuania.'

Starke smiled, amused that Anya should have succumbed to nostalgia. 'Son of a bitch. She's going home.'

'Sir?'

'Never mind,' he amended. 'Get a full surveillance package on this. Aerial and satellite. I want to see every move she makes.'

'We're on it, sir.'

Turning away, Starke fished out his cell phone and put through a call to a man who, he knew, was eagerly waiting for news.

'Get your team ready, Jason. It's time.'

Havana, Cuba

Less than an hour after his call to Anya, Drake arrived at a small private airfield on the outskirts of the city, with Alex in tow. Little more than a single dusty runway and a cluster of support buildings overlooked by a decrepit air control tower, no commercial flights would go near it.

It was perfect for the man he was here to meet.

'This had better be good, Drake,' Cesar Rojas warned, descending from the Gulfstream 500 executive jet with the same cat-like grace as always. 'And by good, I mean well paid.'

Cesar Rojas was a former CIA assassin who had retired years previously, using his lucrative earnings to invest in more 'questionable' businesses. Anya had recruited him in Rio de Janeiro several months earlier.

He had parted company with the team after events in Afghanistan, going his own way. But true to form, the man had landed on his feet, quickly establishing a new business for himself in Cuba. Well-groomed and impeccably dressed, he looked more like a movie star returning from vacation than an assassin-turned-drug smuggler.

Drake, however, was less interested in the man's unsavoury business ventures than in the private jet he used to conduct them.

'Fifty thousand dollars,' Drake said. 'Deposited in your account once we land. Good enough?'

The money left to him by his mother had proven very useful indeed. Much as he was loath to waste it lining the pockets of a man like Rojas, there was little choice if he hoped to get to Anya in time.

He was under no illusions that their call would have gone unnoticed. Starke, with the unlimited resources now under his command, would certainly be gathering his forces to crush her. But in doing so, he just might leave himself vulnerable.

Rojas grinned, always happy to relieve a man of cash. 'Fair enough. Care to tell me what this is about?'

'Anya's in trouble. Every intelligence agency on earth wants her dead. We're going to stop them,' Drake stated simply.

'I see,' the man said, raising an eyebrow. 'How many men do you have?'

'Just us,' Alex answered.

Rojas threw back his head and laughed. 'One hired gun and a computer nerd?'

'Geek, actually,' the young man put in.

Ignoring him, Rojas took a step closer and lowered his voice. 'Look, Drake, I will be honest. I like you. In fact, I'd love to have a man like you working for me,' he added. 'So let me give you some advice – take your money, go home, sit this one out. No good will come of it.'

'I've got enough regrets to live with already. This won't be one of them,' Drake said, staring the former assassin down. 'If I have to go alone, I will.'

He had already parted company with the others, recognising he could ask no more of them. Jessica would stay with Frost until he was able to reunite with them. If not, he had left his sister enough money to make a fresh start under a new identity.

It wasn't much, but it was the best he could give her now.

Rojas was about to respond when his gaze suddenly flicked over Drake's shoulder. Catching his look, Drake spun around and watched as a car pulled up. One of the old, brightly painted but decrepit taxis that plied their trade here, usually ferrying tourists around the impoverished island.

But it was no tourist who stepped out.

'You didn't think we'd trust you assholes to handle this alone, did you?' Frost said, hoisting a rucksack over her shoulder and striding towards them. She glanced up at the jet parked nearby. 'They better have snacks on this flight.'

Dietrich was out next, regarding Drake with his typical brisk demeanour. 'Before you ask, it wasn't my idea.'

Drake couldn't help but smile, looking past his gruff companion to the final member of the group. His sister, Jessica. The woman who had been by his side since this whole thing began, following him from London to Washington, and now to their final destination.

'You sure you want to do this?'

He would do everything in his power to keep her safe, but he wanted her to be clear about what they were facing. Their small, lightly armed group was about to take on an enemy more dangerous and resourceful than any they'd encountered before. There was no guarantee that any of them would make it back.

Jessica nodded, understanding the danger, even fearing it a little. But refusing to be cowed by it. She would never back down from danger again.

'When this all started, I told you I was with you to the end,' she said firmly. 'I meant it, Ryan. Let's find Anya and finish this.'

Smiling despite the gravity of the situation, Drake turned to face the others. They were standing by, waiting for him to give the word.

'You heard the lady. Get onboard.'

CIA Headquarters, Langley

'I don't care about resourcing issues, just have those choppers ready. I want them fully fuelled and armed in time for the assault team's arrival,' Franklin barked into his phone. 'And we need drones flying continuous cover over the target area.'

With the news coming through that Anya's location had been pinpointed from a cell phone intercept, Starke was already dispatching a full assault force to take her out. Franklin, meanwhile, had been tasked with ensuring the necessary logistics and military hardware were in place when they arrived.

'Sir, I have to warn you, launching an unsanctioned operation in Lithuanian airspace is—'

'I know the risks, Kaminsky,' he replied. Lithuania, like the other Baltic states, was now a firm member of NATO, but that didn't mean the US had free rein to do whatever they wanted there. 'Just get it done.'

Hanging up, he let out an exasperated breath and leaned back in his chair. He could practically feel Kennedy's eyes boring into him.

'Goddamn it, Chris,' he said wearily. 'Say what you've got to say.'

'This is all wrong,' Kennedy said, wasting no time. 'Starke sends his own private assault team instead of Agency personnel. No oversight, no questions. Why do you think that is?'

'Surprise me.'

'They're going to kill her. They're not trying to take her down or capture her. They want her dead, just like they want Ryan dead.'

'Ryan's not there,' Franklin reminded him. 'Anya is.'

'You read the transcript. We both know he's going after her. He's walking into a trap.'

'Ryan's made his choices. No one forced him to do anything.'

'This is bullshit, and you know it!' Kennedy snapped.

'What the hell do you expect me to do about it?' Franklin shouted, days of pent up frustration and anger suddenly exploding. 'Scrub the mission? Refuse orders? Arrest the director of the NSA?'

Kennedy sighed, forcing himself to calm down. 'Let me take my team in.'

'Christ, listen to yourself! This isn't some schoolyard fight here. You get caught in the middle of this thing, you and your team could end up disappearing for good.'

'We're willing to take that risk.'

'That's an easy thing to say when you don't have to answer for it,' Franklin reminded him pointedly.

'Look, I know you've got doubts about this thing, even if you won't admit it,' Kennedy said, staring earnestly at the acting CIA director. 'But you can't sit on the fence any longer. If you don't trust Starke, if you think he's dirty, this could be our last chance to do something about it.'

Sighing, Franklin rose slowly from his chair. 'Get out,' he said quietly.

'Excuse me?'

'I said get out, Chris,' Franklin said, giving him a hard, cold look. 'You're relieved of duty. You, and your team.'

Stunned, Kennedy stood up and backed away.

'Take a few days off, get your head together,' Franklin advised him as he headed for the door. 'Oh, and Chris?'

The Shepherd team leader stopped, glancing back over his shoulder.

'I hear Lithuania's nice this time of year.'

He couldn't quite see the smile on the younger man's face, but he didn't need to. Kennedy left without saying another word.

Chapter 68

Lithuania

It was done. After a day of hard physical toil, Anya was tired, hot and thirsty. But at last, she was ready to make her stand. She had done what she could; now all that remained was to await the inevitable.

She knew they would come after nightfall, allowing them to make best use of their superior technology, firepower and the weight of their numbers. They would be well trained, well equipped and confident of their success, as they had every right to be. She would use that against them.

For now, though, she had a little time to rest and gather her strength.

The sun was going down as Anya wearily ascended the slope overlooking her former home, the towering spruce trees casting long shadows across the ground. As a child she'd bounded easily up this hill, leaping over fallen logs and stands of brush, as nimble as a wild deer, but today her steps were slower, heavier.

She was tired in a way she'd rarely experienced in her lifetime, and still hurting from various injuries. She knew that when the time came, she'd rally her strength to do what was needed, just as she always had, but for now she allowed herself to simply experience the weight of her exhaustion.

Reaching the rounded hilltop at last, she lowered herself down onto the grass, grateful to take the weight off her feet. Breathing slower now, she looked out across the vista that stretched before her; the glistening lake waters, the heavy forests shrouded in shadow, the hills and valleys touched by the setting sun. And above it all, the deep azure sky dappled with high, trailing clouds, tinged red by the fading day.

She was grateful beyond words to have seen it one last time.

With her hands resting on the ground at her sides, Anya closed her eyes and breathed deep, feeling the breeze sighing across her skin, lifting her long blonde hair. To anyone watching, she would have appeared utterly at peace with the world.

And for one short moment, she was.

'Who are you?'

Startled, Anya opened her eyes and looked up, confused and dismayed to find a young girl watching her. She must have drifted into a daze, she realised, her usually sharp senses failing her.

Anya looked the girl up and down, trying to discern her origin. She was ten, maybe twelve years old, tall and skinny, with blonde hair tied back in a simple braid. Her facial features, caught between curiosity and wariness, called up such a sense of deep-seated familiarity in Anya that she was certain the girl was native to the area. Probably some local kid out playing, chancing upon Anya by accident.

'I used to live here,' Anya explained. 'This is my home.'

'Nobody lives here,' the girl replied, confused.

'It was long before you were born, child.'

To her dismay, the girl dropped to the ground beside her, sitting cross-legged and watching her with large, intelligent blue eyes. 'Why are you here now?'

'I came to finish something.' Anya gestured off to the distance where, according to her memory, the nearest village lay several miles away. 'You live around here?'

The girl nodded.

'You should stay away from this place for the next few days,' Anya advised. 'Tell your friends to do the same.'

'Why?'

'Bad people are coming. It will be dangerous here.'

The girl thought about that for a moment. 'Then you should leave, too.'

Anya shook her head sadly. 'I can't. They're coming for me.'

'Are *you* a bad person too?' she asked with the open, frank curiosity that only children possess.

Anya's first instinct was to deny it. To give the girl a simple, comforting lie that would allay her fears and reassure her that everything in her world was as it should be. Instead she found herself dwelling on the question, unable to find the answer but unwilling to lie. Perhaps now, at the end, she could finally be honest with herself.

'I have done bad things,' she admitted. 'Things I wish I could change now. But I never really stopped to question what I was doing, or the people I served. Instead I did what I was told, became what they needed me to be. And what did it get me?' She looked down the slope towards the abandoned home, standing alone and forlorn. 'An empty house?'

Anya shook her head, pushing that thought away as she gazed at the sunset. She imagined for a fleeting moment that she held the entirety of her life in the palm of her hand. All her words and deeds, her plans and intentions, her thoughts and emotions. Everything she was, everything she had been, and everything she might become.

'I did what I had to do to survive, for better or worse,' she finally said, facing up to the truth in the only way she knew how. 'It's not for me to decide the value of my life, or how long it should last.'

She blinked, feeling a tear trickling down her cheek, the sun on her skin, the wind in her hair. Her entire lifetime balanced perfectly in a single moment.

'But with the time I was given, the *life* I was given… *I did my best.*'

Anya felt lighter somehow when she finished speaking. She had acknowledged the truth about herself at last, made peace with who she really was, and let go of who she might have been. She had cast aside her fears and worries and regrets.

'It's getting late, child,' she said, wiping her eye. 'You should go home now, before your family worries about you.'

There was no answer.

Frowning, Anya turned around, only to find that the girl was gone. No tracks, no sign that she had ever been there. Anya let out a breath, allowing the moment to pass as the sun dipped below the horizon and the last light of the day faded.

Chapter 69

The mood aboard the Gulfstream jet was fraught and tense as the minutes ticked down. They had crossed into Lithuanian airspace about twenty minutes ago, after a high-speed run across the North Atlantic that had taxed the private jet's service range to the limit.

Drake didn't care how many aviation laws they broke to get here. All that mattered was reaching Anya before Starke and his men arrived.

Through a combination of computer hacking and logical elimination, Frost and Alex had discovered a black flight that had departed US airspace, following a similar course. The two aircraft had been locked in a desperate race all the way.

Based on Drake's educated guesswork, they would be heading for Šiauliai Air Base in the northern part of the country. It was the only NATO facility in Lithuania that could accommodate US transport planes, and it was barely a dozen miles from Anya's location. An ideal staging point from which to launch their attack.

Anya would have to know that too. He was counting on it.

He looked up from the maps and satellite images littering the table as his sister approached, bearing a steaming cup of coffee.

'Thanks,' he said, taking it.

'Don't thank me yet,' she warned. 'The galley's not up to much.'

Drake smiled faintly as he took a sip. 'How are you feeling?'

'Well, let's see.' She thought on it for a few seconds. 'Sick to my stomach, scared, angry and… impatient, I suppose. I can face what's coming. It's the waiting that's hardest.'

'I know. It's always that way.'

'Even for you?' she asked.

'Especially for me.' He leaned forward, regarding his sister honestly. 'Every mission, every time we go into the firing line, it's always the same.'

His sister looked around, taking in the others. They were tired, depleted, nerves frayed, but they were willing to follow him one last time.

'Be honest with me, Ryan,' she said. 'Will this work? Do we have a chance?'

So much of Drake's plan depended on assumption and intuition. But he could be wrong, he acknowledged. He could be leading them all to their deaths.

But if he was right then perhaps, just perhaps, they could still win this.

'No matter how bad it got, no matter what we were up against, we never gave up. We made it this far together,' he reminded her. 'That has to count for something.'

Jessica nodded, understanding his meaning. It was enough for her.

Further aft, Alex was working on his laptop, using the Lithuanian air traffic control network to monitor their rival flight, when Frost approached and sat down opposite.

'Got a minute?' she said when he didn't acknowledge her.

Alex didn't look up. 'If you're here to give me shit, Frost, I'm not in the mood.'

Considering they might all be dead this time tomorrow, reigniting petty grudges and arguments seemed irrelevant now.

'Relax, I'm not here to fight. I came to apologise.'

Raising an eyebrow, Alex glanced up at her.

'For being a dick back in Havana. I know you did your best to warn us. If you hadn't, Jessica and I might be dead.'

Alex sighed, finally laying aside his computer. 'Mitchell was my friend,' he said quietly. 'She saved my life. I wish I could have done the same.'

'You tried, Alex. That's all anyone can ask.' She was about to leave, but thought better of it. 'I didn't mean it, you know.'

'Mean what?'

'That you're not one of us. Truth is, you've helped us more times than I can count. You might not be like us, but that doesn't mean you're not one of us.'

He half expected her to follow it up with some petty insult or sly dig at him, but surprisingly, she remained silent. She'd meant what she said.

Moved by her heartfelt apology, Alex sat forward and held out a hand to her.

'Doesn't mean we're going on vacation together now,' the young woman said, flashing a playful grin as she gripped it. 'You're still an asshole.'

Alex smiled in return. 'Likewise.'

Up front, Rojas emerged from the cockpit bearing news. 'Almost there. Ten minutes.'

Frost cocked an eyebrow. 'Time for the main event.'

Touching down at Istra Aerodrome, a small regional airport in the northern part of the country, the Gulfstream taxied to a stop in a vacant hangar and shut down its engines. The aircraft would be refuelled and, with luck, ready to evacuate the team once their task was complete.

'We'll stay as long as we can,' Rojas advised as Drake descended the steps. The others were checking gear and weapons nearby. 'Don't be late.'

Drake took his meaning. If the shit hit the fan, Rojas would pull out.

'Not coming with us?' he asked flippantly. 'We could use a man like you.'

Rojas had utilised his skills as a former assassin several times during their last mission. This time, however, he flashed a smile. 'I'm a businessman, not a hero. I'll leave that stuff to you.'

'Fair enough.'

He was about to turn away when Rojas spoke up. 'Listen, Drake. If you see her again, tell her...' He trailed off, his usual cocky demeanour fading. 'Tell her she still owes me a bottle of tequila.'

Beneath the humour and the bravado, Drake could see his true sentiments.

'Just hold onto that plane for us.'

Leaving him, Drake strode over to join his companions. The small, disparate group of people who had survived everything they'd been through were waiting for him, hushed and expectant.

'You don't need me to tell you what we're up against,' he began. 'We're in for the fight of our lives. Everything we've done, everything we've faced together, it all comes down to tonight. No more running, no second chances. This is where it ends. This is where we make our stand.'

As he spoke, his teammates looked at each other, taking their measure, thinking about everything they'd been through together. Knowing they had each other's backs all the way to the end.

'Each of you knows what you have to do. I can't say how this is going to play out, but I do know this – it's been an honour to know each and every one of you. No matter what happens, I'll always be grateful for what you did tonight. Thank you. Good luck.'

As the group gathered up their gear, Jessica approached him, well aware this might be the last time they spoke. She knew it, and accepted it.

'Ryan, I…' She swallowed, regaining her faltering composure. 'I know what has to happen now. I know I can't be there with you, but… I want you to know how proud I am of you. You're my brother, and I love you.'

Reaching out, Drake pulled her close and hugged his sister, perhaps for the last time.

'Thanks,' he whispered. 'For all of it.'

Letting go, he took a deep breath, rallying himself for what lay ahead.

'Let's finish this.'

Chapter 70

The hulking C-17 Globemaster transport plane touched down at Šiauliai Air Base, its massive airframe dwarfing the small collection of fighter and utility aircraft stationed there.

The base itself was a modest facility in something of a rural backwater, consisting of a single runway, a scattering of large hangars and hardened shelters dating back to the days of the Cold War, and a couple of support and administrative buildings. Nothing like the sprawling, town-sized bases the US military maintained across the world.

Today, however, it had become a hive of activity, with a pair of Black Hawk transport choppers standing by on the main aircraft ramp. Not far away lurked the massive, brooding shape of an Mi-24 ground attack gunship.

The administrative block had been requisitioned by the assault force and hastily converted into a command and control centre. It was from here that the attack would be coordinated.

Striding out the rear cargo ramp of the Globemaster with the rest of his team in tow, Jason Hawkins made straight for the parked choppers, already armed and geared up. His back was ramrod straight, his face set with dark, focussed determination. He had barely spoken a word on the flight over, and even his own men were afraid of him.

'Where are we on aerial recon?' he demanded.

'We've got a Predator over the target area now,' Sanchez, his new second in command, reported. 'GPS tracking is locked in.'

'And she's still there?'

'Hasn't budged, sir. She's just sitting there.'

Hawkins nodded. 'She's baiting us. Let's see what she has to offer.' Raising his hand, he spun it in a rotating motion. 'Saddle up, gentlemen! This is it!'

In the operations room, Richard Starke stood surveying the bank of monitors in front of him, each displaying footage from the team's helmet cameras. He watched as they piled into the transport choppers, weapons and gear being secured as the chopper's engines spun up to full power.

'Bravo One and Two taking off now, sir,' the technician manning the terminal reported. 'Alpha One is flying top cover.'

Brave One and Two were the Black Hawks, while the Mi-24 attack chopper had been designated Alpha. A Russian-built machine that had once rained death on the battlefields of Afghanistan, it had been requisitioned from the Lithuanians to act as heavy fire support. It was well equipped for such a role, bristling with rocket pods and heavy machine guns, and so heavily armoured that it had earned the nickname 'flying tank'.

'Time to target?' Starke asked, his tone brisk and efficient.

'Five minutes, sir.'

His gaze switched to the monitor showing real-time footage from the Predator drone. Anya was seated on a small hilltop near a dilapidated house, barely moving.

He wondered then if she would even put up a fight.

–

The land was quiet in a way that only the deep hours of the morning can be, the air cool and still. Overhead, the stars were clearly visible between thin ribbons of trailing cloud, the view unspoiled by light pollution.

Nearby an owl called out, the haunting cry echoing through the slumbering forest. The waters of the lake lapped gently at the shore, while further out, a fish splashed at the surface before disappearing silently back into the depths.

And in the midst of this nocturnal stillness, the woman sat with her back against a tree, waiting and watching, barely moving a muscle. She knew what was coming. She knew her chances, and she wasn't afraid.

It started with a low, distant thumping sound coming from the south-west. So faint that it might have passed unnoticed, but after hours of patient waiting, her senses were keenly adapted to her environment.

She heard the distinctive sound of the approaching choppers, and knew her time had come. Leaping to her feet, she took off down the slope, heading for the ruined house.

–

'Tango's on the move!' the technician called out.

Starke watched through the drone's night vision camera as the blurry green shape sprinted down the forested slope, leaping nimbly over obstacles in her path, following a straight and certain course.

'She's heading for the house,' Starke realised, amused and perplexed by her decision to hole up there. 'You can run, Anya. But you can't hide.'

Leaning forward, he spoke into the comms link connecting him with Hawkins. 'Alpha One, are you seeing this?'

'Copy that,' Hawkins replied. 'She's going for the house.'

'Are you in position?'

'Thirty seconds.'

Starke turned his attention back to the drone feed. Sure enough, Anya disappeared through the building's main entrance. Thinking she had avoided detection.

'Alpha One is in position,' Hawkins reported. 'Weapons hot.'

Starke smiled faintly. 'Light it up.'

–

With the two Black Hawks hanging back, the Mi-24 attack chopper swept down out of the night sky like some dark beast born from ancient nightmares, rotors thundering, engines screaming.

The wing-mounted pods opened up, unleashing a barrage of unguided rockets that streaked through the darkness before detonating with multiple concussive blasts. The roof, weakened by decades of neglect, was shattered by the impact, collapsing in on the floors below. The front wall absorbed the bulk of the explosive onslaught, blasted inward in a deadly hail of debris before crumbling apart, taking much of the remaining structure with it.

In a matter of seconds, the house and everything within it had been reduced to a heap of smoking rubble.

Hawkins, watching the destruction unfold with immense satisfaction, smiled as he pressed his transmitter. 'Good hit. Repeat, Alpha One has good hit on target.'

'Copy that,' Starke replied. 'Move in, make sure she's dead.'

'Bravo One, prepare to deploy. We'll cover you.'

'Roger that, Alpha. Bravo One is going in.'

As the Mi-24 circled protectively, the first Black Hawk tilted its nose downward and came in across the lake, heading for the flat, open ground between the house and shoreline.

There was no movement below. Thermal imaging units swept the surrounding woodland and high points, on the lookout for possible sniper or RPG ambushes, yet no targets presented themselves. The Black Hawk continued on its course, flying straight and steady, coming in over the lake before flaring its nose upward to slow its momentum.

What neither the pilots nor any of the troops onboard could possibly see were the four green plastic devices hidden in the long grass. Slightly curved in shape and painted olive drab for camouflage, each plastic casing was stamped with a simple warning.

FRONT TOWARDS ENEMY

Normally, Claymore anti-personnel mines were fixed horizontally, designed to kill or injure enemy infantry who happened to pass by. But in this case, all four had been turned upwards, their explosive detonators daisy-chained together into a single electronic trigger called a clacker.

A clacker that was now in the hands of the woman they'd come here to kill. The woman who had crawled out of the house through a hole broken in the rear wall, making her way unseen along a shallow trench dug into the soft earth, covered over with camouflage sheeting.

The woman who was now watching the approaching troop carrier from a covered foxhole at the edge of the trees, crouched low and silent, her face and body covered with camouflage paint.

Waiting until the chopper was directly over the landing area, the woman braced herself and triggered the clacker.

It took only a millisecond for the surge of electricity to make its way along the detonator wires and into the explosive devices. All four of them detonated simultaneously, ejecting their load of heavy steel ball bearings skyward like giant, overpowered shotguns, straight into the underside of the Black Hawk.

The effect was devastating. In a fraction of a second, the deadly projectiles tore through the chopper's outer skin and through the lower deck, severing hydraulic lines and electrical systems, and perforating the rotor blades above. But it was the effect on the human bodies inside that was worst of all.

Four men were killed instantly, their bodies torn apart by shrapnel, including the pilot, who slumped forward against the control column. The co-pilot, badly injured himself, fought in vain to regain control even as one of the compromised rotor blades sheared off, becoming deadly missiles themselves, scything through nearby trees before shattering into pieces.

The woman watched, eyes gleaming in the darkness as the Black Hawk yawed violently to starboard before pitching right over and slamming into the ground by the edge of the lake.

–

In the operations room, Starke watched in disbelief as the stricken chopper went down, the broken rotor blades churning the lake water around it, steam and smoke rising from ruined engine components.

'What the hell is happening down there?' he demanded. 'Talk to me.'

'I... I don't know, sir,' the confused technician replied. 'Alpha One, status report.'

'Bravo One is down. Repeat, Bravo One is down.'

'Tell me something I don't know,' Starke snapped. 'She did this. Find her!'

–

No sooner had the ruined chopper come to rest than a second firestorm erupted, this one less explosive and more incendiary in nature. Stacks of wood gathered from the nearby forest, placed at intervals around the area and liberally doused with gasoline, suddenly burst into life as if by magic.

The abrupt flare of thermal and visible radiation was like a nuclear bomb going off on the infrared cameras. Within moments, the remaining choppers and the Predator drone overhead had been blinded by the plume of heat and light.

Ignoring this, the woman crouched in her foxhole shifted position, moving behind the bolt-action sniper rifle resting on the edge of the hole. As the first man, injured and panicked, clambered out of the ruined chopper, she carefully took aim and put a high velocity armour-piercing round through his chest.

He was quickly followed by two more, emerging almost at the same moment. She dropped the first with a single shot to the head, though the second managed to tumble over the side of the overturned fuselage and into the water below.

Hefting the rifle up from its bipod, she stood up and advanced, pausing only to fire a third shot that knocked him flat. Her right hand came up and worked the bolt action, drawing a fresh round into the breach. The spent casing fell sizzling into the grass by her feet.

'Please!' she heard him cry out. 'No more!'

Her next shot was enough to put him down for good. Casting aside the heavy and cumbersome weapon, she waded out into the shallow water, grabbed the dead man and yanked his comms unit off his head.

In the gunship overhead, Hawkins heard a new voice on the radio. 'Are you listening?'

He felt his pulse quicken at the sound of the female voice. It was *her*.

'Nice move with the Claymores,' he replied, managing to hold his anger in check. 'Gonna have to pay you back for that.'

Her response was simple. 'Then come and get me.'

Tossing aside the dead man's radio, she reached into his webbing, withdrew a pair of fragmentation grenades, yanked the pins free and tossed both devices in the chopper's open side hatch.

The resulting explosion ignited the fuel tanks, closely followed by the remaining munitions onboard, adding to the near-total thermal white-out on their scopes.

Gritting his teeth, Hawkins switched frequencies to speak with the pilot. 'Take us in. You're weapons free.'

'Sir, we've got no visuals,' the pilot warned. 'We can't see anything down there.'

'Light up the whole goddamn area, then!' he shouted. 'Fire!'

The gunship streaked in once more, rockets and machine guns flaring as it opened fire indiscriminately, strafing back and forth across the area around the ruined house. The woman they were aiming for had already retreated, however, taking refuge amongst the dense tree cover.

As the Mi-24's gunners continued their work, Hawkins radioed the second Black Hawk. 'Bravo Two, move in now.'

'Negative, sir. Area is too hot for landing,' the pilot protested.

'Deploy further out and come in on foot,' he snarled. Already he was starting to see the weakness of her strategy. 'She can't move beyond the fires or we'll see her. Form a perimeter and run that bitch down.'

Finding a suitable clearing about a quarter of a mile away, the second Black Hawk set down, disgorging a dozen operatives in full battledress, protected by Kevlar and armed with assault rifles, light machine guns and grenade launchers. Enough firepower to take on an entire platoon of regular infantry.

As the chopper quickly lifted off, the pilot eager to avoid the same fate as his comrades, the operatives spread out into a skirmish line and advanced, moving swiftly and stealthily through the darkened forest. Heading towards the distant fires that still raged all around the ruined building, closing in on their target.

Chapter 71

Dan Franklin was in his office, anxiously awaiting news from Lithuania. Never in his life had he found himself so torn and conflicted, both professionally and emotionally.

After everything that had happened, he simply didn't know what to believe any longer. Had Drake really turned traitor? Had Cain truly been the corrupt and ruthless renegade he'd come to believe? Was Anya deserving of the death that was coming for her?

A thousand questions tumbled through his mind. Questions for which he had no answers. All he knew was that he was playing a dangerous game, with the highest stakes imaginable.

He practically snatched up his cell phone as soon as it rang.

'Franklin.'

But instead of the call he was expecting from Kennedy, a different voice spoke to him now. 'Don't talk, just listen. If you're the man I believe you to be, you will want to hear this.'

—

The assault force had formed a skirmish line about five metres apart, moving quickly but methodically through the dense undergrowth, weapons tracking back and forth in search of targets. Their eyes had by now adjusted to the low ambient visibility, and they advanced using hand gestures to communicate.

Backing up against a tree about fifty yards ahead of them, the woman gripped the M14 rifle tight, checking the receiver to make sure the first round was chambered. Though long since replaced by more advanced infantry weapons, the M14 was a powerful and accurate semi-automatic rifle, battle tested by decades of use, and still favoured by some special forces groups. Its 7.62mm rounds also stood a better chance against body armour than the lighter shells fired by more contemporary weapons.

They were getting close now. She could hear the faint rustle as they moved through the undergrowth. The moment she started firing, they'd have her position zeroed in. Unless she took their sight away.

Slowing her breathing, she reached for the remote switch in her pocket, disengaged the safety on her rifle and waited.

The lead operatives had closed to within twenty yards when suddenly, light blazed into life in front of them, blinding and intense. Instantly their night vision vanished, their view of anything beyond the floodlights non-existent.

'Cover! Cover!' one of them yelled, dropping to the ground.

His comrade was a fraction slower to react – a mistake that would prove fatal. Rounding the tree, she raised the M14 and put a trio of rounds into his centre mass, dropping him.

As the others returned fire, trying to take out the lights, she took aim at her second target as he darted forward, and put down several more rounds. At least one found its mark, blasting through his thigh, and she saw him fall with an agonised cry.

A sudden crack and a shower of sparks nearby plunged the area into darkness once more. They'd taken out the light. Realising her position was untenable, she turned and retreated, ejecting the half-empty magazine and inserting a fresh one as automatic fire rocketed past her, tearing into vegetation and ricocheting off rocks and tree trunks.

Her heart was beating wildly in her chest, adrenaline surging through her veins as she pounded onward. A fleeting shadow, barely visible as she flitted through the trees. She would fall back to her next defensive position, ready to launch another attack as they closed...

The impact of the bullet striking her was like a giant stone fist slamming into her back, the impact sending her tumbling to the ground. She tried to absorb the fall, rolling through muddy soil and bushes, but she felt as if some great weight were pressing down on her lungs, refusing to let her draw breath.

'Target down!' she heard a voice call out, accompanied by rapid movement. Coming straight for her.

Rolling over, she drew her automatic and opened fire just as a figure emerged from the darkness. The weapon thudded back against her wrist again and again until her target collapsed beside her.

413

He was down, but more would be coming. She had to fall back, draw them in, keep them occupied.

Get up, she commanded herself. *You have to get up now.*

Every second she held out was another tiny victory. That was how she saw it now. It was no longer a case of surviving, but of clawing for each second.

Groaning in pain, she grabbed for her fallen rifle and heaved herself upright. Her lungs burned with breath that increasingly wouldn't come, but she forced herself to move, to push forward, to fight through it. Pain was nothing now. She could take it.

Gritting her teeth, she broke into a limping run as more operatives closed in, drawn to the sounds of the firefight like sharks to blood. It was only a matter of time now.

A matter of seconds.

–

In the operations room, Starke stood in tense silence, listening to the reports coming in. With thermal imaging nullified by the combination of fire, smoke and heavy tree cover, he was reduced to monitoring radio chatter to discern the progress of the battle.

'Target's in the woods, heading west towards the hilltop,' one of them reported. 'Team Two, move left and flank.'

'Copy that, Team Two is Oscar Mike.'

'Get some flares up. Can't see shit here.'

'There! I see her. Heading for that gully on the right.'

'Got her. Move in now. Cut her off!'

Starke folded his arms, his jaw clenched as he pictured Anya's desperate final moments playing out. She had put up quite a fight – better than even he had expected – but it was over now. She was surrounded, outnumbered and outgunned.

All that was left was to fight and die.

–

The forest blazed crimson as a parachute flare shot skyward, illuminating everything for a hundred yards, including the fugitive as she made her desperate retreat uphill towards the summit.

'Target sighted!' a voice yelled out from behind. 'Contact!'

More gunfire erupted from both behind and off to her left somewhere. They must have sent a fireteam around to outflank her. Slowed by her injury, she couldn't hope to outrun them now.

The densely growing trees provided some cover, and many rounds struck them glancing blows that ricocheted off into the woods beyond, but inevitably some made it through. Shots thudded into the ground around her, kicking up clumps of wet earth, and she felt a fresh stab of pain bite into her leg when one grazed her thigh. She stumbled, fell forward, but regained her feet and kept moving.

Reaching up, she keyed her comms unit.

'Anya,' Samantha McKnight rasped as she clawed her way up the slope. 'I can't... hold out much longer. You have to... do it now.'

She had fought for every second, drawing their enemies in and keeping them occupied. Buying time for Anya to do what she must.

She could only hope it was enough.

–

Ten miles away at Šiauliai Air Base, Anya crouched in the shadows behind a refuelling bowser. With her black combat fatigues, and her face and neck smeared with camouflage paint, she was little more than a vague, indistinguishable shape lurking in the darkness. A shape that had approached the perimeter unseen, cutting a hole in the fence and slithering beneath.

As McKnight's desperate transmission came through, punctuated by the sounds of gunfire, she felt a stab of guilt and grief. The woman had volunteered to act as a decoy, knowing it would likely cost her life. All of it to buy Anya precious time. A moment of vulnerability that she could exploit.

'Copy that,' she whispered. All she could offer was a short but heartfelt final message. 'Good luck, Samantha. And thank you.'

'Make it count,' McKnight entreated, signing off.

Forcing her mind back to matters at hand, Anya leaned out far enough to survey the scene beyond. Ahead lay the administration building that was now being used as the assault force's base of operations.

That was where she would find him. That was where she would end this.

A pair of sentries in full combat gear were on station outside, both armed with H&K G36 assault rifles. Powerful and accurate weapons that could easily cut her down. Fortunately, Anya had anticipated this.

Reaching behind her, she gently slid her main weapon off her shoulder. Rather than a rifle or submachine gun, she had put her faith in something far more primitive, but perhaps more effective.

Anya had had a great deal of time to become acquainted with hunting bows in her lifetime. She had practised and trained and perfected her shooting technique until it had become second nature to her.

Never had she used it against human targets, however.

Notching the first arrow, she tensed her arm, closed her eyes and took a breath. When it happened, it would have to be fast. A single mistake, and it was over. Samantha's sacrifice would be for nothing.

For the first time in a long time, she thought of the mantra that had been drilled into her years earlier. The words that had sustained her through the darkest moments of her life, that had given her courage and resolve when everything else had deserted her.

I will endure when all others fail.

Moving out from behind cover, she drew back her arm, took aim and let fly. The silent, deadly missile leapt through the air, impacting in the centre of her target's chest armour. The layers of Kevlar and ceramic plate had been designed to stop anything up to high velocity assault rifle rounds, but a lethally sharp steel-tipped hunting arrow was something its designers had never anticipated.

The missile impacted with an audible thump, carving straight through his chest plate and the ribcage behind it, severing arteries and causing catastrophic internal damage. The man let out a startled grunt of pain and confusion as his legs started to buckle, but Anya wasn't interested in him now.

I will stand when all others retreat.

Reaching for the quiver slung over her shoulder, she drew a second arrow and notched it before the man had even fallen.

Alerted by the sound of his comrade in distress, the second sentry turned his weapon towards her just as she let fly. This time she aimed higher, the arrow passing through his throat, severing his spinal column in an instant. He dropped like a stone, the weapon falling from his grasp.

Weakness will not be in my heart.

Anya was running even as he fell, slinging the bow over her shoulder and drawing her silenced M1911 automatic as she sprinted towards the building. Two shots were enough to destroy the lock, allowing her to kick the door open and move inside.

The central corridor was bare concrete painted a sickly lime green colour, many of the ceiling panels missing, exposing the pipework and electrical cabling above. She moved fast, weapon sweeping left and right, covering every corner and alcove as she advanced to the central stairwell.

Fear will not be in my creed.

She went for it, taking the steps two at a time, rounding the landing to ascend the next flight, only to run straight into another target coming down the other way. She saw the fleeting look of alarm on his face, saw him reach for his sidearm as she raised the M1911 and put two rounds through his head, painting the lime green walls with his blood.

I will show no mercy.

She leapt past his lifeless body as it tumbled down the stairs. Pushing herself onward, breathing hard, she shoved her way through the door at the top of the stairwell and closed in on her target.

So close now. She wouldn't be denied this. She wouldn't be stopped.

I will never hesitate.

As she advanced along the corridor, she heard more voices, hushed and urgent. 'Charlie Three, we have possible hostiles inside the perimeter.'

'Copy that, we're checking it out.'

'Stay sharp.'

Backing up against the wall, she drew a knife from the sheath at her waist and waited until she saw her first target appear around the corner, a suppressed P90 submachine gun up at his shoulder. A second man, similarly armed, was right behind him.

I will never surrender.

The moment his eyes flicked towards her, she went for it, leaping out and slashing at his exposed arm. The blade bit in deep, severing tendons and muscles, and the gun fell from nerveless fingers.

The second man twisted around to open fire, trying to get an angle past his injured comrade. Anya, however, had the drop on him, bringing the M1911 to bear. The venerable old weapon thudded as it spat out two rounds, both of which hit dead in the centre of his forehead, killing him instantly. His finger tightened on the trigger, spraying a random burst into the walls and ceiling that narrowly missed her.

The first man, injured and bleeding, tried to lash out with his good arm, but Anya ducked to avoid it, jammed the muzzle of her weapon beneath his jaw and fired upward. She could feel his warm blood coating the side of her face as she rushed past.

The operations room was straight ahead. This was it.

This was what she'd come for.

–

Clambering over a fallen log and collapsing on the other side, Samantha McKnight backed up against the solid cover, her breath coming in desperate, painful gasps. Adrenaline and sheer determination had carried her this far, but she could go no further.

She flinched as another burst traced its way along the tree trunk, blasting away chunks of rotting wood. They knew her position, and they were keeping her pinned down to prevent further retreats.

Staying down, she pressed a hand against the gunshot wound to her thigh, gritting her teeth against the pain. A flesh wound, but a serious one all the same. It was the chest wound that was making it harder and harder to draw breath.

She could hear shouts all around as her enemies closed the net, coming at her from every direction. No way to hold them off. No way to delay it any longer.

She felt a fleeting sense of disappointment that she hadn't made it to the summit of the hill. She might have held out a little longer on the high ground.

This would have to do. She looked down at the rifle in her hands, smeared with mud and the blood of its owner. One clip left.

Forcing herself upright, she rested the rifle on the edge of the log, sighted another target fleeting through the shadows and opened fire, the powerful gun kicking back against her shoulder again and again. But her shots failed to find their target.

Her enemies were using the abundant cover to their advantage, keeping her occupied while they moved around to outflank her.

Sure enough, she heard movement in the undergrowth behind. This was it. They were coming to finish her.

Breathing hard, she rolled over, swinging the rifle around to face her new threat, only to let out a gasp in disbelief. The figure which emerged from the darkness was a young woman, short and slender, with an unruly mane of dark hair. Of all the people Samantha McKnight had imagined might kill her, she had never foreseen this.

'Covering fire!' Keira Frost shouted, spraying a long burst of gunfire into the woods beyond, the flash of the gunshots illuminating her hard, resolute face.

Moments later, a second man appeared by her side, similarly armed. As he dropped to one knee and put down more fire, temporarily holding their enemies at bay, Frost rushed forward and skidded to a stop beside McKnight.

'You're hit,' she said, quickly assessing her condition.

'Keira,' McKnight replied, her voice a painful rasp. 'What are you doing here?'

'Hurry it up!' Dietrich snapped, ducking down as incoming fire zipped past him.

'We're the fucking cavalry, Sam,' Frost explained, looking her over. 'Let's get you the fuck out of here.'

Chapter 72

Kicking the door open, Anya swept into the operations room. A dark angel, her face marked with war paint and blood, her weapon sweeping between the frightened technicians who had spun to face her.

'Nobody move!' she shouted, looking from one startled face to another but failing to find the one she wanted. 'Where is he? Where is Starke?'

None of them said a word. The seconds stretched out as Anya tried to decide what to do next, where to look, who to interrogate first.

But before she could make a move, the wall-mounted TV that had been displaying live feeds from the Predator drone suddenly changed, showing something very different.

Starke, seated at the end of a plush conference table. The kind to be found in headquarters buildings like Langley.

'Looking for me, Anya?'

–

'Son of a bitch!' Hawkins roared in fury the moment the transmission came through. They had been played. Anya wasn't here, she was at the airfield.

Not only that, but his ground force had just come under attack by unknown enemy combatants, forcing them to pull back and regroup. It was a trap, he realised now. A distraction to keep them occupied.

And he had fallen for it.

'Alpha One, disengage and get us back to the airfield immediately,' he snarled into his headset. 'Ground teams, move in and kill anyone who's still alive down there.'

As the heavy attack chopper swung away from the battle still raging below, rotor blades thumping the night air, Hawkins slammed his fist against the bulkhead beside him.

Anya might have played them, but the game wasn't over yet.

–

Glancing around, Anya spied a small storage room nearby. No windows, no way in or out except the door.

'Everyone inside, now!' she ordered. 'Move!'

As soon as the prisoners were inside, she slammed the door shut and heaved her weight against a filing cabinet beside it. Moments later, it toppled and crashed to the floor, barring the doorway and sealing them inside.

This done, she turned her attention back to the television. She approached slowly, chest rising and falling, weapon gripped tight in her hands.

'You were never here.'

'Of course not. Did you really think I would come all the way to your piss-ant little country just to watch you die?' Starke taunted her.

'I had hoped you would.'

'I'm sure you did.' He leaned forward at the table. 'Not very graceful of you, I must say. After all, you wouldn't be alive today if it weren't for me.'

Two years earlier

'I'll position snipers in elevated positions around the meeting point,' Freya explained, outlining her strategy for what she hoped would be her final encounter with Anya. 'Once I've made contact and I have a confirmed sighting, they'll take her down.'

'And then?' Starke asked.

'Her death is something the Circle has wanted for some time now. It might just be enough to restore their faith in me. After that, we move ahead with our existing plan to access the Inner Circle and take them out.'

Starke was silent for a time, staring into the flames flickering in the fireplace beside him. She had travelled all the way to his own private residence to present her proposal, arriving late at night so that her presence was unlikely to be noticed.

'Are you sure this is what you want?' he finally asked.

'I am.'

He nodded silently to himself, a new course of action already decided upon. Freya had become a liability that now threatened to escalate into disaster. Eliminating her was the most prudent option, and if he could use Anya to do it, then all the better.

Anya's attention could then be directed back towards Cain. And with luck, she would eventually kill him as well.

—

'Why?' Anya asked, knowing this was her last chance to answer a question that had haunted her for the past two years. 'Why did she want me dead?'

'You still don't see it, do you? Freya knew that sooner or later you'd figure out who betrayed you to the Russians: her. Killing you first and using it to gain access to the Inner Circle was a solution to both problems. She was planning to use you in death, just as she used you in life. You were just a pawn in her game, Anya. That's all you ever were.'

'She trusted you,' Anya spat. 'She believed in you.'

'So did you. So did her son,' Starke remarked in amusement. 'A weakness you share, I think. Predictability. That's why you're here tonight, and I'm not.' He chuckled and shook his head. 'I never did understand what Marcus and the Circle saw in you.'

'Something they never saw in you, Starke,' she retorted. 'You're a small, jealous, petty man. You're pathetic.'

She saw a momentary flare of anger in his eyes, an old resentment exposed, but it was quickly masked. 'And yet, here I am. Marcus, Freya, the Circle… all of them underestimated me. All of them paid for it with their lives. Even you, Anya.' He leaned forward, staring intently into the camera. 'Haven't you felt it? Haven't you felt your time running out? You're a relic; a quaint little curiosity from a different world. And this is where your story ends.'

The woman felt herself bristling at his scathing words, sensing the truth in them.

'You know, I don't often let these things get personal. Killing Cain and Freya… those were necessary acts. But I have to admit, knowing you're dead, Anya… well, that *will* give me a certain satisfaction.'

Raising her gun, Anya took aim at his face and pulled the trigger. With a flash and shower of sparks, Richard Starke's image vanished from the screen.

Seconds later, alarms started to blare throughout the building. With his chilling final words delivered, Starke had likely triggered the alarm remotely.

Either way, there was no choice but to evacuate.

Retreating into the corridor, she heard the crash of a door being thrown open, the shouts of operatives closing in on her. She had neither the time nor the firepower to take them on.

Without breaking stride, she sprinted in the opposite direction, looking frantically for another exit just as another cry echoed from behind.

'Contact!'

Barely had she rounded the corner before a short burst of gunfire drilled into the wall, punching straight through the thin plasterboard. But in her headlong rush to escape, she didn't notice the figure in the corridor up ahead until she was in full view.

Skidding to a halt, she raised the automatic at the same moment as her opponent. But then they froze, locking eyes, weapons pointed at each other.

Anya let out a strangled, disbelieving gasp. 'Ryan?'

Somehow, despite everything, Drake had tracked her here, anticipated her plan tonight. And now he stood barely twenty feet away.

For a second or two, everything else melted away as she stared at the man she'd left behind. The man she'd taken so much away from. He'd come all this way, risked everything to find her again.

A sudden movement in the corridor behind broke the spell in an instant. Anya spun around to face the armed operative that had caught up with her, knowing even as she did so that she wouldn't make it. But just as he raised his gun, his head was jerked violently backwards as a round slammed into it.

Anya glanced back at Drake, smoke trailing from his weapon. She gave him a look of heartfelt gratitude, then turned and fled, crashing through the nearest door and into the office space beyond as more shooting erupted.

She needed a distraction if either of them were to get out of here alive. Fortunately, she had one ready and waiting. Reaching into her webbing, she yanked out a radio detonator and flicked the arming switch. Then, taking cover, she triggered it.

Outside, the shaped charge that she'd planted beneath the fuel bowser detonated, rupturing the tank and vaporising its contents, magnifying the explosive force many times over. The concussive blast wave shattered every window in the admin building, knocking the occupants off their feet and showering them with broken glass.

–

'Holy shit!' the pilot of the Mi-24 gunship gasped, staring out through his canopy at the sudden eruption of orange fire. 'The airfield's under attack.'

Unlatching his harness, Hawkins strode forward, leaning into the cockpit to take a look. His face, lit by the glow of the distant flames, slowly twisted in anger.

'Looks like they've been hit by an air strike.'

'It's not an air strike,' Hawkins snarled. 'It's her.'

Chapter 73

'Covering fire!' Dietrich shouted, taking rear-guard position as the small group fell back. Sighting another target darting between tree trunks, he opened fire, spraying a long burst in his direction.

Frost meanwhile was half-carrying, half-dragging an injured McKnight beside her. Her face was resolute, jaw clenched, but her breathing was growing shallow and laboured.

'Come on, goddamn it!' Frost snarled, pulling her onward. 'Don't make me go through all this shit just to die here.'

They were almost at the summit, the trees thinning out around them.

'I thought... you... said you'd kill me,' McKnight gasped.

The young woman glanced at her, seeing how much she'd been willing to sacrifice. 'I was wrong.'

McKnight said nothing to that.

'Changing mags!' Dietrich called out. His shout was immediately followed by a dull, heavy thump. He went down, clutching his shoulder and growling in pain.

'Jonas!' Frost said, leaving McKnight briefly to sprint over to him. He was bleeding profusely from a gunshot wound to the upper right side of his chest. One look at the injury was enough to tell her it was serious. He knew it too.

'Well, fuck,' he said, grimacing.

Frost shook her head. 'Don't be a pussy. Get up and move!'

Helping him to his feet, she hurried over to McKnight. Together the three of them staggered the short distance to the summit, surmounted by a tangle of weathered boulders and long grass. McKnight collapsed against one of the rocks, her strength finally spent.

'They're moving to outflank us,' Dietrich warned, struggling to aim his weapon with one good arm. 'They'll cut us off if we don't move.'

'Sam, we can't stay here,' Frost implored her. 'We have to go.'

McKnight shook her head. The look in her eyes said it all.

'Give me my rifle,' she instructed. 'I'll hold them off… as long as I can. You two fall back and—'

'No!' Frost retorted. 'I already left one friend behind. I'm not doing it again.'

Rather than argue, McKnight looked her in the eye and nodded gently. 'It's okay, Keira,' she whispered. 'I knew what… I signed up for. Let me do this. Please.'

Glancing away for a moment, Frost blinked back tears.

'We stay together,' she said at last, then reached up and touched her radio headset. 'Alex, it's time.'

'Wait a minute,' the young man's crackling voice replied.

'We don't have a minute!'

–

'Sir, we have them on thermal imaging,' one of the technicians reported.

Starke looked up, his attention drawn to the feeds from the Predator's infrared cameras. The small group of fugitives had taken refuge on the high ground overlooking the destroyed homestead, intending to make their last stand there.

But in doing so, they had made themselves visible.

He could see the images of his own strike team moving through the woods, closing the net around them. They would of course overwhelm the three defenders, but it would take time. Time he didn't have.

'You got a target lock?'

'Yes, sir. Hellfires are armed and ready.'

The decision made itself.

'Roll in the drone strike,' he said, preoccupied by the more pressing situation at the airfield. 'Wipe them out.'

'Viper One, roll in strike package. You are weapons free. Ground teams, danger close. Repeat, danger close.'

On the other side of the world, the unmanned Predator drone banked left, lining up for a ground strike. Its thermal cameras quickly reacquired the three targets, passing the information to the four Hellfire air-to-ground missiles attached to the wing pylons.

'Viper One is hot. Target acquired. Fox Two.'

The technicians in the ops room waited for the missile to streak in, obliterating everything on that hilltop. However, no such thing happened.

'Viper One, confirm launch?'

'Negative, Viper One will not launch.'

'Say again?'

Starke glanced over at the screen again with growing concern. The Predator's targeting system suddenly shifted from the three figures crouched together on the hilltop, to the fire teams in the treeline around them.

'Viper One, be advised. You are targeting friendlies,' the comms specialist warned. 'Repeat, you are targeting friendly forces.'

'Viper One does not have control. Repeat, Viper One is non-responsive.'

'What the hell is going on?' Starke demanded. 'Someone talk to me!'

A second later, all four Hellfire missiles departed their weapons racks, streaking down through the dark sky towards their targets. Starke and the others could do nothing but watch as four simultaneous points of light exploded on screen, temporarily blinding the infrared cameras and obliterating the operatives caught within the blast radius.

–

'Fuck, yes!' Alex cried out, punching the air in triumph as the drone feed on his laptop screen displayed the devastating aftermath of his work. 'Take that, you pricks.'

He and Jessica had remained behind at the airport, using the air traffic control system there to pinpoint the Predator drone circling the battle zone. Once he had the aircraft locked in, it had simply been a case of breaking the encryption code governing its control system, and then wrestling command from its operators.

It had been a close-run thing, however. His hands were still shaking.

'Well done, Alex,' Jessica said, squeezing his shoulder before hitting her radio transmitter. 'Keira, Jonas, do you copy? Are you okay?'

–

'We hear you,' Dietrich replied, coughing as smoke from the missile detonations rolled past them. His ears were still ringing. 'We're okay. But maybe you could aim a little further out next time?'

'I'd rather there *wasn't* a next time,' Jessica replied.

Dietrich flashed a sardonic smile. 'That makes two of us.'

Nearby, Frost pushed her hair back from her face and looked up at McKnight, who was lying on her back against one of the boulders. Seeing the young woman close by, she turned her head slowly to look at her.

'You planned this?'

Frost nodded. 'Had no idea if it would work. Guess I really do owe Alex a beer.' Seeing the blood smeared on the rock behind her, she moved forward. 'We need to get you patched up.'

McKnight waved her away weakly. It was a wasted effort, she knew. She was lung-shot, her body giving up on her at last.

'Do me a favour. If you see Ryan again, tell him...' She coughed, leaving a smear of blood on the ground. 'Tell him I'm sorry. Okay?'

Reaching out, Frost clasped her hand tight. 'I will.'

Content at last, McKnight turned her head away from the young woman and looked up at the sky. It was starting to grow brighter in the east, the stars fading as the new day dawned.

A day she wouldn't live to see.

She had fought for every second, and she had won. And that was enough for her.

She smiled contentedly as her grip slackened and her hand fell away.

Chapter 74

Coughing, Drake advanced through the smoke-filled rooms, his weapon up and ready. His ears were ringing, eyes stinging, skin cut by flying glass. But he was alive, and he could move.

He had to find Anya and get out of here.

Flames were licking up the side of the building. Burning fuel from the ruptured bowser was consuming the admin block. If Anya had escaped this way, there was no way he could follow. He had to find another way out.

As he retreated back down the corridor, a figure suddenly leapt out at him from around the corner, tackling him into the wall opposite. One of the operatives who had been closing in on them, similarly disoriented by the blast.

With a surge of rage and fury, Drake drove his knee into the man's chest, hurled him backward against the opposite wall and turned his weapon on him, unleashing a devastating burst into his torso.

Even as the man slid down the wall, Drake hurried past, only to stop in his tracks, hearing frantic screaming and hammering coming from a room up ahead, mingled with plaintive cries for help. People trapped inside. They would burn to death if he didn't help them. Doing so would use up precious time, but could he really walk away and let innocent people die?

'Fuck,' he hissed, hurrying into the badly damaged operations room. The place was a mess, the power cut, smoke billowing from the overhead vents as the building was consumed.

The cries were coming from a door on the other side of the room, blocked by a heavy metal cabinet that had fallen across it. Rushing over, he laid down his weapon down, grasped the cabinet and heaved. It moved an inch or so. Redoubling his efforts, Drake braced himself against the wall and pushed, every muscle in his body straining and trembling. And finally, with a grating rasp, the cabinet shifted.

The door flew open, the occupants forcing their way through the narrow gap. They were unarmed and panicked.

'Get out of here!' Drake commanded, turning away and charging down the stairwell to the lower floor. A wall of flames raged at the far end of the corridor where the exit had been, blocking his path.

'Anya!' he called out, throwing up a hand against the searing heat.

There was no response.

He couldn't stay here any longer. Kicking open the nearest door, he sprinted across the devastated briefing room beyond and leapt through the shattered window into the open air beyond. He landed hard, before scrambling to his feet and looking around, his weapon up at his shoulder again.

The airfield was in chaos, alarms blaring and personnel running back and forth, some trying to tackle the blazing building with hastily deployed fire hoses. A Humvee had pulled up nearby, the occupants leaping out to aid the firefighting efforts.

But as Drake scanned the area, he spotted a figure stealthily leap up into the Humvee's cab. Seconds later, the engine leapt into life and the Humvee took off across the open airfield, heading straight for the perimeter fence. It was Anya, making her escape in a stolen vehicle.

Without even slowing, the Humvee smashed straight through the chain link fence, bumping and rolling across the rough ground beyond.

But Drake wasn't the only one who had seen it. Several hundred feet overhead, Hawkins watched the retreating vehicle through the Mi-24's night vision cameras. He smiled as it broke through the perimeter fence, heading for the dense woodland beyond.

'That's her,' he said. 'Bring us in tight.'

Standing in the midst of the ruined airfield, Drake could only watch in silent horror as the massive gunship swept down, descending on the retreating vehicle.

'No...' he whispered.

'Target locked!' the gunner called out.

Hawkins smiled triumphantly. 'Light her up.'

Disgorging its remaining ordnance, the gunship unleashed a flurry of unguided rockets that streaked down and impacted across the Humvee's path. The effect on the lightly armoured vehicle was devastating, one rocket shredding the rear portion of the vehicle while another near miss flipped it over. The shattered remains cartwheeled over before coming to rest at the edge of the woods, burning and smoking.

'Good hit, Alpha,' Hawkins said, nodding in satisfaction. 'Bring us in. This isn't over until I see her fucking body.'

As the gunship settled into a hover, descent ropes were tossed over the side, allowing Hawkins and a four-man fire team to slide down. Unclipping himself from the harness, Hawkins raised his weapon and nodded to the men beside him.

'Alpha is Splash One on ordnance,' the pilot advised over the radio. 'We have to RTB for resupply. Good luck.'

Hawkins ignored this as the chopper peeled away, focussing on the ruined Humvee. It had overturned, flames licking out of the ruined engine bay, but the main body of the vehicle was still recognisable.

'Cover me,' he instructed, gripping the driver's door and forcing it open with brute strength, eager to see Anya's dead body with his own eyes. The weapon up at his shoulder, his finger on the trigger, ready to finish her if by some miracle she'd survived.

She wasn't there. The Humvee was empty.

A trickle of icy fear ran down his neck when he saw the metal entrenching tool lying on the floor of the cab. Wedged against the accelerator.

Anya wasn't aboard. It was a trap.

'Cover!' he called out, whirling around and dropping to one knee.

Something whizzed through the air, striking the man beside him. He stumbled back, an arrow protruding from the torn, bloody remains of his throat.

'Contact!' Hawkins shouted, firing blindly into the woods.

Backing up against the solid cover of a tree trunk, Anya notched another arrow and drew the string back, waiting for her chance. Stray rounds zipped past her and thudded into the trunk she was hiding behind, but still she didn't move.

–

Drake, sprinting towards the crash site, pounding through the grass and leaping over the crushed remains of the perimeter fence, heard the distinctive crackle of automatic gunfire. It could only mean one thing.

Anya was still alive!

Redoubling his efforts, he forced himself on, exerting every ounce of energy that remained to him in this final, desperate race against time. This was his last chance to reach her.

–

They were wasting ammunition, Hawkins realised. That was exactly what she wanted. He held up a hand to stop the firing. As silence descended around them, he slowly moved behind the ruined Humvee, his eyes scanning the darkened woodland.

Far from being terrified, he smiled at the situation in which he now found himself. Anya was toying with them, picking them off one at a time, evening the odds. But he was the one she really wanted.

That was how he'd beat her.

'Come out, come out, wherever you are,' he said mockingly, edging closer to one of his fellow operatives. 'I know you want to.'

Anya held her position, breathing hard, forcing herself not to lose control. Waiting for the perfect moment, just like a hunter should.

'So this is how it ends,' Hawkins went on. 'The great Maras, the best operative the Agency ever had… How does it feel to have nothing left? To lose everything you ever cared about?'

Anya could feel her heartbeat quickening, her muscles trembling, desperate to act. With a great effort of will, she held on, waiting.

Nearby, Hawkins readied himself. 'Cain gave his life to save yours. I have to admit, I'm gonna enjoy sending you to him.'

Now.

Rounding the tree, Anya's keen eyes scanned her targets, found the one she sought, and swung the bow into position, already taking tension on the string. A single second was all it took to line up her shot, then she let fly.

At the same moment, Hawkins grabbed the operative beside him and pulled him backward, right into the arrow's path. As the missile impacted and he let out a cry of agony, Hawkins' assault rifle spat out a short, vicious burst.

Anya felt the fist-like impact, the familiar burst of cold numbness as the round struck her. The bow flew from her grasp and she went down, bleeding from a gunshot wound to the abdomen.

Releasing his grip on the dying man, Hawkins strode towards his injured prey as she tried feebly to crawl away, leaving a trail of blood in her wake. The other two operatives converged on him, their weapons up, fingers on triggers.

'Nobody kills her but me,' Hawkins warned them.

She could no longer use the hunting bow. Rolling over, Anya reached down and drew her M1911 automatic. Hawkins was ready for her. Taking careful aim, he snapped off a shot that tore into her upper arm, jerking it backward. Anya groaned as a new wave of pain assaulted her, stubbornly refusing to cry out.

Taking no chances, Hawkins clamped his boot down on her arm, pinning it to the ground and preventing her reaching for the gun. Teeth bared, Anya glared up at her enemy.

'You were quite something in your time, but your time's over,' Hawkins said, shaking his head as he surveyed his beaten enemy. 'And you know something? I was always better.'

Relishing the moment, he raised his other foot and pressed it against her injured abdomen. There was no holding back the pain this time. Anya screamed in agony as Hawkins twisted his boot and blood flowed freely from the wound.

By the time he withdrew it, she was close to passing out, her vision blurring, her world one of tortured anguish assailing her on all sides. Bending down, Hawkins plucked the automatic from the ground and looked at the venerable old weapon.

'I wonder how many lives this old piece of iron's taken,' he mused, turning it over in his hand. He smiled and tossed his assault rifle aside. 'Seems only right that it takes one more.'

He raised Anya's gun, taking aim at its owner. Injured and bleeding, Anya could do nothing but stare back at him: a huge, powerful figure silhouetted against the fires behind him, his eyes gleaming with absolute hatred and malice.

This was how it was going to end. This was how she would die.

'This is all you ever were, Anya,' he said as his finger tightened on the trigger. 'Expendable.'

Suddenly a sudden burst of automatic gunfire exploded from off to his right, the two operatives behind him crumpling to the ground. Startled, Hawkins whirled to face this new threat, bringing the weapon with him.

The silenced automatic thudded as Drake leapt in, one wild shot biting into his shoulder as he swept his empty assault rifle around like a club, catching the handgun just as Hawkins was squeezing the trigger.

The impact smacked the weapon out of his hands, a second round barely missing Drake as it fell.

Vaguely he was aware of the sharp stinging pain of torn flesh, but pushed it aside, focussing everything on his enemy. Bringing the butt of the rifle back around, Drake swung for his opponent's head. But Hawkins had recovered from the shock of his sudden appearance and caught the gun just as it was coming at him, wrestling it aside.

For a second or so the two men were eye to eye, glaring at each other with unrestrained hatred and vengeance.

Gritting his teeth, Drake drove a knee into his adversary's side that elicited a grunt of pain, then leaned back and butted Hawkins full in the face. The impact was like driving his head into a wall, but he heard the faint crunch of cartilage breaking, and felt warm blood spray his face.

Hawkins gave vent to an animalistic growl as blood gushed from his broken nose. But along with the sudden flare of anguish came a surge of pure rage.

Exerting every ounce of his considerable strength, Hawkins heaved the weapon up, pulling Drake with it, then shifted all of his momentum forward, slamming the smaller man into the ground. Drake's breath exploded in a violent gasp as the air was forced from his lungs, and pain blazed across his back as he impacted the rocky ground.

But there was no time to think about pain or injuries now. Yanking the weapon from his grip, Hawkins hurled the assault rifle aside and came at him as Drake scrambled aside, narrowly avoiding a kick that would have dropped him like a stone. Hawkins was like a man possessed, raining blows on him, forcing him to cover up and block. Drake, already tired and hurting, couldn't hope to weather this attack.

A stinging punch to the ribs nearly doubled him over, putting him off balance, setting him up for the boot that swept around and hit him like a freight train. He buckled and went down, falling to his hands and knees.

'You really thought you could stop this?' Hawkins snarled as he closed in, blood dripping from his mouth and nose. 'You just gave me the best gift of all, Ryan. Two for the price of one.'

Hawkins' face was twisted with fury and vengeance as he moved in to deliver a knee to the face. But his momentary delay had given Drake a precious few seconds to recover. As he came in, Drake suddenly rose up and twisted aside, using his opponent's momentum against him.

With a furious, enraged cry, Drake drove a fist into Hawkins' back that sent shockwaves down the man's spine. A kick to the back of the leg buckled his knee, allowing Drake to clamp an arm around his neck. Muscles and tendons strained as Drake tightened his grip, crushing and twisting, gritting his teeth as he put everything he had into it.

He heard the man snorting and gasping, blood bubbling from his broken nose as he gasped for air that wouldn't come.

I've got you now, you bastard, Drake thought in that moment of wild, frenzied anger. He knew then that he'd crush the very life out of Hawkins, break his neck, collapse his windpipe.

He didn't notice Hawkins reach for something at his waist, didn't have time to react as steel rasped and something glinted menacingly in the firelight. In a heartbeat, something leapt out, striking him in the side.

And just like that, the world seemed to slow down. He looked down in confusion, watching as Hawkins pulled a bloodied blade from his flank, and felt a strange coldness wash over him.

'No!' Anya cried out in horror as Drake's grip slackened and he staggered back, blood flowing from the knife wound at his side.

Hawkins rose up in front of him, a terrifying figure in the glow of the flames. The knife clutched in his hand dripped with Drake's blood.

Don't think about the pain, Drake told himself as Hawkins readied himself. *Pain is nothing.*

Smiling a bloody grimace, Hawkins came at him again, swiping with the knife. Drake dodged and tried to catch his knife arm, but his enemy abruptly changed direction and the blade sailed past his grasp. A renewed flash of pain tore into his side as the knife slashed at his flank again, cutting through skin and muscle.

As Drake turned to face him, bent over slightly to protect his injured side, Hawkins circled his prey at a thoughtful, almost leisurely pace, fingers flexing and tensing on the knife hilt. He was in control now, able to pick and choose when he struck. Able to make it last.

Drake stared back at his enemy, weakened by injury but defiant to the end. His hands were still raised, his fists clenched, his battered body readying itself one last time.

Hawkins' face darkened once more and he leapt in, coming in low this time, the knife slashing into Drake's thigh as he rushed past. There was no way he could have stopped it. As Drake sank to his knees, Hawkins turned to face him again, his expression triumphant.

He had won, and he knew it.

Nearby, Anya watched Drake's final moments through blurred vision, pain radiating through to the very core of her being. She had been hurt before, had taken every kind of punishment life could throw at her, but even she had limits of endurance. And she was past them now.

She had done everything she could, had fought to the last, tested her strength to its end. It hadn't been enough to carry her through this last battle. She could feel the darkness closing around her, slow and insidious and inviting. A deep and endless dark without pain or fear. She felt herself sinking into it, felt her eyes start to close.

Then, unbidden, a voice leapt into her head. A voice that seemed to be all around her, driving back the darkness, forcing clarity in her thoughts. A voice that spoke to her, commanding her, as it had so many times before.

Remember what you told him.

You would rather die for something, than live for nothing.

This is the last fight of your life.

Her dimming eyes snapped open, clear and focussed once again.

Get up.

Bloodied hands clawing at the ground, she managed through some supreme effort to pull herself upright, watching as Hawkins circled around behind Drake, the knife dripping with his blood. She had no weapons left. None except the arrows for her bow.

Reaching behind, she yanked one free and, gritting her teeth, muscles trembling, pushing aside the pain and the exhaustion, Anya fought her way up from the ground. Inch by inch, heartbeat by heartbeat.

Get up.

'Oh, Ryan. I imagined killing you so many times, I actually thought it would be a disappointment when it finally came,' Hawkins said, wiping the blood from his face as he looked down on his vanquished enemy. 'But I was wrong, man. This is better than I ever could have imagined.'

Poised to strike once again, Hawkins hesitated. He heard the movement coming at him from his right, and spun just as Anya leapt at him, thrusting at the arrow into his stomach. She was close, but Hawkins' reactions saved him. He turned aside just as the arrow came at him, tearing a gash through the fabric of his Kevlar vest and exposing the armour plating beneath.

Realising she'd missed, Anya slashed desperately at his throat with the improvised weapon, but this time he caught her arm, twisting it backward with his vastly superior strength. The arrow fell from her grasp as Hawkins, eyes blazing with anger, drove a fist into her injured stomach.

Anya fell, crumpling to the ground, her vision swimming. Out of the fight for good.

'Goddamn you, you just don't quit,' Hawkins snarled, surprised and infuriated by her last, desperate effort. 'You stubborn bitch.'

Grabbing Drake's hair, he yanked the man's head back, exposing his throat. The bloodied knife gleamed in the darkness as he raised it up.

'I want you to remember this moment,' the man said, glaring at her. 'Remember the look in his eyes when I kill him.'

But Anya's last effort hadn't been in vain. While Hawkins' attention was focussed on the woman who had so vexed him, Drake felt on the ground, closed his fingers around the arrow she'd dropped, and snatched it up.

And as Hawkins leaned in to slash his windpipe, Drake reversed his grip on the weapon and plunged it deep into his thigh. The man threw back his head and let out a howl of agony as Drake twisted it viciously, the sharpened steel point slicing and tearing his flesh.

Hawkins sank down. And as he fell, Drake leapt on top of him with a burst of desperate, frantic strength, grabbing for his knife hand and turning the weapon against him. The two men, both injured and bleeding, were locked in a final deadly struggle, their eyes fixed on one another, their breathing coming in heaving gasps as they strove for survival.

Drake was on top, forcing the blade down with every ounce of strength he could muster. Hawkins likewise strained to turn the knife away as the tip crept closer to his neck, his powerful arms clenched in one last Herculean effort. And for a few seconds, the two men were perfectly balanced, the knife trembling motionless between them.

Images of everyone this man had killed flashed before Drake's eyes as he forced the knife fractionally closer. Everything Hawkins had taken from him. Everything he'd destroyed.

Every ounce of hatred and vengeance rose up within him as an unstoppable tide.

'I told you, Jason,' Drake whispered, the veins in his arm standing out hard against the skin as he strained with all his might. 'I told you… I'd be the last thing you ever saw.'

Finally, as the desperate struggle reached an unbearable peak, he saw what he'd been waiting for in his enemy's eyes. He saw fear.

With a primal, enraged cry, he forced the knife through skin and windpipe, arteries and tendons. Hawkins' eyes grew huge as agony flared through him. His mouth gaped open to scream, instead emitting only a choking, gurgling surge of blood.

Then, at last, his struggles ceased and he lay still.

Rolling off him, Drake collapsed onto his back on the cool earth, completely and utterly drained, his breath coming in ragged, agonised gasps.

It was over.

He could almost feel his body quietly surrendering to it at last.

'Ryan…'

The weak, plaintive sound roused him from his growing exhaustion.

Anya.

Rolling over, he managed to crawl over to her. She was slumped against a tree trunk, a bloodied hand pressed against the wound at her stomach. She looked up at Drake as he neared.

'You came back for me,' she whispered.

He nodded, wincing in pain.

'Why?'

Why had he come back? Why had he risked everything for the woman who had taken so much from him? Why had he fought with every ounce of his strength to protect the person who killed his own mother?

'Because some things are worth dying for.'

The distant wail of approaching fire trucks warned Drake that they weren't safe. 'We have to get out of here.'

Anya shook her head weakly. 'I can't, Ryan.'

The sad acceptance in her voice hurt almost as much as the injuries he'd taken. She knew what it would mean if he left her behind. She'd always known what tonight would cost her.

'Bullshit you can't. I won't give up on you now,' he said firmly, hooking an arm beneath her. 'Get up! Come on!'

With some great exertion of will and whatever strength remained to him, he pulled the injured woman to her feet, ignoring the pain that flared through him, ignoring her groan of agony. Anya, realising he wouldn't leave her behind no matter what she said or did, reluctantly complied. And together, bleeding and clinging to each other, they limped slowly away into the forest.

Chapter 75

Richard Starke strode out of the ops room and headed towards his personal office. He would have to make a lot of phone calls and draw upon many favours in the next hour if he expected to come out of this intact.

Somehow it had all fallen apart. His plan had collapsed into chaos and disaster.

But it wasn't over. He still commanded enormous power and resources. Even if he'd failed today, he knew there would be other opportunities. There would be a good deal of explaining to do, of course, and more than a few people who would need to be silenced, but he could manage this crisis.

Just as he had managed so many before it.

'Dan,' he said, taken aback to find the acting CIA director waiting for him in his office. 'What brings you here?'

'You, actually,' Franklin said, taking a step towards him. His look of naked hostility was enough to give Starke pause.

'Excuse me?'

Reaching for his cell phone, Franklin selected an audio file and hit play.

'*You know, I don't often let these things get personal,*' he heard his own recorded voice say. '*Killing Cain and Freya... those were necessary acts. But I have to admit, knowing you're dead, Anya... well, that will give me a certain satisfaction.*'

Hitting the pause button, Franklin lowered the phone. 'We've got the whole thing, Richard. Your whole confession. It's over.'

Starke closed his eyes, a thin, bitter smile forming as he realised the full magnitude of his folly. Anya had known all along that he wouldn't be at that airfield in Lithuania. She hadn't gone there to kill him, she had gone to do something far more permanent – destroy him. And in his arrogance, he'd walked right into it.

'And what do you think you've really got there, Dan?' he asked. 'You think any jury in the country will convict me? Son, we own them.'

'There is no "we" anymore,' Franklin reminded him. 'Your little cabal is dust. Nobody's going to help you now.'

Starke raised his chin defiantly, though he couldn't keep the quaver out of his voice when he spoke again. 'You're about to make the biggest mistake of your life.'

'We'll see about that. Come!'

At his summons, a pair of FBI agents waiting outside strode into the room. 'Director Starke, you're under arrest for treason, conspiracy to commit murder and planning acts of terrorism,' Franklin stated as his hands were wrestled behind his back and cuffed. 'You have the right to remain silent. Anything you say can and will be used against you in a court of law.'

'Give it a few years,' Starke said, glaring at the younger man.

'You have the right to a lawyer. If you can't afford one, one will be provided for you.'

'Give it a few years,' he repeated. 'And you'll be just like me.'

'I'm nothing like you.'

Holding his gaze for a second or two, Franklin nodded to the two agents.

'Get this piece of shit out of my sight.'

–

Stumbling and limping through the slowly brightening forest as the night waned and the new day approached, Drake forced himself through the pain, forced himself to keep moving. If they could get clear of the airfield, they might reunite with his team and find a way to escape...

Deep down he knew it was futile, that neither of them would make it far now, but he wouldn't allow himself to accept it.

Just keep going, he told himself. *Keep going and you'll get out of this.*

Emerging from the woodland, they passed through a small wild meadow. The scent of damp grass and wildflowers stirred as they trudged slowly onward, making for the far side where a small stand of trees grew.

'Ryan, I can't… keep going…' Anya gasped, her steps growing slower, her breathing laboured.

'It's going to be okay,' he replied, one hand pressed against the wound at his side, his shirt damp with blood. 'Everything's going to be okay now.'

Only when they passed beneath the trees and saw what lay beyond did Drake finally stop, letting out an exhausted, defeated sigh.

The river flowing lazily past was at least thirty feet wide. No way across. No way out.

'Oh, no…'

Beside him, Anya sank to the ground, slumping against a fallen tree trunk. With no way forward, Drake collapsed beside her, the last of his strength deserting him.

'No more,' she gasped, shaking her head. 'No more, Ryan. Please.'

They had gone as far as they could, fought to the very last, but this was it. This was the end of the path they'd started on all those years ago. They had done all they could.

There was no need to fight it any more.

Her breathing slowing, Anya looked around, taking in the peaceful river flowing by, the wildflowers and trees around them. Overhead, the infinite blue sky was growing brighter, the sun rising above the horizon to the east. The dawn of another day.

The end of the old world, and the beginning of a new future.

It was a good place to die.

'Another life,' Drake whispered, echoing her earlier words to him.

Anya looked at him then.

'I wish we could have met in another life. Maybe things could have been different.'

There was so much in her life she wished she could have changed, so many choices and mistakes she wished she could have undone. But out of all of it, meeting Ryan Drake was one thing Anya would never regret.

'Maybe we will,' she acknowledged. 'But I'm glad I could be with you… at the end.'

Reaching out, Drake found her hand and closed his bloodied fingers around it. After everything they'd been through, everything they'd endured together, perhaps it was fitting that it should end here like this. Just the two of them.

Nothing left to fight for. Nothing left to fear.

He was disturbed by a noise carried to him on the breeze. Shouts, coming from the woodland behind. The sound of people moving, calling to each other, drawing closer. It wouldn't have been difficult to track them, following the trail of blood and broken undergrowth they'd left in their wake.

'They've found us,' Anya said. Reaching into her tunic, she pulled out her old M1911 handgun, ejected the magazine and checked the rounds left in the clip.

'How many?' Drake asked as the shouts grew closer.

Her eyes met his. 'Two.'

He didn't need her to say it. He knew what she was thinking. She wouldn't be captured, wouldn't spend the rest of her life in prison, or endure some show trial and summary execution. She had come too far, been through too much for that.

And so had he.

'We both knew it would come to this, Ryan,' she said quietly. 'This is where we were always meant to be. This is how it was meant to end.'

He looked down at the weapon, marked and scratched by long use, stained with blood. His, or hers, he could no longer tell.

Without saying a word, he reached out and took it from her.

'It's all right,' she promised him, gently encouraging. 'I'm ready.'

She nodded to herself, taking in the river, the wildflowers around them, the sun rising into a perfect sky. And high above, she caught a glimpse of something moving slowly in the vast sea of blue; starkly white, straight as an arrow. The contrail of some high flying aircraft. The sunlight glinted off its hull, bright as a shooting star.

She thought of the days she'd spent lying in the long grass as a child, staring up at aircraft like this and marvelling at what far-off destinations they might be heading to. Dreaming of what might be out there. Picturing the adventures that lay ahead.

She smiled softly as Drake raised the gun.

'I'm ready.'

He closed his eyes as he pulled the trigger.

'Ryan!' a voice called out. 'Ryan Drake!'

With a gasp, Drake took pressure off the trigger and turned back towards the meadow, where a trio of armed operatives were moving towards him through the long grass. Two men and a woman. They were armed, but their weapons were lowered, their expressions filled with concern rather than anger.

'Anybody got eyes on?' the leader asked. 'Talk to me!'

The woman suddenly caught sight of Drake and pointed. 'There! I see him!'

With that, the leader broke into a run, sprinting forward. Skidding to a stop beside him, the man laid aside his weapon and looked at the two injured fugitives, quickly assessing their condition.

'Shit,' he said under his breath. 'I need a medic here!'

'On it!' the woman called out.

'Kennedy?' Drake said, incredulous at the sight of a fellow Shepherd operative. 'What are… you doing here?'

Kennedy grinned at him, though his smile was tinged with concern. 'Franklin sent us for a bit of unofficial R&R. Looks like he made a good call.'

The female Shepherd operative was already tending to Anya. 'I need you to keep pressure on that wound,' she instructed, speaking with the cool, calm efficiency of a medical professional. 'We're gonna get you out of here.'

The second man was speaking into his radio. 'Zulu One, we've found them. Repeat, we've found them, but they're injured and serious condition. We need immediate evac.'

'They're looking for us,' Drake mumbled, his vision starting to blur. It was such an effort to focus on the man in front of him, but even now he was aware of the agencies still hunting for them both. 'They'll find us.'

'Don't worry about that, buddy. We've got it covered.'

Reaching out blindly, Drake touched Anya's hand again and felt her clasp it tight.

The last thing he saw before darkness closed around him was her, staring up at the dawn sky. Finally at peace.

Part Six

Something to Live For

We know what we are, but not what we may be.

William Shakespeare

Chapter 76

Arlington National Cemetery – one month later

With the trees and bushes in full summer bloom and the sun shining down from a cloudless sky, it was a pleasant evening to be outdoors, breathing fresh air and feeling the warm breeze on one's skin. Even more so for Ryan Drake, who had been largely confined to a hospital as he slowly recovered from his injuries.

Emergency surgery at a hastily set-up operating theatre in Lithuania had saved him from fatal internal bleeding, though it had been a close-run thing, as Kennedy had made a point of reminding him while he lay convalescing at a safe house in Vilnius.

Still, he was well on the way to recovery now. He wouldn't be back in the field for a while, and was tired by the time he'd ascended the gentle grassy hill at the centre of the cemetery. But as with most things, it was simply a matter of time.

Anyway, he would not be discouraged from his visit here today. Some things were more important.

Tracing his way along the rows of neatly arrayed tombstones, he found the section he was looking for and stopped to take in the four pristine white headstones laid out before him, each with the name of one of his fallen comrades carved in them.

John Keegan (1956–2008)
Cole Mason (1970–2010)
Olivia Mitchell (1972–2011)
Samantha McKnight (1976–2011)

Four friends who had each given their lives in the line of duty. His family, who he had trusted and cared for as if they were his own blood.

His gaze lingered the longest of all on Samantha McKnight's grave. Whatever her conflicted history, whatever decisions she'd been forced to make, she had redeemed herself and more, sacrificing her life for theirs. Nobody could ask more of her, and Drake himself would never forget what she'd done.

He only wished he could have been there for her at the end.

'Good to see you up and around,' Franklin said, moving up to stand by his friend's side. 'I'll be honest, I wasn't sure you'd pull through.'

'What do they say about bad pennies?' Drake replied.

Franklin smiled faintly at the joke.

'Do you have any idea the shitstorm that enveloped this place while you were relaxing in a hospital bed? I think I might have traded place with you.'

Drake was well aware of the turmoil that had erupted in the wake of the deadly confrontation in Lithuania. Everyone was up in arms, wanting to lay the blame somewhere else, everyone was out for blood.

But somehow, through some great feat of diplomacy, deception and selective deployment of the truth, Franklin had managed to navigate these perilous political waters and wrestle a decent outcome from it. The recording of Richard Starke's damning confession had gone a long way towards shifting the blame away from Drake and the others, convincing most people that they were simply victims caught up in the machinations of far more powerful men.

In the end, they'd found their scapegoat.

As for the man himself, Starke had been awaiting trial on multiple charges of treason and conspiracy, with a life sentence looking like the most optimistic possibility. But it wasn't to be. His guards had found him lying dead in his prison cell two weeks earlier, having ingested a lethal dose of cyanide. To this day, no one knew how the poison had found its way to him, or who had supplied it.

And they never would.

Marcus Cain, meanwhile, had been laid to rest in a simple, formal ceremony that Drake had been more than happy to avoid. Though he had never been officially sworn in as CIA director, his death and the events leading up to it had still attracted a great deal of interest and controversy from the news media, especially online conspiracy theorists who were working doggedly to uncover his secrets.

The CIA, acting in its own best interests and eager to avoid a scandal that would rock them to their core, were likewise doing their best to thwart these efforts. Marcus Cain's complex life would remain, for most people at least, an enigma.

'I'll stick with my end of the deal,' Drake conceded. 'Anyway, isn't that what this place is all about? One big shitstorm after another?'

'I think I've earned a break, don't you?'

'You might want to get used to it,' Drake suggested, hinting at the man's ongoing, and so-far successful, tenure as acting director. 'Director Dan Franklin. It's got a decent ring to it.'

Franklin thought about that for a moment, imagining the possibilities that lay ahead, then let it go. Those were concerns for another day. 'What about you? You thought about what you'll do next?'

'Yes, he's going to live a very quiet, boring and sensible life,' Jessica said, moving forward to speak with the two men. 'Preferably somewhere I can keep an eye on him.'

Drake smiled at that. He was still adjusting to the reality that he was no longer a wanted man, being able to move around again without the constant fear of surveillance and attack. Part of him wondered if he'd ever really get used to it.

Some habits were too hard to break.

'I second that!' Frost called out, standing alongside the others a short distance away. 'And by the way, you still owe me a shit ton of hazard pay, Ryan.'

'Keep dreaming,' Drake shot back.

'Well, if you ever find yourself looking for work, give me a call,' Franklin advised him. 'We can work something out.'

He knew Drake well enough to know that 'quiet' and 'sensible' were two words that didn't belong in his vocabulary. Sooner or later he would find himself back in this world of theirs. It was part of him now. Maybe the best part.

'Thanks, but I've got something else in mind,' he remarked cryptically. 'Something a little more... independent.'

Franklin raised an eyebrow but said nothing further on the matter, guessing Drake wasn't ready to give him more just yet. That, too, was a conversation for another day.

'Well, I guess I'd better get back. Never know when the next shitstorm will erupt,' Franklin said, looking out across the city before giving his friend a nod. 'I'll see you around, Ryan.'

He was just turning to leave when Drake called him back. 'Dan?'

'Yeah?'

Stepping forward, Drake clasped his hand and shook it. 'Thank you. For everything.'

Nodding acknowledgement, Franklin let go and walked away down the hill, leaving Drake with his small group of friends.

They smiled with relief, with elation, with longing as he approached. This was the first time they'd been reunited since parting ways at that airfield in Lithuania. And now, with their fallen comrades by their side, they were all together at last.

Drake almost felt like he could sense them, watching over the friends who yet had their lives to live. Grateful for the time they'd had together, and knowing that one day they would see each other again. And that was a comforting thought.

'You think *now* we can rest a while?' Jonas Dietrich asked sardonically. 'I'm getting too old to run around with you fools.'

Drake smiled at his gruff, abrasive comrade. Their friendship might not have begun under ideal circumstances, but somehow Dietrich had always come through in the end.

'Don't want you getting complacent, Jonas,' he returned with a grin, before turning his attention to the younger man by his side.

Alex Yates, the computer hacker reluctantly recruited into their team. A young man plucked from obscurity, thrust into a world he couldn't possibly have prepared himself for. But rather than shrinking from it, he had grown, becoming a stronger and braver man than he ever could have imagined.

'What about you, Alex? Will you go back home to the UK?'

Alex thought on that briefly, remembering the life he'd left behind, then shook his head. 'It's not my home anymore,' he decided. 'There's nothing there for me to go back to. Maybe… I don't know, maybe there's something better out there.'

'Shit, don't tell me you're getting a taste for this stuff?' Frost snorted.

Alex grinned, shrugging. 'We'll see.'

Last of all, Drake's attention came to rest on Keira Frost. The fiery, temperamental, impetuous, abrasive and irritating young technical expert he'd been forced to work with for years now. A comrade who had risked everything for him. A friend that he loved with all his heart.

'There's something I want you to know, Keira,' he said, his voice soft and quiet. 'Something I never told you.'

Frost waited, hushed. Expectant.

Drake leaned closer, his face brightening in a grin. 'You're not entitled to hazard pay. Sorry.'

'You asshole!' she cried, punching him in the arm.

'Take it easy!' he protested in mock pain. 'I'm still an invalid.'

'You will be if you pull that shit again.'

But her playful banter faded a little as she looked at him, allowing the memories of everything they'd been through together to rise to the surface at last. There was no stopping it. Throwing her arms around him, she pulled him as tight as he held her, her face buried in his neck, tears streaking his skin.

They didn't say anything. They didn't have to.

When at last he let go, he paused to take in the small gathering. His friends. His family. The people who had followed him to the end, and stayed together.

Perhaps they still would work together, he reflected. There was much still to be said and decided once they were finished here. Experiences to recount, memories to share, thanks to give. And perhaps, plans for the future to be made. He certainly had some ideas on that front.

But as he glanced up the hill towards the Tomb of the Unknown Soldier and saw a lone figure standing at the entrance to the amphitheatre, Drake knew those things could wait. There was one last person to meet with today.

Taking leave of his friends, he ascended the last stretch of the hill, passing the Marine honour guard standing watch over the tomb, and entering the towering white archway to the empty amphitheatre beyond.

She was waiting for him there, standing alone as she so often had been.

Anya. The woman who had changed his life forever.

She, too, had largely recovered from her injuries over the past month, her body well acquainted with pain and hardship. Physically she was recuperating well, and looked to be healthy and rested. As for what lay behind that strikingly beautiful visage, Drake had yet to find out.

This was the first time they'd spoken since that morning in Lithuania.

'How's it feel to be dead?'

According to the Agency's official report, Anya had been killed during the operation in Lithuania, her body vaporised during the air strike on her former home. Though it had taken some careful manoeuvring and outright deception on Franklin's part, most of the agencies hunting her had been persuaded that she was finally dead, abandoning their manhunts to focus on more pressing concerns.

'Surprisingly liberating,' Anya acknowledged with a wry smile. 'I should have tried it a long time ago, I think.'

Her demeanour, however, turned more serious when she spoke again. 'It doesn't feel real. After all this time, knowing it is finally over...'

Drake knew exactly what she meant, because he had wrestled with the same doubt.

'It's hard to imagine a life without it, right? The running, the fighting, the fear. After a while, it becomes a part of you. Now its gone, you feel like you've lost something.'

She nodded, surprised by his insight.

They were quiet for a time, each knowing they had things to say but neither quite sure how to bring it up. In the end, it was Anya who made the first move.

'I was ready to die there, Ryan. I had made peace with it.'

He knew that well enough. Death had held no fear for her.

'Did you want it?'

She thought about that, considering the question carefully. 'I had always known that was how it would end. So that was how I lived – for the mission, the fight, the moment. Never the future. Because if there *was* no future, there was nothing to lose, and nothing to fear. Now... I feel lost.'

'Maybe that's not such a bad thing,' Drake coaxed. 'Not everything ends the way we think it should.'

It certainly hadn't for him. Drake too had listened to the recording Anya had made, had listened to Starke's confession about his mother. She had tried to have Anya killed, leaving the woman with no choice but to do what she had. Once more, his understanding of Freya Shaw had been changed, along with his perception of the woman who killed her.

Neither one had been perfect. Neither had been without blame. But he accepted this truth without condoning or condemning either of them.

Anya nodded thoughtfully, sensing his double meaning.

'Do you remember what you told me once?' Drake asked. 'That you would rather die for something, than live for nothing?'

Anya swallowed. That had been her mantra for most of her life. To have her death mean something. To end her life on her own terms, with purpose and resolve.

'I do.'

Taking a step forward, Drake reached out and touched her hand, taking it in his. 'Maybe it's time you found something to *live* for.'

Anya smiled faintly, turning her head away. He couldn't say for certain, but he thought he saw her eyes glistening.

Perhaps she might at last start to lay aside the armour that had protected her throughout her troubled life. Armour that had now become a burden, weighing her down, holding her back.

'So what will you do now?' he asked.

She glanced at him curiously. 'Do?'

'Well, you're officially dead,' he reminded her. 'You've got a fresh start. You can go wherever you want, do whatever you want… *be* whoever you want.' He paused, leaning in closer. 'The only question is, who do *you* want to be, Anya?'

The woman glanced downhill, taking in the rows of headstones. The warriors of past generations that had fought and died and been laid to rest here. The place where some of her own comrades were buried. The place she had always imagined ending up.

'All my life, I have been a soldier,' she said, her expression pensive. 'Living in this world, but… never part of it. Seeing it from the outside.'

She sighed and raised her face towards the sky, summoning up everything she'd been, every decision she'd been forced to make, every aspect of the identity she'd created for herself. Bringing it all to mind.

And, at last, laying it aside.

Frankfurt, Germany

Yasin was passing through the school gates with the small knot of kids who had gradually become his friends over the past six months, all chattering and laughing together as they made plans for the summer ahead.

He was tired after a long day of studying, having thrown himself into schoolwork with even greater determination recently. Doing his best to keep his mind occupied. Doing his best to forget the woman who had come to visit him a month ago.

'What about you, Yasin?' one of his friends asked. 'What will you do?'

But Yasin wasn't hearing him. He had seen something on the open playing fields that backed onto the school. Something that stopped him in his tracks.

—

'I want to live a real life,' she whispered. 'No more missions, no more Agency, no more hiding in the shadows. I want to be better than that.'

Drake nodded, sensing that perhaps a little piece of the armour had been discarded. Another little burden cast aside. Perhaps she might finally see beyond the darkness and struggle of the past, to make a better future for herself. Not by fighting and killing, not by hiding herself away from the world, but by doing something good with the time she had left.

'I might suggest a vacation first,' he added with a grin. 'I'd say you've earned it.'

That's when it happened. For the first time in a long time, Anya laughed. A true, honest, uninhibited laugh of joy, of relief. Of life. Just the sound of it was enough to make his heart swell.

'And you?' she asked as her laughter faded. 'What will you do with *your* life?'

Drake shrugged playfully, then glanced back down the slope at the small gathering of people. His friends. His family. The new path they might chart together.

'You know me. I always find a way to cause trouble.'

Stepping closer, Anya reached out tentatively, placed her hands on his shoulders and just looked at him for a long moment. Taking in everything he was. Then, unable to hold back any longer, she pulled him close, holding him tight as if she would never let go.

Drake too felt the gravity of this moment, the significance of this embrace.

They had been many things to each other. Comrades, allies, enemies, lovers. But perhaps, here at the end, they were none of those things. Perhaps they too had earned a clean slate.

—

'Go on without me,' Yasin replied absently. 'I'll catch up.'

Leaving his friends behind, he changed direction, heading across the open expanse of grass, ignoring the other kids who were running and laughing and playing around him. His eyes were fixed on the woman ahead of him.

A woman he'd said goodbye to.

'I thought you weren't coming back,' he whispered, standing face to face with her.

Anya nodded. 'So did I.'

'You said yours was no life for someone like me.'

And then, for almost the first time he could remember, Anya smiled. 'Then perhaps it's time I made a better life.'

It was more than he could take. Dropping his school bag, Yasin rushed forward and threw his arms around her.

—

'You know your problem, Ryan Drake?' Anya whispered as she stepped back. 'You're a good man.'

With a final, wistful smile, Anya turned and walked away. Drake stood there watching her leave, thinking about everything that had changed because of her. Everything he'd done, everything he'd lost and gained, everything he'd become. Because of her.

He heard footsteps beside him, felt his sister draw near.

'Do you think we'll ever see her again?' Jessica asked gently, watching Anya depart.

For so long, the two of them had been like magnets pulling inexorably together. No matter how much time and distance opened up between them, somehow they always found their way back to each other. And maybe they still would. Perhaps one day their paths would cross again, or perhaps this was to be their last encounter. Only time would tell.

'I don't know,' Drake confessed. 'But she's free now, just like us. And that's good enough.'

Whether he saw her again or not, Drake knew one thing as he watched her departing, her back straight and her head held high — Anya had found something to live for.

And so had he.

Acknowledgements

'Part of the journey is the end.'

Never have those words felt more relevant than when I sat down to write this book in the summer of 2019. It's a journey that started for me more than a decade ago. I was a young unpublished author lying awake one night, with a hundred jigsaw pieces of ideas floating around in my head. When suddenly, in one of those little chance events that can change the course of a person's life, everything seemed to come together in a moment of clarity and Ryan Drake, Anya and so many of their friends and enemies were born. It's a journey that carried me through nine books, two novellas, many long, frustrating, rewarding hours at my computer, and more cups of coffee than I care to think about. It's a journey that's changed my life for the better, in more ways than I can begin to express.

And it's a journey that's inevitably brought me here, to the end. Writing *Something to Die For* was always going to be a bittersweet experience, taking these characters who have been such a big part of my life for so long and sending them on their last adventure, but even I wasn't prepared for how demanding, draining and exhausting this book would prove to be. It's my sincere hope that I'm able to do them justice, and give them the send-off they deserve.

But producing a book like this isn't just down to me. It's an undertaking that requires the combined efforts of many others behind the scenes, and it's only fair and right that I acknowledge them here. Firstly, my sincere thanks go to my editor, Craig Lye, for his tireless work, his boundless enthusiasm for this series and his excellent suggestions and ideas. This book is far better (and shorter!) because of his efforts.

Likewise, I'd like to thank Iain Millar and everyone at Canelo for bringing me into their vibrant, positive and wonderfully supportive publishing house, for seeing the potential in my work and for allowing me to tell this story my way. And for understanding when I missed my deadline!

Also, my appreciation as always goes to my agent Diane Banks at Northbank Talent for taking me on all those years ago, for pushing me to be better at what I do, and for her help and guidance in this strange, often confusing world of book publishing.

Last of all, I want to thank my wife, Susan, and my two boys, Daniel and Matthew, for keeping me grounded and focussed, for understanding when I locked myself away in the office night after night, for their love and laughter, and for reminding me of what's really important.

To all of you who have helped, advised, supported and encouraged me over the years, I thank you.